THOSE
TWO
WORDS

RONNIE MATHEWS

Copyright © 2024 by Ronnie Mathews

All rights reserved.

No part of this book may be reproduced in any form or by any electronic or mechanical means, including information storage and retrieval systems, without written permission from the author, except for the use of brief quotations in a book review.

All names, characters, businesses, places, events and incidents in this book are either the product of the author's imagination or used in a fictitious manner. Any resemblance to real persons or events is purely coincidental.

Cover Design by Melissa Doughty at Mel D. Designs

Editing by Paisley McNab at Perfectly Write

Proofreading by Caroline Palmier at Love & Edits

ASIN: B0D1R5STFS (Ebook)

ISBN: 978-1-3999-8932-9 (Paperback)

This one's for me.
I'm glad I didn't listen to that little voice in my head that said I couldn't do it.
If you want to do the thing, do the thing!

author's note

Thank you so much for deciding to read Those Two Words. I hope you love this story as much as I loved writing it.

I highly recommend you read the prologue, not only because it's cute, but it sets the scene perfectly for Johanna and Patrick's story.

Those Two Words is the first book in the Sutton Bay series and can be read as a standalone. All books in the series will be interconnected standalone stories, but I suggest reading them in order to get the full feel of the stories.

Johanna's journey with her mental health may not be a reflection of everyone's experiences, but it is a reflection of my own and many others, so I kindly ask that you respect that.

This is an open-door romance and intended for readers who are eighteen years or older. All characters written are consenting adults and you will find explicit, on-page sexual content, explicit language, and real life situations. I ask that you always look after yourself, and if you wish to see a full list of content and trigger warnings, please visit: www.ronniemathews.com

playlist

When We Were Young - Adele
Maine - Noah Kahan
Strangers - Mt. Joy
Decimal - Novo Amor
Happier (Stripped) - Marshmello, Bastille
Lose You To Love Me - Selena Gomez
Long Time - Wild Rivers
The View Between Villages - Noah Kahan
Bad Life - Sigrid, Bring Me The Horizon
Believe - Mumford & Sons
All We Ever Knew - The Head And The Heart
All Fired Up - Matt Corby
Not Good At Not - Morgan Wallen
Skin - Rihanna
You & Me - James TW
Wild Love (Acoustic) - James Bay
Back To You - Twin Forks
Only Love - Ben Howard
Constellations (Piano Version) - Jade LeMac
Sweet Love (Acoustic) - Myles Smith

PLAYLIST

I Don't Want To Lose You - Luca Fogale
Pink Skies - Zach Bryan
In A Heartbeat - Ryan McMullan
I Swear - Mother's Daughter, Beck Pete
An Evening I Will Not Forget - Dermot Kennedy
Missing Piece (Acoustic) - Vance Joy

Scan QR code below to listen on Spotify.

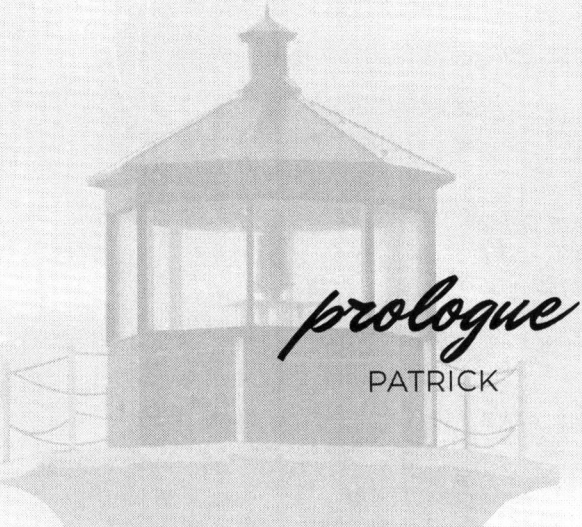

prologue
PATRICK

TWENTY-SEVEN YEARS AGO

"WE CAN'T BE IN HERE," A HUSHED VOICE SAYS FROM BEHIND ME. I fumble to open the door as quietly as possible, but the jangling of keys is going to get us caught soon if I don't hurry up.

Turning around, I shush my best friend, who scowls back at me. Annoyingly, she's two inches taller than me, and I only know this because our moms measured us against the stockroom door frame this afternoon. I'll be taller than her soon, though, because Mom says I take after my dad and he's really tall. Plus, I'll be *seven* next month and she'll still be six until August.

"I know that, YoYo, but there's no more candy left at the buffet. I'm sure there's some Starburst in my dad's desk."

"My name is *Johanna*, for like the gazillionth time, you dork." She's trying to whisper but isn't doing a good job.

I try to hide my giggle. Obviously, I know her name, but teasing her is my favorite thing to do. Well, after playing with my Hot Wheels.

I try another key, and when it doesn't get jammed in the

lock, I let out a little cheer. "AH-HA! Quick, come in before someone hears us."

"Well, they have now, Patrick. You're like a foghorn," she says as we hurry into my dad's office, and I push the door shut behind us. Hoping the loud music from the party covers up any noises of our break-in, I turn to face Johanna. Her long blonde hair is up in two twisty things with some shiny stuff wrapped around them. I told her she looked like an alien bride, and she told me I smelled like her grandma's one-hundred-year-old cat. She's wearing a sparkly silver dress and shoes to match her hair. She's very *shiny,* but I suppose she looks kinda pretty. My mom put me in a long-sleeved button-up shirt, tie, and pinchy shoes. She said I look handsome, but I feel dumb, and the tie around my neck is starting to strangle me.

It's New Year's Eve and the first ever party being thrown at our dads' new restaurant. It's fun and all, but they keep playing really old music about love and other mushy things.

It's dark in here, but Johanna glows in the corner of the room as I tiptoe over to the desk. Her dark blue eyes glare at me, hands fisted at her sides—she looks a little mad. "I'll only help you look for the candy if you let me have all the orange-flavored Starburst."

"Fiiiiine. But I want to be the first one to hold a sparkler at midnight. Deal?"

"Deal." She walks over to me and holds out her hand. I spit into mine to seal the deal, but before I can close it around hers, she jerks away.

"Ewwwww! Gross, Patrick! I'm not shaking it now. You'll give me cooties," she cries. My other friends think it's weird my best friend is a girl, and I get it when she doesn't like to do cool stuff like this. But most of the time she's pretty awesome.

"I will not, and like it matters, anyway, when we're husband and wife, you'll have to do lots of gross things with me. Like holding my hand and trimming my nose hairs. That's what Mom does for Dad," I say with a shrug.

"Yes, but that's when we're married. I can't hold it now, silly, you haven't asked me yet."

What's the big deal? I think as I wipe my hand on my pants.

I walk around my dad's desk and pull out the chair tucked underneath, revealing the drawer hopefully full of candy, and pray he forgot to lock it. Taking a deep breath in, I pull with all my strength. I have a lot of it because Mom says that I eat more vegetables than Graham, so he won't be as strong as me. Booth eats lots of vegetables, but they're blended up since he's still a baby. I must not have eaten enough green bean casserole tonight, because when I pull on the drawer, it doesn't budge.

With a frustrated sigh and sad expression, I look up at Johanna. "I'm sorry, I think he locked it."

"I did," a voice booms from the shadows.

"AHHHHHHHHH!" Our high-pitched screams bounce around the small office.

A deep chuckle comes from the now-open doorway. Johanna's and my parents are standing there laughing at us, but I can't tell if my dad's angry face is serious or not.

My palm slaps against my forehead when he holds up the set of keys I left in the lock.

"What are you two weasels up to this time?" Johanna's mom, Valerie, asks.

She's tucked underneath the arm of Johanna's dad, George, and rests a hand over her big round belly that looks like a basketball. Johanna hopes it's a girl, but I think it's a boy, which would be great. I'm so glad it's just my brothers and I, no stinky sisters for me.

My dad has a sleepy Graham in his arms, while my mom has Booth strapped to her chest. I have no idea how they're both sleeping with the party going on.

I peek over at Johanna, who looks so nervous she might

puke. She kinda looks like Casper, the ghost from that movie we watched the other week. I quickly try to come up with an excuse as to why we're in here.

"Umm...YoYo had to go number two, so I said she could use the toilet in your office." *Good save.*

"PATRICK!" My shoulders shoot up to my ears at Johanna's screeching.

Oh, maybe not.

Our parents try to hold back their laughter, before ushering us out of the room, and my dad locks his office back up. I look at him guiltily, but he just chuckles and ruffles my hair as he pockets the keys.

"C'mon, you two, it's nearly midnight and you don't want to miss the celebrations," my mom says as she walks ahead with everyone else.

We walk back to the party and my dad pulls Johanna and me into his side. I think he's about to tell us off, but then he presses something into my hand. I look down at the yellow wrapper of my favorite flavor of Starburst before grinning up at my dad.

He is *so* cool.

"Patrick, you can't be telling people about a lady's...business," my dad says quietly—probably talking about when I told everyone Johanna needed to go poop.

"I'm sorry, Johanna," I mumble and peer around my dad at my best friend on his other side. "You forgive me, right?"

"Hmmm." She thinks for a second and then smiles. "Yeah, but only if you let me have the first sparkler now."

"Okay," I agree, because that seems to make her smile, and I like making my friend smile.

Everyone is still dancing around the room when we get back to the front of the restaurant. The tables have been pushed aside, people are singing at the top of their lungs about some

THOSE TWO WORDS

summer that happened a long time ago, and the lights from the DJ booth flicker across the room and reflect off the disco ball hanging from the ceiling. The room is covered in a hundred specks of light, like the dance floor is made up of little stars.

I think it's pretty cool that our dads own a restaurant, because we get to hang out here after school and eat as many lobster rolls as we want. Johanna and I decided we would run this place together when we're older. She's my best friend, so who else would I do it with? Plus, I don't like any other girls but her, so it makes sense that we'll be married too.

"Okay, kids, let's take a picture of you both and then you can run off to cause more trouble. The clock is about to strike midnight," Johanna's mom tells us and makes a shooing motion with her hand as my dad stands in front of us with his Polaroid camera. "Huddle up close."

We stand in front of the big driftwood bar in the restaurant, ready to pose for the picture. Once we're standing next to each other with smiles on our faces, I whisper in her ear, "I know how I can make it up to you."

"For what?"

"For saying what I said back there."

"How?"

"Close your eyes."

She looks confused but after a moment she closes her eyes and stands there.

"Okay, keep them shut," I command.

"Ten," everyone begins to shout around us. I realize we're seconds away from midnight, so I need to act fast.

"Patrick, what are you doing?"

"Nine. Eight."

"I know we're not married yet." I have to shout over everyone counting down.

"Seven."

"But I won't embarrass you like that when we're husband and wife."

"Six. Five."

"We'll be a team when we run this place."

"Four. Three."

Ignoring my clammy hands, I lean in closer to her. I really don't want her to be mad at me.

"*Two.*"

"*One.*"

People around us cheer and the flash of the camera goes off right as I kiss her on the cheek. Her eyes shoot open when I pull away and I smile at her nervously. She looks a little shocked. We saw a couple kiss like that in a movie once and Johanna said it was cute.

"See. I can be a good husband, like my dad is." She still looks confused, but then giggles, so I guess she liked it. Which is good, because I'm not doing it again—it was gross, and she smelled like flowers.

Our parents are cheering around us and kissing each other now. *Yuck.*

"I'm your best friend and you're mine, right?" I ask, checking for sure that she isn't mad anymore.

She gives me her biggest smile and it lights me up like the fireworks flashing outside in the street. Flashes of blue, red, green, and yellow streak across her face, turning her into a rainbow. Her eyes are bright and shining, and seeing her smile like this has my own cheeks hurting as I smile back.

"Yeah, Patrick." She throws her arms around me and squeezes tight. "I'm yours."

one
PATRICK

PRESENT DAY

"SPUD! WE'VE GOT TO GET A MOVE ON OR WE'RE GOING TO BE late," I shout up the stairs, glancing at my watch. Almost five years in and we still don't have this timing thing buckled down.

"I'm almost ready. Don't rush me, Daddy," a sassy voice hollers back.

Sighing, I remind myself that women of all ages don't like to be hurried. I take a quick glance in the hallway mirror to see how much being a girl dad has aged me. Answer: it's a lot, but totally worth it. My dark blond hair is its usual shaggy self and a little damp from my morning shower, making it appear darker in shade. Grabbing a beanie, I pull it over my head and grab our coats from the rack, ready for when my daughter graces me with her presence. We're against the clock this morning, so I haven't had the chance to shave the day-old stubble decorating my jaw.

I'm about to shout up for the fourth time when, right on cue, Lottie hops down the stairs, her dark chestnut braids bouncing with each step. The angelic face she makes has me forgetting all about how late we're going to be. She might be four, but she knows she has me wrapped around her little finger. Blackmail by cuteness.

"What do you think?" she asks with a twirl that almost has her tumbling backward but saves herself by finishing off the move with some jazz hands. She's paired a bright orange T-shirt with an otter printed on the front, with a pink skirt, and hiking boots. Quite the ensemble—and not the outfit I laid out this morning, and definitely not appropriate for the snowstorm we got hit with over the weekend. Hopefully the last one of the winter.

She looks up and flashes me a toothy grin. Vivid green eyes matching my own stare up at me, eagerly waiting for approval. There's a glimmer of mischief in them too.

"So pretty. Don't you think you're going to be a little chilly during recess?"

She lets out a sigh of her own, reminding me I need to watch how I act around her. She's at the age of repeating *everything* she overhears.

"How about we put a sweater and some tights on, whaddya think?"

She taps her pointer finger on her chin a few times, contemplating her decision, even though we both know this is nonnegotiable.

"I think...okay!" she shouts, then hurries back up the stairs and slams her bedroom door shut behind her. Privacy is very important to her now, and I must always knock before entering or face her wrath.

I can't wait until she's a teenager.

When she returns, I double-check her outfit before helping her into her coat and heading outside, thankful the snow isn't as heavy now. I load her into my truck, and without any more delays, we finally get going.

Ten minutes later we're almost at her school as some song

about unicorns and sharks is playing through the speakers. The one thing no one warned me about when you have a kid, is how they dictate every song you listen to. We've been listening to this one for almost four weeks and I'm confident it's melting my brain cells.

As we turn into the school, I check my rearview mirror to see if Lottie's braids are still intact from her outfit change. When I don't spot a hair out of place, I nod my head in quiet congratulations that I've finally cracked the French braids she's been begging me to do for months. *Thank you, YouTube.*

Once we reach the front of the drop-off, I put the car in park, and the school admin opens Lottie's door to help her out of her car seat. I roll down my window and wave goodbye.

"Have a great day, spud. Don't forget to listen to what—"

"Daddy, what's for dinner tonight?" she interrupts.

This kid.

"I haven't decided yet, but try not to interrupt people, remember? Listen to your teachers, and Grandma will pick you up after school. Love you, kiddo."

"Love you more than s'mores. *Oh, oh,* can we have s'mores for dinner?!" she asks and nods her head enthusiastically. I laugh and blow her a kiss before the admin takes her by the hand and walks her over to join her prekindergarten classmates.

My daughter has the appetite of a hungry hippo, just like her uncle Booth. I'm grateful she's not a picky eater like my little sister, Florence, was when she was her age.

I make my way off the school property and check the time on my dashboard. The restaurant opens later on Mondays, and I doubt a lot of people will be venturing out of their homes with all the snow we received. The extra time allows me to catch up on admin work and finalize some vendor issues we've been having.

As I cruise back through town, I take in the view through

my windshield, which is, hands down, the best in town. Robin Road is the main road leading into the town and ends right at the edge of the bay, and from the top of the hill, you can see the town in all its glory. The bay is about two miles wide and curves with the town until it meets the secluded beaches nearing Acadia National Park. The town is surrounded by cliffs, bluffs, and towering pines; permanently enveloping us in evergreen colors. Wherever you are, you get a sweeping view of the waterfront as you watch the fishing boats come in and out.

Robin Road is the heart of Sutton Bay. The road is lined on either side with mismatched brick buildings, painted in an array of colors, and right now, the small businesses are opening their doors to start a new week. We have fewer tourists this time of year, except for the town's annual Christmas markets, and it gives the businesses some time to recuperate before they come swarming back in spring. One of the newest is a small bakery called Just Brew It. Despite it being the new kid on the block, it seems to be doing well from the small crowd forming out front.

I push the jealous pang that hits me when I spot the line of people outside the bakery. Something we haven't seen in a *long* time.

When I see an empty space outside of the restaurant, I turn on my blinker and pull into it. With the collar of my parka high above my ears, shielding myself from the biting air, I make the short walk and avoid piles of snow along the way.

Once I'm standing in front of the brick building I know better than the back of my hand, I glance up and read the bold, white lettering stenciled across the navy-blue, wooden sign. OUR PLACE. Dark red bricks decorate the two-story building that's tucked between the town's post office and hardware store. I glance left and right and can't help but cringe at how neglected the outside of the restaurant looks. The exposure from the salt air doesn't help, but giving the restaurant a facelift is on the long list of things I've been meaning to do for months.

The glossy blue paint is chipped, and the white lettering on the glass-paned front door is starting to peel. The *O* and *L* look sad and deflated from where they're sitting above the restaurant's logo. A lobster. Because what else would we use for a seafood restaurant in New England? Cupping my hands around my eyes, I peer through the window of the front door. The rising sun glares off the glass, making it hard to see inside the dark restaurant. But I know exactly what you'll find inside. It's the same as it was when I was running in between the tables with my siblings and best friend...

The rattling of bike chains stops my mind from wandering down memory lane. I turn to find my youngest brother, Booth, pulling up along the sidewalk, looking way too cheerful for this frosty morning. He takes off his helmet and shakes out his hair. Out of all four kids, Booth is the only one of us not to take after our mom's dark blonde locks, instead inheriting our dad's dark brown—before he went bald, that is. Ironically, he is the only one to have our mom's icy blue eyes. Like me, he keeps his face clean shaven, though his reasoning is to show off the "money makers."

Or dimples, as most people call them.

"What's that face?" he asks.

Staring flatly at him, I ask, "What face?"

"That face." He points and chuckles. "Did Lottie put dirt in your French press again?"

"No." I nod toward the front doors and grimace at the reminder of my sweet daughter *kindly* adding extra flavor to my coffee a few weeks ago. "C'mon, we've got work to do before Mom and George get here. Did you finalize all your ideas for the spring menu?"

Booth chains his bike up at the stands by the front of the restaurant and nods with his gloves between his teeth.

Something that sounds like *most of them* but comes out like *moft ov dem* comes from behind the wool material.

"Great, because I really want to have it nailed down and ready to present this afternoon." I struggle to pull out the overflowing set of keys from my coat pocket and unlock the drab-looking front door. The rattling of keys between my trembling fingers must give away my nerves, because Booth sidles up next to me and takes them from me to unlock the door himself.

The gnawing feeling in the pit of my stomach hasn't disappeared since this meeting was arranged a couple of weeks ago. I've tried not to overthink what Mom and George want to discuss with us, but for the last eight months I've been dreading and expecting this day. Every time our middle brother, Graham, reports back the restaurant's monthly profits, and it remains in the red, the knot in my stomach grows in size.

"It'll be fine," Booth says as we step into the restaurant. Reaching for the beeping security alarm, I enter in the six-digit code, the action now a habit. "It's been a tough few months, but what do they expect during winter? April will be here soon, and we'll see more people coming in."

I shrug because I don't know how to respond. It's a good thing Booth is optimistic about today, because one of us needs to be. The lack of customers has nothing to do with the season, but I also have no clue as to why we're struggling to get people through the doors. Finding the time to get to the bottom of that issue is yet another item on my never-ending to-do list. The rising costs and people having to make certain cutbacks in their finances definitely doesn't help, and unfortunately, eating out is one of the first things people stopped doing. When other businesses in the area are thriving, it's hard not to feel like you've failed and question what you've done wrong.

This place, Our Place, holds so many memories from my childhood, teenage years, and adult life. I like to think it's those memories that keep the building standing, not the brick and mortar. It's also the place that reminds me of two people I lost in my life almost six years ago.

From the day my father and his oldest friend, George, decided to make their dream of going into business together come true, they wanted to create something special. Where families like their own could come to celebrate birthdays or anniversaries, couples could have awkward first dates, and friends could catch up over dinner and drinks. They did just that, but they also created a safe space for their own families to be raised. Somewhere my siblings and I could come to escape if we'd had a bad day at school or needed a home comfort away from home.

That's what Our Place is—a home away from home.

I only wish my dad and George's wife, Valerie, were here today to see what their dream has turned into.

Or perhaps it's best they're not.

two
PATRICK

"WHAT THE FUCK ARE *FIDDLEHEADS*?"

"They're furled up baby ferns. Really nutritious and cheap because we can forage for them in the park. They're perfect as garnishes," Booth says, like I should know exactly what they are. I'm too busy staring at the screen of my laptop and reading over his final menu proposal to catch his expression, but I know he's rolling his eyes.

I open the search engine and warily type in *fiddleheads*. When the results come up, it's not as bad as I thought, but I still recoil in disgust as I scroll through the images.

"Booth. They look like dead caterpillars. We're trying to encourage people to eat here, not have them call pest control on our asses. Can't we stick to cilantro like other restaurants? I don't want Martin Willis to claim we're probing his backyard for herbs again."

Booth snaps his head up from his laptop. "That dude has it out for me and you know it." A smile curves his lips. "Did you just say probing his backyard?"

"Shut up, man. I know he's a bit of a nuisance, but he gives us a great deal on vegetables, and we can't afford to lose that—

plus, he owns a lot of the buildings on Robin Road. Let's keep next season's dishes more home comfort than fine dining, okay?"

"This town wouldn't know *fine dining* if it smacked them across the face," he whines.

While sulking over his weird insect plants—and begrudgingly deleting *fiddleheads* from the menu—I look over last week's sales report that Graham has sent over. I scroll through the figures and when the red numbers continue their depressing pattern throughout the spreadsheet, my hand slams the laptop shut. Red for under profit. And for failure.

We're sitting at one of the two large oak tables in the restaurant today. The white, wooden chairs we're sitting on match the smaller tables dotted around the restaurant floor. Exposed brick covers the wall behind the bar, while the other walls are paneled and painted with a whitewash effect. If you didn't know Our Place was a seafood restaurant at first, you would when you walk in. Decades old fishing gear adorns almost every surface—buoys, fishing nets, and lobster traps decorate the space, along with pictures of the restaurant and the town over the years. In total, we can seat up to forty covers when it's a full house; though, I can't remember the last time we were at capacity.

My favorite part of the restaurant is the bar. Being along the coast, Dad and George wanted to give a nod to our town's location and history. Together they crafted a driftwood bar from random pieces of wood they collected over the years, right here in Sutton Bay. It took three weeks, one trip to the emergency room, and a lot of dollars in the swear jar. My dad always told me it was worth it and swore he could smell the Atlantic every time he walked in here. That, paired with the array of fresh seafood dishes, made this place a fisherman's wet dream.

Looking around, the wave of emotions and memories I'm hit with seems extra intense today. Something feels *off,* although I can't put my finger on it. Stepping in here is like walking through a time warp back to my childhood. There have been a few small changes over the years, but for the most part, it's exactly as it was the day it opened almost twenty-eight years ago.

In a way, this place is like a memorial for my dad and Valerie. It's hard not to be reminded of their memory whenever you're here. The interior might appear a little dated, yet if there's one thing my siblings and I can agree on, it's that we don't want to change anything about the decor—keeping Our Place forever frozen in time and holding onto whatever memories of our dad we can. He was the one to hang the black-and-white photos of fishermen on the walls. He was the one to beg our mom to pick a shade of white paint, even though he was adamant they were all the same. Even the tables with their wobbly legs hold memories: doing homework, eating lobster rolls, or jigsaw puzzles on rainy days.

A lot of other memories rise to the surface when I look around. They're not all happy ones, and I tend to tuck those away in the corner of my brain where they can be forgotten.

My dad and George were the official owners back when it opened, but their wives were very involved and had a big say in the direction of the restaurant. Mom and George are now the co-owners, however, have taken a backseat over the years and left a lot of the decision-making to Booth and me. Graham helps out as the restaurant's accountant, but he also has a long list of demanding clients to keep in check, so he isn't as involved. Florence, while she loves this place, is too busy jetting off around the world, and I think she prefers it like that. When responsibility was first handed to us, I recall pride swelling in my chest, so determined to prove to them and myself that I was cut out to run the restaurant. Only now, the pressure of those responsibilities has me snowed under with worry.

I wonder if they regret their decision.

I'm so deep in my thoughts that I don't notice my phone vibrating on the table at first. I look down to see Graham's name light up the screen and answer it before it rings out.

"What's up?" I ask.

"You won't believe who I just saw in town," he gruffs, his voice serious and deep as usual. Graham is the polar opposite of Booth. Night and day. Where Booth is smiles and jokes, Graham is brooding stares and grunts.

"Well hello to you too, sweetheart. How's your morning going?" Graham isn't one for salutations, so I decide to taunt him a little.

"Hello, hi. Did you hear what I said? I saw—"

A knock on the front door has me pulling the phone away from my ear, cutting off what he's saying. I look to the front of the restaurant and see my mom and George standing outside. I wave at them and point at the phone, but Booth is already walking over to unlock the door and let them inside.

"Listen, I've got to go; Mom and George are here. We'll catch up later."

"Patri—"

I end the call and cut off whatever he was about to say. He knows how to send a text.

A flurry of fresh snow follows behind Mom and George before Booth can shut the door. They shake off the snow from their hair and coats, dusting the floors in white specks that melt immediately from the warmth inside the restaurant. Their pink cheeks and noses are a reminder of how cold it is today.

"Hello, darling," my mom says as she unwraps herself from a knitted scarf that looks double her height. She's a petite woman, with dark blonde hair like mine, only hers is now streaked with gray and cut short, sitting just below her jawline. It's difficult not to feel anything but love and kindness when you look at her, although I wouldn't let that fool you—she's as honest as they come and won't hold back if she thinks you need putting in your place.

"Hey, Mom." I bend down to kiss her on the cheek, my six-foot-one frame towering over her. My brothers and I are all above six feet, and we constantly tease her about it, usually earning us a pinch to the back of our arms.

The swinging door to the kitchen opens, revealing Booth with cheeks stuffed full like a chipmunk—he must have snuck to the back when I wasn't looking—a bread roll in one hand and a plate in his other. He was recently promoted to head chef after his long-serving predecessor, Gloria, retired after twenty-seven years. She was the first employee the restaurant hired when they first opened their doors and was famous for her signature clambake, and blueberry pie.

Having my brother by my side has been such a blessing, especially as I tried to navigate life as a single parent and work full-time at the restaurant as bar manager. More recently, I've been balancing the role of both bar and restaurant manager, after the last one resigned in the summer. We've had lots of restaurant managers walk through the doors, but they've never lasted. My standards aren't high, I just have certain expectations, and most didn't make the cut.

We're not a huge restaurant but trying to juggle everything has been challenging and tiring. I admitted defeat two months ago and finally gave in to my mom and Booth's pestering to put an ad out for a restaurant manager.

So far we have had a whopping *zero* applicants.

I look at Booth, who is still stuffing his mouth. "Do you ever stop eating?"

Gulping down the bread roll almost whole, he shakes his head. "No, and that's why I'm taller than you."

"By one inch." I give him a blunt look.

"Every inch coun—"

"Booth Sadler!" my mom shouts, voice raised, but there's

zero vehemence behind her words. Booth is an absolute Mommy's boy, something even he doesn't deny.

"Sorry, Mom," Booth says as he settles back in his chair and places a plate of whoopie pies on the table.

"Can I get anyone a tea or coffee before we start?" asks George from behind the bar. George is a mountain of a man, and like my mom, his outward appearance is extremely misleading. Despite being built like an ox, he wouldn't hurt a fly. He's been like a father figure to me over the years, helped out so much with Lottie, and has been an amazing friend to my mom since Dad passed away.

We put in our orders, and Booth and I clear the table of papers and menus to make space for the drinks. We chat among ourselves about nothing in particular, until George places our drinks down on the table, the smell of freshly brewed coffee filling the room.

Once we're all settled around the table, I open my laptop and clear my throat. My mom and Booth sit opposite George, while I sit at the end, with my back to the door. "Shall we get started?"

"Well..." George hesitates and checks his watch. "Sure. Why don't you boys go over your proposal for the spring menu and then we can move on to other topics."

His tone and vagueness have me pausing for a second, but I ignore it, letting Booth talk over the changes he wants to make to the menu—something he's been pushing since he became head chef, with little success.

When he's finished, he looks up with a hopeful gleam in his eyes. My brother has worked extremely hard over the years, and to be in his position at only twenty-seven is a great accomplishment. He's always itching to try new and exciting dishes, but a lot of the people around town are quite happy with keeping the menu as it is, not wanting to move away from the classics we currently serve.

"So what do you think?" he asks eagerly.

From the look my mom's face, it's going to be the same response they've been giving him for months. She places a hand on top of his before answering. "It sounds fantastic and very modern. Although I'm not sure the town will be on board with this idea." Sympathy is laced through her words, and I know she hates seeing disappointment cloud his features.

My brother's shoulders practically drop to the floor with that response. His culinary skills and ideas are way beyond his years, yet when a lot of your regular customers are fishermen or people who have lived in Maine their entire lives, they'd rather see clam chowder on the table than *foie gras* and anything that sounds remotely French. *No offense to the French.*

"I get people don't like changes around here, but we've had the same menu for over twenty years, it needs to be spruced up a little bit," I say, trying to convince them to give this a shot.

"I'm not sure right now is the time for such a drastic change," George adds, which isn't the usual excuse they give Booth for denying his proposals.

"What else did you want to talk about?" I ask hesitantly, hoping this is the end of the meeting and they're not about to tell me the news I've been fearing for the past eight months.

"I noticed we haven't had any applications for the restaurant manager position," George replies with caution, which makes me shift in my seat. He looks to my mom and back to me before continuing. "You've done a great job at spinning all these plates recently, but we've found someone who has some great experience and will be a perfect fit."

"Okay...so who is it?" I ask. *Why are they being so cryptic?* The air in the room feels like it's shifting right before an angry storm rolls in without warning.

"Well, that's what we wanted to talk to you about first," my mom says, but before she can continue, the sound of the front door opening draws everyone's attention behind me. Booth must not have locked it and now I'm going to have to politely turn a customer away. Before I turn around, I notice the strange looks around the table: my mom looks apologetic, George looks relieved, and Booth looks like he's seen a ghost.

The moment a timid, yet familiar voice carries across the room, my head spins, and my heart plummets to my feet.

"Sorry I'm a little early."

It seems one of those memories I've tried my best to forget has just walked in.

I collect myself, school my face, and hope that no one can hear my thundering heart. I take a deep breath and turn in my seat toward the owner of the voice.

Honey-golden hair spills down her back. Deep, navy-blue eyes so dark they could hold a galaxy. Flushed pink cheeks to match her full pink mouth. A mouth I have no business knowing is as soft as it looks. And a constellation of freckles across her nose and round cheeks. They've been dulled by the lack of sun, however, I know they'll be back come summer.

It's strange that something so beautiful can cause such melancholy.

"You're fine, sweetie. We haven't gotten to the important stuff yet. Come in and get settled first," my mom says, and stands to greet her. It's not just anyone. No. Because standing in front of me is my childhood best friend.

The only woman I've ever given my heart to.

And the same woman who walked away and never returned it.

three
JOHANNA

I do my best to avoid the slushy puddles as I hurry down the sidewalk, but when the orangey-red hand flashes above me, I come to a sliding halt. My black tweed coat is covered in long blonde hairs, and I pluck them off as I wait to cross, which is when I notice the tremble in my hands. Shoving both hands in my pockets, I keep my head down and walk down the street. My fingertips rub incessantly together in my pockets, a nervous habit I've picked up over the years that helps quell my nerves.

It's only when I reach my destination that the nervousness threatens to spill out all over the sidewalk.

Our Place.

Simply reading the words has my chest tightening in longing and dread. My breathing quickens and I rub my fingers together so fast, I wouldn't be surprised if a fire broke out in my pockets.

I can do this. If not for me, then for my dad.

It's been too long. And though I don't hold the same fears and regrets I did six years ago, the mismatched red bricks and dark blue paint still tug at memories I thought were buried deep in my chest.

THOSE TWO WORDS

Today will be easy. Meet with Dad and Claire and discuss the job opening they have. Zero pressure. *Take your time.* That's what my dad said when he called last month asking for my help.

He's never pressured me to come back. I know he misses my sister and me and just wants us to be happy. My younger sister, Harriet, is definitely happy in Tennessee, living her dream in a small town on the outskirts of Nashville, playing her guitar and touring with artists across the country.

Me? I'm as happy as I think I can be.

Tennessee has been my home for almost six years, and although it was never supposed to be long term, I made friends out there. Had a good job. Spent lots of time with my baby sister. So yes, I was happy. I somewhat considered it home, but when Dad called to say the restaurant was struggling and my old job was available, I knew it was time to go *home*.

So here I am, back in my hometown of Sutton Bay. The place I've avoided for so long and at the same time yearned to return to. It's not a totally impulsive move, and I've talked about it to great lengths with my therapist, Amanda. I just never saw myself *actually* doing it. If anything, I wanted to feel brave enough to return here for the holidays or my dad's birthday. Amanda and my sister were as shocked as I was when I told them I'd quit my job, bought a one-way ticket, and was moving back. Harriet even tried to talk me out of it, but something deep down told me this was the right thing to do.

I'd put it off long enough.

I squeeze my hands into tight fists before pulling them out of my coat pocket, the cold air instantly nipping at my fingertips. With a deep breath, I push open the front door to the restaurant. As it creaks open and I step into the warm, open space, the first thing I notice is how much it *hasn't* changed. The hot air blasting from the overhead heater makes my eyes water, obscuring the four figures sitting in front of me—two more than I anticipated. When my vision clears, I see the mix of emotions across three of their faces. Guilt. Delight. Shock.

"Sorry I'm a little early." I wince at the wobble in my voice, needing to at least feign confidence today.

"You're fine, sweetie. We haven't gotten to the important stuff yet. Come in and get settled first," Claire says with such a warm smile it immediately puts me at ease. She stands and walks over to where I'm still standing by the front door. I love that she doesn't hesitate to pull me into a hug, her small frame somehow enveloping me like I'm not double her size.

I look back to the table and smile at my dad, who I expected to be here. I've been staying with him since I arrived back in town Saturday afternoon, so it's not the first time I've seen him today. Booth Sadler's face was not one I was expecting to see, although, I suppose it makes sense with him now being the head chef. I give him a hesitant smile and an awkward wave before my gaze drifts to the fourth person around the table. He hasn't turned around yet, but I don't need to see his face to know who it is. I'd recognize those wide shoulders and dark blond, shaggy hair anywhere.

Patrick.

I don't know if everyone in the room has gone silent as they wait for him to acknowledge me or if the beating of my heart has drowned out all the noise. When he finally turns around and looks at me, everything falls away. The moment those dark green eyes lock with mine, I suck in a sharp breath. It's like some invisible force of nature has me glued to the spot, because I want to look away from his scrutinizing stare, but I can't. Green like the towering pine trees that surround this town. Only these eyes don't hold any desire or kindness in them now. The usual warm glow has been swept away and replaced with a coldness, a lot like the cold winds blowing outside.

I'm not naïve to think he'd welcome me with open arms, no

matter how much I'd love to have them wrapped around me again. I don't know what I was expecting. Perhaps surprise or anger, but this hurts more. That nervous energy morphs into anxiety, and my fingers tap against my thigh.

A firm hand on my shoulder draws my attention away and I turn to find my dad looking down at me with kind eyes. Despite his calm presence easing my anxious thoughts, they still simmer beneath the surface.

"Hey, kiddo." My dad kisses the top of my head, and then turns toward the bar while still talking to me. "Take a seat and I'll grab you a coffee. Iced, I presume?" I don't miss his teasing tone, because yes, I drink iced coffee all year round.

"Yeah, thanks, Dad." Looking toward the table, I find the only two seats available are next to Patrick or at the other end of the table—where I will be sitting directly across from him, with no chance of avoiding eye contact. I shrug off my coat and hang it on the coat rack, summon all my courage, and sit to his right. Awkwardness hangs in the air, and I know everyone can feel it.

My dad comes over, places a tall glass in front of me, and as I watch the condensation run down the edges, I take some steadying breaths before properly taking in my surroundings. My eyes drift to Booth and Claire, who are both smiling at me from across the table. *At least they want me here.* Memories of my childhood come rushing back as I take in the familiar décor, paintings, and photographs, but I'm drawn to one photograph in particular that sits above the bar. The sharp sting in my sternum has me clamping my eyes shut and I try not to let my racing thoughts feed my anxiety any further.

A throat clears to my left and I jolt at the noise. Patrick's gaze darts between mine and the photograph, and I swear that frigid stare starts to thaw, but it's gone before I can blink.

"Why are you here?" he grits out. His words hit me right in

the chest. It feels as though someone is injecting ice-cold water directly into my veins with how quickly that all-too-familiar feeling spreads from my fingertips and up my arms.

"Patrick," Claire scolds, but the buzzing in my ears blocks out his reply. I breathe in deeply through my nose and let out a shaky breath through my mouth. My dad's hand rests on my arm as I concentrate on my breathing.

Look for something red. Look for something red. Look for something red. I internally remind myself as my eyes dart around the room.

Red buoy.
The red of a miniature lighthouse.
Red ketchup bottle.
The red polish on my nails.
The red notebook sitting on the table.

The distraction does exactly what it's intended to do—to help my mind focus on something else, other than the rising panic. I understand why he's reacting this way. I really do. It doesn't lessen the blow, though.

Only once the buzz of anxiety settles does Patrick's question hit me.

"I'm here about the restaurant manager job..." My voice trails off as I take in the confused expressions from Booth and Patrick. *Do they not know?* I look to my dad, who is finding the grooves in the table very interesting all of a sudden.

"Well, you'll need to apply and send in your resume, like all the other applicants." Patrick's tone is cool and his face void of emotion.

"What other applicants?" Booth asks, but he promptly clamps his mouth shut when Patrick snaps his head toward him. *Busted.*

Before Booth has the chance to say the wrong thing again, Claire cuts in. "Nonsense, we haven't had any applications in months. Johanna would be perfect for the restaurant manager position. It was her job before she—"

"Left. Before she left," Patrick interrupts. "Do I not get a say in this?"

"Of course you do," Claire says. "But we need someone experienced and available now. Johanna is both of those things."

"What's the rush?" Patrick asks.

"Well, that's the other thing we wanted to discuss with you all today," my dad continues. He isn't a shy man and has always been careful with his words. From the unease in his voice, I don't think we're going to like what he has to say. "The restaurant is struggling."

My stomach drops and I allow my eyes to drift to Patrick. He doesn't look surprised by this news, but from the rigidness in his shoulders, it's not welcomed, and neither am I.

Claire must sense the hurt in his gaze. "There are lots of reasons why this is happening. Costs are rising but we've always been adamant we don't want that to affect the fair wage we pay our employees. Plus, a lot of larger neighboring towns are opening up restaurants. It's competitive, and the market is very saturated right now."

I'm not sure if her words comfort Patrick, but he nods his head slowly anyway.

"Either way," my dad says. "We need to do something fast, and this is why we called this meeting. We need to get people back into the restaurant, and you both need to work together to do that."

"Together?" I say, just as Patrick asks in a shocked tone. "What do you mean *both*?"

"Together," my dad confirms with a nod. "We have until May to see some big changes or..."

"Or?" Patrick asks, leaning in closer to my dad, waiting for his response.

Call it daughterly instinct, but I know exactly what my dad is going to say as he glances at Claire. They share a look of discomfort, before my dad looks back toward Patrick and me.

"Or we'll have to look at selling the restaurant."

four
JOHANNA

When I was in third grade, Tommy Gillespie told me that Santa Claus wasn't real. I was devastated and spent the rest of the day at school and the bus ride home crying my little heart out. Once my parents calmed me down and had the "talk"—not that one—I was in a state of shock for about a week.

The shock of that news feels minuscule compared to the bombshell my dad just dropped.

"What do you mean sell?" Patrick asks, panic seeping from his tone.

"We mean, it's been almost a year since we've had a profitable month. The cost of produce is rising and with competitors opening their doors every week and large chains in the city, we don't see this being a viable business for much longer," Claire explains.

So many questions zip around in my brain, but I can't seem to find my voice to ask them. I knew things hadn't been great from what Dad told me over the phone, but from the worry etched into his face now, it's clear things are much worse than he let on. Guilt hits me hard at that realization, and I wish I asked him what was happening sooner, because while I haven't worked here in almost six years, this place means the world to me.

My dad and Patrick's dad, Ted, put so much passion, love, time, and money into Our Place. To hear they're thinking of selling after nearly twenty-eight years feels like my childhood is disappearing before my eyes. It's a different type of loss I didn't expect to face when returning to town. I won't deny that this place is a painful reminder of my mom and Ted no longer being with us—something I struggled to acknowledge at first—but I would never want the restaurant to stop being a part of my life.

Every surface of this place reminds me of my mom. If you look closely at the parquet floor, you can spot a crimson-red stain from where my dad dropped a crate of wine after she jumped out and scared him one Halloween. Or the paneled wall by the bar, you will find about twenty poorly patched-up holes from where she tried and failed to hang up picture frames. It's a bittersweet pillar to her memory.

Every corner, surface, and crevice reminds me of her absence. It may have been almost two decades since she died, though sometimes I feel like that lost and shattered seventeen-year-old when I think too hard about it. Which is why I don't talk about her often.

This is where Harriet took her first steps. Where Ted and Claire told their friends and family they were expecting Florence. Where we all came to take pictures before prom. Where I came to cry on my mom's shoulder after my high school boyfriend dumped me. Where I realized my feelings for Patrick went much further than friendship.

This place is both a safe haven and a reminder of some of my hardest days.

Patrick and Booth are in a state of shock and haven't uttered a word since the news broke out. Booth is uncharacteristically quiet, and Patrick is hyper focused on something in front of him—I don't think he's blinked for minutes.

I decide to break the deafening silence. "Surely hiring me isn't a smart business decision then? That's going to cost you more money."

That brings Patrick back into the room, because his eyes whip to mine. He just stares at me, and my god, I can feel all the words he isn't speaking. I knew today would be hard. That seeing him for the first time in years would have those feelings I'd hoped had been pushed aside racing back to the surface at full force; I'm surprised they haven't toppled me backward off the chair.

It's crazy what time can do to someone, because there's no way I ever thought of this *man* as boyish. I'm sure as heck not complaining, though, because Patrick is really pulling off the fine lines and creases around his eyes. I'd like to presume those lines are from laughing, I wouldn't know though. It's been so long since I heard it, and I'm not sure I even deserve to anymore.

The crooked nose he's always hated after breaking it during a lacrosse game is still as endearing; so perfectly imperfect against his handsome features. The white scar on the cleft of his chin. Dark brows. A sharp jaw he used to keep clean is shadowed with stubble today. Perhaps *she* likes the stubble.

No, I'm not going down that road. I have no right to be angry or jealous.

"Listen, kids, I know this is a lot to take in right now, but please trust us on this decision." Dad looks at me before casting his eyes to Patrick. "Hiring Johanna is the best thing for the restaurant right now."

I almost want to laugh that my dad still refers to us as kids, considering I'm older than he was when he had me. *Almost,* because I'm too busy feeling weighed down by the sudden pressure from his last words.

"Take a couple of days to think about it. Both of you. If we can all agree, Johanna will manage the front of house, Booth the kitchen, and Patrick can oversee the general day-to-day and bar. The more hands on deck will free you up and give you the time you've struggled to find, Pat. It's not a punishment, we know how hard you work." I don't know what his relationship with Patrick and Booth is like anymore, but from the looks on their faces, they trust my dad.

Both brothers nod their heads in unison, giving their silent agreement. And then four sets of eyes land on me. So much for *Take a couple of days,* because I'm feeling the pressure to make a decision here and now.

I think about what's at stake. My family's business. Memories of my mom and Ted. My already hopeless heart.

This isn't what I expected to sign up for when Dad asked me to come back to town, and I'm still surprised I'm sitting here at this table despite all my fears and regrets. Maybe this is a way to prove to not only myself but everyone around me that I'm not the disappointment they think I am. It's clear Patrick doesn't want me here; a truth I'll have to ignore for now.

This is definitely something I need to unpack with my therapist, and while my brain is screaming at me to slow down and think this through, I know this is what I need to do. Pride and heart be damned.

Pushing back my shoulders, I take a deep breath before speaking, my voice no longer wobbly.

"I'm in. Tell me when and I'm yours."

five
PATRICK

I'M YOURS.

Words whispered in the dark of night. Two words that were breathlessly repeated over and over again when limbs were tangled in bedsheets. Two words that felt like a promise.

Words that quickly turned into a lie but have been branded on my heart and embedded in my brain since they were spoken. The burn still feels as fresh as the day I was marked.

I shake myself out of the somber memories and walk toward Lottie's bathroom. I can't see her putting up a fight at bedtime tonight, considering she spent the evening at my mom's and chasing Graham's dog, Curly, around in the snow for over an hour.

There are three bedrooms on the second floor; mine has the en suite bathroom, and Lottie has taken over the small one down the hallway. The other room is technically a guest room, but since all my family lives in town, it doesn't get used much. There's also one smaller room on the ground floor that I use as my study and home gym. The open plan kitchen and dining area is my favorite spot in the house, letting me catch up with

Lottie about her day while I'm cooking dinner and she's coloring at the dining table.

I might be a single guy, but I like to think my house is decorated with good taste; though, I have my mom and sister to thank for that. I began looking for a house to buy when Carrie was halfway through her pregnancy, knowing I'd need somewhere bigger to raise a child. Two months later I moved out of my one-bedroom apartment in the middle of town and closed on this four-bedroom, Victorian-style coastal home, on the outskirts of town. I wanted to make sure my kid would have a childhood similar to mine; with the ocean at their doorstep, endless space to get up to no good, and unconditional love at every corner of their life.

Carrie only lives a short drive away in Jacob's Bluff, one of the neighboring towns, making it easy for Lottie to share her week with us both. She usually spends Wednesday to Saturday with Carrie and Sunday to Tuesday with me, though we're pretty flexible. Carrie is an EMT, and her schedule is just as unpredictable as mine sometimes, but we try to keep it consistent for Lottie's sake.

Although Lottie wasn't planned, there would never be any doubt in anyone's mind that she is loved, cared for, and supported. Carrie and I pride ourselves on showing her that even though we aren't together like other parents, we show a united front and act like a team. I have never seen Carrie as anything more than a friend—and I know she shares the sentiment—but I love her for bringing my daughter into the world. Something I will forever be grateful for. Years ago, I saw myself raising a child with a different woman, but life had other plans for me. *Young and naïve.*

No one stuck around after the tense meeting today, and I'm not ashamed to say I went and hid in the back office while George went over some final details with Johanna.

My new coworker.

THOSE TWO WORDS

Jesus, what has my life come to? If someone had told me my week would start with *her* not only walking back into my life but that we'd be forced to work alongside each other at such high stakes, I would have laughed hysterically in their face. It appears that fate is now laughing in mine.

Peeking around the door frame to Lottie's bathroom, I check to see how she's doing. I find her making funny faces in the mirror, looking a lot like a rabid raccoon, thanks to the toothpaste foam lining her mouth. She catches my reflection in the mirror and her goofy face breaks out into the biggest grin, instantly erasing the sullen mood I've been in since leaving the restaurant. I like to call it *Lottie therapy*.

"Excuse me, miss, have you seen my daughter?" I ask in faux confusion while looking around the bathroom dramatically, even whipping back the shower curtain.

She looks a little concerned for a nanosecond but then quickly catches on to my joke. "She doesn't live here. I do, the *bon-don-ible* snowman." She curls her fingers, raises them in the air, and growls.

"Oh my! Well, *a-bom-i-na-ble* snowmen don't need bedtime stories. Guess I'll get going." Thumbing behind me, I back slowly out of the bathroom.

She scrambles down from her stool and wipes her mouth on the hand towel hanging next to the sink. "Dadd-eeeeee! It's me, it's me. I love story time. Come on." She grabs my hand and pulls me down the hallway toward her bedroom, with a lot of strength for someone so tiny. "We have to get a move on."

I laugh because this is exactly what I said to her this morning when we were running late.

Once she's tucked underneath her mint-green comforter, surrounded by her favorite stuffed animals and her twinkling night-light is on, I settle my large frame beside her. We read her favorite dinosaur princess bedtime story—voices and all—but she drifts off to sleep before I get to the last page.

Pushing her hair back, I drop a kiss to her forehead and shut off her overhead light. "Sweet dreams, spud," I whisper, before tiptoeing out of her room.

As soon as I'm outside her door, my phone buzzes in my back pocket and my smartwatch shows me it's Graham. *Don't I have a bone to pick with him.*

Making sure I'm far enough away from Lottie's room so I don't wake her, I accept the call and don't bother with niceties.

"Thanks for the heads up, you prick!" I whisper-shout.

"Whoa, now hold up. If this outburst is about this afternoon, I would like to remind you that I called to *warn* you about the town's newest arrival. It's not my fault you hung up on me before I could tell you. Do you want to apologize?"

"Well...you could have tried harder. I walked right into that meeting looking like the biggest fucking idiot. I could barely look at her without wanting to..." *Strangle her? Hold her? Kiss her?*

My eyes widen at that last one, as if my internal thoughts were broadcasted through the phone to my brother, and I'm glad he can't see the heat warming my cheeks.

"Without what?"

"Nothing, nothing. This is a total mess. I'm guessing Mom told you about what she and George proposed?"

"Mm-hm. She sure did. I'm sorry I didn't let you know how bad the finances have gotten. Mom swore me to secrecy until they had spoken to you." I hear the hurt in his own voice, and I know how hard it would have been for him to keep that information under lock and key. "How do you feel about it all?"

I know he's not only referring to the restaurant. I've spent all day playing today's meeting on repeat in my head and the only conclusion I've come to so far is that I have no idea how I'm going to handle being in such close proximity with Johanna and stop myself from asking that burning question.

Why did you leave?

I wish I didn't care, yet there are so many reasons why I do. Not knowing what happened all those years ago has slowly eaten me up inside, to the point that I feel numb anytime I hear her name or see something that reminds me of her.

She's exactly as I remembered her, if not more heartbreakingly beautiful. Something about the way she carried herself and reacted to certain things had me pausing. The sudden stiffness to her muscles, the way she avoided eye contact, the glint of panic in her eyes when I first spoke. I hated the way I reacted and how I spoke to her, but I was completely blindsided by her arrival.

"Honestly? I have no idea. The restaurant is a punch to the throat, but I knew we couldn't carry on pretending that the number of customers wasn't dwindling each day. Jo, on the other hand? Yeah, didn't see that coming." It's been over five years since we last spoke and I'm still none the wiser as to why she left. Last my mom said she was doing well in Tennessee, so why would she abandon that life at the drop of a hat and move back to town?

Graham hums in agreement down the line. "What are your plans for the restaurant then?"

"Apart from avoiding her as much as I can, I don't know where to start. I never knew things were *this* bad."

Graham is silent, and I know he's thinking of the best way to respond. This news is hard on all of us, and I know Graham will be quietly stewing in his thoughts.

"Well, be careful. I know how close you two were and I don't want you to get hurt again." Something about Graham's tone makes me think he has more to say on the matter, but he doesn't press me on the subject. He's never vocalized it, but I know Jo's leaving cut Graham much deeper than he let on. He doesn't know the full story about what happened between us before she left, and it's not something I'll be sharing with him anytime soon.

"You've got nothing to worry about. I can't see her sticking around for long."

"I don't know, Pat. Mom said something this evening about going easy on Jo and not judging her too quickly. Maybe you guys can finally talk about what happened."

"There's nothing for us to talk about. She made that clear enough."

I decide to change the topic, not wanting to dwell on Jo's return and my failing as manager. We make plans to go for a drink later in the week, and Graham offers to pick Lottie up from school tomorrow. We hang up, I let out a long sigh, tilt my head back to rest against the cushion, and stare up at the ceiling. My eyes follow the path of a crack in the crown molding, and for once I allow myself to think back to the weeks following my dad's death, his funeral, and Jo's departure.

The memories leave my jaw aching from how hard I'm grinding my teeth together. I try not to think about one day in particular, but as always, fail miserably. I acted on impulse, allowed my emotions and bruised heart to lead me, and I saw something I didn't want to see. And it was the straw that broke the camel's back.

Weeks later, I was in an even worse state. I lost myself in the restaurant and was working over sixty-hour weeks. My family dealt with the loss of Dad in their own way, but I knew they saw the additional loss I was carrying. For whatever reason, they knew better than to ask.

Only my best friend, Dex, called time-out on my pity party when he saw I was practically dead on my feet and losing weight. Deciding I needed a change of scenery, he took me out for a few drinks in Jacob's Bluff, rather than our usual drinking hole, Shirley's. Only a few turned into too many. I wasn't blackout drunk, but it was enough for me to reveal all to Dex as I held back the tears in the middle of the bar. I don't remember much after that. I do remember meeting Carrie and going home with her.

The guilt of that night was acidic, eating me from the inside out. Betrayal and hurt still riddled my mind and heart from the loss of Jo, but never in my life did I see myself trying to get over it like that. We weren't official, but it still felt like cheating. I'd somehow convinced myself that everything I saw was a mistake and perhaps if I tried to reach out to Jo again, she could explain it all as a complete misunderstanding. I just needed to get my head straight first before contacting her.

Only I never got that chance, because a few weeks later, Carrie called me out of the blue asking to meet up. I wasn't proud of the night we spent together and wasn't interested in a relationship with anyone. Probably because I still held out hope Jo would realize she belonged in Sutton Bay with me.

When Carrie told me she was pregnant, my world was flipped upside down. I didn't forget about Jo—that's a skill I will never be able to master—but I knew I had to show up for Carrie and the baby we were now expecting. It didn't feel right to reach out to Jo, and guilt still ate away at me. It might not have been planned, but the idea of becoming a father felt so right. After weeks of heartache, the unexpected news brought light and happiness to my family and me. And the loss of my dad and Jo hurt a little less as each day passed.

Two months before Lottie came into the world, I received a text that answered all the self-doubting questions that had been running rampant in my mind for months.

I guess you're done waiting. Don't worry about me, I'm not your problem anymore. Now I know why your calls stopped.

It took all my willpower not to pick up the phone and demand answers from her. To tell her she *was* my problem and I'd never been done waiting. She was the one who had clearly moved on.

I knew nothing good would come from making that call or

responding to that text. What I wanted wasn't a priority anymore, because I had to step up and put my past behind me. That was the last time we spoke, and before I knew it, I was the father of a little girl. She was the one thing that now held all my attention and love. The moment my eyes fell on my daughter, nothing else mattered. Everything I did was for her.

Only after seeing Johanna Thomas for the first time in years, two things are clear.

The burns from her leaving never fully healed.

And she still lights me up like no woman ever has.

I might not *like* what my mom and George are proposing, but I won't let my damaged pride get in the way of working together to save the restaurant. If I don't do it for myself, I'll do it for my dad.

As I struggle to fall asleep, I forget about Graham's warnings to be careful. Because when sleep finally finds me, I dream of a woman with golden-blonde hair and dark blue eyes.

The only difference between the woman in my dreams and the one I saw today is their smile.

Because the smile I remember rivaled the sun. The one I saw today was fake and dulled.

And I wish I didn't care so much to find out why.

six

JOHANNA

I HUFF OUT A BREATH AS I FINALLY SQUEEZE THE LAST OF MY clothing into the small walk-in closet.

My first week back in town has gone much quicker and better than I anticipated. I managed to secure a three-month lease on a one-bedroom apartment above the new bakery on Robin Road. Unlimited iced coffee and pastries at my doorstep? Say less. When my dad helped me drive over some of my old things from the house this morning, the smell of fresh bread and coffee was the first thing to greet us.

I couldn't believe my luck, and while I've loved spending time with my dad, at thirty-three years old, staying in your childhood room doesn't scream *I have my shit together*. I was surprised to find out the entire building was owned by Martin Willis, the town's produce supplier, and was even more surprised he gave me such a good deal. Growing up, the man was known as the town's pariah, always standoffish and blunt, but he seemed quite happy to rent out the apartment to me.

The closet looks like it's ready to bust open and I have to shove my shoulder against the door to shut it securely. Once everything is unpacked, I walk into the open living space and look around my new home. The apartment has a small bathroom, and the kitchen, living, and dining areas are open plan. Looking out of the window, I take in the warm glow from the streetlights below, spotlighting the piles of slowly melting snow. I make a mental note to add a couple of plants to my online shopping cart, knowing they'll look cute on the windowsill and get plenty of sunlight.

While this move didn't feel impulsive at first, it sure as hell does now. Less than two weeks ago, I was living with Harriet, working the same job and living a quiet life, with no clue what was on the horizon.

This whole week deserves a little celebration, so I pour myself a hearty glass of sauvignon blanc, make up a small plate of cheese and crackers, and sit on the floor with my back against the small sectional the apartment came with.

I unbox one of my new jigsaw puzzles and tip the pieces out on the hardwood floor in front of me. This one is of Paris skyline. As I set aside the outside pieces, my mind wanders to this week's events.

I knew my return would prompt some chatter among the locals, but most people have greeted me with a smile or asked how Harriet and I were. The unease of seeing everyone slowly disappeared as the week progressed. It came roaring back on Thursday when I was running some errands for my dad and ran into Mrs. Stewart—one of the town council members and local busybody. When she realized it was me, she spent a long time examining me before shaking her head slowly, *tsking*, and walking away.

I abandoned the items in my cart and called Harriet from my car, who helped calm me down. Her parting words were, "*Tell that old bird to stick her judgy eyes where the sun don't shine next time.*" She has a special way with words even outside of songwriting.

The next day, I spent my first online therapy session overthinking every single interaction I had so far, convinced people were judging me for leaving and abandoning my dad and the Sadlers during their time of need. Amanda reminded me that people don't know the full story and will make their own assumptions about why I left—I just wish they wouldn't presume I did it happily—and I get to decide who and when I tell people. It's my story to tell, but in that moment, the shame and fear I used to feel about people finding out the truth started to show its ugly face.

Leaving this town was one of the hardest decisions I ever made, but at the same time, the best thing I could have done for myself.

I felt settled after my forty minutes of word-vomiting to Amanda, and we finished the session going over my preferred coping mechanisms, should my anxiety and panic become unbearable. I haven't had an attack in two years, and I know it's important I'm always prepared for the unexpected and to not ignore the signs. It took me a long time to acknowledge what was happening and to stop brushing it under the rug.

It's pure luck I'm still able to have sessions with Amanda. She isn't licensed to practice in Maine, but one of her colleagues, Davis, knew a member of the state's licensing board and we were able to agree to some short-term virtual sessions. It sucks that I'll have to find a new therapist eventually, but the process of finding someone I click with isn't as daunting now.

Since the meeting at the restaurant, I haven't seen or heard from Patrick, which comes as no surprise. That will all change tomorrow, because Monday morning is my first day as restaurant manager—and our first shift together. Looking back on our last shift together, there's no doubt it's going to be the polar opposite experience. Flirty banter swapped for awkward silence.

I'm about to top up my wine glass, when my phone vibrates

with an incoming video call. I turn it over and find a picture of Harriet riding a mechanical bull. Holding my phone up to my face, I click accept and I'm greeted with the sight of her ear canal. For a twenty-seven-year-old, she is worryingly inept when it comes to technology. A disappointment to millennials everywhere.

"Harry, you *video*-called me, you nugget!" I shout at the screen.

She changes the angle of the camera, and it pans to her scrunched-up face of confusion. I see the second realization hits her, and then she's smacking the palm of her hand to her forehead. "It's actually embarrassing how many times I do that."

We both take after our mom with our bright blonde hair, freckled skin, dark brows, and tall frames. Our dad always said he was grateful for that, but I'm glad we share his blue eyes.

My baby sister has been my constant since I left Sutton Bay. It was my job as Big Sister to console her and try to fill the huge gap our mom left after she passed. We found our roles reversed when I followed her to Tennessee after Ted's funeral. She held me tightly as I cried silently during our flight to Nashville, and even slept in my bed that first week. During the hardest days, she would comfort me, but she also gave me the push I needed to be honest with myself and get the help I needed. That was the hardest step, and though it still felt like I was walking through molasses, it eventually got easier as each day passed.

She never made me feel like a burden. She helped me find a job at one of the local restaurants and let me infiltrate myself into her small friendship group. I wasn't sure I would ever see the light at the end of the tunnel when I left Sutton Bay, but she stood by my side, holding the flashlight every step of the way.

She's flown home a few times over the years, but Dad usually chose to come visit us for the holidays. There'd been a few occasions I was close to joining Harriet during her visits home, but the anxiety always got the better of me. I also knew there was no avoiding Patrick in this small town, so I stayed put.

"I swear Dad would have better luck navigating a smartphone than you," I tease.

"Hey! My brain works where it counts."

"I can't argue with you there. To what do I owe this pleasure?" I ask in my over-the-top British accent. It's my default when I get nervous and can feel my anxiety creeping in. Not that this phone call induces that, I just know she's going to want to talk about tomorrow.

"So, how are you feeling about tomorrow?"

See?

I stand, abandoning the puzzle, and sit cross-legged on the sofa. "Nervous. Excited. Antsy." I run my fingers down the stem of the wine glass, keeping my eyes trained on the movement. "Worried how he's going to act around me."

"Hmm. I think you've got to let him ride out those feelings. Maybe...never mind." She shakes her head, and her evasion piques my interest.

"Maybe what?"

She lets out a big breath before continuing. "I'm so proud of what you're doing. Honestly, I thought you were joking at first, but I know how happy Dad is that you're back. A lot of time has passed, maybe it's time to talk things out with Patrick."

"You didn't see how he looked at me on Monday. Like we were strangers. I doubt my reason for leaving is enough to wipe away everything that went down. I left him during one of the worst times in his life."

Even through the phone I can see the gears turning in her head. "Okay, so you might not get the response you're hoping for. But isn't telling him better than holding it in? Please don't forget that you had a lot on your plate too."

"He's not going to care, Harry!" I snap. "Sorry, sorry. I know you're trying to help. Let's drop it, I'm too tired to try to predict what mood he'll be in tomorrow. One day at a time."

"You're fine, I get it. Really." She blows a kiss through the screen, the topic dropped. "Well, how is everyone? I haven't been back since this tour kicked off, but hopefully I can come visit later in the summer."

The idea of Harriet visiting perks me up, even if it's months away. "They're good. I haven't seen anyone apart from Dad since Monday. Graham is around, though he's keeping to himself as usual. Dad said Flo is somewhere in South America right now. As for the people of this town, well, they're exactly the same. Nosey and everywhere you look."

She laughs at that, throwing herself backward onto her bed. "I'm hoping you haven't seen much more of Mrs. Stewart?"

"No, thank god. There's the cutest new bakery below my apartment though. I met the owner, Quinn, and she makes the best iced coffees."

"Oh, Jo..." My sister sighs. "Still with the iced coffee in below-zero temperatures? Could you get more basic?" I gasp in mock horror. "Seriously though, don't let that old fart bother you. You've worked so hard and only the people closest to you need to know the truth. It's up to you if you tell Patrick. For what it's worth, I know he's not going to pass the same judgment you've experienced from others. You're going to do great tomorrow. Chin up and show them you don't care what they think."

"Thanks, sis. I'll try. I'll text you tomorrow when my shift ends. Love you."

"Love you too. I'm proud of you. Give Dad a hug and say hi to Mom for me." We share a sad smile and I promise her that I will.

I finish off my wine and go through my nightly routine before cocooning myself into my comforter, ready to get a good eight hours. Only I find myself staring aimlessly at the small picture frame on my bedside table. *How did we ever get here?* I think to myself. From best friends to the man, I...well, whatever we were is so far from what we are now that I can't see us ever finding our way again.

After hours of tossing and turning, my brain finally switches off. The last thing I think is Patrick Sadler will never be a stranger to me, no matter how much we act like it.

Taking in a deep breath of salty, crisp air, I watch the waves retreat from the tips of my boots at Piper Beach. Snow still covers the beach, but patches of golden sand peek out along the water's edge. The crashing of waves and distant cries of seagulls are sounds I didn't know I missed until this moment. A strong sense of nostalgia carries with the wind.

Summer barbecues. Sand-covered hot dogs. Water fights in the shallow waters. Hot cider on cool fall nights.

I managed to get a few hours of sleep, but my body decided it was time to wake up before the sun today. That would have been fine had I remembered to stock coffee in my apartment, but not having any gives me a good reason to pay Quinn a visit this morning. For now, the cold winds whipping across my face will have to do its best at waking me up. Trudging down the beach, the satisfying sound of snow crunching beneath my feet, I try to remind myself of Harriet's words last night. That confidence is now overshadowed by nerves the closer the clock ticks to the start of my shift.

My brain seems to be working overtime this morning and a swarm of negative words and questions swirls around my brain like an angry hurricane.

Selfish. Disloyal. Heartless.

What would her mother think?

It's hard not to presume people think the worst of me, when I spent years thinking the same things about myself.

A sudden gust of icy wind hits me in the face, making my eyes water and ears ache. Calling time-out on today's morning outing, I walk back to my apartment. I look up the hill that is Robin Road, leading right through the town, and puff my chest to prepare myself for the steep walk. The view is always better going down, plus, my thighs aren't used to such steep inclines anymore.

The sun breaches the horizon as I reach my apartment, the sky now a hue of pinks, purples, and oranges. As I'm unlocking my door, a smiling face waves at me through the window of the bakery. Quinn gestures to the coffee machine and I nod my head and hold up my hands, letting her know I'll be ten minutes.

We hit it off immediately. She is probably the bubbliest and most welcoming person I have ever met, and is a tiny little thing, with envious curves and an infectious smile.

Unlocking the first door, I jog up the small flight of stairs, unlock the main door to my apartment, and strip out of my clothes. I trade my leggings and fleece for a pair of distressed jeans, dark green sweater, and black ankle boots. I'm not short at five foot nine, but a little heel gives me that extra boost of confidence. I glance at myself in my bedroom mirror. I did my best to hide the shadows under my eyes, and my hair is thrown up in a messy bun as usual. A quick swipe of mascara and blush makes me look less ghoulish, and I accept it's the best I'm going to look today.

"You've got this," I reassure my reflection. I throw on my coat, head back downstairs, and walk into the bakery just as Quinn is setting my take-out cup of iced coffee on the counter.

"Oh my goodness, you are a fairy godmother sent by the coffee gods," I groan in excitement. I make grabby hands toward the cup, before grasping the cold plastic between my fingers, and taking a long sip.

"I'm cold from watching you drink that." She laughs as she wipes down the coffee machine.

I let out a sigh as the sweet, coconut flavor bursts across my tongue and the first hit of caffeine enters my bloodstream. Nothing, and I mean *nothing*, beats that first sip of coffee in the morning.

"I don't care, it's good three hundred and sixty-five days a year, and I'll never stop." My voice is much cheerier now that I've had some coffee.

"Well, this is on the house." She places a paper bag with a little bit of grease staining the middle. I'm about to tell her I can't accept it for free, but she stops me when she points a finger at me and looks very stern for someone so chirpy. "For your first day—a good luck ham and cheese croissant."

"You had me at cheese." I take hold of the bag and inhale the melty, gooey goodness that's definitely Swiss cheese. "Thanks, Quinn."

"You're welcome. Knock 'em dead!" She cheers, and I can't help laughing at her enthusiasm as I wave goodbye and make my way back outside.

Making a new friend since coming back to town—something I didn't see happening—makes me feel a little lighter and puts a pep in my step. My commute to work is short and I reach my destination in seven minutes flat; one of the best things about my new apartment is that it is exactly two blocks away from the restaurant. It would probably take me less time on a normal day, however, the sidewalk is still extremely icy, so my steps are taken with caution.

Although I'm still a ball of nervous energy and feel like I might puke any second, this day has started off okay, and I shimmy on the spot in celebration when I reach the front door of the restaurant. Only I forget that the sidewalk is moonlighting as an ice rink today, and it's too late to right myself, because in a split second, I'm on my ass and covered in iced cold coffee.

Feeling momentarily dazed from my fall, I lie there motionless, waiting for my vision to clear. Only, when it does, I'm met with the angry stare of my new coworker.

Yay first day!

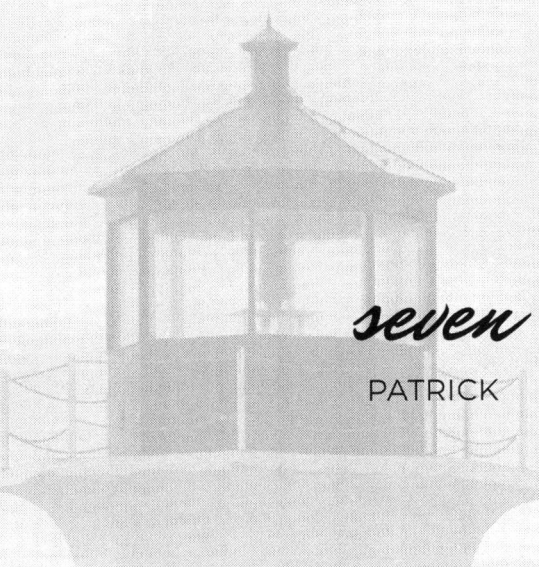

seven
PATRICK

Watching Jo do this little dance from across the street makes me forget who we are for a second. The elated look on her face and wiggle of her hips remind me of the old Jo, and I don't have the grit to tear my eyes away—which is fortunate, because in the blink of an eye she goes careening backward and almost cracks her head on the concrete.

Cursing, I check for cars and run across the street, trying not to meet the same fate as her. Once I get to her sprawled-out body, I stand over her and stare down at the sidewalk. Even covered in gray slush and brown liquid I'm captivated by her.

And that pisses me off. These feelings have no right to show themselves after years of being hidden away.

From the hesitant look on her face, I know I'm doing a shitty job at hiding my irritation. Before she can say anything, I lean down, grab hold of her hands, and haul her to her feet. Whether I underestimate my own strength or forget how light she is, she ends up barreling into my chest and we almost go flying backward into the snow. I manage to right us and hold her steady with my hands resting on her hips. Even with a thick winter coat on, I can feel the flare of her hips and where it tapers into a small waist.

Like I've been burned, my hands shoot back to my sides, and I clear my throat.

"You're here early," I point out. Avoiding eye contact, my gaze stays lowered and that's when I notice the take-out cup and squashed paper bag on the ground. "Shit, did you spill coffee on yourself?"

"Ugh, yes," she grumbles as she tries to shake off the snow and coffee residue. "It's a good thing I don't drink cappuccinos."

"I cannot believe you still drink iced coffee in this weather."

Her movements halt at my comment, and I try to hide my wince. I shouldn't know or care what she drinks all year round. Just like I shouldn't be thinking about how the blush on her cheeks is probably spreading across her chest right now.

Begging my brain to shut up, I turn away abruptly, pretending for both our sakes that I didn't say that. Once the front door is unlocked, I gesture for her to go in first and follow close behind. Reaching out for the security alarm, I take my time entering the code, and will myself to chill the fuck out before turning to face her.

Yeah, that doesn't help.

She removes her coffee-stained coat with a defeated look on her face, and it takes every cell in my body not to reach out and try to cheer her up. That's what I would have done years ago, and clearly, the time apart isn't enough for old habits to die. Draping her coat over her arm, she pulls her lips between her teeth and averts her eyes before speaking.

"I, umm, thought I'd come in early and try to get a head start on the day. I hope that's okay. If it's not, I can come back later."

I raise my hands as if I'm going to grab hold of her shoulders but stop myself a moment before I make contact. They

THOSE TWO WORDS

hang between us awkwardly, palms up like I'm surrendering—and I don't know, it kind of feels like I am.

"It's fine. You're an employee here. *Again*. You can come and go as you please. Jules is on shift today. She's the assistant manager, so you can shadow her for the first few days. I presume you still know your way around a restaurant, and they don't do things that differently in Tennessee." Jo tries and fails to hide how she recoils at my words, and only then do I hear how harsh they sound.

"That sounds smart," she replies and ignores my jab—which makes me out to be even more of a dick. Her eyes bounce around the space until they settle on a spot to her left. I follow her line of sight and find the framed picture of her mom and my dad embracing each other above the bar. I can only see her side profile, but I don't miss the sadness creeping across her face.

My heart drops when I hear her sniffle, but when she turns her head, I'm surprised to see a small, tentative smile.

And shit, if that hint of a smile isn't enough to floor me.

I was convinced years of separation would quell my body's urges toward her. Yet seeing her standing in front of me with her honey-golden hair piled on top of her head, rosy cheeks, and a soft look in her eyes, I'm met with the sudden realization this is going to be much harder than I thought. Six years clearly means nothing when it comes to Johanna Thomas, because like all those years ago, she demands all my attention.

AFTER I SHOWED JO WHERE THE NEW BREAK ROOM IS, WE DID A quick walk around, and I gave her a new set of keys and abandoned her in the office. I practically ran out of there, because no way in hell could I stand to be in such a small space with her for another minute. Her jasmine scent, all-too-polite smile, and well, simply being around her was driving me insane. I left her to go over some new employee paperwork and get up to date on all the safety manuals. I won't lie, I gave her some that aren't relevant, hoping it would give me time to collect myself. My emotions are uncontrollable; one minute I want to demand why she left, the next I catch myself staring at her without caution.

Am I avoiding her? Yes. Does that make me a coward? Yes again. I'm so erratic and unpredictable around her. I make a mental note to switch some of my shifts around over the next few weeks, so I'm working with her as little as possible.

Making my way to the front of the restaurant, I search for Booth so we can have our weekly catch-up while we're closed until lunchtime. Now that I think about it, Johanna should be attending this meeting as the new restaurant manager. I glance back to the closed office door and decide she can attend next week.

Master of evasion over here.

"Sooooo," Booth drawls from his spot behind the bar as I walk into the empty restaurant. "Where is our little YoYo?"

"*Johanna* is in the office filling her paperwork in and reading over some...manuals."

"Why couldn't she do it out here?" he asks suspiciously as I settle myself into a chair and open up my laptop.

"It's quieter back there. Fewer distractions."

"For her or you?"

There's no point in answering him, because from the beguiled look on his face, he knows the answer. He slaps his hands on the table as he plonks himself down in the seat across from me. "You absolute fucking chicken, hiding her away so you don't have to face her." He's full on laughing at this point, like my discomfort is a standup act.

"I am not avoiding her." *Lies.* "It's just weird."

THOSE TWO WORDS

"Weird, how?" The hint of mirth in his tone makes me think over my next words carefully. No one but Dex knows the full story about what went on between Jo and me. Though, since we were teenagers, Booth would always tease us about our friendship and how he suspected there was more than meets the eye. His accusations were wrong up until six years ago.

"I'm not getting into that now. Listen, she left and didn't look back. Just because she's back now to help us out doesn't mean all can be forgotten."

Out of all my siblings, Booth seemed the least affected by Jo leaving. He was in the same class as her sister, Harriet, and they even dated a little in high school. I was clear I didn't want any updates about Jo's new life, though he would drop little tidbits of information from time to time. And I'd be lying if I said I didn't relish those updates, treating them like gold dust.

My thoughts on Jo are so polarized, which only makes me more agitated. "Can we get on with business? I need to clock out early today. Carrie is dropping by with Lottie later this afternoon, and I said I'd take them for dinner."

"Just one second," he says. "I really don't know what went on with you two, but I've made a few logical guesses over the years. I know her leaving after Dad was tough, I mean, fuck, it hurt us all, but what I don't get is how years of friendship were thrown away because she moved to another state. You guys were attached at the hip as soon as you both could walk, from what I've heard. What gives?"

Booth might act like a goof, but he's annoyingly intuitive.

"Listen," I blow out, my head falling between my shoulders with a sigh. "People change, and for whatever reason, this town wasn't enough for her anymore." *I wasn't enough for her,* but I keep that last part to myself. "She's here to help us get back on track, and to stop this place"—I throw my arms up, gesturing around the restaurant—"from falling into the hands of some greedy property developer. I've accepted that she is going to be working here, whether I like it or not. I have made peace with it. She's a *coworker,* and that's all she will ever be to me now."

When I look at Booth, I'm hoping to see he's gotten the message, instead, he's staring at something over my shoulder with pity and apology written across his face.

The blood drains from my face. Without following his gaze, I know what he's looking at. Or who, for that matter. It's like my body senses her—that, and the subtle smell of jasmine and ocean air.

When I turn around and find Jo standing there, frozen and with moisture brimming in her eyes, I feel sick. From the shattered look on her face, I know she heard every word.

eight
JOHANNA

I WILL NOT CRY. I WILL NOT CRY. I *WILL* NOT CRY.

I knew he didn't want me here. The truth and finality in his words hit their mark, slicing me right down the middle. I ran out of there before he could see me fall to pieces. So much of what he said wasn't true, but I understand how my leaving would look that way.

This town wasn't enough for her anymore.

How wrong he is. This town was more than enough for me. It was also too much for me at the same time. If the telling sign of my anxiety didn't warn me that I needed to get out of there, I would have stayed and corrected him. Told him he was why it was so hard for me to walk away in the first place. But I'm not brave enough for that conversation, and I don't know if I ever will be.

Tears cloud my vision as I sit defeated on the dusty stockroom floor. My head falls against the wooden shelves behind me—rows and rows of liquor, wine, beer, and sodas line them.

The callousness and indifference is so unlike him, and I know this is as hard and confusing for him as it is for me. He's nothing like the man I remember, but perhaps what he said is true.

People change.

I'm wiping away my tears with the sleeves of my sweater when the door cracks open, allowing a sliver of light to illuminate the space. The specks of dust I've disturbed dance around in the air like floating glitter, but what catches my eye is the row of initials and dates etched into the frame of the door. PS. JT. GS. BS. HT. FS. Each set of initials working its way up the wood as the years go on. Booth drops to the floor next to me, while I keep my eyes trained on the letters.

I'm not disappointed that he's the one to come find me, but a small part of me hoped a different Sadler brother would be the one to do it.

He leans in until we're shoulder to shoulder. "Hey, you."

"Hey." My voice cracks from either crying or inhaling dust mites.

It's pretty dark in here, and when I finally turn my attention to Booth, I see the sympathy in his eyes. I haven't spoken to him much since I arrived back in town, and I know he speaks to Harriet regularly. Growing up, Booth was always an energetic kid who expressed his feelings freely. As he got older, it was clear he wore his heart on his sleeve and was loyal to the core, and the fact he's sitting on this dirty floor with me now shows that hasn't changed at all.

He tilts his head slightly and reveals one of those dimples I loved to poke when he was younger. "He didn't mean it, you know." I do a bad job at hiding my sadness, because he bumps his shoulder with mine when my face falls. "I'm not going to apologize on his behalf, he's a big boy; he's trying to come to terms with this all. He's changed a lot since you left and I'm not saying it's your fault, he's just different. A little quieter; a lot more serious. His heart and brain are competing over what they think is best."

"I suppose becoming a parent will do that to you." There's no bitterness in my tone, and I allow my mind to drift back to the day I found out he was going to be a dad. It gutted me for so many reasons, and though we never really got to see where our relationship could have taken us, I pictured parenthood going a lot differently for us both.

"Weirdly, Lottie is the only one who seems to bring out the old Pat and she didn't even know that version of him. Probably because she is in no way quiet or serious. You'll love her."

The name of Patrick's daughter stings less than it did when I first heard it, and I bob my head in agreement, because I'm happy for him, but seeing him play house with another woman is too much for my tattered heart to take. One brutal truth at a time, please.

"He just needs time to adjust to things," Booth continues.

"You mean to me being here?"

"Yes...but he knows it's a good thing."

"Does he?" I scoff.

"He will," he corrects. "We've all missed you, and I'm not going to ask what happened. God knows I've asked my dumbass brother enough over the years, but he's tight-lipped about whatever went on between you two." He gives me a side glance, almost like he's waiting for me to fill in the blanks. I quirk my brow at him, and his shoulders shake with laughter. "Just like my big bro. I'm glad you're back." He slings his arm over my shoulder and tucks me in close to him. "How have you been?"

"I'm..." I stop myself from defaulting to old ways.

I never knew how to truthfully answer that question, and my auto-response was always "I'm okay." What does it even mean?

Compared to a few years ago, I'm more than okay. It wasn't an upward battle, and the one thing I've learned is that you might take a few stumbles back to move forward again. Being honest with myself was the biggest step. Knowing how to be kind to my mind, my body, and not bottling it all up inside was both difficult and necessary in being *okay*.

"I think I'm a little different too." It's a genuine response, but I poke him in the ribs to shift the attention from myself. "What about you? Harriet says you're quite the ladies' man now."

His chest puffs and shoulders pop back like some alpha male. "Pssht, YoYo," he teases. "You have so much to catch up on. I'm the town's hottest bachelor, I'll have you know. Tourists' panties are dropping—"

"Ugh, gross. You're like my little brother; please keep a lid on those sordid details. I'm sure you were a virgin when I left."

Chuckling, he stands and offers me his hand, hauling me to my feet. He grabs me by the shoulders and looks me dead in the eyes.

"I want you to know that I saw you during one of the most difficult times in your life. Seeing how you handled the loss of your mom with such grace—" His voice breaks a little and I appreciate that he doesn't try to hide his vulnerability. "It helped me a lot when we lost Dad. I'll always be grateful for that."

He places a kiss on the crown of my head, squeezes my shoulders, and walks out the door. Fresh tears spring to my eyes for a different reason now. On the outside it might have appeared I handled the passing of my mom well, but behind that façade I was drowning, with no idea how to come up for air.

What no one knows, is that it took over a decade for me to break through the surface.

THOSE TWO WORDS

After Booth left me in the stockroom, I took a few more minutes to collect myself, plastered on a smile, and headed to the front of the restaurant to meet Jules, the assistant manager.

We've spent the last couple of hours together, going over what you would for a typical new employee, though there wasn't much to teach me I didn't already know. Bless her heart, she even tried to explain that FOH stood for Front of House, until she remembered I was practically raised in this building. What I have learned is the menu is still the same as it was over twenty years ago. Even the customers are the same, just aged with time. We still don't have a point of sale system, taking customers' orders the old-school way, which I'm hoping is something I can help with.

She didn't see it taking long for me to pick things back up, and I couldn't disagree with her. I know this place inside and out, and it helps that nothing has changed, though, maybe one of the reasons it's in its current state.

Now, I'm sitting at one of the tables in the restaurant and observing the team at work during the lunch rush. Only it isn't much of a rush at all. Sure, Mondays are slow, but we've only had three tables in since noon. I watch the team stand around, trying to stay busy with odd jobs, and I'm sure one of them has wiped the same table five times.

It's painful, and I now know exactly what my dad meant when he said they're struggling.

Movement on my left catches my eye, and I watch Patrick as he carries in a crate of beer from the stockroom. There is one change around here, and I am in full favor of it; it's the muscles Patrick is now packing. His biceps flex and ripple against his long sleeve shirt, and I am not ashamed of my unabashed perusal. He was always lean, but he's now filled out in all the right places. His expression is also different. Unless he's speaking to a customer or a member of the team, it's solemn.

The skin between his brows is permanently creased, and years ago, I would have rubbed that spot away with my thumb.

My ogling is interrupted when a woman and a young girl walk in. I think nothing of it at first. Watching them chat back and forth is quite sweet, reminding me of days out with my own mom. When the little girl makes a beeline for Patrick, my heart sinks.

The slapping of her feet across the floor catches his attention, and the moment he spots her, he crouches down and spreads his arms wide just in time to catch her. His expression lights up when she wraps her little arms around his neck, and they hug each other tightly. She might not have the same hair color as Patrick or the woman standing and laughing next to them, but there's no doubt in my mind who they are.

I'm so absorbed in watching them I almost don't notice when Patrick's gaze flicks to mine as he talks to the woman. Girlfriend? Partner? *Wife?* No. I would know if he was married. Wouldn't I?

I avert my eyes, needing to look anywhere else but at the happy little family on the other side of the room. I keep myself distracted and check the delivery updates for my new throw cushions when a small hand creeps into my peripheral and taps me on the arm. When I look up, the shade of green in the little girl's eyes would be a dead giveaway as to who she is, if I didn't know already.

"I'm Lottie! How is your food today?"

At first, I'm startled by her question, but I have to suppress the laughter bubbling in my throat when she stares at me with such seriousness. Her lines are clearly rehearsed, because I don't even have any food in front of me. My heart might be aching in the knowledge of who she is, but when she flashes me a toothy grin, I can't help but be charmed by her.

"Do you know what?" I reply with my own grin to match

hers, because how could I not? "This is the best iced coffee I've had in a long time."

"*Iced?* It's so *brrrrrr* outside," she says, shaking her arms and looking outside. "Don't you want some hot cocoa?"

"Your daddy would say the exact same thing."

Her eyes go comically wide, and I regret my response immediately.

"You know my daddy?!" she asks excitedly, bouncing on the balls of her feet. "He works here with my uncle Boo. Do you know him too? Sometimes I play waitress and I check on the customers. Did you know the customer is always right?"

I have no idea how to reply to her rambling of words, but god, if she isn't the cutest. I'm so distracted by her chatter I don't see Patrick approach us until he's standing directly behind her.

"Spud, don't forget, only a quick question and we move along. Don't bother people too much," he says, resting a hand on her shoulder. She looks up at him with a cheeky smile, and I wish seeing the affection warm his eyes didn't make him even more handsome.

"She's really not bothering me at all," I supply.

"And she knows you, Daddy. Is she your friend?" Lottie asks eagerly.

"No, umm, she's a…"

It's a slap in the face that he can't even put a label on us, but I've always told myself to be better, not bitter.

"A *coworker*," I finish for him, echoing his earlier words. "I'm the new restaurant manager." Patrick's shoulders drop. In relief or regret, I'm not sure.

"Ooooooooh," Lottie replies with a lot more enthusiasm than my job title deserves, before a look of confusion washes across her face. "What's a *cow-worker*? Do you work with cows?"

We both laugh at that, but when our gazes meet, the smiles slip from our faces. The laughter falling to flat silence. Jesus, this day needs to be over if we can't even laugh in front of each other without it being awkward.

"Okay, spud, that's enough for today. I'm going to meet you and your mom soon for dinner, say goodbye."

Her shoulders drop and she curls her bottom lip but does as she's told and gives me a little wave as she returns to her mom.

Before Patrick can join them, I call out, "Pat, umm, sorry, Patrick. I don't want to overstep, but I have a few contacts with a till company that works in the Northeast. Have you ever looked into upgrading?"

He raises an eyebrow, prompting me to continue. "It should help the staff work more effectively, and I think I can get us a good deal."

"I don't really have time to install and train the staff on something new right now."

"That's why I'm here," I quickly say, plastering on a smile. "I can handle it all, I'd just like you onboard before I go inquiring."

I half expect him to shoot me down, and I know it would be out of pure stubbornness. And if there's one thing I still know about him, it's that he's not a guy to act out of spite, no matter what he thinks of me.

"Okay, get some quotes over to Gray and me, and we'll think about it. There's a pot of money aside for things like this." He doesn't give me a chance to respond before he's turning and walking away.

It's something, but overall, this day is a big bag of dicks.

I don't let myself watch Patrick and his family for much longer. And I certainly don't cry myself to sleep that night thinking about what could have been.

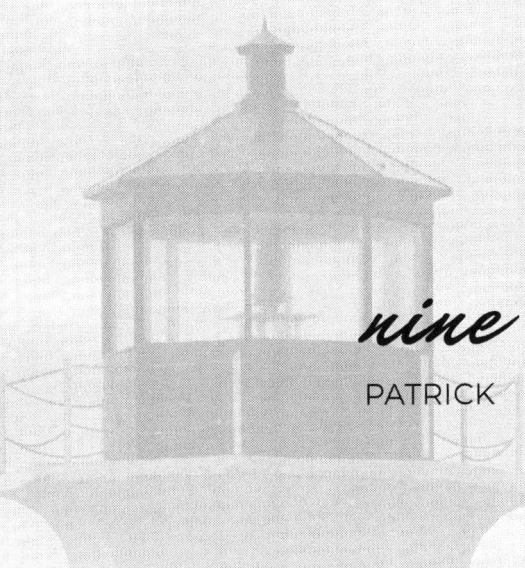

nine
PATRICK

"Uncle Boo, manners," my daughter reprimands my brother. Although she's now learned how to pronounce words with *th* in them, the cute nickname she gave Booth when she first started talking has stuck.

Booth joined us for dinner tonight after his date had canceled last minute. It might be his night off, but he still ended up cooking after Lottie convinced him to make her favorite pasta dish, which is what the three of us are currently eating around my dining table, the smell of cheese and garlic filling the air.

"Pssht, table manners are boring, you little toad." He shoves two breadsticks in his mouth and makes noises of what I presume is a walrus. She breaks into a fit of giggles and tries to chomp off one of his doughy tusks when he gets too close.

Lottie has a different relationship with each of my siblings but loves them all equally. They've all played a huge part in helping me raise her, especially as I wrapped my head around fatherhood. Even now I'm learning something new each day.

I watch them and laugh behind a bite of pasta when Lottie

successfully steals a breadstick and bonks him on the head with it.

"C'mon, children. Lottie, you know better than that. Show Uncle Booth how to behave."

"I don't need to be taught how to behave. I'm her cool uncle." He nods his head toward Lottie. "My only job description is to be funny and handsome; nailing both of those, aren't I?"

"Uh-huh. The moms at school say they like your buns." A little frown forms between her brows. "Because you a chef?"

Booth and I try to stifle our laughter. Her innocence is hilarious, even when she's referring to her classmates' moms ogling her uncle's ass.

"Those moms are relentless." He laughs. "Surprised one of them hasn't tried to snatch you up yet." He quirks his eyebrows at me suggestively. The moms in Lottie's school have tried a number of times to ask me out, and while I'm flattered, I've never been interested.

"Yeah, no thanks." I look at Lottie, who is inhaling her dinner as usual. "Great job with your food tonight, spud. A few more bites, then you can have two scoops of ice cream."

"Oh, so the women we grew up with are off limits all of a sudden?" he asks and waggles his eyebrows again. He's trying to catch me out, and I will not take the bait.

I throw Booth an unamused look, letting him know to drop it before turning my attention back to Lottie.

"How was your day, spud?" I ask.

She swallows her bite of food and sighs very dramatically for a four-year-old. *Just wait until you're thirty-four, kid.*

"My best friend, Nora, ate a tuna sandwich for lunch, and I don't like tuna, do I, Daddy? It smelled *soooo* bad. Then Mrs. Hargrove taught us about the rainbow. There was no pink. Why isn't there pink in the rainbow?"

Before Booth and I can get a word in edgewise, Lottie is off again, her endless babble is a good distraction. I'm not sure she took a breath in the five minutes it took her to tell us about her disappointment in the color spectrums and how, despite disliking tuna, it would make a good pet. As Booth clears our plates, I explain the dynamics of the rainbow and tell her owning one would be a *really* big responsibility.

I envy how quickly she gets over things and wish I could take a page out of her book.

Once the table is cleared, Booth and I sit around the dining table, both nursing a bottle of local IPA while Lottie has an hour of screen time. From his grin alone, I know he is itching to grill me about Jo.

"Just ask," I groan, and take a long pull from my bottle.

"How have things been with Jo this week?" *Like fucking clockwork.*

"Fine." I shrug.

"Last Monday was a little tense," he observes. I hold back my wince as I recall that awful morning. It took all my strength not to chase after her when she ran to the back, but Booth thought she might have needed some space from me. *Because apparently, she hasn't had enough already.* "She seems to have taken to the role well. Like riding a bike, hey?"

He's not wrong.

When she finally emerged from the stockroom to train with Jules, her red-rimmed eyes were a giveaway that she'd been crying. Knowing I was the cause behind those tears devastated me, and I didn't know how to even begin to apologize to her. She didn't let it deter her though. I watched her listen attentively to Jules, even though I knew none of this would be new to her. From that day she's been professional, patient, and capable —just as she always has been. She's already convinced me to install a new till system, and once Graham and I agreed it was a smart investment, she already had a technician lined up and ready to go. Discount included, because she *knew a guy*.

Whoever this guy is, he better be fifty years old and happily married.

We shared a few words and acted professional around the team. After Booth told me about their encounter in the stockroom, I promised myself I wouldn't be dismissive or unkind. Just...elusive.

We might have a long, unspoken history, but we're adults and have got to learn to work with each other.

"She's always been like that." I know how sentimental my next words are, but I can't seem to stop myself. I don't look Booth in the eye, but concentrate on the label of my bottle, which I've shredded to pieces. "Even when we were younger, you only had to explain something to her once and it was like she'd been doing it her whole life. I always envied that about her."

He hums in agreement. "It's been nice having her back, and the staff likes her. She's been getting along well with Simon."

Now I look him in the eye. He's not smiling, so it's hard to work out if he's trying to goad me again, so I keep my tone disinterested.

"How so?"

"I dunno, joking around and catching up after work over a beer or coffee. They're both new to town, something they have in common. It's been good for Jo to meet new people; I know she's been getting along well with Quinn too."

Simon is Booth's sous chef, who recently moved back to New England from Arizona after a messy divorce. He's not from Sutton Bay, and I found out recently he went to school with Carrie. He seems like a nice guy, hardworking, but something about him bothers me and I can't put my finger on it.

Weirdly, my suspicions started eight seconds ago.

"Hmm." I nod, maintaining the cool guy persona, because why should I care? Nor do I want to give Booth another reason

THOSE TWO WORDS

to meddle in my life. Jo is free to hang out with whomever she wants. Totally fine with it. The *finest*.

"Where do they hang out?" I rush out. *Okay, not so cool.*

"At Lenny's place or the bakery."

Lenny owns one of the oldest drinking spots in town, Shirley's, which he named after his first love. This would be a sweet sentiment if his old flame wasn't a fishing boat from the eighties and his wife wasn't called Edith. While the tourists love to flock to the brewery out of town, this is where all the locals come to spend their Friday nights. Everyone from fishermen, schoolteachers, the mayor, and my mom can be found there. It's no surprise that this is where Jo ended up on her evenings off; it's where we spent our nights off together back in the day.

"Oh, right. We should look at joining them one night, be good for morale and all that jazz." *Liar, liar, pants on fire,* my conscience chants. Not that I don't care about my staff's morale, it's just rare you would catch me at the bar for anything outside of family gatherings. Since Lottie entered my life, going out for a beer and playing pool with my friends isn't as appealing. When Lottie isn't with me, I'm usually catching up on sleep, work, or slaving over a jigsaw puzzle. Riveting, I know. I still hang out with Dex, my brothers, and a few other guys, but I'm more of a homebody now.

"Really?" Booth asks in surprise.

"Yeah, why not? Maybe we can organize a team bonding night. Some pool, darts, and food," I suggest. "I'll check when Carrie is free, and we can do it on a weekday and close the restaurant early."

"Nice, okay. It'll be good for Jo to hang out with all the staff outside of the restaurant. Leave it with me."

"Who is Jo?" a small voice from behind us asks.

We turn to find a curious-looking Lottie staring up at us, twirling one of her pigtails around her fingers.

"She works with your dad and me," Booth replies.

"The new lady?" The fact she remembers who Jo is from over a week ago but can't tell me where she left her sneakers two hours ago is astounding.

"Yep, that was Jo. She helps get all the food out from Uncle Booth's kitchen to feed the customers," I explain.

"Cool. She was so pretty. She looked like Rapunzel. Can she come to my party? It's a princess party, so she would like it. I think she's my friend now." Smiling brightly, she rocks back and forth on her fuzzy-socked feet. My girl has the biggest heart, but I'm hesitant to let her get too attached to Jo. I know the pain of that all too well.

"She is prett—" Without even looking at Booth, I can picture his cocky grin at my slipup. Scratching my cheek with my middle finger, I continue talking to Lottie. "I don't think she has time to come to your party, but all your friends will be there. Do you know what princess you want to be yet?"

She brings her shoulders up to her ears in a slow shrug and lets them drop, upset that she can't invite her "new friend." Luckily, her birthday is almost two months away, and I'm sure she will have forgotten about Jo by then.

"We can go shopping for a princess dress and tiara next week," I say with a boop on her nose, cheering her up immediately. Not only does this have Lottie deciding on her birthday party outfit, she also declares that her uncles and I will also be wearing matching tiaras and tutus. No arguments.

After Booth leaves, I get Lottie ready for bed. Once her bedtime routine is done, we choose a story to read in my bed. She begged to fall asleep in my room tonight and demanded I carry her to her "big girl bed" to wake up in the morning.

"This one!" Lottie announces proudly from her spot at the foot of my bed, where she's dumped out her entire book box at my feet. She skips over to where I'm lying down, waiting for her to decide, and shoves a book in my face before throwing herself on top of me. Despite being a tiny thing, she still knocks the wind out of me.

I look down at the book she's chosen and see that it's an older version of Rapunzel that my mom gifted her.

"This one, hey?"

"Yup! It's like JoJo, that's what I'm gonna call her," she says cheerfully. It's not lost on me that my own daughter would coin a nickname for Johanna that's so similar to the one I gave her when we were Lottie's age.

With a nod, I tuck Lottie in close, and we read about the girl with long golden hair, trapped in an ivory tower.

ten

JOHANNA

Today is looking to be a great day already.

My hair did that thing where you put in zero effort and it ends up looking like you've spent hours grueling over it. Quinn had my usual waiting for me downstairs and even complimented my hair and freshly painted nails. And to top it all off? March is here, the snow has melted, and spring is around the corner.

It's my favorite season in New England. We might be known for our fall time, but there's something so magical and revitalizing about seeing the flowers bud and bloom after surviving another harsh winter. Patrick always teased me for this, but I swear you can smell the sweet, almond flavor of the maple trees as the days get warmer.

I breathe in deeply as I walk down Robin Road, humming along to Dermot Kennedy playing through my headphones, hoping to catch that scent in the air.

Nodding hello to a few people headed to work, I can't help but smile at how things have picked up since my first week in town. I'm feeling more at ease; those moments of overthinking my decision to move here have now passed, and I've made a few new friends who aren't my dad. Even Amanda told me during yesterday's session how impressed she was at how I've transitioned into a new routine and settled into my new job. It's not to say I haven't struggled, it's how I cope with it and look after myself during those moments that's key.

I reach the front door of the restaurant and pull my set of keys out of my coat pocket. When the song reaches its crescendo, I don't hold back singing the chorus out loud, zero shame, because *Dermot Kennedy!*

A tap on my shoulder has me screeching like a banshee, and I whirl around with my fists raised to defend myself.

I'm about to punch the creeper in the throat and educate him about not sneaking up on women but stop myself before I pop them in the nose. Because I recognize this creeper.

"Well, hello, stranger," they drawl as my fists drop.

"DEX!" I shout, and throw myself into the open arms of one of my oldest friends.

Chuckling, he returns the hug in a bearlike grip and picks me off my feet with ease.

"Oh my god, I didn't think you were in town for a while. When did you get back?" I ask as he places me on my feet.

"Two days ago, but I made the most of not having any jobs lined up and slept yesterday away." He tugs his beanie off his head and runs his hand across his shortly cropped hair. Swirls of black and intricate lettering peek out from the collar of his army-green parka. When Dex turned eighteen, he got his first tattoo, and I don't think he's ever stopped. His gray eyes shine bright against his sun-kissed skin from hours of working outside.

Dex is a hard guy to miss. His six-foot-five, husky frame towers above everyone, and his biceps are bigger than my thighs. He might look intimidating, but the guy is the epitome of the *Big Friendly Giant*. Soft and kind to his very core.

I notice he isn't wearing his hearing aid—something he

would always forget when growing up—so I make sure he can see my lips as I talk to him. He hasn't lost all his hearing, but he's completely deaf in his left ear, and I know speaking to him face-on makes it a lot easier for him.

"What was the job?" I ask.

"A couple of new cabins are being built near the Canadian border. Was up there just shy of seven weeks and then decided to take a detour on the way home." He flashes me a megawatt smile that pulls out a grin of my own. Knowing I'm still worthy of those smiles adds to this already great day.

Dexter—or Dex, as most people call him—grew up a few houses down from my family home. We met on our first day of kindergarten. He was technically Patrick's friend first, but because the two of us were inseparable, I easily forced my way into their friendship. Dex complained that because I was a girl, I would give him cooties, but I won him over eventually.

A lot of my childhood memories consist of riding our bikes around the neighborhood or playing hide-and-seek in the woods behind our houses. Once we all graduated from high school, Dex didn't go to college but continued his job at the local lumberyard and later taught himself carpentry in his spare time. What started off as a summer job and a passion for woodworking, quickly turned into a successful carpentry business of unique and bespoke pieces. From dining tables to fully livable log cabins, you name it, he can make it.

"Are you on your way to a job now?"

"Sure am." He jerks his chin toward the restaurant. "Just got here."

"Here?"

"Mm-hm. Your dad asked me to measure some shelving in the kitchen. Once I heard a certain *someone* made a dramatic return to town, I pushed this job to the top of my list. Patrick sure kept your arrival quiet," he says with a teasing nudge to my shoulder, and that's when I notice the small toolbox at his feet.

"Hardly dramatic." With a roll of my eyes, I ignore his last comment. I give him my back for a second and continue unlocking the door. Once the alarm is off and I've switched on all the lights, he drops his stuff on the parquet floor.

"You wouldn't think so hearing all the gossip around town. *Scandalous,* Johanna." He places his hand across his chest in mock aghast. "I'm sure I heard Mrs. Stewart whispering about how you'd run away to a convent and got kicked out."

"*Har-Har.* That woman is a fuc—" My sentence is cut short when the woman herself slowly walks past the large glass window, eyes slowly examining us both. "Jesus, that was creepy. Well, do you have time for a coffee and to catch-up? I might have a little favor to ask."

"For you, I have all the time in the world." He pulls me into his side and squeezes me gently, smelling like wood shavings and home. "Missed you, slugger."

"GOD, HARRIET HAS NOT CHANGED AT ALL BY THE SOUNDS OF IT." Dex laughs from where he is kneeling in front of the sink in the ladies' restroom. I'm leaning against the wall next to him, on hand with the wrench as he works. Or I think that's what it is. I told him one of the sinks was leaking and he offered to look at it. It's a good thing I came in early today, because it's been great catching up with Dex for the last hour. He sent me a few texts when I first left, checking in on me, but like so many messages, I didn't have the heart or energy to respond. I'm sure he knows everything that went down between Patrick and me. He could've easily given me the cold shoulder, considering we haven't spoken at all in the time I've been gone. It's so refreshing that it feels like no time has passed between us.

"She is a walking oxymoron; has the style of a trendy

teenager yet can't work out how to find an email she drafted the day before. It was great staying with her, but I always worried I was cramping her style. This move home came at the perfect time."

"Are you glad you're back?" He peers up at me, as he waits for my reply.

"I am. It kind of happened out of the blue, but I'm glad to be close to Dad again and to be helping out however I can. I didn't realize how much I missed this town until I stepped back in it."

"I'm sure you're helping a lot. Some people just take a little time to recognize that."

I don't miss the insinuation in his words. I've been trying to find the right words for the last hour, but rather than think them over, I blurt them out. "I'm sorry I never texted back. I-I...A lot happened."

It shouldn't surprise me that Dex's response is full of empathy. "This might not be the same thing, but remember we didn't speak for about a year when you and Pat moved away for college?"

My fingers run across the cold metal of the wrench as I nod my head.

"That time apart didn't mean jack shit in the grand scheme of things, and neither do the last few years. You're like family, Jo. I'll never see you any differently, no matter what happened."

"Well shit, now I'm going to cry," I say with a teary smile. It's clear Patrick has told him *everything,* but why wouldn't he? Dex is his best friend.

"Please don't. It makes me uncomfortable." He stands and tests the faucet, makes a few adjustments, and gives the sink a tap before turning toward me. "All fixed."

"My hero."

"Anything for the damsels in distress around this town. Hey, what are you up to tonight?" he asks and wipes his hands down the front of his pants.

THOSE TWO WORDS

"I'm meeting up with some of the team at Shirley's, you?"

"I was going to see if you wanted a beer and a slice of pizza at Dough. Maybe next week?"

"Oh, I've missed Dough so much. Their pepperoni pie was always wicked good. I'm off on Thursday and Sunday next week." Dough is the town's pizzeria, somewhere Patrick, Dex, and I would hang out on weekends or after school.

"Thursday it is. Pick you up at seven?"

"It's a date." I lean in and flutter my eyelashes at him.

Just then, the restroom door swings up, and we turn to find Patrick standing in the doorway. His eyes sharpen as they dart between Dex and me, his jaw ticking in irritation. It's then I notice how close we're standing, but I don't move away, and neither does Dex, who has a weird smirk pulling at his lips.

"Am I interrupting something?" Patrick asks brusquely, with a look that gives nothing away.

This day might have started off great, but seeing his stupid, handsome face reminds me how hard he's been trying to avoid me at every turn. I walk into a room; he finds an excuse to exit it. I've tried not to let it bother me, but whenever he refuses to acknowledge my presence, a piece of hope I clung to over the years falls away.

So, this whole giving-a-shit-all-of-sudden thing he's got going is not going to fly. *No sirree.*

"Pat! You sure are, just catching up with Jo here." Dex throws an arm around my shoulder and ruffles my hair. I take a little bit of satisfaction in seeing Patrick's jaw work overtime. I hope he cracks a tooth. "Managed to score a night of fine dining with her. Isn't that right?"

He looks down at me and winks, suddenly becoming very flirty and nothing like the friendly banter we've been tossing back and forth all morning.

"Umm..." I look at Patrick, and that passiveness is long gone, because he's looking at Dex in silent warning. The subtle widening of Dex's eyes triggers a lightbulb moment, and I know to go along with the rouse. "I mean, if you're paying," I reply innocently.

"I always pay for my dates."

Even I'm momentarily distracted by the smoothness in Dex's tone, however, when the heat coming off Patrick's glare warms my face, I take a small step away. I don't want to poke the bear *too* much.

"Right, well, as much as I hate to break this up, I have work to do in the office, and Jo should be opening up in"—Patrick glances down at his watch—"forty minutes, so she better get a move on." His gaze morphs from fiery to stony when he glances at me. "The rep from our wine supplier is coming in at one o'clock. Don't forget."

Dex laughs, shakes his head, and begins to pack up his tools. He can't seem to believe the fucking nerve of Patrick's dismissive tone either. He might find it funny, but me? I am trying to find my inner peace and not say what I'm thinking out loud.

Which is, *You're a massive asshole!*

Instead, I put on the fake smile I've been using around him and push down the sassy attitude. "Sure, *boss*. I'd appreciate if next time, you talk to me, not through me," I say and give him a salute. Maybe the sassiness wasn't completely bottled away, but he hasn't bothered to utter more than a few curt words to me since I returned, and now he decides to start spitting orders at me. *I think not.*

I whip around and give him my back, hoping my long ponytail flicks him right in his dumb face. I look at Dex and give him a wink of my own.

"See you next week, Dex." With a pat on his chest, I turn to walk out of the restroom, not even sparing Patrick a glance. I swear Dex mouths, *Good job,* before I walk out.

THOSE TWO WORDS

Once the door to the restroom closes behind me, I check no one is around and raise my middle fingers at the door before stomping away.

eleven
PATRICK

She shouldn't look so cute marching out of here in a huff, and I spend too long watching the sway of her hips as she does it. Once the door slams shut behind Jo, I whirl on my best friend.

"What the *fuck* was that?" I demand.

"What was *what*?"

I know he's playing dumb right now. And from the smug look on his face as he closes the latch on his toolbox, he knows he's got me all riled up.

"You know what. You were all over her. And *a date*? She's like your sister; you practically grew up with her."

"Oh, I'm sorry. Is there a rule that we don't sleep with women who are *like* sisters to us now?" he asks with a shrug of his shoulder. "She looks good, too, don't you think?"

Dex has been conspiring with my younger brother, I'm positive. I inwardly cringe at my behavior minutes ago. I might as well have beat on my chest and claimed her as mine.

"What are you getting at, Dex?" I ask.

"Nothing, nothing at all. Just catching up with an old friend. I've missed her. Haven't you?"

"That's irrelevant, because she clearly didn't miss us." I try and fail to hide the pain lacing my accusatory tone.

Dex's face morphs into that of sympathy and he places his hand on my shoulder. "I think if you gave her the time of day, you'd be surprised to find out that's not the case. I worked that out after spending one hour with her." With his other hand, he runs it over his buzz cut. "I know a lot went down between you two. It was messy, but it's also been left unresolved. Don't you think now is the perfect opportunity to speak to her and find out what happened? A lifetime of friendship swept away over what you think you saw?"

"I know what I saw," I grit out, pulling my beanie off in frustration.

"Okay, okay. You saw what you saw. Maybe now is the ideal time to ask her what it meant though. Shit, only your mom and me know that you flew—"

A gasp behind us has him pausing, and we turn to find one of the servers standing in the doorway, no doubt shocked to find two grown men in the ladies' restroom. We apologize and relocate to the office.

Throwing myself into the chair behind the desk, I crack my neck and wait for Dex to continue his friendly lecture.

"Can you honestly sit there and tell me you're not curious? Or don't want to see if you can get a modicum back of what you once had?"

Like my next breath. It's been brutal silently missing Jo all these years, almost as difficult as secretly pining after her. To have her in my life again and all these memories resurfacing, that's even tougher.

"I want to do my job and not let this place be ripped away from us all."

"Spend a little bit of time with her. She's...I don't know. Something felt off, like she was..."

"Lost," I finish for him.

"Exactly." He dips his head to the side and observes me from where he's sitting on the leather sofa in the corner. "So you have been paying attention to her?"

Of course I have, I want to shout. I notice everything about her. Always have and always will. But Dex is right. Things have changed since she left; I'm a father, for one. I can't continue blackballing her. The way she laughs and smiles seems muted, like something in her has been snuffed out and it's been eating me up inside to find out why since she stepped back into my life.

"I work with her, so it's hard not to notice her."

"Go easy with her, man. We were all shocked about her moving away. What good is it going to do keeping her at arm's length? You've not dated or shown an interest in any woman since she left. You're really over her?"

"God, of course I'm not!" Dex doesn't flinch at my outburst. "I haven't stopped thinking about her. Not a day has gone by where I haven't wondered what she's doing, how she is, or if she still thinks about me. I've typed out hundreds of texts over the years and then talked myself out of sending them. I let six years pass. I think it's too late for anything, even a friendship."

"If you aren't going to ask her those burning questions, then you need to move past all this man. It's not fair on either of you. Sure, you might not get back what you lost, but isn't it better than walking on eggshells around each other? Try to see past everything that went down, and maybe you can be friends again."

I shut my eyes and slump down into the chair. My head feels like it's trapped in a vortex as I try to sort through my thoughts. My wallet digs into me, and I pull it out of my pocket, flinging it on the desk. I hate that he's so right. But I also don't, because Jo and I can't carry on like this.

She has never been just a *friend*. Hell, we were more than that before she left. We can't go on pretending there isn't an

THOSE TWO WORDS

ocean of unspoken words between us now that distance is no longer an excuse.

My worn leather wallet screams at me, but I don't dare open it up in front of Dex. Because that's a little piece of Johanna that I want to keep for myself.

I'M AN IDIOT. A FUCKING IDIOT.

As I sit in a dark corner of Shirley's, I repeat those words in my head. I have no idea what I'm doing here, but after Dex let it slip where Jo was headed tonight, I decided *now* would be a good opportunity to speak to her. He tried to talk me out of it, but the moment the seed was planted, there was no telling me otherwise.

He never pushed me to reach out to Jo after I told him the truth. I think he sensed how torn up I was over losing my dad and how things turned out the last time I saw Jo. Perhaps I did jump to conclusions, but I was not in the right headspace to even begin unpacking that. My impending fatherhood was on the horizon, and Jo had made her intentions clear.

I know he's right. If we can't move past the history between us, working together is going to be painful for everyone around us and undoubtedly blow up in our faces. We owe it to our parents to not let that happen.

Looking over the rim of my glass, I take a sip of ice-cold IPA and watch the other customers from my hiding spot. The room isn't big, but the bar itself curves around the room and I'm currently hidden behind the row of liquor bottles and glassware on the back bar. The sound of laughter, glasses clinking, and pool balls ricocheting off one another fills the room. It's not a fancy establishment, and always smells like a strange combination of stale beer and fresh air.

A small group of people crowd around a couple of high-top tables, but my eyes are only drawn to one person.

Jo is wrapped up in some cream sweater dress that hugs every one of her sweet curves. The temptation to walk over there and run my hands across each dip and bend to test if the material is as soft as it looks is driving me crazy. From the way my knee is bouncing below the bar and how I've been half-hard since I spotted her, I'm unsure if going over there is the best thing to do right now.

Seeing her laughing in the middle of the stuffy bar is so different from the last time I saw her in one.

The moment I get her voicemail for what feels like the hundredth time, I hang up. I slowly lower my head to the countertop, the cool granite easing the pressure building between my eyes.

It's been one month since I felt on top of the world. One moment and one kiss led to what I'd only ever dreamed of happening. Then another moment for that world to come crumbling down until all that remained was a pile of chaos and devastation.

It's been one month since I last saw my dad. Three weeks since his funeral. And three weeks since she left.

I can't work out where the pain of one loss starts and where the other one ends. All I know is that it hurts, and I don't know how to get it to stop.

I have no idea if she's even seeing these texts, but I type out another one anyway and press Send.

> Patrick: Your dad says you still need some time and I want to give that to you. But I miss you. I meant what I said, I want to give this a go between us. I'll wait for however long you need.

I know she's safe, George tells me that much, I just can't wrap my head around why she would leave without a word, and on the evening of my dad's funeral. It was a hard day for everyone, and we barely got a second to talk after the service. By the time I'd spoken to everyone and helped my mom get home, Jo had already left. With a one-way ticket to Nashville, it turned out.

George reassured me she was okay, said she needed some space, but I've heard that so many times in the last few weeks, I worry she actually wants space from me. I respected it at first, but I now reek of desperation and his words do little to stop my mind from overthinking everything that happened since that night.

I want to give her the space, but why can't she have it while still in this town? Why can't I help her with whatever is going on? Am I the reason she left?

Before I know it, I'm scrolling through my phone looking at the next available flight to Nashville and entering in my credit card information.

I tell myself that when I set my eyes on her and see that she's okay, I'll give her what she needs, but not without letting her know I'm here on the other side waiting.

FANNING MY T-SHIRT AWAY FROM MY STICKY CHEST, I PAY THE DRIVER and step out of the cab. When I turned up at the apartment Jo and Harriet shared, she wasn't there. After calling Harriet and asking her where Jo was and arguing for ten minutes, she finally relented and told me. I'm sure she only caved out of pity.

I look up and spot the name of the bar Harriet gave me. The strum of a guitar greets me as I step through the doors, and I look over to where a man is playing an unfamiliar song—likely his own—on the small stage in the middle of the room.

It's crowded, and the heat is no better in here than it was outside, but I know she's here. I buzz with excitement and nerves. Excitement at seeing her after weeks of zero contact and nerves at how she's going to react.

As I scan the room for a familiar head of bright blonde hair, the guy on stage finishes up and thanks the crowd. He steps off the stage and shakes the hands of a few people, and when his eyes drift to the other side of the room, I follow them.

And that's when I see her. She's still so beautiful, it makes my chest ache, but she looks thinner and has dark shadows underneath her eyes.

I had no idea what I'd find when I saw her, but embracing another man was not it. When they pull apart, her head is bent low as he whispers in her ear. I can't see her face, but I've already seen too much.

The sound of my heart breaking even further would have been audible if it weren't so loud in here. I'm certain what was at first a crack, has now fractured right down the middle and split in two.

If this is the space Jo needs, it's clear I am not welcome in it.

The heat and noise become too much, and when I finally manage to pull my eyes away from the two of them, I spin on my heel and walk right back out of there. As much as I want to walk up to her and demand what the fuck is going on, I don't have it in me. All the fight and hope I had has evaporated into the humid air.

It took one minute for Johanna to wordlessly tell me that even though I was happy to wait for her, waiting for me wasn't an option.

I drop Harriet a text and thank her for letting me know where Jo was but that I couldn't find her. I ask her not to tell Jo I was here and ignore her follow-up text asking what happened and why. And every text that follows.

Hours later, I'm staring at the city lights on my return flight home and bid farewell to my heart, where I've left it broken and bruised in Tennessee.

For whatever reason, those memories don't have the same gut-wrenching impact they've previously had. Perhaps it's the idea that we can move past it all, or the idea that I might finally get the answers I've been looking for.

If anything, it confirms that tonight I need to ask her what happened all those years ago, and I'm not leaving without an answer.

Dex was supposed to meet me here, but I've been waiting around for almost half an hour with no sign of him. I'm about to try his cell again when someone settles onto the stool next to me.

"What time do you call this?" I huff out, yet when I turn to face my best friend, I find an unamused Graham instead.

"Evenin'," he mumbles, and waves at Lenny, the owner of the bar.

We were mistaken as twins a lot growing up, with only eleven months between us; we're easy to tell apart now though. He has the same hair and eye color as me, though his hair is trimmed short, and nothing like the messy waves on top of my head. Plus, he's permanently scowling behind his signature tortoise shell glasses.

"What are you doing here?" I glance around for Dex's towering form.

"Booth invited me," he answers with zero explanation.

"Booth isn't here."

"Yes, I am," a voice whispers down my ear. The sensation of his creepy breath against my neck almost has me falling backward.

I'm getting dizzy with how many times I've spun around on this stool. Booth grins at me, and I know that look means trouble. "For fuck's sake, is this some brotherly reunion I didn't know about?"

"Of sorts," Booth replies as he sits on the empty stool to my left, as Lenny takes Graham's order. "Hey, Lenny, can I add a gin and tonic to that?"

The surly bar owner grumbles under his breath, mixes up Booth's drink like he has all the time in the world, and slams the glass on the bar top. No one flinches at the questionable hospitality; it's just how he is. "Loada' bull that is. Stick to beer and whiskey, boy."

"Always a pleasure," Booth calls as he shuffles away.

Looking left and right, both my brothers have a hint of concern in their eyes, and I sense a conspiracy. My head thumps against the sticky bar as it falls forward.

"Dex sent you, huh?"

"We've been watching you gawk at Jo for the last thirty minutes. I wish we intervened sooner. What's your plan here, Pat?" Booth says, though there's no teasing in his voice now. When Booth uses a serious tone, you know he means business.

Peeling my forehead off the bar with a groan, I raise my head and keep my eyes trained forward. "I've been trying to work that out since the moment I got here. This is dumb." I go to stand up, but a strong hand grips me by the elbow and yanks me back.

"Dex texted me. Said you might need some support tonight. He didn't say much, but from the way you've been staring across the room, I think I know what help you need. Just go and talk to her." Graham's gaze doesn't break with mine. His perception is spot on. Despite me thinking I kept my feelings under wraps—even before Jo left—it's clear I wasn't as sly at hiding them as I thought I was. Apparently even now I look at her like a lovesick puppy.

"I've been such a monumental dick to her. I don't even know if she'll *want* to speak to me."

"Why don't we stop creeping on our coworkers in the shadows and join them for some darts? If you talk to her, you talk to her. If you don't, you don't. The call is yours, buttercup." Graham and I jump as Booth slaps his palms on the bar, droplets of warm beer hitting me in the face with the impact. "Let's get groveling."

As he walks toward the table, greeting everyone with a smile or handshake, I suck down my obvious discomfort and stand to follow him. Graham is close behind, who's more of an introvert than me, and the minute he sees his escape, he'll be out of here.

Booth must have warmed them up to our arrival, because they're all smiles and friendly greetings when we join them. Even Jo cracks a small smile at our approach, though it's one of those fake ones I've seen her use over the weeks.

Everyone makes room and drags some extra stools around tables. It's a tight squeeze, and by the time Booth and Graham have settled, the only spot left is next to Jo.

"What brings you in, boss man?" Simon asks as I perch on the stool. He's on Jo's other side, and when I see how close they're sitting, I'm reminded that I don't like him.

"Just a beer with colleagues, you know," I say, raising my glass at him.

"I'm guessing Carrie and Lottie are having a girls' night?" Simon asks.

"They sure are. She's probably on her fifth rewatch of *Encanto* by now." I love my daughter, but when does a movie you've watched over forty times get boring?

Jo shifts slightly in her seat, and when I glance to her lap, I notice her fingers tapping on the outside of her thigh. I've seen her do it a lot lately and it's not something I ever witnessed before she left.

A nervous tick?

"I didn't know you and Jo went so far back," Simon continues. Because he never seems to shut up. "She only told me George is her dad the other day." He pokes her in the ribs from her other side, and *nope*, don't like that.

She looks at the group sheepishly. "I didn't want anyone to think of me as a nepo baby."

"You're clearly a pro in the restaurant field and the team loves you," Jules adds and gives Jo a genuine smile. She's not wrong; Jo's been a huge asset to the team and already I've felt a weight lifted off my shoulders. *I should probably tell her that.* And now I feel like an even bigger dick. I've been so busy obsessing over how to avoid her while simultaneously creeping on her, that I've failed to acknowledge what amazing work she's been doing.

"I think it's so cool George's and Ted's kids are working at Our Place again. I bet it's a massive relief for your mom"—Jules nods to me—"And your dad"—now to Jo. "Ted and Valerie would be so proud."

"Thanks, Jules. We miss them both so mu—"

"Excuse me."

Everyone's eyes dart to Jo as she rushes to get off her stool—almost toppling backward into a young couple in her haste to escape. Her eyes are as wide as saucers and skin practically translucent she's so pale.

Without any explanation, she runs out of the bar, leaving behind her coat and bag. I don't even realize I'm standing to follow her until I see Simon rise from his seat, but Booth quickly grabs his attention and gives me a nod.

Then I'm rushing out into the cold night in search of her.

twelve
JOHANNA

THE FIRST TIME I HAD A PANIC ATTACK, I WAS SEVENTEEN.

It was three weeks after my beautiful mom passed away suddenly in her sleep. No warning. No goodbye. No time to prepare for the indescribable loss and heartbreak. One second, we were laughing at dinner together, the next we were grieving her. When I look back, I don't think I ever got to that fifth stage of grieving. I stuck with the first, thinking that denial was the best solution, because if I didn't acknowledge it, it didn't exist.

I'd been falling asleep with my mom's robe wrapped around me every night, quietly crying myself to sleep so I didn't worry my dad or upset Harriet. Only that evening, I'd gone into my room and couldn't find her robe. Within seconds, my room was in disarray. And the next moment, I was lying on my bedroom floor, hands clutched to my chest as an invisible fist squeezed so tightly, I was certain I was having a heart attack. Ice filled my veins. Cold sweat coated my skin. Everything was trembling uncontrollably.

And then it was over.

Convincing myself I was coming down with something or that it was a normal reaction to losing a loved one, I shrugged it off. I continued to do this for another decade, and it was only at twenty-eight years old that I finally acknowledged it for what it really was.

As I stand with my shaking hand pressed against my chest, I know this isn't a panic attack thanks to years of experience, but I still beg my body to calm down. I glance around the eerie parking lot, and once I spot the blue Ford Explorer under the streetlamp, my thumping heart finally slows.

"And five," I whisper, my lungs deflating with a whoosh of air.

"Five what?" a deep voice asks from behind me.

His sudden appearance doesn't startle me, it makes me mad. It's about time he made himself known. He's not as stealthy as he thinks, hiding in the dark corner of the bar. I wondered why my gaze felt drawn to that side of the room, and when my eyes landed on his broad form, face all serious and solemn under the poor lighting of the bar, I'd hoped he was here to join us.

Only he stayed tucked away for almost an hour, and I cursed my stupid heart for being so reckless with its affection.

My eyes remain fixed on the midnight blue sky as I hear the crunch of gravel under his feet. The moon is out in all its glory tonight, reminding me why I love living in a small town, away from all the light pollution that smothers the twinkling stars. The Milky Way is teasing us tonight, so I concentrate on the smudge of white and yellow, rather than the tingling sensation building at the back of my neck.

"What were you counting?"

"Nothing." I don't look at him, even as his shoulder brushes against mine. Keeping my eyes skyward and hoping he doesn't notice how my breath hitches at the subtle touch.

"Are you okay?"

I drag my gaze away from the twinkling lights and turn my head toward Patrick. I hold back my laugh at his awkward posture; boots dragging across the loose stones and eyes flicking from me to his toes. He's spent weeks avoiding me, so why is he here now? I voice that exact question.

"Why are you out here, Patrick?"

It's only as his head shoots up that I spot genuine concern in his eyes, alongside what looks like guilt. "You ran out and, umm...left your stuff. I wanted to check you were okay." I glance at his hands to where he's clutching my bag and coat.

He slowly raises them toward me, but when my hand wraps around the coat, he doesn't loosen his grip. I frown at him in question as his eyes bore into mine. "Johanna, I need to know. Are you okay?"

His concern doesn't stop the emotions from bubbling over, spilling on the dusty stones between us. The professional and unaffected mask I've been wearing falls to the ground too—everything I've been holding in bared to the world.

"You don't need to know anything. Don't act like you care. No one is around for the act." I pull at my coat again, but he doesn't budge. "Are you really making me play tug of war for my stuff?"

He lets out an exasperated sigh. "It's not an act."

"Oh, good to know. At least I know the hate you have toward me is genuine."

"You know that's not true."

I tug. He pulls.

"Could have fooled me."

The hold on my coat slackens, and the fractured look in Patrick's eyes halts my movements. "Do you really think I could ever feel that way about you?"

"Then what is this? Because whatever it is, it's tiring. I know this isn't easy. Believe me, *I know*. Do you really think we can continue going on li—"

"You left."

The coat slips from his grip and my arm falls limply at my side. Both of us weighed down with anguish and defeat.

We stare. Eyes locked. Blue meets green. Heartache meets sorrow.

"I never wanted to leave, Patrick."

"But you did." And god, does the brokenness in his voice fracture my heart right open.

"I *had* to leave. It was killing my dad to see me like that."

"To see you like what?"

I bite my tongue so hard at that slipup and shake my head. "It doesn't matter, you're right, I did leave. I needed ti—"

"Time. I know. And I gave you that. I said I would wait... clearly it wasn't enough."

"*Waited?*" I shout. The space I wanted from him disappears as I step forward. "You might have waited, but there was clearly an expiration date on how long. Harriet told you I didn't want to speak to or see anyone."

Despite the rage that flares in his eyes, I stand strong. With every word, we step closer. "We said we would give this a go between you and me. I would have waited however long you needed, but you moved on. You made a happy little life for yourself in Tennessee. Without me." His voice rises, ricocheting off the brick wall of the bar and my heart.

I rear back at his words. "Happy?" I whisper. Patrick's accusation extinguishes all the heat in my voice. "You think I was happy?"

"From what I saw, you looked pretty happy to me."

And at that, the remaining embers are smothered by his words.

"You saw me? When?"

Vulnerability sparks in his eyes. His gaze falls away for a second before it swings back to me. "I flew out to see you. A month after you left."

My heart stops.

His hands run through his messy hair, gripping the strands so tightly I worry he's hurting himself. "I came over to your apartment right after I landed, but Harriet wouldn't tell me where you were at first. I just wanted to see you; check you were okay. She told me you needed time away from everyone, that you needed space, but I'd heard those words on repeat for weeks on end from your dad. It drove me crazy not knowing what was going on with you. Not knowing why you left. I told myself once I knew you were okay, I'd give you what you wanted. Maybe it was selfish of me, but I wasn't thinking straight."

"You came to see me?" The words are barely audible. "Why didn't I know this?"

"I didn't stick around once I saw you."

"Did Harry know?"

He doesn't reply, but from the guilty look on his face, she did.

It takes a second for his words to make sense in the tornado that is my brain. He came to Tennessee. To see me. To check on me. But what did he see that made him leave without making himself known?

"W-what did you see?" A very small and unguarded part of me worries that he saw me at my worst. That somehow he saw me in the middle of a panic episode.

"Does it matter? What I saw was enough." From the pained look in his eyes, I think it does matter.

"Patrick, whatever you think you saw it wa—"

"A guy. I saw you with another guy."

The drop in my stomach is so sudden, I sway backward with the sensation, my foot slipping on the gravel, but he doesn't let me fall. No, he grabs hold of my shoulders, steadying me, and doesn't let go.

I had friends, but in the first month, I only hung out with Harriet, so who did he—*Davis*. He must have seen me with

Davis the night I went to visit him at the bar where he was playing. That's the only explanation, because I haven't been on a date or with another man in a long time. Almost six years, to be precise, but Patrick doesn't need to know that.

"Whatever you saw that night wasn't what you think. I promise you. I wish I knew you were there or let me explain. But I definitely wasn't happy, far from it."

"So, who was he? You never responded to my calls and texts. You can't blame me for seeing you wrapped up in his arms and putting two and two together. The only time you contacted me was months later."

It makes sense why his constant texts and calls stopped now. His silence hurt, but I was also grateful I didn't have to continue avoiding him. The second I reached out to him after months of ghosting, I regretted it. The text was fueled by anger and heartbreak. I'll never forget how the news of Patrick becoming a father unraveled all my hard work. It wasn't his fault; I was barely hanging on as it was. Dad was visiting for Thanksgiving, and I overheard him and Harriet talking. *Patrick. Carrie. Pregnant. Baby.* They didn't know I was listening, but it didn't matter.

Yeah, I didn't take it well.

I'd convinced myself I'd be returning to Sutton Bay after Christmas—seven months after I left—but gosh, was I wrong. Even without the news of Patrick, I was far from ready. It took two years for me to even entertain the idea of going home, but by that point, I'd found a good routine, a great therapist, and made somewhat of a life out there. I felt too ashamed to go back, plus, there was no way I could watch Patrick raise a family with another woman. I knew my limits.

"I regretted that text the moment I sent it. I wasn't in a good place, Patrick, and I'm sorry I ignored your calls, but then I found out about..." I gesture toward him, not wanting to volley his own words back at him. *You're the one who moved on.*

THOSE TWO WORDS

"That night was a mistake." He shakes his head vigorously and clamps his eyes shut. "*Fuck.* No, it's not, because we have Lottie. I never intended to go home with anyone that night, but I was drunk. Hurting. Confused."

Guilt rips through me. Of course he was hurting, he'd just lost his dad and his best friend wasn't there for him. I remember the night he came to see me so clearly, and I know exactly what he saw. Me hugging Davis. But that hug didn't hold an ounce of attraction or romance. As much as I want to explain who Davis is, he's too agitated right now and I'm too exhausted.

"I'm sorry I left you to deal with that grief alone. It killed me inside to leave you when I did. Leaving this town. Leaving you was one of the hardest things I've ever had to do." The pressure behind my eyes builds, but I hold back the tears.

"Losing my dad hurt, it still does, but that night was fueled by a completely different pain." He steps closer, the space gradually disappearing until our chests brush. The scent of him surrounds me. Pine and juniper. "I was grieving the loss of you that night. Waiting for you was never a question. I was happy to give you the time and space your family told me you needed, because I was certain you'd come home. To me. But when I saw you with someone else, I took it badly. Drank myself stupid to forget you. But there is no *forgetting* you."

"I don't understand," I breathe out, the words leaving my mouth in a puff of air. My hand is gripping so tightly onto his arm now, I'm sure I'll leave a mark. "Why? Why come to see me when I left you and your family during one of the worst times in your lives? Why do you care after all these years?"

There's no anger, frustration, or sadness in his gaze now. He shakes his head like the answer is obvious. But how could it be?

The pause makes me think he's not going to answer me.

Then I hear three words my teenage heart dreamed of hearing from his lips. Words I never thought I'd hear.

In another universe, another life, I imagined this declaration being whispered to me sweetly. Words I could wake up to in the morning and fall asleep to at night.

They're whispered, but not sweetly. And they aren't meant to be spoken in the past tense.

"I loved you."

thirteen
JOHANNA

Patrick's confession echoes around us, floating into the night sky. It rattles in my hollow heart, and when it settles, the tears I've been holding in trail down my face, and his eyes follow each one with equal agony.

He looks as wrecked as I feel. His confession drains whatever argument or words of persuasion I had to convince him he's wrong. I think we're done for the evening, but our unspoken words still speak volumes.

Is he sorry he loved me, and no longer does? Maybe I should be lucky he ever felt that way. Being loved by him once is better than never at all, right? I wonder how he stopped, though. Because for me, loving Patrick Sadler is chronic. No cure for the heartrending love I spent years trying to ignore.

After months of regret, guilt, and doubt over the move to Tennessee, I accepted that my decision meant that my love would never be reciprocated. I didn't think I would ever see him again. But here he is, standing in front of me, having stopped loving me before I even knew it was possible.

This type of love hurts, but it didn't always feel like this. It was gentle and soft, like a cool spring breeze. One minute the grassy fields are bare, the next they're flooded with new life.

I can pinpoint the exact moment my love for Patrick started to bloom.

Smoothing out the layers of tulle on my baby-blue dress, I try to ignore the horde of butterflies taking flight in my stomach.

I'm not much of a girly-girl, that much is obvious considering two of my best friends are boys, and I've never been into makeup and all that jazz. But when my mom offered to take me into the city to get my hair and makeup done, I couldn't say no.

Because tonight is my junior prom.

When Brody Dixon walked up to me as I was about to step on the bus, and asked me to be his date, I couldn't believe it. He didn't make a big fuss about it like I'd seen some of the other boys in my class do, but who cares? I had a prom date!

Patrick also looked super surprised, and I was a little bummed he didn't seem as excited as I was. He just sat there staring out the window for the entire bus ride home. I don't know if it's because he didn't have a date yet or was tired after a long week of school.

My blonde hair is curled in tight ringlets that fall down my back, and a few diamanté clips hold back my bangs. The curls bounce around as I turn in front of the mirror, checking that my dress and makeup are perfect before heading outside. Brody is picking me up in his new truck, and when I check the time, I realize he'll be here soon.

I swipe one more layer of gloss across my lips, smack them together, and leave the restroom to join Patrick and our parents.

Patrick's dad wanted to get some pictures of the two of us together at the restaurant. We begged him not to, finding the whole thing embarrassing, but it's rare you find Ted without his trusty camera. When I walk out and I'm met with a chorus of gasps and coos, my cheeks heat.

"Johanna," my mom chokes out. "You look stunning, my little Mayflower."

Even my dad tries to subtly swipe away his tears.

THOSE TWO WORDS

My face drops and I chew my lips to hide the shy smile pulling at them. When a pair of black, shiny dress shoes steps into view, the bashfulness vanishes.

I slowly drag my eyes up to find a wide-eyed Patrick. As he looks me up and down, his mouth parts slightly, but no words come out. He's in a silver two-piece suit and I know he hates how his hair has been styled like that.

Is it normal to think your best friend looks hot?

His tie is a little lopsided and I reach out to adjust it, which snaps his gaze to mine. I watch him swallow as I straighten the silky material. "Well don't you clean up well."

"T-thanks. You look beautiful. No! I mean, yes, you do. Your dress is beautiful. You look okay. No, grea—oh fuck."

"Patrick!" Claire scolds from across the room. Ted shakes his head with laughter as he fiddles around with his Polaroid camera.

He's not usually nervous like this, but the red tips of his ears and the way he stumbles over his words make me think he is. Because of me?

"Your tie kinda matches my dress," I point out, giving it a pat, letting him know I'm done. It's a darker shade of blue, but it looks nice against the poofy tulle between us.

"Is that okay? I know I'm not your date, but when you said you were wearing blue...I can change, it's dumb."

He goes to turn away, but I drag him back with the grip I still have on his tie. He falls into me but steadies himself when his warm hands land on my bare shoulders. My heart pitter-patters at the contact, and now I'm the one blushing.

"No, keep it on. I like it." The rhythm of my heart doesn't slow when his panicked face morphs into a big smile, flashing his straight white teeth.

We take photos, our parents fuss over us, and then Patrick heads over to the school with a few of his lacrosse teammates and Dex, leaving me to wait for my date at the restaurant.

When the clock on the wall chimes at seven o'clock, my ears perk up every time I hear a car outside. After ten minutes of waiting, my knees bounce in anticipation. After half an hour, my mom is giving me a pitiful look from across the table. And after one hour, my dad doesn't put up a fight when I beg him to take me home.

As we step out into the cool night, the tears of mortification I've been holding in finally fall. My prom is ruined, and everyone will be talking about how I got stood up by Brody on Monday morning. I tug at the clips in my hair, not caring about the sharp sting in my scalp, when shouting from behind me has me pausing.

"Wait!"

My dad and I turn to find a red-faced Patrick running toward us with something white clutched in his hands, arms flailing in the air.

Quickly wiping at my tear-stained cheeks, I look at my dad in question, who shrugs.

"Patrick, what are you doing here?" I ask once he reaches us. His styled hair is now a mess of curls, and he bends at the waist trying to catch his breath.

"Wow. The school is much farther than you think." Did he run here? "My dad texted me. Brody Dixon is a fucking idiot, and you can do better. Don't let that little turd ruin your night," he rushes out breathlessly. He holds out his elbow to me, but I just stare at him in confusion. "C'mon, YoYo. We're gonna be late."

Still unsure of what's happening, I take his arm and he escorts me to where my dad is standing by his truck. Patrick jogs ahead and opens the back passenger door for me, and I can't help but giggle at the bow he gives me as I climb in. I expect him to sit in the front seat, but to my surprise, he rounds the truck and slides in next to me.

"George, my good man. Take us to the prom!" Patrick calls to my dad, who is now sitting behind the wheel.

My dad rolls his eyes in the rearview mirror, starts the engine, and pulls a U-turn to head in the direction of the school.

I look at Patrick, who's face is still pretty flushed as he smiles brightly. He holds out a fist and uncurls his fingers to reveal a white flower sitting in the middle of his palm. It's a little crushed and bruised now, but it's still recognizable.

"A corsage?" I whisper, my eyes flicking between the delicate flower and my best friend.

"Yeah." He scratches his cheek and glances between us. "Dex was holding on to it for me. That's why it's, umm, a little squashed. I didn't think that tool would get you one, and I didn't want you missing out."

He shrugs his shoulders like it's no big deal, when this is the biggest deal ever. The pitter-pattering from earlier is nothing compared to the herd of horses now galloping in my chest.

He takes hold of my left hand and slips the elastic band around my wrist. He's leaning so close to me, his minty breath coasts across my face and the subtle scent of his aftershave fills my nostrils. Pine and something else?

"You didn't need to come back for me."

"Of course I did," he says and squeezes my wrist gently. "You're my best friend. And I guess this makes me your prom date now, huh?"

Chuckling softly, I stroke the soft petals of the corsage before smiling at Patrick so wide, my cheeks hurt. My humiliation is long gone, and Brody Dixon forgotten. "And I'm yours."

A sudden gust of wind whips across our faces, pulling me back from the memory. We're still standing impossibly close to each other in the middle of the parking lot.

"Why didn't you say anything?" The wind picks up as my voice pitches with emotions.

I can't bring myself to look at his face right now, so I keep my eyes trained on his throat. He swallows deeply before speaking. "I never got the chance, and it was all so new between us."

Whether it's from the cold or the devastation, Patrick notices the shiver that ripples through me.

Taking hold of the coat still hanging from my fingers, he

drapes it over my shoulders and rubs his hands up and down my biceps. The way he looks after me, even when there's so much strain between us, reminds me of that same seventeen-year-old boy.

He gives me a sad smile before he backs away. My body screams at him to come back as he walks toward a row of trucks. My legs have a mind of their own as I follow him silently. Pulling out his keys, he stops in front of a very familiar-looking blue Chevy and slides the key into the lock. Turning toward me, my face must give away my shock at seeing his dad's old truck.

He taps the roof and opens the passenger door for me. "I'm as shocked as you are that this old thing is still running."

Flashbacks of school pickups, camping trips, and drive-in movies come racing back to me as I walk to where he's holding the door open for me. A small dent in the passenger door has a watery smile appearing on my face, remembering the first time Patrick drove it and within the first yard, hit his neighbor's mailbox. He freaked out for a good hour, but in classic Ted fashion, he didn't care and was just glad we were okay.

"Get in, I'll crank the heat."

I hesitate for only a second before sliding past Patrick. There isn't much space between his truck and the one next to it, and when my hip grazes his, he plasters himself against the car door to escape me. I can't decide whether to chuckle that he's trying to be a gentleman or cry that he's trying his hardest to stay away from me.

He rounds the truck and climbs in as I slide into the passenger seat, then chucks his phone and wallet on the bench between us.

"Here," Patrick says as he reaches behind me to the backseat. He's wrapped in a black parka, and when he leans back, his navy Henley rides up to reveal a sliver of muscle and a trail of hair disappearing under his dark blue jeans.

I immediately snap my eyes forward. My emotions are all over the place. From panic, to anger, shock, and now...I have no idea what's hanging in the air between us. Something scratchy falls in my lap and I meet Patrick's meek gaze.

"Sorry, that's all I have in this truck."

"This is fine," I say and drape the blanket over my knees.

He nods and turns to face the windshield. The interior lighting turns off after a few seconds and we're blanketed in darkness, both staring out across the blueberry field in front of us. I hate the awkward tension between us, so thick you could cut it with a butter knife. The younger versions of us would be so confused at it all, but I guess time and distance can do that to people.

"I don't want it to be like this," Patrick murmurs, breaking the silence. We stay facing forward, but from the corner of my eye I can see his fingers flexing against the steering wheel. "I handled you coming back badly and I'm sorry."

"My dad and your mom didn't exactly prime you for my return. And maybe I shouldn't have pretended that...well, that everything could just be ignored," I offer.

"I know why they didn't tell me. But I think I've done my fair share of pretending too."

The side of my face warms, and I know he's looking at me. I want to meet his eyes, but I drop my head and play with the frayed edges of the blanket instead.

"I've been unfair to you, and you won't be surprised to hear that my brothers have been giving me a hard time for it. And Dex. I want to make this work between us. For the restaurant," he rushes out. "If you're here to stay—"

"I am," I blurt out. I need him to know that I'm not going anywhere.

His head rests against the seat; he looks tired, handsome, and so familiar. I want so badly to wipe away the frown line etched into his face, erase all his worries and doubts. We were always that person for one another, someone we would go to for validation, to vent, to laugh, or to cry with.

He has Carrie for that now.

I watch his throat work as he mulls over his next words. When he turns his head to face me, I swear I see relief. "Okay. I've had a lot of time to go over what happened all those years ago, I've gone through all the motions, and I'm not mad at you for leaving. I might not know or understand why you left, and I'd still like to hear you out. I don't think tonight is the time for that. If we're going to continue working together, I think a clean slate is what we need."

"I agree. There's more I want to say, but I struggle to open up sometimes." The worry in his face deepens and I'm quick to assure him. "It's nothing bad, or anything you need to worry about, just some things I had to work through. I don't find it easy to share...but I want to tell you when I'm ready."

"Whenever you're ready, I'll listen. I know I acted like a prick, but I'll never stop worrying about you."

How does one even begin to respond to that? "I'm not here to make things difficult for you. I want us to move forward too." My stubborn heart will hate me for what I say next, but it seems crucial if we really want to move past this all. "I know we have history, but Carrie can rest easy knowing I'm not here to rekindle anything."

His head rears back and he sits up straighter, his entire body now turned toward me. "Wait, what? Jo, that's no—"

"It's fine, Patrick. If I don't say it now, I never will," I interrupt, though the words taste bitter and ashy. "I have spent almost six years coming to terms with it and...it's okay. I'm glad you're happy. Lottie seems like a great kid."

He looks so dumbfounded. Is it that hard to believe that I could be happy for him? At least one of us hasn't been a total disaster and has moved on.

"How about that heat?" I ask, needing to change the subject.

It takes him a moment to shake himself out of his stupor, and once he does, he places the key in the ignition but doesn't turn it. He opens and closes his mouth before shaking his head. I'm about to ask him what's wrong when understanding and disbelief shadow his features.

"You've got it all wrong, Jo."

fourteen
PATRICK

She thinks Carrie and I are together.

How she's come to that conclusion, I don't know, but I feel like a fucking fool for not putting it together sooner. When I felt her anger around Carrie getting pregnant, I got it. But has she really spent all this time thinking we were a couple?

Clearly, we both did a good job of avoiding news about the other. And I don't blame her. After the trip to Tennessee blew up in my face, I made it clear to everyone I wasn't interested in any updates about Jo. Just so long as she was safe and well.

It hits me then how wrong we've been. My grief and whatever was going on with Jo clouded our judgment. I've seen the way she blanches whenever Carrie is mentioned. Could it have been jealousy? Some deep, primal part of me wants that to be true. Because how can she sit there and say it's okay I've moved on? It's anything but *okay,* and far from the truth. If the last few weeks have taught me anything, I was never over Johanna Thomas, time and distance be damned.

And I haven't the first fucking clue what I'm supposed to do with that revelation, so I bury it where it belongs.

"Jo. I think you've misread the situation. Carrie and I, we

aren't together. We never have been, well once, umm..." We both know I don't need to finish that sentence.

"You're not...together?" she asks, her eyes widening ever so slightly.

I shake my head slowly.

"Oh."

What does oh *mean?*

"We have a good thing going; she's a good friend and a great mom. She lives in Jacob's Bluff, but we make it work. Trust me when I say nothing has ever been romantic between us."

"Oh."

I really wish she'd stop saying that word and tell me what she's actually thinking.

"I just wanted to set the record straight, so yeah." I raise my thumbs and point at myself awkwardly. "Single dad."

Her lips quirk, but there's still a stiffness in the air. "Okay then. How about that heat?"

"Oh shit, sorry." Hand still on the key, I finally turn it, only to be met with the screeching chorus of Lottie's playlist. I curse and fumble to reach the dial to turn off my daughter's most recent musical obsession—a song about unicorns and glittery poop. We wince and reach for the volume dial. Jo reaches it first, and the rational part of my brain knows I can pull away in time, but I don't, and my hand engulfs hers.

She doesn't move her hand back like I expect her to, and I slowly turn my hand—and hers—until the cab is bathed in silence. We're impossibly still, and the feel of her hand in mine awakens something in me.

As if it has a mind of its own, my thumb starts tracing small circles on the inside of her wrist. Her breath hitches, but she still doesn't move as we watch our intertwined hands, the feel and softness of her skin like a comfort I didn't know I missed. I don't question whether she's as affected as me, because when my thumb finds her pulse, it's wild like mine.

When I slowly circle that spot, she whips her hand away and severs our connection.

Fuck. What am I doing?

She tugs at the sleeves of her coat, like she's trying to hide any traces of where our skin met. I clear my throat, willing my dumb heart to chill out. My head is all over the place, because not fifteen minutes ago we were laying it all out, right in the middle of the parking lot.

"Let me drive you home." I put the car in reverse, placing my hand on the back of her headrest, and check it's safe to pull out. These last few minutes have clearly gone to my head, because I'm dizzy for her. Drunk on her. It would be so easy for me to slide my hand behind her head and run it through that honey-golden hair.

An image of my hands in her hair for a totally different reason flashes in my head, and I have to shift in my seat as my cock thickens at the filthy thoughts. Her on her knees. Eyes watering. Pouty mouth open and swollen. Swallowing me down.

Yeah, that doesn't help. My dick strains against the zipper of my jeans, and I hope the darkened cab hides the effect she's having on me without even trying. *Jesus, it's been a long time.*

"How's living above the bakery?" I genuinely do care, but I'll talk about anything at this rate, just to stop my mind from wandering into the gutter.

"Unlimited coffee and pastries? I'm living the dream."

"It's a nice spot. Great grilled cheeses," I say and throw her a wink. Suddenly, the cab is filled with the sweetest sound. A sound I haven't heard in so long. *Her laugh.* And god, have I missed it.

"Coffee and cheese. I'm so basic."

I shake my head and laugh as she singsongs the last part in that over-the-top British accent; something she's done since we were younger, and it's comforting to know she hasn't lost that little quirk.

"You could never be basic."

At this rate, it's futile trying to filter anything that comes out of my mouth when she's around.

"I've been meaning to ask if I could sign the restaurant up for the Easter fair in April? It might be good to showcase some of our staple dishes, but also give Booth the chance to show off his talents. It's a great way to give back to the community too."

"That's a...really good idea." I laugh, even though I'm annoyed at myself for not thinking of it first. "I'll see if Graham knows anything about the permits we'll need and how to apply for a table."

"How is Graham? Tonight was the first time I've seen him."

"Same old. Always scowling, but still no bite."

"Are he and Jenna still together?"

I hiss through my teeth. "Tough subject. It ended about a year ago. And not well either, but Mom doesn't know that, so keep that to yourself."

"Permission to speak honestly?"

"Go ahead."

I catch her glancing around the cab, like Jenna is hiding in the backseat waiting for her. "*Ialwaysthoughtshewasabitchface.*" I almost don't catch her words, but when I brake at a stop sign, I turn to see her biting her lip.

"Johanna May Thomas. The mouth on you." Her shoulders slump like she's been carrying that weight around for years. "You're not alone there. It just took us a few years to figure that out."

She hums in what I think is agreement but then a gasp has my eyes darting to her shocked face. "First the truck, and now I see you have the same old, ratty wallet?"

She reaches to where I haphazardly threw my wallet

between us. Panic has me intercepting her, and I snatch it up before she can grab it. *And see what's inside.*

"Oh. Sorry, that was rude of me," she says, hands recoiling back to her lap, and I hate the shocked confusion on her face.

"No, no. It's just old and falling apart. I need a new one." I hope she accepts the little white lie as I tuck it away safely in the glove compartment. I've already confessed my past feelings to her tonight, no need to add to the list of things I'd rather she didn't know about.

The rest of the drive is filled with silence, nothing like the days spent riding around in this truck as teenagers, goofing around or riding along the coast. Everything between us was always easygoing and honest. Well, apart from the long-standing crush I had on her, but that never disrupted the good thing we had going on. We've sure as heck been honest tonight, but the easy part is still missing.

When we approach the block where her apartment is, disappointment floods my veins. What excuses can I make so she has to stay a little while longer? Left my coat at the bar? Nope, wearing it. Maybe I could fake a flat? Also dumb, as I can see her apartment from here.

"This is me," she calls out as I pass her building. *Is this classed as kidnapping?*

"Oh yeah." Pulling up a little down from the bakery, I park the truck.

"Thanks for the ride." She goes to unbuckle herself but struggles with the seat belt that I now remember is busted.

"Ah, fuck, I should have warned you. That one's broken. It's usually only Lottie with me, and I'll drive my other truck then so she can sit in the back," I explain as I lean over to help her, secretly giddy that she has to stay a while longer.

My hand slides along the strap across her chest right when she yanks at it, pulling it taut. Taking me with it. *Anddd now I'm touching her tit.*

THOSE TWO WORDS

Her mouth drops open, and I try my best to pretend like I'm not feeling her up.

"Umm, sorry. Just a second," I stammer out and slip my hand out from where it was snug against her. It takes a few sharp tugs, but neither of us attempts to move once she's free.

"I thought I'd have to take you home with me tonight," I joke, but when I hear it out loud, I know how it sounds.

I don't miss the blush on her cheeks as she laughs nervously. A small smile on her lips, but once again, not the one I want to see. What will it take to see that smile again?

How can I bring it back? I want to ask.

"It's your day off tomorrow?" I ask instead, and she nods in response. "What do you have planned?"

"I'm up early for a hike with Quinn in Acadia. I'm going to take her to the lookout." The corners of her lips pull down at that. I know what caused it, and what the lookout means to her.

"That'll be nice. Tomorrow is supposed to be a good day for it too."

She nods slowly and reaches for the door handle. "Well, thanks. I'll see you next week?"

"Yeah. I'll be around."

"Goodnight, Patrick." She steps onto the sidewalk and gives me a timid smile as she shuts the door behind her.

I shouldn't want to haul her back into my truck when she climbs out. I shouldn't have a list a mile long of ways I can get that bright smile to light her face again.

But I do.

As I wait to pull away until she goes inside and the upstairs lights turn on, I realize no one knows that we left. I drop a text in the group chat I have with my brothers.

> Patrick: Sorry to bail. Jo and I got talking. We left about twenty minutes ago.

> Booth: YOU LEFT TOGETHER?!

> Graham: Rude.

> Patrick: Not like that. I drove her home.

> Booth: And?

> Booth: I see you've read the message.

> Booth: Don't ignore us.

> Graham: Booth is getting upset. Can you please answer him.

Ignoring them, I make the short drive home, recalling what it felt like to have my hands on her again. How the touch of her skin still has mine tingling. How the subtle scent of jasmine and ocean still lingers. But I also remember how badly it hurt to lose her.

If we have any chance at making this work as friends, those feelings that have been sitting dormant for years need to stay asleep.

fifteen
JOHANNA

"I THINK MY LUNGS ARE GONNA FALL OUT OF MY BUTT," Quinn huffs out next to me.

"Yup," I agree, trying to catch my own breath. "I kinda forgot how steep the incline was." I know this trail like the back of my hand, but I swear it's gotten steeper. "Sorry, I don't remember it taking this long to get to the lookout."

"Oh, don't sweat it. It's so nice to be out of that tiny kitchen and get some fresh air," she says in her usual chipper tone.

"So, the Rockies, hey? I've always wanted to visit Colorado. What's it like?"

"Definitely in my top three of places I've lived. I haven't been back to San Diego for years, not since I was eighteen, but that's a great place to visit too."

Quinn is originally from California and has lived in twelve different states since she left. Her dream has always been to run her own bakery; she just needed somewhere to start it. She has zero connections here, but a dart thrown drunkenly at a map made the decision for her. I'm grateful it landed on Sutton Bay.

"This view will put the ones you saw in Colorado to shame."

We have mountains here, but we're known for our vast forests and breathtaking ocean views.

"Oh, it already has—what more could you want." She throws her hands up in the air and spins around in a circle.

"I've missed this place like crazy. You'll love it in the summer. We'll have to go camping as long as you don't mind the mosquitoes."

"Bah, they're just hungry. I heard fall is pretty spectacular around here?"

"Yeah, it's something else. Watch out for the leaf peepers come October."

"The *what* peepers?" she asks.

Chuckling at the look on her face, I step over a large muddy puddle. "Tourists who flock to New England to look at the changing colors of the trees. It's a whole thing, but I know the best spots to avoid them."

"Ooh, I cannot wait. I'll be knitting us the cutest sweaters for fall."

"I didn't know you could knit?"

"I can't," she says. We stare at each other for a beat, before breaking out into a fit of laughter.

The path ahead narrows, so I walk in front and pull back some overgrown ferns, letting Quinn pass by first.

She really is the most sunshiny human I've ever met and has a wardrobe to match her personality. It's been really nice getting to know her and making a friend who doesn't know me as the girl who abandoned her friends and family.

"I'll have no issue finding you if you get lost," I say with a glance at her outfit. She's wearing a bright pink raincoat, paired with purple space leggings.

She shoots me an overly dramatic look of worry. "You will *not* lose me today, Johanna. *Shit,* the bears can probably smell the sugar on me."

We walk and talk for another ten minutes, planning a wine

THOSE TWO WORDS

and cheese night at my apartment soon. When a set of jagged rocks comes into view, I know we're near the top.

"Almost there." I'm unsure if I say that for my sake or hers, but as the horizon breaches the hill, the ground below our feet flattens and the breath in my lungs stalls. This view never fails to take my breath away, but after not seeing it for years, I'm immobilized by how awestruck it leaves me.

This is home.

Stopping a few feet from the scraggy cliff edge, we stand between a small opening in the trees; pine, aspen, and fir encircle us. The water reflects the clear, blue sky, making the horizon appear seamless. Lush green and cerulean blue. The water is choppy today, and the waves crash below us, lancing up into the sky when they hit the small islands dotted around the inlet. Sea birds dip and dive into the water with ease, cresting the surface minutes later with a fishy dinner.

Calmness sweeps over, all the stress that's built up in my muscles dissipating as I soak up the picturesque view. A splash of water lands on the back of my hand, and I look up at the clear sky in confusion, only to realize I'm crying. These are sad tears as much as they're happy. It feels therapeutic, like a weight is being lifted with each tear that falls and every breath of pine and salt water I take in.

It's easy to forget the days when I couldn't see myself escaping the black hole of anxiety and depression when I'm standing here.

My eyes drift to a large pine tree that stands out from its neighbors, its trunk thicker and rougher, showing its age. Where all the other trees have started to tilt from being exposed to the strong winds, this one stands steady. That's exactly why my dad, Harriet, and I chose it. Resilient, with a striking presence, just like Mom.

Forgetting that Quinn is standing next to me, I brush away the tears, hoping she isn't weirded out by my sudden outburst of emotion. But when I turn to her, she gives me a knowing look.

Smiling softly, she takes hold of my hand and gives it a squeeze.

"We all need a good cry now and again. Happy, sad, angry, excited—you name it. It's healthy. Don't feel ashamed when you need to let it out."

Her words of acceptance abolish the shame I know I shouldn't hold about being vulnerable, and I squeeze her hand back. And then I do exactly as she says. I let it out. The tears track down my face and I don't know how long we stand there, but she doesn't let go of my hand the entire time. When the well of emotions is empty, I let out a watery laugh as the wind cools my tear-soaked cheeks.

"It's just so good to be home. I never thought I'd be here again and feel so...so content. It's been a rough..." I pause, but her encouraging smile gives me the push I need. "It's been a rough few years. I'm sure you've overheard people talking about it."

"I try not to listen to town gossip. From personal experience, nothing good ever comes from it. I won't pry, but if you ever want a judgment-free zone, I'm all ears. We all have our ghosts."

I nod my thanks and pull my backpack off my shoulders. Pointing to a few smooth boulders, we make our way over. "Let's get set up over here, it's a great spot to eat lunch, and you can see the whole bay."

"Wow," she says, taking in the view as we sit. "So this is Anakiwa Lookout? It's special to you, huh?"

Maybe it's the familiar scenery, the tranquil sound of waves crashing, or birds calling overhead. Or perhaps it's Quinn's assurances that it's okay to be unguarded, for whatever reason, I tell her all about Anakiwa Lookout. The hikes we took every month, the camping trips, and how this is where we came to scatter my mom's ashes.

"FUCKING STUPID DOOR!" I MUTTER TO MYSELF AS I WIGGLE THE key in the front door of the restaurant. I'm trying to be quiet, not wanting people to think I'm breaking in and call the cops on me, but my impatience is getting the better of me.

It's almost 1:00 a.m. on a Saturday and well past my bedtime. We closed hours ago, and I'm so exhausted from working a double and experiencing serious brain fog, that it took me hours to realize I left my phone here. Or I hope I did.

That's why I'm standing outside the restaurant, in my pajamas, freezing my tits off, and very close to kicking down the door if it doesn't open in the next five seconds.

I'm trying to remember what Patrick said about the front door getting stuck sometimes. Something like, *"Pump the handle up and down, then turn the key as soon as you hear it click."* Honestly, I don't remember. I was too busy looking at his arms flexing with the motion he made when he said *pump*.

I'd find it funny that I was so distracted by his biceps if I wasn't so tired and having an all-around shitty day. Nothing seemed to be going right. I got a flat tire driving to my dad's. Burned my breakfast. Chipped a nail. All microscopic, but sometimes they just add up. I'm about to force my way inside when I hear a *snick* and feel the handle pop. Not wasting my opportunity, I twist the key and almost cry in relief when the door swings open.

Wincing at the alarm blaring louder than usual, I scramble over to the keypad and clumsily type in the six-digit code. It takes me three tries to get it right, my mind somehow drawing blanks every time I press the numbers. *God, I need to sleep.*

My feet drag across the floor to the back, and once I'm inside the office, I flick on the light. A big sigh leaves me when I spot my phone sitting on the desk. I grab it, switch off the light, lock up, and trudge my way to the front. In and out, no issues.

Each step toward the front door is another step closer to my warm bed, where I plan to sleep until mid-afternoon. As I walk alongside the bar, my feet dragging behind me, I run my hand along the multicolored surface of the driftwood. The feel of the different textures beneath my fingertips usually comforts me, but not tonight. I'm so on edge, and I snatch my hand away when the lights of a passing car shine through the window and reflect off something on my left.

My steps falter before being rooted to the spot. A chill runs through me, like I've been plunged into an ice bath. Front and center, in the middle of all the liquor bottles, sits my mom and Ted, forever frozen in time.

I've seen that photograph every day when at the restaurant, and my heart has never seized like it is now. Grief is fickle like that. It sits below the surface of your mind on some days, barely noticeable, then hits you out of nowhere.

Their smiling faces are a stark reminder that they're no longer with us. Ripped away too soon. And there was nothing I could do about it. That last one is something I try not to think about too deeply, but I've triggered the thought now, and the roots of anxiety and grief burrow deep in my chest.

Mom has been gone for almost two decades, but sometimes that pain is as fresh as the day we lost her. Those roots now creep down my arms, my legs, and remind me of how all my loved ones will be ripped away from me in the same way.

Dad. Harriet. Patrick. Claire.

So many people I care so deeply about, and I have no control over how long they will be on this earth.

I try to remind myself these thoughts are unhelpful, that everyone I love is fine, but the pressure in my chest and tingling in my fingers lets me know the anxiety has got a good grip on me now.

"It's fine," I mumble to myself. "I just need…"

My words drift off when I realize my anxiety medication is all the way back in my apartment, which sets off a whole new wave of panic. It isn't far, but as I take a shaky step toward the door, I know it's too late for the meds to do their job.

Discarding my phone on top of the bar, I crouch, running my hands through my hair in frustration, willing the beating of my heart and the shaking in my hands to stop. I slowly massage my temples, but it all feels useless. All of this because of one photograph. I grip the edge of the bar and pull myself up to standing, eyes landing on the framed photograph. If I can just get it out of sight so their memory stops haunting me, this will all go away. *Right?*

With shaky legs, I make my way around the bar until I'm standing directly in front of the shelves of liquor bottles and glassware. The photograph is higher up than I anticipated, but I use the bottom two shelves to climb up until it's in reach. As my fingertips graze the cold edges of the metal frame, the bottom of my sneaker slips.

As if in slow motion, I watch the picture frame tip forward. It tumbles off the shelf and brings a bottle of bourbon with it. The moment the glass cracks and shatters against the wooden floor, so does my heart. The floodgate holding back the tidal wave of emotions splinters open.

"No, no, no, no," I repeat frantically. Falling to my knees among the mess of broken glass and bourbon, my hands hover over the broken frame, like I might do more damage. Mom and Ted stare up at me, their happy faces now tarnished. I try my best to shake the glass and sticky liquid away, but the damage is done.

In more ways than one.

Heartbreak and panic aren't a good combination.

The pressure in my temples increases.

The tingling in my fingers spreads all over, leaving me numb in its path.

My already quickening breathing turns to desperate gasps for air.

The corner of my vision fades to black, and icy panic seizes up my muscles. I try to slow my breathing and think of a color, any color.

Green.

I clench my eyes shut, count to ten before opening them again, and search the small space in front of me.

Five things. Just five green things.

I manage to find four from my spot on the floor but come up short when I try to find that fifth and final item. It's too dark in here.

Why didn't I turn on the lights?

Will anyone find me?

Do I want anyone to find me?

I sink further into the floor. The panic truly has its claws embedded in me.

I'm drowning in grief. In darkness. In sadness. In hopelessness.

There's no use fighting it anymore, so I succumb to it.

Then all I see is black.

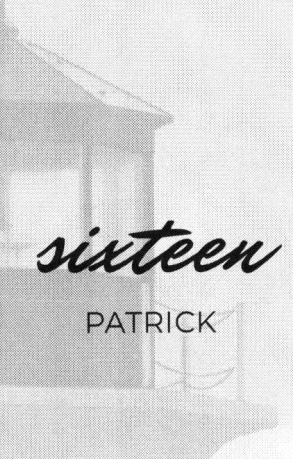

sixteen

PATRICK

SHUTTING THE DOOR BEHIND ME, I TIPTOE AWAY FROM THE GUEST room Lottie is sleeping in tonight, carefully avoiding certain floorboards like landmines. One wrong step and the creak of the old boards will wake her up and we'll be back to square one.

I make my way downstairs and find my mom in the kitchen, even though it's past midnight.

Carrie had to make an emergency trip out of town, but I'd already made plans with Dex to help him pick up some timber a couple of counties over. My mom would never say no to a sleepover with her granddaughter, so Lottie stayed with her tonight. The long drive and heavy lifting have left me exhausted and sore, and I was about to crawl into bed when my mom called to say Lottie wasn't well and had been crying for Carrie and me. When I heard Lottie's muffled sobs over the phone, they just got me to haul ass in my truck quicker.

Three hours later, after lots of tears, and me begging her to take some medicine and rocking her to sleep, she's finally down. She's a good kid, but she's never been great at taking medicine; pair that with her being overtired—yeah, it's been a long night.

"Hey," I whisper. She's making two cups of tea, and the strong smell of peppermint fills the air. She offers me a cup and I take it, hoping it will help me find a few hours of sleep tonight.

"How's our baby doing?" my mom asks.

"Exhausted, emotional, and grumpy. Lottie is the same."

My sarcasm isn't welcomed, and she smacks me on the chest before I walk away, chuckling.

"Ouch." I rub at the spot. "Am I not your baby?"

"My first baby, but she is *the* baby," she replies with an eye roll. I don't argue with her there. Lottie has everyone wrapped around her pinky without even trying.

"She's feeling better and finally settled; I doubt she'll wake up now until the morning. She came down with it fast. Carrie said it was spreading like crazy in her class."

"Let's hope it's a twenty-four-hour bug. Are you at the restaurant tomorrow?"

"Nah, day off. Jo has the afternoon shift covered. I was hoping to take Lottie out to the creek. One of the customers mentioned some bald eagles had hatched nearby," I say, turning to make my way into the living room.

I take a seat on the sofa and Mom settles in her recliner. The empty chair next to her hasn't been touched in years, and you can still make out the indentation of when Dad last sat in it.

We get talking about the restaurant and other things, when a buzz from my pocket interrupts us. Pulling out my phone, I'm surprised to see a notification from the security system app telling me the restaurant alarm has just been disabled. *After two failed attempts.*

The alarm was set hours ago, so what's this? Neither my

brothers nor George have told me that they'd be heading over, and I can't see why they would at this hour.

My mom must see the concern on my face. "What's wrong?"

"I don't know, but the alarm was just turned off at the restaurant."

She looks at her watch and the confusion on her face now matches my own.

"Who closed up last night?"

"It was Jo..." I answer, but my words trail off. Surely she's not at the restaurant? If it is her, is she alone? Dread sits heavy in my stomach. Jo, more than anyone, knows why it's not safe to be alone in the restaurant, and my mom must be thinking the same thing from the worry lining her face.

"I'm gonna go and check it out. I'm sure it's fine and there's a glitch in the system or something." I'm already on my feet and halfway to the front door.

"Be safe and call me if you need anything. I'll wait up."

"Don't worry, I won't be long. Thanks, Mom." I pull on my coat and boots before jogging out the front door to my truck.

The roads are quiet at this time of night, and I drive a little over the speed limit. The gnawing feeling grows with each minute that passes. I haven't taken my dad's old truck, so I'm able to call Jo's cell phone through the Bluetooth, but I'm met with her voicemail each time. I try to assure myself that she's asleep in her bed, a few blocks over, but my gut is rarely wrong.

Once the restaurant comes into view, the worry doesn't disappear. It looks shut from the outside, but it still leaves me to question why the alarm has been deactivated. I park my truck, turn off the engine, and sprint up to the front door. My worries grow tenfold when I test the handle. *Unlocked.* I make a point of opening the door loudly and hope it scares off anyone who shouldn't be here. It might be stupid of me to go storming in like this, but my mom knows I'm here.

When I'm met with silence, I shut the door behind me and keep the lights off. I take hesitant steps along the bar, looking for anything out of place. Everything looks as it should, but then something catches my eye. A pale blue phone case. *Jo's phone.*

"Jo! Johanna! Are you here? It's Patrick." I don't even stop to think before I'm shouting her name through the restaurant. If there are burglars, they know I'm here now. Storming into the kitchen, I look around but don't find her. The same goes for the stockroom, restrooms, and office.

Maybe she left it here by mistake, but it still doesn't explain why the building is unlocked. I'm about to go check the security footage when the smell of liquor hits me. Following the scent toward the bar, I pause when my boot crunches against something. Lifting my foot, I see shards of glass, and my breathing stops. The trail of glass leads me to a small puddle at the end of the bar, and as I look down the narrow space, following the river of what I presume is bourbon, my heart stops altogether.

A small, huddled form lies shaking on the ground, surrounded by shards of glass.

Jo.

I don't think, I just do; never moving so quickly in my life. Doing my best to avoid the bourbon and glass, I crouch in front of her and run my hands along her arms, back, head, hands. Anywhere I can reach. It's only when I lean in closer to her that I hear her raspy, uneven breathing. I know she's not unconscious, and I can't see any visible injuries, but I need to see her face. Her eyes.

With the gentlest of touches, because I'm still not sure if she's hurt, I place my hands on her trembling shoulders. "Johanna, what happened?" She doesn't respond and the shaking of her body ripples right through me. "It's Patrick. Look at me, please." Over and over, I repeat her name, tell her I'm here, but she doesn't lift her head from where it's tucked between her knees.

Her pants are soaked through, and I know I need to get her away from this broken glass, but from her unresponsive state, I'll need to do it myself. I push back on her shoulders gently and encourage her to sit upright. When she finally raises her head, the panic-stricken look on her face guts me. It feels as if someone has reached inside my chest and has a brutal grip on my heart.

She looks almost catatonic, looking straight through me as her lips tremble with each harsh breath she tries to suck in. Only whenever she does, her eyes widen, like the air is getting trapped in her throat.

"Johanna, I need to move you, okay? I'm going to pick you up."

When her hand claws at her chest, searching for that lost breath, I act fast. Scooping her up in my arms, I step over the small picture frame and broken bottle. Once we're clear of the mess, I hold her close to me as I sit on one of the chairs, her legs hanging over my thighs. It's then I notice she's in a pair of flannel pajamas and sneakers. *Did she come here straight from bed?*

Bringing my other hand to her chin, I tilt her head back. If I thought her brightness was dulled before, it's been completely doused out now. Her dark eyes swim with panic, drowning them. Her skin is clammy and pale. The tremors in her body haven't lessened, and I don't know what to do.

But I know I need Johanna back.

I'll do anything to bring her back. Putting that light back where it belongs. Because sadness and terror are not emotions that should ever be on the beautiful woman breaking in front of me.

Not my Johanna.

The best I can do for her is let her know I'm here. Stroking my hand down her spine, I shush her quietly, rocking us from left to right. "I'm here. I'm not going anywhere."

From where her face is pressed up against my chest, I just about make out her mumbling.

"Say that again?"

"Green," she murmurs against my neck, so quickly I almost don't catch it. But then her breathing intensifies again, and she repeats that one word. *Green. Green. Green. Green. Green.*

"Johanna, look at me, c'mon. I need you to slow your breathing." I place her hand on my chest. "Feel me breathing. Feel that. Match my breathing."

At first, I thought it was fear, and I suppose it is, but it's taken hold of her and doesn't want to let go.

Because she's having a panic attack.

seventeen
JOHANNA

The familiarity of the vise-like grip around my heart isn't welcome. My mind greeted that crippling fear like an old friend.

It's a discomfort I've spent years learning how to avoid. But today it won. It's been so long since it conquered me, I worry I've forgotten how to escape. Everything seems like a feeble attempt. Right now, I'm the prey. Anxiety is the predator.

I almost found my way out of the darkness, but even that failed me.

Green plant.

Green gin bottle.

Green bottle opener.

Green apron.

Green...nothing.

With that loss, my fight gave out and I let it take over.

Only when I sensed him did a sliver of light break its way through the clouds. But the fear and overpowering sensations playing havoc on my body and mind don't let me take him in properly. All my senses feel muddled. I try to cling to them, like a buoy in stormy waters.

Touch returns first. A gentle brush on my shoulders, and then a warm hand on my chin.

Sound next. His voice; deep and soothing.

When my nose fills with the scent of pine and juniper, my heartbeat slows.

"P-P-Patrick?" I stutter out.

"It's me, I've got you. Do you know where you are? Should I call someone?" The sound of his voice pulls me through that crack of light in the darkness, but I slip back in when his hand retreats. I fumble for him, needing his touch. Needing to know he's got me.

I frantically shake my head, the pain in my chest pulling taut again, and I bury myself into his chest.

"I-I need...green," I rasp.

"Green what?"

"It's too d-dark. Need to see green."

"Here, I'll put on a light." He stands and places me down. Bright light filters through my eyelids and I cringe away from it. His absence is short, and when I'm in his arms again, I don't let go. The strong hold and comforting words he whispers in my ear help, but my mind is still so determined to find my something green.

"It's not dark anymore, love. I'm here."

He's here.

Those words give me the courage to open my eyes, the bright, white light is startling at first, but I soon take in my surroundings.

Gentle hands take hold of my face, strong and firm fingers gently stroke along my ears, jaw, and cheeks, and soft lips brush against my forehead.

"What do you need? Let me help you."

"Green," I repeat. Not having the energy to explain myself.

"I don't know what that means. Green what? Please look at me, Johanna. You're worrying me and I don't know how to help.

Show me your eyes." The pleading tone in his voice tells me I need to fight this. I need to find a way out. Not to let it win.

It takes a few seconds for him to come into focus, and even his silhouette is a comforting sight.

Strong jaw. Crooked nose. Scarred chin. Wavy, dark blond hair. Pine-green eyes.

Green eyes.

Green.

A sob rips through me, and it must shock him because he tightens his hold of me, but all I feel is relief flooding my system. My body goes slack with sudden exhaustion. The panic doesn't completely disappear, but I repeat the five green items repeatedly in my head. Patrick's eyes being the lifesaver in the dark ocean that tried to wash me away.

My eyes fall shut, I'm in his arms, cold air hits my face, and he doesn't once let me go.

For the first time, the darkness doesn't feel that lonely.

He's got me.

eighteen
PATRICK

Jo remains cradled in my arms as I walk down the hallway to my bedroom.

My hands have hardly left her since I found her curled up on the floor like my worst nightmares come to life. Her hand was in mine the whole ride over. I planned on taking her back to her apartment, but the need to have her in my space, safe and under my watch, had me carrying her to my truck and driving in the opposite direction.

I dropped a text to the cleaning company to apologize for the mess, one to my mom to let her know we were okay, but I'd be heading to my house tonight, and another to Jules to see if she could cover Jo's shift tomorrow. Knowing Lottie is safe with my mom also meant that I didn't have an excuse not to bring Jo to my house. Not that I needed one, but it meant I could give her my full attention and take care of her.

There's no doubt in my mind that she was in the middle of an intense panic attack. So intense, that I was close to calling George or an ambulance. But what caused it?

The moment I turned the lights on and our eyes met, I

could see the panic ebb, and her entire body seemed to relax. The way our eyes locked on each other for those few seconds felt like I was peering into the ocean from one of the bluffs. But today, the sky above the ocean was stormy, and her eyes weren't the deep blue that I love.

She slept the entire drive, and I'm sure I could have woken her to get her into my house, but something about having her in my arms felt right. I carried her from my truck, through the house, up the stairs, and here we are. The guest room behind us is an option, rather than my bedroom, but the decision is made for me when she reaches up and wraps her hand around the collar of my coat.

I step over the threshold into my darkened room, and her eyelids flutter open. A small frown forms between her brows as she tries to take in her surroundings. It feels bizarre that she hasn't been in this house before, considering we grew up in each other's homes.

"We're at my place," I assure her. "I didn't want you to be alone tonight."

She blinks up at me and speaks for the first time in what feels like hours. "Okay." Her voice is hoarse, and I make a mental note to check if I have some ginger tea in the pantry.

As much as I don't want to, I slowly lower her to her feet, and she must have the same reservations, because her hand stays glued to my coat. Placing my hand over hers, I smile at her. "I need to take care of a few things. Why don't you take a shower?" I nod toward my en suite bathroom. "I'll grab you some clothes; I think I have some of Florence's old things here."

Her lips curl inward and she lowers her head slowly, looking both insecure and nervous. Placing the tip of my pointer finger under her chin, I tilt her face up. "I'm not going anywhere, but if you want me to take you ho—"

"I want to stay here."

I shouldn't love hearing that, but I'm a fool around this woman. She pads across the hardwood floor, glancing back a few times, looking so vulnerable, and shuts the door behind her. When the shower starts to run, I turn around and jog down the stairs, throwing my coat over the banister on my way into the kitchen. Flipping on the kettle, I place my hands on the cool countertop and let my head hang between my shoulder blades.

Only now that I'm alone do I begin to break down tonight's events.

Seeing Jo in that state, lying on the floor of the restaurant, looking so small and broken, brought back so much heartbreak and trauma to a day I'm sure neither of us want to remember. A reminder of finding someone else I cared for lying hopeless in that building. I know she isn't broken, but it doesn't stop me from wanting to help her.

In the years I've known her, I've never seen Jo in such a way. Sure, she had her moments of stress over work things, or worries like the rest of us, but nothing that would come close to being a panic attack. *Was this the first one? When did they start? What caused it?*

With a cup of tea, bottle of water, and some aspirin in hand, I head back upstairs. Jo still isn't out of the shower when I put the items on the bedside table, so I head into the guest room closet and pull out some clothes for her. I'm about to grab one of Flo's sweaters, when I spot my old lacrosse T-shirt folded up next to it.

Ten minutes later, I'm scrolling through my phone, looking at pictures of Lottie while I wait for Jo to finish in the bathroom. When a text pops up on my phone, I shouldn't be surprised that my mom is still awake; she won't be able to sleep until she knows we're home safe.

Mom: Is she okay?

THOSE TWO WORDS

> Patrick: Yeah, we're at my place.

> Mom: Look after our girl. Don't worry about Lottie, you stay with Jo as long as she needs.

I want to reply that she isn't my girl. *Not anymore.*

> Patrick: I will. Give Lottie a big hug for me in the morning please.

The steam coming from under the door reminds me that she's been in there for a while, and I don't want to overstep, but something doesn't feel right. Taking cautious steps toward the door, I rap my knuckles against the wood. "Hey, everything okay in there?"

Silence.

I try not to panic, because that's not what she needs right now. With my ear against the door, I listen carefully. After a minute I hear a faint sound above the running water. When I hear it a second time, my hand is already on the handle, steam hitting me in the face as I barrel into the room.

"Jo?" I call, louder this time.

It takes me a second, but when the steam clears, I see her. Sitting in the middle of the shower stall, her legs pressed to her chest, arms wrapped around them tightly. Seeing her so small and fragile like this again has my heart careening to the floor. Her skin is mottled red from the hot water, but even through the cascade of water, I can tell she's crying. I'd hoped I was wrong about hearing her broken sobs through the door. Her tears disappear down the drain, but they're not gone quick enough. I'd sell my soul not to see her cry ever again.

Approaching her slowly so she knows I'm here, I slide off my shoes and step onto the tiled floor. Her head shoots up from where it was resting against her knees, and her eyes go wide, mouth opening like she wants to protest, but a heart-wrenching whimper leaves her instead. Not caring about the hot water as it pelts down on me, soaking my clothes instantly, I crouch in front of her. I ignore the fact she's naked and keep my eyes locked with hers.

"Hey, hey," I say in a hushed tone. I brush the wet strands of hair from her face and cup her damp cheeks. "What can I do?"

"I-I-I can-n't do-o-" Her words come out in short gasps, her chest heaving with the effort to get them out. She's going to have another panic attack.

"Johanna, love, I need you to breathe for me. Like before, you remember? Look at me, watch me breathe in. Watch me breathe out." I lean over her and turn off the water, before reaching behind me to grab a fresh towel from the hamper. Wrapping it around her, the white terry cloth swallows her, and then she's back in my arms. "That's it, nice and slow."

Like it's the most natural thing in the world, I press my lips to her forehead. She smells like me, and I have to tamper down the wild thoughts that triggers and how I can make her smell like me in other ways. Wrapped up in my sheets. Wrapped up in *me*.

The tremors slow again, her breathing calmer now. "Let's get you in bed," I whisper into her hairline. I stand with her in my arms and shuffle out of the bathroom, leaving a trail of water behind us with each squelching step.

"You're soaked," she whispers.

"I needed a shower anyway." I pause at the foot of the bed. "I'm going to put you down."

When I place her securely on her feet, she glances around warily, like she's forgotten where she is.

I point to the pile of clothes on the dark gray comforter. "I thought you could sleep in those. Not that you need to sleep in here, but it's the biggest bed."

Her long hair clings to the towel in a knotted mess, but there's color in her cheeks now, and not just from the heat of

THOSE TWO WORDS

the shower. Her eyes aren't glassy and unfocused anymore. Seeing her return to herself comforts me.

She walks toward the clothes and looks over her shoulder at me, grasping the towel close to her chest. "Thank you," she says, her voice clearer now. Her eyes dart back and forth from me to the hand that's resting on the sweatpants. And that's when I notice I'm just staring at her and she's waiting to get changed.

"Oh, sorry." I turn on my heel, almost slipping in my wet socks. "You get changed and make yourself at home." *In my bed.*

Shut up, brain!

Once the door shuts behind me, I collect myself and peel off my drenched clothes on the way to the laundry room. Drying off my hair quickly before pulling a fresh T-shirt and some pajama pants from the dryer, I slip them on and head upstairs after I lock up. I'm passing Lottie's room when a thought pops into my head.

I beg the rapid beating in my chest to stop. I have no clue if my heart rate is still high from seeing Jo in such a state or from having her in my space, but it needs to slow down.

Tapping lightly on the door to my room, I hear a soft "Yes" through the wood. My foot has barely landed when my heart rate picks up to an unhealthy rhythm again. Perhaps I'm dreaming. No, because my dreams have never looked like this. This is somehow better and worse. Johanna is wearing my old, baggy T-shirt, snuggled up in my comforter, and on my side of the bed. I haven't shared a bed with another person in a *long* time, but I do have a preference for which side I sleep on.

For tonight, that's her side, and damn, does she look perfect there.

Her hair is still a tangled mess and I know she'll hate going to sleep like that. I hold up the hairbrush I grabbed from

Lottie's room in question. "I thought you might want to brush your hair."

"Oh." She runs her hands over the damp strands. "Wow, I must look like a wreck."

Never in your life.

My lip stings with how hard I bite it not to let those words slip free. I sit in front of her and twirl my finger around.

"I can do it," she argues and sits up straight to prove her point.

Pulling my hand backward and shaking my head, I stare at her with pleading eyes. "I know you can, but let me do this. I don't know how else to help you."

Her head tilts to the side, and she looks like she might protest again, and I'm glad she's got some of that spark back. She chews on the corner of her rosy lip and turns, the comforter twisting with her until her back is to me.

Moving to my knees, I shuffle forward and gently pull the wet strands over her shoulders. Bringing the brush up to the ends that sit at the small of her back, I drag it through her hair, the bristles gliding through easily with each pass. I slowly work my way upward, being careful not to tug on her scalp.

"You do help," she says out of the blue. "You said you didn't know how to help. But you just being here with me now. It helps. Having you close helps."

I'm at a loss for words, concentrating on my task while I try to find the right ones. I don't want to open up old scars, not like the other night at the bar, but I have to let her know what I've always wanted to say. What I'd planned on telling her when I flew out to see her.

"That's all I've ever wanted. To help, to be there. To be the person you needed." *To be the person you wanted.*

Her hair is now smooth, like woven gold, so I place the brush on the mattress. My hands come to the base of her neck

THOSE TWO WORDS

and collect the sleek strands; my fingers threading and twisting through them like muscle memory, something I've done countless times with Lottie.

"Are you...Are you braiding my hair?" she whispers.

My fingers continue to work methodically through her hair until I come to the ends, and I take in the braid running down her spine. With my teeth, I pull at the pink scrunchie wrapped around my wrist and use it to secure her hair. "I did a pretty good job, too. You have a lot more hair than Lottie."

With my hand still holding on to the ends of her hair, I slowly stroke my fingers against the soft material at her back. She relaxes into the touch, melting into the bed, until she's resting against my knees.

"That feels so good," she breathes, and with those words, we freeze.

Clearing my throat, I climb off the bed. She turns around to settle against the pillows behind her, a pink hue creeping across her neck. The moment that I shouldn't have allowed to happen has ended. Slowly backing away from the bed, I point toward the bedside table.

"I made you some ginger tea, but it's probably cold now. There's also some water and aspirin. I'll let you get some sleep. I'll be across the hall if you need me."

She shoots up, the dark gray comforter pooling at her waist. "Don't leave."

How can I tell her it's not a good idea, when she stares up at me like that? The pleading in her voice makes it hard to say no. She's much more herself now, but vulnerability and unease still swirl in her eyes.

"Please," she whispers.

My eyes fall shut, because I don't have the will or the way to deny her. When I open them again, her shoulders slump as I turn toward the door, but I only make it as far as the light switch. The room is bathed in darkness, but a streak of light from the streetlamps outside cuts across Jo's face. Her shoulders visibly relax as I walk back to the bed.

"I'll stay," I assure her and point to the floor next to her. "I'll be right down here."

"No, up here. Please, Patrick. I need to know someone is next to me right now."

If she says please one more time, I'll give her the world and ask her what more she wants.

Reminding myself I'm here to comfort her and this means nothing, I round the bed and take a deep breath. I know she needs me right now, so I pull back the covers and climb in beside her. Her hands are tucked underneath her head, the raw terror and panic long gone. Her face is bare, making her look so much younger. So like the Johanna I remember before she left, but also different.

Mirroring her position, I give her a small smile. She looks like she could fall asleep any second, so I don't expect one in return. But when a soft smile pulls at her lips, that stupid organ in my chest takes off again.

Distracting myself from our closeness, I absorb all the details of her face. The constellation of freckles across the bridge of her nose remains the same, but there are new additions on her cheeks and forehead, tempting me to trace each one. Her hair is the same sun-kissed shade of honey, just longer. She always wears it up, but I love it when it's free, flowing down her back endlessly. And those eyes. Such a hypnotizing deep blue, that you could get lost in them and be thankful. Like me, the lines around her eyes and mouth are a little more prominent, only adding to her loveliness.

As I file away every detail—new and old—bitterness blooms. I'm bitter about the years we've missed together. Bitter that I don't know which summer she gained a new freckle.

Bitter that I don't know if the lines on her face are from laughing at another man's jokes.

A tender touch to my forehead drags me from my sullen thoughts.

Jo runs her thumb between my eyebrows. "Why the frown? You look like Graham." There's a lightness in her tone, and like a calm breeze, it blows the unpleasant feeling away.

"I take great offense to that," I say and poke her teasingly in the side.

A carefree and airy laugh leaves her lips. But it's not her laugh that threatens to tilt my world on its axis. It's the blinding smile that breaks across her face. The smile I've been waiting to see since she came back to town. Would that smile taste as good as it's making me feel? Are her lips still as soft as it makes my heart?

A few inches are all it would take to answer those questions.

But now isn't the time. And perhaps that's the soundtrack to our story: "Never the Right Time." That thought doesn't stop my next words, though.

"That makes me happy."

She looks puzzled for a second. "What does?"

"Seeing that smile again."

I register the candidness in my words too late, because the smile slips from her lips. It wasn't my intention to make her feel bad, but as I watch regret contort her features, I wonder if she thinks the same. That our chance has passed, and perhaps that one night was all we were meant to have.

I'll be her friend, the person she can lean on in tough times like today, and I'll find peace with it. Eventually. I have to; for Lottie, for my own sake, and hers.

Pulling the comforter up around us, I stroke my fingers across her cheek, before joining our hands together. I've gone from wanting to build a pillow fort to needing her touch. "C'mon, YoYo, let's get some sleep."

As I watch her eyes close and hear her breathing even out, I think back to that night together. I'll savor that night for the both of us, knowing we'll never get another. I take comfort in the fact that I know of the pillowy softness of her lips. That we spent so many summers together collecting new freckles. That hundreds of her smiles were put on her face because of me.

That for even a fraction of our life, she was mine.

nineteen

JOHANNA

My body and mind float in that space between sleep and consciousness. The downy weight of my comforter and the cloud-like texture of the pillow hold me in that limbo, and I'm almost tempted to let myself be pulled under and sleep for the rest of the day.

Almost.

Because something about the texture of the comforter and the height of the pillow doesn't feel right.

Cracking open one eye, I see the sun pouring through the gaps in my curtains.

But I don't have curtains and suddenly I'm barraged with flashbacks. Losing my phone. The photograph. The panic. The darkness.

Patrick.

Carrying me to his house. Finding me in the shower. Holding me. Braiding my hair. Staying with me all night.

My heart aches at the memories.

Opening both eyes, they feel puffy and raw. I stroke the braid hanging over my shoulder, feeling grateful it isn't a mess thanks to Patrick's gentle braiding. As my morning fog clears, I stretch my arms out and arch my back. A moan almost slips free with the movement, but when my butt brushes against something hard, it gets cut short.

I forgot this isn't my bed, and the owner of said bed currently has his arm slung over my waist and is now dragging me toward him. A small squeak escapes me once my back is flush to his chest, every curve of my body pressed against the hard planes of his.

And other hard things.

Thinking I can wiggle my way out of his hold is quickly disproven, because it only causes him to tug me in closer, and my ass is now nestled nicely into his lap. The layer of clothes between us does little to hide his erection.

He's still asleep, but it doesn't stop my body from heating up all over and my mind from thinking very indecent things. Mumbling something incoherent, he nuzzles his face into my hair, and his hand drifts under my borrowed T-shirt until it lies flat against my stomach, fingers splayed against my heated skin. I suck in a breath at the contact and look at where his strong forearm disappears underneath the gray bedding. I've always found the darker hairs on his arms oddly attractive. Throw in the sinewy muscles running down his arms and wrists—well, it does a lot.

My mind is wandering into dangerous territory. I lie as still as possible, hoping he loosens his grip. But he doesn't, and before I've even finished that thought, the hand that was resting on my stomach ventures to my breasts, which have been heavy from the moment he pulled me into him. My nipples are painfully hard and sensitive, aching for a touch that I shouldn't want to chase.

I squeeze my thighs together when his thumb brushes along the underside of my breast. Biting my lip to muffle my light whimper, I hungrily lean into his touch, delirious that he's inches from my peaked nipples.

I'm desperate. It's been so long since someone made me feel like this, and it's almost laughable that he was the last one to do it.

I didn't plan for it to be this long, but when depression and anxiety are your companions, those types of needs take the back burner.

Under Patrick's caress? Those desires come roaring to life.

His rough fingertips run across the curve of my breast, trailing higher and higher. I should wake him and not let this get any further.

The wetness between my thighs can't be ignored now, and I rub them together to ease the slightest bit of pressure. That only forces Patrick's hand to travel farther north. My eyes close at the feel of his warm hand now cupping my breast. His fingers gently toy and squeeze, sending a zap of pleasure to where I crave him most.

It takes every modicum of self-control not to grind my hips into him. But when his thumb runs across my nipple, those quiet whimpers turn to a loud moan.

"Shit," he curses, no longer asleep. His hand whips out from under the T-shirt.

Biting back my protest at the loss of his touch, I risk a glance over my shoulder. He's not guilty or outraged like I was expecting. His pupils are blown wide, hair messy and wild, and his eyes burn with desire, I worry a wildfire might take light in them.

I go to open my mouth, but what do I even say? *Sorry for rubbing up against you like a bear needing a back scratch from a tree.*

"I, umm, Jesus, Jo. I'm so sorry. I think I forgot where I was for a second." He lets out a deep breath. "That wasn't...staying here...that wasn't my intention. I swear."

My mood instantly shifts when I see the guilt morph his

face. He's worried he's taken advantage of me, which is not the case.

"Hey, it's fine. It takes two to tango, right?" I wince as the words leave my mouth in that dumb British accent, hinting at my unease. It's not that being close to him makes me uncomfortable, far from it, but we clearly have no clue how to navigate our way around each other. We're constantly fumbling around in the dark and bouncing off one another.

He huffs out a little laugh and scratches the dark stubble on his jaw. It's such a contrast to his usual clean-shaven look, and I can't help but wonder how it would feel against my...

Nope! Not going there.

"How are you feeling?" he asks.

"I'm pretty tired, but it looks like I slept for..." I squint at the clock hanging on the wall. "Crap! Ten hours! Patrick, you should be with Lottie or doing something better with your day. Oh my god, I'm due at the restaurant soon." I shoot up in bed, untangling myself from the comforter when his fingers curl around my wrist, halting my escape.

"She's with my mom. Making sure you're okay is my top priority right now. Jules has got your shift covered too." His fingers begin stroking my wrist—just like that evening in his truck—as he looks at me, brows furrowed. "You scared me last night, but please don't tell me you're okay because it's easier."

Jesus. How does he know exactly what to say?

I'm so used to putting up a façade, worried about how my true feelings will impact others. No one has ever called me out on it before. "I'm tired but embarrassed more than anything. Thank you for everything, and I'm so so—"

"Don't you dare say you're sorry," he interrupts. His tone isn't angry, but I hear the warning, like the idea of me apologizing is absurd. "You have nothing to apologize for or be embarrassed about. I'm just sorry I didn't get to you sooner."

This man. He would take on the burden that he didn't help

me sooner, as if he knew where and what I'm doing at all times. Like I'm his responsibility. Then a thought enters my mind. "How did you know I was there?"

He reaches behind him and waves his phone in the air. "I have an app linked to the security system. A notification came through early this morning saying it'd been turned off. That reminds me, your phone is downstairs."

My phone. The whole reason I got myself into this mess. Though, I hardly expected to have my first panic attack in two years when searching for my missing phone. Anxiety loves to be unpredictable and unforgiving like that. I made a rookie error. I should have known better than to go somewhere that tends to trigger me without my meds, especially when I was already in such a low mood.

Patrick looks at me intensely, but he isn't staring at me like I'm a delicate piece of porcelain ready to crack at the slightest knock. He's trying to peel me back, layer by layer; to work out what's different about me. Dropping my head to avoid his gaze, I run my fingers across the faded lettering of the T-shirt, secretly soaking up how much I love being in his clothes.

He ducks his head, and there's no avoiding him now. Patrick takes my hand in his, caressing his thumb across my knuckles as he holds my eyes captive. "Don't do that, love." His voice is so tender, it makes my chest ache. "We all have our days, and while I'm sorry you had to go through that last night, I'm glad I was the one to find you. We can talk about what happened, or we can move on to something else?"

This. This is exactly the conversation I spent years avoiding. That self-conscious girl I've grown from shows her face. She was so ashamed and embarrassed about how she was feeling. But I'm not that same girl, and I trust the person in front of me. I thought he'd changed since I moved back to town, and in a way he has. But he's the same seven-year-old boy who kissed me at midnight just to make me smile. And the teenage boy who raced through town to save my junior prom.

"Can I freshen up and have some coffee first, before I answer that?"

The corner of his mouth picks up and he nods, before leaning forward and placing a kiss to my forehead. "Iced coffee?"

That small brush of his lips leaves me speechless, and all I can do is nod in response.

"I'll get right on that. We know how grumpy you get without your caffeine. There's a spare toothbrush under the sink. Help yourself to anything else in there, I'll use Lottie's bathroom."

He climbs off the bed and with the sweetest smile, saunters out of the room, while I sit there stunned from his words and actions.

A short while later, feeling less like a zombie after splashing some water on my face and brushing my teeth, I head to the bedroom to make the bed, but the sight of a Post-it note on the pillow I slept on last night catches my eye.

The last time he left me a note was also on a pillow in his bed. Specifically in the bed where we had slept together for the first time. Where I gave him my heart and he gave me his. The most memorable night of my life.

It was quickly followed by one of the worst few weeks of mine, and no doubt his.

The point of no return.

It's not the same message, but the words are just as powerful.

It's okay to not be okay.

I doubt he knows the power of those words, but it's a

mantra I think most people should carry with them. One I wish I'd followed sooner.

Tucking the note into the pocket of the sweats for safekeeping, knowing exactly where I'll be putting it. I head downstairs and take in his house for the first time. It doesn't scream *single bachelor*, but a family man. The walls are covered in family photos from over the years. Ones of Lottie as a newborn to more recently. His siblings. His parents. A blushing Patrick, next to...squinting, I rear back. Jesus, my mom actually let me go out with that much makeup on? Despite the orange glow from the foundation three shades too dark, there's no hiding the smile splitting across my face. And it's directed right at the boy standing next to me, his arm slung gingerly over my shoulder, like he wasn't sure of the safest place to touch.

A kernel of hope drops in my stomach, because if he'd wanted to forget about our history, why would he hang this photo up in his home?

Following the noise of a radio, I wander to the kitchen and come up short when I spot Patrick in a pair of dark navy pajama pants hanging low on his hips, washing the dishes. *Gray sweatpants, who?* There's something delicious about a man who can pull off a pair of loose, plaid pajama pants. The cherry on top? He's topless, water splashing on his muscular stomach as he scrubs at something in the sink.

Oh, to be a plate.

I'm treated with the view of his strong back, the muscles shifting with his movements. *And* he's barefoot. This might not be the best way for me to recover from last night, because I'm now light-headed.

The whole visual is quite the morning treat and when he spots me over his shoulder, the sheepish grin he gives me as he dries his hands does all sorts of things to my insides.

"I spilled some coffee on it," he says and nods to the stained white T-shirt on the counter. "I was trying to mix your coffee in the blender how you like it." He walks to the fridge and pulls out a glass, holding it out to me. "It only took me two tries. Coconut milk and one sugar, right?"

"Yes. You remembered?"

"I'll never forget your weird obsession with iced drinks." I then notice the two plates of eggs on the counter. He grabs them and walks toward the dining table in the open plan space, where the light from the early afternoon sun streams through the large glass doors leading out into the yard.

I follow Patrick and sit opposite him. He pushes a plate toward me and digs into his breakfast as I take my first sip of coffee, the zing of caffeine alleviating the dull headache. He grabs a sweatshirt from the back of the chair beside him and pulls it over his head—much to my disappointment.

We settle into a comfortable silence, drinking our coffee, eating our food, and sharing small smiles across the table. The domestication of it feels bizarrely familiar. We shared a lot of meals just like this over the years and would stay over at each other's places on occasions.

When we're finished, I sense his hesitancy to start the conversation.

So, for once, I'm the one to do it.

"It's not the first time it's happened." He seems surprised at first but then settles in his chair, so I continue. "The panic attack, that is. It's been a couple of years since I've had one. I have medication for when I feel one coming on, but I didn't have it with me last night."

Debating my next words, my fingers tap against my thigh under the table. Patrick's eyes catch the movement, but he doesn't comment on it. He sits there patiently, with an encouraging look on his face.

"I have Generalized Anxiety Disorder. I got diagnosed in Tennessee, but, umm...I think I'd been dealing with it long before then. I had some pretty intense ups and downs with the diagnosis, but with the right support and meds, I've been good the last two years." Holding his gaze, even though every cell in my body wants me to look away, I wait for the disapproving look or eye roll.

You just need to stop thinking so much.
Life can't be that hard?

But Patrick's gaze doesn't waver. It doesn't shift from the kind and thoughtful look he's pinned me with since we sat at the table.

"I'm sorry you had to go through that, I can't imagine. But I really appreciate you trusting me enough to share." His hand finds mine across the table. "Do you know what triggered it?"

Now that's a question I'm not prepared to answer today. Not because I don't trust him, but because I'm so mentally exhausted from last night, I worry how I'll hold myself together when telling that side of my story. So I keep my answer simple. "Being tired, frustrated at myself, and the photograph."

"The photog—Oh." From the knowing look in his eyes, he's slowly piecing together what happened, and I'm grateful he doesn't press me on it. "I'd like to know how I can help, if you ever need it. And if you ever find yourself in a position like that again, you call me, okay?"

"I'm sorry." He shoots me a glare, reminding me I shouldn't apologize for last night, but I also can't imagine how finding me like that would be for him. "I'm not your concern, Pat. You have enough on your plate already."

"You absolutely are my concern. You're my friend, and we look out for one another." *Knife, meet heart.* But it's one step better than when I first arrived back in town.

"Wow, you really have that *daddy* glare nailed down."

"Johanna," he warns me.

I resist the urge to tell him that his tone makes him sound even more *daddy*.

"Honestly, waking up to breakfast and coffee really helps. I can't wait for a bubble bath and cheesy rom-com later. The attacks usually wipe me out, so I really appreciate you getting my shift covered today."

"Was the color thing a way of coping?" he asks hesitantly. I shouldn't be surprised at how observant he was, and from small snippets I remember of last night, I was very vocal in my search for that something green.

It doesn't always work, but the second my panicked eyes found his, it did its job. Sometimes it's less of a distraction and more a sense of accomplishment, like my brain is happy we found our way out.

"Umm, yeah. It's kinda like the five-four-three-two-one technique. I don't know if you know it." I shrug. "Only I like to find five things of the same color. For some reason, I picked green."

Understanding dawns in those same green eyes. "Green's a good color."

"I think it saved me last night."

He goes to say something but stops himself and stands. Collecting the dishes from the table, he tilts his head toward the hallway behind us. "I left your phone by the front door. Let me get these dishes done and I can drive you home." He turns away but then pivots. "Not that I'm saying you need to leave, you can stay. I need to get Lot—"

Laughing, I hold up a hand. "Patrick, it's fine. I could really do with a soak in the tub and another ten hours of sleep."

"Only if you're sure, but I'm driving you. Your clothes are in the washer, but I'll drop them by tomorrow."

Lifting the hem of the worn, maroon T-shirt I'm still wearing, I shrug a shoulder. "I think this suits me better. Don't you think?"

Something flares in his eyes, similar to the look he was giving me this morning, but rather than overthinking it, I go in search of my phone.

I find it sitting on a wooden sideboard by the front door, but when I spot the open door to what looks like a study, my curiosity is piqued. Dumbbells and a treadmill sit in one corner, while a large desk sits in the other. The desk isn't covered in papers and menus like I'd expect, but something that makes me question if fate likes to fuck with me.

On top of the dark, oak desk sits a half-completed jigsaw puzzle.

As far as coincidences go, this one is pretty unbelievable. Because this is the exact same jigsaw puzzle I started the other week. You can make out the bottom of the Eiffel Tower in this one, and I'm a little envious that he's made more progress than me.

"Hey, there you are—Oh," Patrick says from the doorway, but I don't turn to look at him. I'm too busy picking up a stray piece and slotting it in place.

"Do you still like doing them?" he murmurs.

"Yeah. I never stopped." I run my fingers along the cardboard landscape. "It's one of the earliest memories I have with my mom. It's a good distraction when things get a little...tough."

This puzzle reminds me a lot of the one framed at my parents' house, forever missing its thousandth piece. I moaned about it for months to Patrick, who thought it was hilarious. He even convinced my dad to frame it in the hallway downstairs, so it was the first thing I'd see when I stepped through the front door.

"I started this one the other week." I turn to face him, only to find he's standing much closer now. Inches away, in fact. His finger traces the piece I just placed, and I can feel the heat from his body as he leans in close.

We know how close we're standing, but I don't think either of us holds the willpower to pull away. Or the want.

"What are the odds." I think he's still talking about the

puzzle, but being this close to him jumbles my brain. "It reminded me of you. That's why I bought it." His hands move to my shoulders with a soft touch, and even through the material of the T-shirt, the heat of it is dizzying.

"So did the one before that. But everything reminds me of you. Wherever I look, there you are. How did you do it?" He must see the question in my eyes. "How have you kept such a tight hold of my heart, my mind, after so many years?"

He swallows hard with the admission, and I watch in fascination as his throat bobs. Slowly dragging my gaze up his neck, past his chin with the tiny scar on the cleft, and up to lips so full they don't belong on a man. When I meet his eyes, I find them glowing with longing.

"Patrick," I whisper.

"It was useless, wasn't it?"

"What was?"

"Trying to not be pulled into your orbit again. I was always going to end up back in it."

"I never wanted to leave yours," I murmur.

"We've made a mess of this, but you must know, Jo." His hands slip up to frame my face, long fingers clasping the back of my head while his thumbs stroke across my cheeks.

"Know what?" I ask breathlessly.

"That I never stopped..." He trails off, but before I can ask *What*, his lips are on me.

I cling to his sweatshirt, trying to keep my balance as his lips mold over mine, the ferociousness of his kiss feeds the roaring need in me. My knuckles must be white from how hard I'm clutching his sweatshirt, and it only tightens when his tongue run against the seam of my lips. I open willingly, and his tongue spears into my mouth. The taste of him sends me wild, because *god*, have I missed this. One night wasn't enough to soak up everything that he is.

This kiss is eager, hungry, and unforgiving.

THOSE TWO WORDS

What he gives, I give right back.

Our hands don't know what to do, roaming all over one another. His tangle in my hair one second and grip my face the next. Mine lock behind his neck and then fall to his pounding chest. We're everywhere at once. He walks us backward until I hit the edge of the desk, my grip on him never loosening. His hands glide down my sides, then he grabs the backs of my thighs and hoists me up on the desk. The jigsaw puzzle and my brain in disarray.

Our tongues continue their dance as his fingers slip underneath the T-shirt, but pause above the tops of the sweats. He lazily runs the backs of his fingers along the exposed skin of my belly, such a contradiction to the punishing pace of his kiss.

Teeth. Lips. Tongues. We give it everything, because this kiss isn't hello.

It's a homecoming.

He grinds the hardness growing in his pants against the inside of my thigh, but I need more. Crave more. I widen my legs until my hips cradle his, and I can feel all of him. Long, hard, and thick.

I'm so lost in the moment, I'm not sure what causes it, but suddenly Patrick rips himself away and stumbles back. Our chests are heaving, and his lips are swollen and glistening from our kiss. The few feet between us and the guilty, torn look on his face create a chasm in my heart.

He's the first one to speak, and boy, do I hate his words.

"I can't do this with you again, Jo."

twenty
PATRICK

I loathe the words the second they leave my mouth, and from the crushed look on Jo's face, so does she.

Half of me wants to snatch the words still hanging heavy in the air between us, shove them back down my throat, and kiss her senseless again. The other half, the half I wish wasn't making the most sense, tells me this isn't a good idea.

That I never stopped...

So close to finishing that sentence and contradicting what I confessed outside the bar the other night.

There's no point in trying to come up with some half-assed excuse, like *I don't know what came over me.* Of course I do. *She* came over me. Pulling me and tempting me with everything she is. I'm hardwired to need her.

I should know better. The bruises on my heart should be warning enough.

All the progress we've made eviscerated. It's written all over her face. I saw glimpses of my old friend today, and it felt monumental that she trusted me enough to share something that clearly made her feel uncomfortable and exposed.

This is why you should never let your heart take the lead. It goes in blindly and has you making stupid decisions.

Like kissing the woman you've tried to forget.

I take a step toward her. "Jo."

That snaps her out of whatever daze she was in. Her eyes lock with mine, but as I take another tentative step forward, she skirts around me and darts out of the room.

I'm hot on her heels, calling her name, and when I catch up with her a few feet from the front door, I step in her path, blocking her exit. She seems so intent on escaping me that she's about to run out of my house with no shoes on.

"Johanna, stop. Please."

"We have stopped. And now I'm going to go," she says flatly, crossing her arms over her chest. The hurt in her eyes is gone and I only see determination. I'll take that over sadness any day, but it still doesn't make me feel better.

"How are you going to get home?"

"I'll call a cab. It's really not your concern. Nothing is your concern actually, and I'm sorry I dragged you into my mess. Forget this happened."

I know I'm sending mixed messages when I take her hand in mine, but I can't bear for us to part ways like this. "Nothing about you is a mess, and I meant what I said earlier—I want to be there for you. What happened just then can't happen again, though. There's so much at stake with the restaurant."

"The restaurant?" she asks with a tilt of her head, challenge burning in her eyes.

I'm an open book to her, and she sees right through that pathetic excuse. It's not *just* the restaurant; it's also my daughter and my heart at stake.

When I don't answer, she yanks her hands away and throws them up in exasperation. "Patrick, can I please remind you that you're the one who kissed me."

"I know, and I'm sorry. I can't let whatever is happening

between us distract me. I have so much on my plate. But I also can't do it again."

"Do what again?" she asks.

"To know what it's like to have you and then find out it's too good to be true. I care about you so much, but losing you again isn't something I think I can survive. I've got to keep my priorities in order, and right now, they're Lottie and the restaurant."

Her eyelids flutter closed, and I watch as she takes a steadying breath. I know the honesty in my words hurts her. They hurt me.

When they open, I'm met with a blank stare as she nods slowly and swallows. "Thank you for last night and for breakfast."

"I don't want to leave it like this. Stay, we can talk this out, or at least let me drive you home," I plead, but she holds up a hand.

"I think you've said enough for today. We both have, and I'd really like to go home."

The finality in her words tells me it's pointless fighting her on this, she's made up her mind.

Ten minutes later, she's climbing into a cab, and as I watch the car pull away, I worry we've gone right back to the beginning again.

I'VE BEEN IDLING IN MY MOM'S DRIVEWAY FOR ABOUT TWENTY minutes, playing this afternoon over and over in my head. Another example where I haven't thought my actions or words through, and acted on impulse. It seems every time we interact, I come away regretting something.

But not that kiss.

Because *that kiss* was everything and more.

The memories of our last kiss didn't do this reunion any justice.

I can still taste her on my tongue. The subtle sweetness from her coffee and a taste I know only as Jo. The delicious moans she made when I backed her up against the desk, the way she clung to me and met my lips with as much zeal.

While my heart might be skipping in my chest, my brain is screaming at me to slow down, always in conflict with one another. I wish I knew which one I want to come out on top.

Deciding I've spent enough time stewing over what I said and did, I turn off the engine. The moment I shut the door behind me, a small body collides with me.

"Daddy!" a muffled voice shouts into my thigh. The chaos in my head vanishes the second I lift Lottie into my arms and squeeze her tight. "Ugh, you're squishing me."

"Sorry, spud, but you're just so squishy." I give her one last squeeze before pulling back to look at her. She grins up at me, her cheeky smile doing wonders for my mood. It also reminds me why drawing a line between Jo and me is the right thing to do. As much as Jo says she's here to stay, I can't let Lottie become attached to her. I have firsthand experience with how badly that can turn out.

"How are you today? Grandma said you're feeling much better." We walk up the path to the house, and I spot my mom, who's watching us from the doorway.

"Uh-huh. The bugs is gone from my belly now. Were they like spiders?"

Laughing, I shake my head. "Not real bugs like you see in the forest, tiny ones that make us a bit sick sometimes. But you fought them off." I poke her in the belly. "My big, strong girl."

"Oh, man. I like bugs. Is JoJo feeling better? Grandma said she was sick too."

I glance at my mom as we walk up the final step. "Umm, yeah, she wasn't feeling too good either."

"Hey, sweetheart." My mom greets me and looks over at Lottie. "Hey, why don't you go and finish that picture you started drawing for Johanna?"

"Okayyyyy," she says excitedly, before wiggling out of my hold to run into the kitchen.

"Mom, you shouldn't have said anything." I follow to where she is walking into the living room.

"Pfft, all I said was Jo was a little under the weather too. I'm not lying to my grandbaby. Now sit your ass down and tell me what kept you out all night. Is she okay?" She might be bossing me around, but I catch the concern in my mom's voice. My mom has cared for Jo like another daughter since, well, forever.

I tidy up a few of Lottie's toys, hoping to stall the interrogation coming my way. My mom sees right through it and throws a cushion at my head. "Ass. Sofa. Now," she instructs. Even at thirty-four years old, her *Mom* voice still does the trick and I do as she says without argument.

Dropping myself on the sofa, I get a sense of déjà vu. Not even twenty-four hours ago we sat in these exact spots before I ran out of the house, knowing something was wrong.

"Is she okay?" she asks again.

"Yes, she's okay now." *Well, she was before I kissed her and fucked it all up.* "I found her at the restaurant, and she wasn't in a good place."

"Oh, Patrick. I should have come with you, I wasn't thinking. Are you okay?"

"I'm good. Truly," I assure my mom. Seeing Jo like that, in the restaurant alone, brought up a lot of old trauma, but I don't need my mom worrying about that.

"I don't know what you know…"

"Hm. I know a little from her dad. I've pieced a few things together over the years too. I get the impression it's been happening for a long time. Well before she left."

THOSE TWO WORDS

My head drops, and guilt stirs in my chest. Guilty that my mom somehow understood what was going on with Jo, but me, her *best friend*, I was clueless. *Maybe I didn't try hard enough.* I could tell Jo didn't want to divulge any more details about her anxiety than she already had, but I was able to make my assumptions.

"Don't think like that, Patrick. I'm not one hundred percent certain what had her moving away, or what went on between you two. That's for her to share. The one thing her dad said to me was that Johanna did a good job of pretending she was okay for a long time."

Is Jo's anxiety the reason she left? *No.* I would have noticed the signs, I know her. She was happy, always at work or out with family and friends. Even in the years we were away at college, she was out at parties or telling me about the next dickhead she decided to date. She had her ups and downs, but there were more ups, right?

Nothing about her behavior would lead me to believe she had an anxiety disorder back then. My rapid thinking must be written on my face, because my mom shuffles forward, catching my eye before she speaks.

"I'm not sure you could have helped, for all that it's worth. She's home now, but I think this time away was for the best. Maybe for the both of you. You had so much to deal with as well."

"I want to believe that."

"Sometimes, the heart wants what we're not ready for. We have to heal first before going after what we want."

My mom pats my shoulder and gives me a sympathetic look, before standing and leaving the room. Once again, I'm left with my thoughts.

The idea of being with Jo again scares the shit out of me, my injured heart has never let me forget that, but it's also never stopped the feelings that should have died when she left this town. They've never gone away, and it's what drove me to kiss her this afternoon.

There was no denying she wanted that kiss as much as I did, but does she still feel the same way? How many more chances do we get before the universe says enough? Looking back now, we've missed out on plenty. The classic, *right person, wrong time* scenario.

I stare down at the bouquet of flowers at my feet and cringe. I've debated throwing them into the trash can across the quad for the last twenty minutes, but then I remember her telling me that her idiot of a boyfriend didn't buy her flowers once during their two-year relationship.

Good. Fucking. Riddance.

I hope she likes them.

I hope she likes dinner. Actually, *I know she will because I found a restaurant in the city that cooks everything with cheese. Literally every item on the menu has cheese in it.*

I hope she likes that I've turned up unannounced outside her last class of the day.

The biggest hope I have is that she realizes this is the first time we're both single and maybe, just maybe, she feels the same way I do.

My flight was already booked when she texted me to say that she and Aaron had broken up. It made this impromptu trip to Florida that much more important.

The moment I spot a long blonde ponytail swinging in the crowd of students, I shoot to my feet and scoop up the sad-looking white tulips that now slip between my sweaty fingers.

"Hey, YoYo," *I shout, and all heads turn my way. It's only one person I want to see, and when she turns toward the sound of my voice, my heart somersaults. How is she prettier now then when I last saw her during Spring Break?*

She squeals and runs toward me. "What are you doing here?"

Before I can answer, she's catapulting herself into my waiting arms. The second I have a hold of her, I don't want to let go. My face is pressed against her neck as I hold her tight, drinking in her scent.

"You only turn twenty-one once. Happy birthday, Jo," I whisper. How easy it would be to lay a soft kiss right here. Or on her cheek. Her mouth. I pull my head back and take her in. Her freckles, bright smile, everything. I can't take it in fast enough or get enough of her, needing to catalog every small detail, as if I don't have her face memorized already.

"I can't believe you're here! And for my birthday. Oh my god, I think I might cry." She punches me in the arm. "How dare you make me cry on my birthday, Patrick Sadler."

"Ouch. You can't get your present if you beat me up."

"Oh, gimme gimme," she says, holding out two grabby hands toward me.

"Ah-ah. After dinner. I booked this great place and I would love to take you out. Whaddya say?" I don't have it with me anyway, it's back at my hotel. My parents helped cover the cost of the trip, but the tickets to see Green Day in the fall were all me.

"Oh. Patr—" I hate the way her voice deflates with disappointment, but her words are cut short when two arms loop around her from behind, pulling her back abruptly. Right into the chest of a guy I don't know. I'm about to ask what the fuck he thinks he's doing, but when he opens his mouth, my heart drops.

"Babe, you need to get ready. The party starts soon," he says before slapping her on the ass and making her jump. The laugh she lets out is fake. "Oh, hey, man, didn't see you standing there. I'm Aaron."

Clearing my throat, I hold out my hand to him, hoping Jo doesn't see the devastation seeping out of me. "Hey. I've heard a lot about you. I'm Patrick."

"Ohhh, Joey's little school friend, right?"

Joey. She hates that name, so why doesn't she correct him? She just stands there awkwardly in his hold, her dejected stare never leaving mine.

"Yeah, that's the one. Umm, you guys headed to a party? Is it for you?"

"Oh nah, this is my buddy's. He got this sick apartment off campus and we're going to check it out, right, babe?"

"Yeah. You should come, Patrick?" Jo asks with pleading eyes.

This fucking douche isn't even taking her out on her birthday. He's dragging her to someone else's party. And by the looks of it, Aaron is no longer an ex.

"No, I don't wanna ruin your plans. This was just a flying visit, I'm headed home tonight." Jo knows I'm lying, but I can't stand here for a moment longer. Thrusting the flowers toward her, she takes them slowly. "These are for you. I think they're dying, though. I hope you have a great birthday. Good to meet you, Aaron."

I take a step back and go to turn away when she pulls herself from Aaron's grasp and grabs hold of my hand.

She steps into me, lowering her voice, but Aaron is already too busy chatting to some guy behind him. "Pat, is your flight really tonight?"

"Yeah, Jo, I wish I could stay. Really. I'll text you when I land, and I'll see you at Thanksgiving." Leaning down, I place that small kiss after all, laying it softly on her cheek. "You deserve better than him," I whisper, but give her the best smile I can muster up, even though it's cracking at the edges. Cracks are breaking out everywhere. Even where she can't see.

Her eyes widen at my words, and her mouth opens and closes as she fumbles to find her voice.

I take that as my cue. Turning on my heel, I hightail it out of the quad. I don't dare look back.

Because if I do, I'll see all the hope I had splattered on the floor where it spilled from my chest.

Groaning, I scrub a hand down my face, wincing at the memory. We were young, seniors in college, and that was the summer I decided to seize the day. I'd finally let Jo know how I felt—how I'd felt for a while.

It didn't work out, clearly, and from there, we found ourselves cemented in a "friends only" status that only became more concrete the older we became.

Until that night.

Those years of friendship are ones I cherish, I just wish we'd acted sooner on our feelings.

But the thing is, she's here.

Back in Sutton Bay.

I convinced myself almost six years ago that we had clocked in all our chances. Convinced she was happy in Tennessee, the memories of our time together a thing of the past. But no, she's here, and *friends* don't kiss each other like that. We've proven that before.

I know we're scared. Fuck, I'm petrified, but maybe it's more about her not feeling the same way, and less about our past. We can't change what happened, but we can decide our future. I have questions, she has answers. From what I've pieced together, I can't rush Jo for those answers, with the fear of pushing her away.

If I let this chance pass us by, I fear it's the last one we'll ever get. It would be the biggest regret of my life if I don't at least speak to her and see what she wants. My mom says that we have to heal first, and I don't know if it was Jo or me that needed to do the healing. Perhaps both.

If we're done healing, what do our hearts want?

Mine wants her. It never stopped yearning after Johanna Thomas.

Now all I have to do is convince her to give this another chance.

To give us another chance.

twenty-one
JOHANNA

"Okay, you bring the crackers, I've got the cheese."

"Gotcha!" Quinn says to me as I walk out of the bakery.

Waving goodbye to her, I shut the door and step out into the street. In five short steps, I'll be at my front door. Exhaustion hit me like an 18-wheeler about an hour ago, but when Quinn spotted me climbing out of the cab, she called me inside. I ran up to my apartment to get changed out of Patrick's clothes and headed back down to see her, and time got away from us planning our wine and cheese night next week.

Now, I'm ready for bed, the aches in my muscles quickly setting in from my attack. I'm so relieved I'm not scheduled in the restaurant until Monday, because despite the long sleep in Patrick's bed, it always takes a day or so to fully recover.

Reaching for my keys, I spot a large paper bag sitting at the base of my front door, my name written in large, messy letters. I hesitantly pick it up, worried about its contents—I've read enough crime thrillers to know how this goes. Only, once I open the bag, there's nothing inside that scares me. It does make my heart gallop in my chest, though.

Bath bombs, scented candles, trashy magazines, a couple of

DVDs. It doesn't take a genius to guess who left this here, but the brand-new jigsaw puzzle confirms it.

My phone buzzes in my purse and I pull it out, juggling the contents of the bag in my other arm, and I'm surprised to see it's a text from Patrick.

> Patrick: Hope you can use some of these things for a relaxing weekend.

I'm still confused, but I've had time to cool down, and I understand why he would react the way he did.

> Johanna: I love How to Lose a Guy in 10 Days. Thank you.

It's a lame response, but what else do I say?

His next text has me blinking repeatedly at my screen in confusion. It also makes my stomach dip. Like when you reach the top of a long, drawn-out incline on a rollercoaster before falling over the edge. It's scary. Has your heart racing like crazy. Leaves you breathless.

But it doesn't stop you getting right back on it, to experience all those things again.

> Patrick: I don't regret kissing you. I regret not doing it sooner.

> Patrick: I'm not trying to send mixed messages and I'm sorry for how I reacted today. Can we talk soon?

I want to tell him *he is* sending mixed messages, and I'm now suffering from whiplash.

> Johanna: I want to talk too. I need to recharge after last night and then I'm working most of next week.

The speech bubbles dance across my screen, disappearing and returning for a few minutes before he finally replies.

> Patrick: Okay. You tell me when and where and I'll be there.
>
> Patrick: You look really pretty, but you looked better in my T-shirt.

My head snaps up and I scan the street for him. My eyes land on his blue Chevy and I can't help the laugh of disbelief when I spot him.

Patrick raises his hand from the steering wheel, before pulling out in the street and driving away.

"Oh, Jo. You're in trouble," I whisper to myself.

Do I let the fear of Patrick seeing me for all that I am stop me from getting back on the roller coaster, or do I take the chance that this trip could be the best decision of my life?

A LOW WHISTLE SOUNDS FROM THE SOFA AS I WALK INTO MY living room.

"Miss Ma'am! Who would have thought you'd just put away a full wheel of brie? Those jeans were made for you."

Laughing, I try to hide my slight blush at Quinn's compliments. Tonight was our wine and cheese night. A few bites into the cheese board I'd whipped up, I realized I'd double booked and forgotten about the team's pool competition at Shirley's. It would look bad if I didn't show, so I asked Quinn to come with me, who didn't need much persuasion.

A little buzzed from the bottle of wine we shared, we've changed out of our sweats and into something more appropriate. Well, I thought my original outfit was perfect for tonight.

After I told Quinn what happened between Patrick and me the other week, she pulled out a pair of tight, black skinny jeans and a black silk corset, stating, *"This will work up his appetite."* Quinn is likely to get some heads turning tonight from the knee-high boots and faded, blue denim dress hugging her curves.

I wanted to dress up in something nice, knowing Patrick would be there.

It's been almost a week since my panic attack, and we haven't had the chance to talk much since I found the care package at my door. We've seen each other at the restaurant, it just hasn't been the right moment to talk and I'm secretly grateful, because it's given me time to prepare myself for whatever he wants to discuss; the questions he might ask. I also don't want to get my hopes up and overthink it all.

When I came back to town, kissing Patrick was the last thing I expected to happen. It doesn't mean I haven't thought about it for the last six years. Do I want it to happen again? Yes. I'm cautious to put my heart on the line, no matter how much it aches for him. It's a defense mechanism I've picked up over the years. It has nothing to do with trust and more with how he's going to look at me if I shed that last wall of vulnerability.

Although he's been on my mind a lot, it's easy not to let myself overthink everything with how busy the restaurant has become. We've seen an increase in customers, with reservations being made through the automated system I introduced. I also set up a social media account and asked a friend from Tennessee if they could help build a website for us. All in a week's work. It's been hectic, but I'm proud of myself for the positive impact it's having.

I just hope it's enough. As we near the end of March, I'm getting more and more nervous that no matter what we do, my dad and Claire will still have no choice but to sell the restaurant.

"Okay, the cab's ordered. What's the plan?" Quinn asks, looking way too excited for a night at the local dive bar.

"Um. Not to make a fool of myself?"

"Nope. One goal. Make Patrick feral. Flirt a little. Maybe get some dick, I dunno. The last part is negotiable." She shrugs.

"That's three things? And I highly doubt I'll be getting any *dick* tonight." I laugh as I slip on my heeled boots, pushing the concerns of the restaurant aside.

"A shot of something will change your mind."

"I forget you're still in your twenties until you say stuff like that. My days of shots are over, unless you want to hand-feed me greasy fries tomorrow morning."

"The only person who will be eating is Patrick. Right outta' the palm of your hand."

Oh boy.

Twenty minutes later, we're walking into the bar. It's not typically this busy on a weekday, but with all the restaurant staff here, plus some locals and wandering tourists, it's more crowded than usual.

"Okay, I'll do one shot," I announce, deciding I'll need something stronger if Patrick wants to talk tonight.

Quinn squeals and pulls me over to the bar. I spot most of the team in the corner, crowded around the pool table, but don't see Patrick.

We order two lemon drops, though Quinn has to explain to Lenny how to make them. When the fiery liquid glides down my throat, I shoot her a worried look. "I don't think that was a lemon drop."

She looks like she's going to hurl but recovers quickly. "Yeah, that might have been paint stripper. You're going to need it though."

"Huh, why?"

"Because a certain single daddy is looking at you like you're his next meal. *Shit,* even I'm getting hot and bothered from the way he's looking you over."

I don't need to look to know he's staring. His eyes are burning a slow path up my body. Despite the warmth of it, my skin pebbles in the wake of his gaze.

Slowly turning my head, using my hair to shield my face, I find him across the room. His hand is clenched around a glass of beer so tightly it might shatter. Even from where he's standing, I can see his throat working as his eyes flit between my neck and chest, until we finally lock gazes.

I don't look away, thankful for the liquid courage Quinn served me, and why would I want to? Having him look at me like this, desire brimming in his eyes, is thrilling. The way his jaw clenches is emboldening, sparking something in me that I've only ever felt with him.

He's the only person to ever strike that match, and right now, those embers from our first night together are ready to be rekindled.

twenty-two
PATRICK

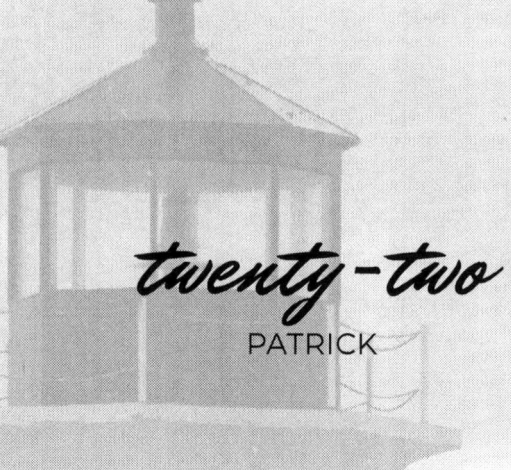

"Thanks, Lenny, put it on the tab and I'll settle it at the end of the night." I place a few dollars on the bar mat and grab the tray of drinks. "Thanks for letting us use the bar tonight."

"Better you all than all those *flatlandahs* and busybodies from away. Always causin' trouble."

He's always had a problem with people from out of state, but he knows like all business owners in town, we rely on them returning every year. "Maybe next year they'll stay away."

"If you are gonna stay late, I'll leave ya my keys. Just make sure you close the lights off before you lock up." He doesn't wait for my reply before dumping a large set of keys on the bar, grumbling something and shuffling away to serve more customers.

Lenny might not be the most welcoming to his patrons, but the bar and the restaurant have always had a really good relationship for as long as I can remember. He and my dad were old school friends, and they helped each other out a lot over the years. Lenny was also a huge help to my family and me in the weeks after my dad's passing.

He knows we're good for settling our tab, so it's not the first time he's given us the keys and told us to lock up after ourselves.

I pocket the keys and carry the tray of drinks over to the small crowd at the back of the room. The scoreboard tells me that the front of house is still beating the kitchen by one game, and I intend to keep it that way.

As people collect their drinks and thank me, I look around, disappointment settling when I still don't see Jo in the crowd of people.

I'm about to cave and ask Booth if she's coming when the front door of the bar swings open. The first thing I see is a pair of long, lean legs wrapped in tight black denim. I follow the denim higher, coming to soft, supple thighs. A sliver of creamy skin peeks out from the top of the jeans. Up and up, my eyes travel. Tempting, full hips, small waist, and perky tits that I know are the perfect handful and are close to spilling out of the black ensemble holding them up.

My jeans get tighter as I imagine what they'd look like with my cock sliding between them.

I track her movements, even as she's pulled toward the bar. Her infectious laughter rings across the room at whatever Quinn is saying before they throw back a shot of something with a grimace. A small trickle of liquid escapes, falling from her chin, trailing down her slender neck, and disappearing into her cleavage. What I would do to be that drop of liquor.

Her pink tongue peeks out, and it's then I should stop watching. My thoughts are too filthy to be in the company of others right now, my brain only transmitting messages to one organ in particular the moment she walked through the door.

She turns her head, a curtain of golden hair partly obscuring my view, but I still see the flare of her eyes when they find me checking her out without care.

And I couldn't give a shit.

If she's going to turn up looking like *that,* she deserves to know exactly what it does to me. No other fucker better be looking at her the same way though.

My eyes dart around the room, checking I'm the only one, which is when I meet the amused gaze of my little brother. The pool cue is slung over his shoulders and his arms are perched on either end as it rests behind his neck.

I ignore the smug smile slowly growing on his face as I make my way over, after one final glance back at Jo.

"Christ, Pat, you were a smitten kitten in high school. I'm not sure what to call you this time around. Eager beaver? Lovestruck buck?" He pokes me in the ribs with the cue.

"Fuck off. It's not what it looks like."

"Oh, so what did it look like?"

Walked right into that one.

"Exactly." Giving me a wink, he strolls away to take his shot and pockets the solid yellow ball with ease, before ending the game and sinking the eight ball, making the score between the kitchen and front of house even.

I make a conscious effort not to let my eyes follow Jo as she makes her way over to where the rest of the team is sitting. The moment she sits next to Simon, however, I find myself stomping over to them before I even realize what I'm doing.

Fucking Simon.

Poor guy hasn't done anything wrong; he just needs to not exist around Jo. I'm not asking for much.

Quinn is already deep in conversation with some of the bar staff, leaving Jo and Simon to their own private conversation. There's an empty stool next to Jo, which Booth makes a beeline for. Before he can sit down, I shoulder check him and claim the seat for myself.

Everyone murmurs their "hellos," as Jo's eyes flick between Booth, hauling himself off the floor with a chuckle, and me. Ignoring my brother, I lean in close and whisper in her ear. "I didn't think you were going to join us."

Her hair is pulled to the side to reveal the delicate skin of her neck, tempting me to run my tongue across it to see if I can still taste the shot that trickled down her throat. Her shoulders draw back and breath hitches at my proximity, telling me she's just as affected as I am. She's removed her jacket to reveal a strappy-looking thing, that does little to hide her temptingly soft skin. This close, I can smell the floral scent of her perfume, but it's the subtle hint of ocean that overrides my senses.

"I won't lie," she says, her eyes staying trained on the drink in front of her. "I forgot until this afternoon."

"Are you going to play?" I nod toward the pool table.

"Nope, the front of house doesn't need me helping them lose," she chuckles, her shoulder bumping mine with the movement. She goes to scoot her stool away, but I grab the padded cushion with one hand and drag her right back, if not closer.

"Patrick," she whispers, eyes darting around like we're doing something wrong.

"Don't do that." I keep my voice low.

"Do what?"

"Move away from me."

When she finally turns to look at me, her face is inches from mine. Her glossy lips are so luring and the black stuff around her eyes makes the dark rings in her irises pop.

"I didn't want to give anyone the wrong impression. I'm confused as well, Pat. One minute you're pushing me away, the next *literally* pulling me close."

"I know, and I'm sorry for last week." My fingers brush against her hip as I hook my thumb through her belt loop. "Can I drive you home? We can talk then. I'll drop Quinn off too."

I'm not even flirting, but *fuck* she blushes at my words anyway. Like the thought of being in a small space with me again has her heating up. She ducks her head, trying to hide her heated cheeks, but I don't let her get far.

175

"Don't do that either." With a finger on her chin, I raise her gaze back up to meet mine.

She peers up at me with a questioning look.

"Hide from me, love. There's no part of you I don't want to see, especially when your cheeks turn pink like that." Maybe I'm being too forward, but I can't control myself with her. "It's my favorite color and I've missed it so fucking much." I see the apprehension in her gaze, it's the same one I saw across my dining table when she opened up about her anxiety. "If we talk or don't talk tonight, just know that nothing you say will scare me off. I promise you that. I don't know what we're doing, what this is. I think you can fee—"

"Hey, sorry to interrupt," Quinn jumps in. "I could use the restroom, wanna come with?"

Jo's mouth drops open, and she looks between Quinn and me. "It's fine." I give her a genuine smile, but feel the opposite of fine as she walks away with my sentence left unfinished.

I think you can feel it too.

Maybe her feelings aren't as strong as mine, but I'll never know if I don't make mine clear. Even if for a day, I held her. Kissed her. Felt her. I know the sounds she makes when I sink into her. How that blush on her chest spreads when she climaxes. That she loves when I whisper dirty things against her skin.

There's so much more I want to learn about her.

Years of biding my time, and all for one night? I curse my younger self for not acting sooner as Booth calls me over for my round of pool.

"I WANT TO THANK MY TEAM, BECAUSE WITHOUT YOU GUYS, I wouldn't be standing here," Booth shouts from where he's standing in the middle of the room, a plastic trophy clutched to his chest. From the engraving that reads BOOTH SADLER 2001'S PLAYER OF THE YEAR, he swiped it from Mom's house and brought it here.

"I'm not sure how we're related to him," Graham mumbles beside me.

He showed up a couple of hours ago, much to my surprise. It's nice to see him out, even if he has only uttered ten words all night.

He's been glowering from the high-top table he's been stood at all night, clearly regretting his decision to socialize. I could have sworn it slipped just a fraction when Quinn skipped over to him and introduced herself. Her smiling face was such a contrast to his scowling one. When she laughed, his eyes widened in amazement. I don't think he looked at anyone or anything during their whole interaction.

"I'm pretty sure he was swapped at birth. Florence has the same energy, so at least we know they're related," I comment.

Jo and I haven't spoken much more tonight, either getting pulled into other conversations or having to play our round of pool. Much to my chagrin, her last game was against Simon, and she lost spectacularly. I'm both bitter about the loss and the fact it was with Simon.

I watched the entire game. My eyes weren't on what balls she was aiming at, though. No. They were glued to the way she was bent over the pool table in front of me. Her tight ass sculpted to perfection in those black jeans. I was a fucking goner when she wiggled her hips before sinking the white ball and was barely able to hold back my whimper. Everyone found her performance hilarious, but I was close to breaking the skin of my fist with how hard I was biting it.

Booth finishes up his speech and bows dramatically, before people start to say their goodbyes and head out. Lenny left about an hour ago and the only people remaining now are from the restaurant. I'll be the last one to leave, to make sure everything is clean and locked up safely.

Quinn waves goodbye to everyone, stumbling slightly on her feet, but I don't see Jo anywhere. Has she left already? Why didn't she say goodbye? Maybe she's outside waiting for Quinn?

I'm about to go check on Quinn, partly for my own selfish reasons, when Graham abruptly stands from his stool beside me. He downs the rest of his club soda, slams the glass on the table, and slaps me on the shoulder.

"I'm headed out." He doesn't give me a chance to respond and heads to the front door that Quinn has just disappeared through.

"Okay, bye," I call sarcastically to no one at all, and finish my glass of water.

I make sure the last few people have rides or aren't walking home alone. When it's just me left in the bar, I collect the empty glasses and tidy up our mess. Booth offered to stick around, but he has an early shift tomorrow, so I sent him on his way.

Once the glasses are loaded up in the dishwasher, the tables are wiped down, and all the back exits locked up, I head toward the front door, ready to call it a night. I'm about to flip the last light switch when the sound of a door opening and a quiet "Oh" from behind me has me pausing. I turn toward the voice and find Jo standing in the doorway of the ladies' restroom with a surprised look on her face.

"Everyone left?" she asks.

"Yeah, a while ago. I didn't know you were still here...wait, have you been in the restroom this whole time?"

"Umm, yeah. Well...great night, thanks for everything. See ya," she rushes out and steps sideways like a crab toward the front door, keeping her back to the wall.

"Hey, wait, how are you getting home?"

THOSE TWO WORDS

"I was going to walk."

"Not by yourself. I thought I was going to drive you?"

"No, honestly, I'd rather you didn't. The fresh air is good for me." She tries to duck under my arm from where it's still hovering above the light switch, but I step into her path.

"Jo. What's going on? Did I do something?"

Her shoulders drop in defeat, and she lets out a loud sigh. "No, you didn't do anything. Promise you won't laugh?"

I hold up three fingers. "Scout's honor."

Her eyes squint at me in suspicion before she ever so slowly does a one-eighty turn, and the reason for her crustacean-like walk is made clear. I try my best, I really do, but a snort breaks free before I can stop it.

"Patrick! You promised," she cries and spins to face me, her hands flying backward and slapping against the exposed skin, which only makes me laugh harder.

"Jo, you know I was never in the Scouts. That honor meant jack shit. What did you do?" I attempt to grab her shoulders to turn her around, but she scurries away from me.

"I don't want to talk about it. Hurry up and do your thing so I can go home and hide away forever." She covers her face behind her hands and shakes her head.

"It's really not that bad."

She drops her hands and gives me a dubious look. "Patrick, you can see my ass cheek."

I most certainly can.

She has a huge rip in her jeans, from the top of her back pocket to halfway down her thigh. I didn't acknowledge the sight of her exposed skin, no matter how soft and firm it looked, or the hint of black lace peeking out either. I'm a gentleman.

"Can you imagine if this had happened during my round of pool?"

With that, an idea pops into my head. I'll take her home,

just not yet. I don't have it in me to say goodbye. Not when this is the first time we've been alone since that afternoon in my study.

Reaching behind the bar, I pull out an apron and throw it over to her.

"Problem solved. Now, I think you could do with some pool lessons."

"What?" Despite her confusion, she ties the apron around her waist backward.

"Your performance tonight was painful to watch." Painful because of how she was bent over like that. "How can someone be that bad? I swear you played better when you were twenty-three."

"Oh god, please do not remind me how old I am," she groans.

"You've aged like a fine wine. Your pool skills, on the other hand," I pause to cringe. "They need some work."

"Okay, wiseass," she says and walks toward the felted table. The fact she isn't putting up a fight to leave is a good sign. I follow behind her, wishing I hadn't given her the apron as her hips sashay from left to right.

Grabbing two pool cues, I hand one to her. "Atta' girl. Now, let me show you how to rack the balls."

A giggle bursts out of Jo's lips and I roll my eyes. "That's immature, even Booth is more well behaved than that."

"You said rack *and* balls in one sentence. How was I supposed to react?"

Thirty minutes later, I've talked her through the basics and we're playing our own game. I have two stripes left, while the table is littered with solids. I've lost count of how many times she's pocketed the cue ball. She even managed to chip it off the table, narrowly missing *my* balls at one point.

We take our time pocketing our balls, not paying any mind

to the time. I try to show off with some fancy shots, because I'm only a hot-blooded male after all.

When Jo somehow manages to scratch again, I stroll up behind her and shake my head.

"Johanna," I scold mockingly. Taking hold of her shoulders, I maneuver her body so it's at the right angle. With the cue between her hands and my chin hovering above her shoulder, I whisper my next words, "Have you forgotten how to shoot your shot *again?*"

"Like this?" she breathes. Before I can make a joke about her poor technique, she leans into my touch, and her back brushes my chest as we bend over the table.

"Mm-hm," I hum, because how am I supposed to form sentences when I'm pressed up against her like this.

It's a dangerous game, but it doesn't stop me from draping myself over her back, my chin propped on her shoulder, and arms bracketing hers. I feel the rise and fall of her chest, and I'm sure she can feel the growing hardness in my jeans.

Trying to keep up the charade that this is all about teaching her how to play, I slowly skate my hand down her arm. "That's it, just like that. Do you remember what to do now?"

I know she knows what to do, I've watched her do it badly for the last half hour. She shakes her head anyway, and because I take education very seriously, I show her.

"Here, let me remind you."

twenty-three
JOHANNA

"Here, let me remind you," Patrick says, the deep timber of his voice vibrating through to my bones.

"Remind me?" It's possible my brain has melted. *The game.* Of course. I asked him to show me how to hit the ball with the stick-thing. *Cue.* He's told me that like eight times.

I'm pulled from my internal rambling when Patrick's palm glides from my elbow to my wrist, where the cue is balanced, and his hand envelops mine. His support doesn't stop me from shaking, and I think my whole body is pulsing with need at this point.

With his chest flush to my back, he helps aim the cue at the white ball. I try to funnel all my concentration into what he's showing me, but my mind is on anything *but* the game. I've had a one-track mind since the moment he came up behind me.

And I remind myself he's just teaching me. Nothing more.

Get your head out of your vagina, Johanna.

He brings our arms back in tandem. "Just like that." His breath coasts across my shoulders, and goose bumps rise on my arms that he's sure to notice.

Without warning, he pops our arms forward, and the cue

follows our movements, hitting the ball dead center. The satisfying crack reverberates around us, and the air leaves my lungs in a rush as the solid green ball drops into the pocket with a thud. I can't even remember if I'm solids or stripes at this point.

I should be excited that I've *finally* pocketed a ball. My mind and body are too distracted by the way Patrick remains draped over me. He could step away now if he wanted to.

But he doesn't.

The air is so thick around us, like a fog of anticipation. The crackling energy surrounding us is enough to shake the foundations of this empty bar and bring it tumbling down, with no care in the world.

I try to ignore my arousal, but it's difficult when I can feel Patrick's dick nestled against my ass. Every hard plane of his chest and abs is pressed against me, keeping me pinned between him and the pool table. This first innocent game now feels anything but. A buzzing starts beneath the surface of my skin. My breaths are coming in fast. Wetness pools between my legs.

We've tried to pull back the reins on what's going on between us, both aware that there's a lot to discuss before diving headfirst into the whirlwind of this unquestionable magnetism. We lose all sense whenever we're alone, and right now, no one is here.

The edge of the table digs into my hips, causing me to shimmy them to ease the discomfort, but a groan from behind stops me and I realize I'm grinding my ass into him. I should be mortified that I've just rubbed myself up against him like a dog in heat, but I'm not. I also don't stop myself from repeating the movement, because I'm desperate to hear that noise from him again. All deep and throaty.

Before I convince myself this is a bad idea, my ass shifts against him again, and I hold my breath, waiting to see what he does. He allows me a few seconds of stolen pleasure, and then his hands fly to my hips to halt my movements.

"Jo," he grits out, as though he's in pain. "What are you doing to me?"

"I don't know what you mean." I try to sound innocent, but he sees right through it.

"I think you know exactly what I mean." Dropping his head to the crook of my neck, he lets out a breath.

"Just for one night." Maybe I say it to give him an out? To see if he's only looking for *one night*. With every fiber in me, I hope he isn't. I twist my upper body around, our mouths a whisper away and eyes hazy with lust. "It doesn't have to mean anything."

"It'll mean everything, though," he whispers, the movement causing his lips to brush against mine.

I regret not doing it sooner, that's what he said about our kiss in his study. And *god*, I share that same regret. My lips brush against his, testing the waters, before pulling back. I practically preen when his eyes fall heavy with want and he presses himself into me harder.

"I don't want to fight this anymore."

We're toeing the line. If we do this, there's no forgetting tonight.

"We need to talk." His movements contradict his words, because he grips my hips harder and trails his lips across my shoulder. "I want you so fucking badly, you have no idea, but...*Fuck it.*"

And that's all it takes.

Large fingers splay across my hips in a bruising manner as he grips me from behind. He presses himself into me with a light thrust, the cold metal of his belt buckle cools my overheating skin, and a gasp slips free when I feel just how badly he wants me.

Another gasp escapes me when Patrick grabs my nape with

his left hand and directs my hips to where he wants them with the other. He's using my body for his own pleasure. It's filthy and depraved, and I can't stop myself from thrusting my hips backward to meet his. With a firm grip on my neck, he turns my head and crashes his lips into mine. This kiss doesn't start off slow—it's needy and aggressive. It's as if someone has told us we have seconds to live, and this is all the time we have left to savor each other.

He pulls his mouth from mine. "Jesus, Jo. Why does this feel so good?" he rasps.

"Don't stop, whatever you do." I lean forward and spread my fingers across the green tabletop. We're grinding up against each other with no resolve, fully clothed, no care about where we are.

"I'm not stopping unless you tell me to. Please tell me you're sober enough for this?"

"I haven't drank in hours. Don't you dare fucking stop."

And he doesn't. He takes control.

The hand at my nape slips around to grip the front of my throat with the slightest of pressure, guiding us back so we're standing upright. His other hand slinks around to my chest and yanks at the cups of my corset top, causing me to pant harder when the cool air caresses my aching nipples. He wraps the hair hanging over my shoulder around his fist, giving himself full access to my neck and bare chest. A shiver breaks out when he leaves a trail of hot kisses from my shoulder to the sensitive skin behind my ear. I reach behind me and grip his shirt, belt, anything I can to stop myself from floating away from how high he's making me feel.

"No fucking bra, I knew it. Did you wear this outfit for me?" He drops my hair and brings his hands to my rib cage, dragging them up my sides until he's cupping my breasts, his rough palms skimming against my nipples. He's going to drag this out, torture me with the barest of touches, but he changes tactics as he starts to play with the hardened peaks. Pulling, twisting, pinching.

"You did wear this for me. You knew exactly what it would do to me when I saw your tight little ass molded in these jeans. It's a good thing they're already ruined, because I'm this close to ripping them off you." He holds out his pointer and thumb to accentuate his point. And *god,* do I want him to tear the denim from my skin, because there are too many layers between us.

"I wore it for me."

"You're lying. That's okay though, because I enjoyed the view anyway. You drive me insane, and I think you know it."

The weight of Patrick's body disappears, and I fall forward. I look over my shoulder, but he hasn't gone far, and the sight before me steals the breath from my lungs.

He's on his fucking knees.

"Stay facing the front," he commands. "And bend forward for me, love. Let me take a look at this perfect ass."

He hums in appreciation as I follow his order. His hands inch around to my front and begin to untangle the knot in the apron. Patience isn't his virtue though, because after two seconds he grasps hold of the strings and pulls, snapping it instantly and throwing it on top of the pool table. Deft fingers flick open the button of my jeans and ease my zipper down. He's acting like he has all the time in the world as his fingertips glide and caress across the exposed skin above my lace underwear. The featherlight touch has my stomach hollowing and goose bumps erupting across my body.

I don't want slow caresses or careful touches. I want deliberate and desperate.

The fucker chuckles behind me as I squirm in his hold. "Patrick, stop teasing me, you shit."

His laughter rings around the bar, like I'm not about to spontaneously combust.

"Why? What's up, Johanna?" He places and gentle kiss to

the pebbled skin revealed behind the rip, and then tugs my jeans until they fall to my knees. "Oh, I see the problem." A kiss to my other cheek now. "You've soaked through your panties." A slow lick this time. "Should I help you?"

"Please, yes. *Please.*" The ache between my legs and tightness in my belly is so intense now.

"Okay," he croons. I jolt when he grazes my pussy through the damp material of my underwear with his knuckles. With my jeans locking my legs together, it's a tight fit for his hand, but he's nothing if not attentive. I don't question him when he gently removes my boots. That care is such a contrast to the way he yanks my jeans and panties down to my ankles, freeing one foot. The moment my feet are firmly on the ground, that commanding tone returns. "Now open those legs nice and wide for me. I never got a taste last time, and I need my fill."

Leaning forward and balancing on my forearms, I spread my legs wide. The way I'm standing in front of him, completely bare but for the rumpled corset around my waist, is so lewd. It's obscene.

And I love every second of it.

I crave his touch. I'm desperate for him to feed the hunger pulsing through my veins and between my slick thighs. There's no doubt he can see how much I want him. When he palms my cheeks to pull them apart, I'm completely at his mercy, bent over a pool table, half-naked, ready to be worshipped by him.

"Fuck, you're as beautiful as I remember," he murmurs into the crease where my ass and thigh meet. His tongue runs leisurely across my skin, and being blind to his next move only intensifies the pleasure. "I have always wondered how you taste. Thought about it every time I wrapped my hand around my cock. Did you think of me when you touched this pretty pussy, love?"

"Every time."

"Right answer," he growls.

We're done with words now.

His mouth moves to where I need him the most, and I fall forward, the felt rough against my nipples. All inhibitions fall away when he reaches my soaking entrance. I try to gain purchase on anything but come up short. His tongue circles around my center languidly, and I muffle my cries into my arm, while my other hand darts backward to clutch to the soft strands of his hair. Groaning in appreciation, he moves to my clit and sucks on it before circling it with the tip of his tongue. Over and over, he does that. Ecstasy fills my veins, and my legs threaten to buckle, and they probably would if the firm grip he has on my ass wasn't keeping me upright.

"More. *God.* There. Harder," I cry out, and I don't have to ask twice. He's everywhere at once. Licking, biting, sucking, nipping. Building me up higher and higher, I might be out of this atmosphere. I'm *so* close, my orgasm is cresting, but something is missing. My whining and wriggling must tell him that.

"I remember what you need. Don't be afraid to ask for it. I'll always give it to you." And does he ever, because two thick fingers slide into me from behind and slowly pump in and out. I'm dripping down my thighs, I'm so wet. The fullness of his fingers and the attention he's giving my clit makes me delirious, but I'd kill to feel the fullness of his cock gliding into me instead. To experience that again. We might have spent years apart and only one night together, but this man knows exactly how to play my body.

When he turns his wrist and crooks his fingers inside of me, my hand shoots out, the balls from our forgotten lesson ricocheting against each other. Black spots float in my vision as I chase my orgasm, bringing my hips back in time with the thrust of his fingers. The slap of his palm meeting my skin and the cries from my lips echo off the walls.

"God, you should see how you look right now. Your tight, pink pussy is gripping on to my fingers so hard. Keep fucking my hand like that, baby. Find it." He rewards me with faster and deeper thrusts of his fingers. "Do you want to come?"

I turn my head and try to look at him, but from this angle, it's difficult. I nod my head frantically anyway. "Yes, Patrick. Please."

"Please what?" He removes his fingers and I cry out in frustration.

"God, you're so ann—" *SMACK*.

"Please what, Johanna?"

Oh. My. God. He just spanked me. He spanked me, and it pushed me closer to the edge of the cliff I'm ready to fall from. He soothes the sting with a kiss, leaving me delirious from the sweet torture. I want to come, but I also love this game we're playing.

I bite my lip to stop the plea escaping them, and when another sharp slap finds my other cheek, my head falls forward onto the felt, groaning from the mix of pain and pleasure.

"If you don't answer me, I'll leave you bent over this pool table without giving your greedy cunt exactly what it wants. What'll it be?"

I don't want to test whether he'll be true to his words. "Come. I want to come. Please, Patrick," I beg, pushing my hips back to show how eager I am for him.

"Okay." And then he's on me. Spreading me wide open again and licking me from bottom to top. One of his hands leaves my ass and moves to my front, where his fingers find my clit, wet from my pleasure and his mouth, and he starts massaging in tight, small circles.

I'm so close. Wound so tight, I could break in half. The pressure low in my belly is building, and the tingle at the base of my spine tells me I'm close to shattering.

And I do.

Because the second his tongue comes to my center and the pressure on my clit increases, I snap.

I fall.

I scream.

The orgasm rips through me, sending shockwaves from my core to every cell that makes up my very being.

Patrick doesn't let up until the aftershocks stop, even when I protest that I'm too sensitive. With a kiss at the base of my spine, he removes his fingers and stands, but I still feel him close behind me.

I'm too spent to turn around and look at him, still folded over the table like a lawn chair. When he helps me into my underwear, jeans, and boots, my heart increases in tempo again.

The act of him dressing me makes me blush. Not the fact he was going down on me over a pool table in a public place moments earlier, but the tenderness in his touch. How he's domineering and filthy one minute, and sweet and considerate the next.

Finding the energy to push myself off the table, I settle my top back in place. My body is heavy and weightless. As I turn around, I worry what expression I'll find on his face. Regret like that afternoon at his house?

What I find when I turn around surprises me. There's not an ounce of regret in sight. His eyes are glazed over, pupils wide, hair mussed from my hands, and lips glistening from me. He looks relaxed, if not a tiny bit bashful.

Me, on the other hand, I don't know what to do. Where to look or to put my hands. I curse myself for offering this up as a one-time thing. I watch as his hand comes up to brush a few strands of hair from my face, his thumb grazing my cheek.

"I don't know if this makes me better or worse at pool," I joke, sounding like some stupid British aristocrat. He brings his lips to my forehead and laughs against my skin. When he pulls back, I see some uncertainty in his eyes as he thinks his next words over.

"Hey, are we good?" I ask.

"What does this mean for us?" He doesn't miss a beat. A question for a question.

My next words are all lies, and it's stupid of me to even suggest it. Shrugging, I avoid his gaze when I mumble, "Just for tonight, remember? It doesn't mean anything. A moment to get whatever is going on between us out of our systems."

He's instantly in my space, hands cradling my face. "No. I want this, fuck, I need it. What if this is our last chance? I want to give this a go. To really try." I go to open my mouth, but he presses his forehead to mine, silencing me. "I know there's a lot of unspoken history between us, and that's not me trying to rush you. More than anything, I want to see where this could take us, and I don't want to hide from it. Please tell me this isn't one-sided. I don't want *just for tonight*, love. I've already had that and it wasn't enough. It will never be enough."

I shake my head, hoping I look relaxed despite my heart beating erratically in my chest.

I'm an idiot for even suggesting it. Because it took only one night for me to realize I wanted all his nights.

I run my fingers along my swollen lips. The lips Patrick just kissed.

Or did I kiss him?

I look up at my best friend, still hovering above me. His face looks shocked and wild; probably mirroring my own. Not because it didn't feel good, but because it felt so good.

A kiss with your best friend of over twenty years is meant to be awkward, right? Like you're kissing your brother. It wasn't anything like that. And maybe this is the bourbon speaking, but I think it felt so good because I've imagined doing it before a hundred times over.

"Jesus. I shouldn't have done that. I'm sorry, Jo." He groans and throws himself back on the arm of the sofa, staring up at the ceiling.

"Why are you sorry?" *I'm certainly not sorry he kissed me. The way my lips still tingle and heart races upholds that.*

"Because you're drunk and—"

"If you say you took advantage of me, I'll knee you in the nuts."

He lets out a deep chuckle and his head drops forward. His eyes are ablaze, tracking my movements as I shuffle toward him on my knees. I reach out and trace his slightly crooked nose, before leaning in closer.

"I'm not sorry," I whisper. "And I'm not sorry for this."

The kiss is tentative at first, checking to see that the first time wasn't a fluke. Then we dive right in. He groans into my mouth and moves me to straddle his lap. The kiss becomes eager, messy, and so, so right.

"Do you want this? Please tell me I'm not the only one who feels this pull between us?" he asks against my skin, his lips skating across my collarbone now. Soft kisses to teasing nips.

"More than anything. I've wanted this for so long," I confess.

When he raises his head to look at me, his pupils are so wide, his eyes look more black than green. "You have no idea how long I've wished to hear those words."

Without breaking the kiss, he stands and walks us to his bedroom.

That was the night that changed it all. Nothing was one-sided, that was made clear.

The dance we'd spent years choreographing finally came to an end. The one where we tiptoed around our feelings or found ourselves with the wrong partners.

I was ready to dance with him forever until it was cut short, and the music stopped.

But here we are, ready to take those steps together again. We need to take it slow, and I'm unsure who is taking the lead. I just hope this isn't our final dance.

It's up to me to help break down this last barrier between us, and it starts with me being brave enough to answer the one question he hasn't dared to ask. *What made me leave?* The first thing I expected him to collar me with, yet all he's shown me is patience and empathy. He deserves to hear the truth, no matter how much it makes my skin itch to think about sharing my vulnerabilities with him.

For him, I need to be strong. I need to overcome my insecurities, or I worry the music will stop again.

"I want to try too. With you."

He places a chaste kiss between my brows, hands still cupping my cheeks. When he pulls back, he looks calmer, more settled in himself.

"Okay. Now I don't know about you, but I need some sleep."

I laugh and the yawn that follows confirms that sleep is calling my name too, though, I have no idea how I'm going to find it after what we just did.

Once he's locked up, driven me home, made sure I'm safely in my apartment, I go to sleep praying we find our rhythm again.

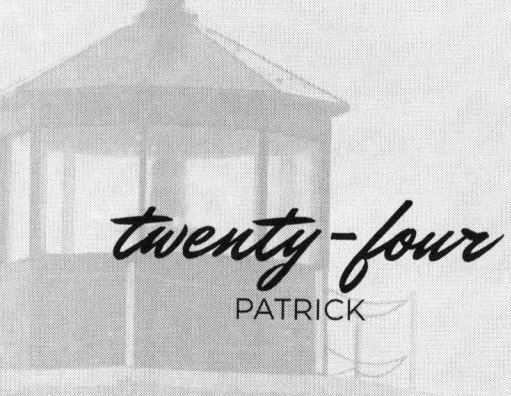

twenty-four
PATRICK

"Hey, spud. Can you get your bag from your room and then we can head out?"

Lottie stands at the bottom of the stairs, with a scowl that shouldn't look cute. She lets out a tiny huff before running up the steps to her room without a word, clearly mad at me still. I didn't get home until 3:00 a.m. after dropping Jo off at her apartment, and even then, it took me hours to fall asleep. Thoughts of Jo played on repeat. Her taste. Her sweet moans. *Her.*

I was so pent up and only managed to find sleep after replaying the night's activities over in my head and coming all over my stomach.

Jo is turning me back into a horny teenager.

When Lottie stays at Carrie's, she likes to call me in the mornings to tell me about her dreams, even though she doesn't remember them half the time. It's my favorite way to start the day, but today, I slept through the call and the dad guilt is coming in strong.

"Did you have fun last night? She said you had a girly sleep-over planned," I ask Carrie, who is standing by the front door

THOSE TWO WORDS

holding Lottie's coat and shoes. Friday is her day with Lottie, but I asked if I could take Lottie out today after school, wanting to show her some of the ducklings at the park.

"I mean, if watching *Tangled* three times and her stealing all the popcorn makes for a good sleepover, then yes, we had a great time." She laughs and shakes her head. "I asked if we could watch something else, and she told me it was 'her turn' to pick. I tried to explain it's always her turn, but apparently you pick the movies at your house?"

"Yeah, you've been played, because it's always her night to choose when she's with me too. *Tangled,* huh?"

"Her current Disney princess obsession, apparently. When I asked her why, she said it reminds her of her new best friend, JoJo." She tilts her head, her tone curious. "Who is this friend?"

I could lie and say it's a teacher from her school, but I'm sure Carrie will work it out eventually. "Just George's daughter, Johanna."

"*Just* George's daughter? Really, Patrick? God, men are so dense sometimes."

"I—she is George's daughter." I take off my baseball hat to scratch my head, feeling like I'm on the wrong side of an interrogation suddenly.

She walks up to me, places a hand on my shoulder, and looks me right in the eyes. "Patrick. You might not have shared much over the years, but don't be an idiot. We both know she was never *just* anything."

Carrie disappears upstairs to check on Lottie. I'm left there in the hallway, speechless at her observation. Here I was thinking it was only my brothers and mom with suspicions about Jo and me. Carrie knows about Jo from family get-togethers she's attended, but clearly my attempt at hiding the truth was futile.

Pulling out my phone from my pocket, I unlock the screen and type out a message.

> Patrick: Hey, hope you got some sleep before your shift today.

Her reply comes instantly, and I feel like a teenage boy texting his crush—which, fifteen years ago, is exactly what I was.

> Johanna: The 4 hours I got were good, I'm dead on my feet now though. I have a lot of regrets about working a double today.

It's almost midday on a Friday, no doubt in the middle of the lunch rush. This is the earliest we've seen tourists flock to the town, and I'm not complaining, because it's the first time in months we've experienced such busy afternoons.

Before I can respond, another text from her comes through.

> Johanna: Booth is giving me a look *side eye emoji*

Fucking Booth.

> Patrick: If it makes you feel better, I have to entertain a 4-year-old on only two hours sleep.

> Patrick: Also, I haven't told him anything. I swear.

> Johanna: I don't think he needs to be told anything. He keeps doing this weird thing with his eyebrows.

> Johanna: What are we gonna do about the cameras?

Fuck. I didn't even think about the security cameras at the bar, and I hope to god Lenny doesn't check the footage. Lottie won't be happy about being dragged to a bar before the park, I'll just make it up to her with sugar and watching *Tangled* as many times as she wants. I totally get the infatuation about women with long blonde hair.

> Patrick: Leave it to me. Can we talk next week?

I tap the side of my phone in anticipation, waiting for her response. When I drove us back from the bar, I felt intense relief that we were on the same page. I know I can't rush for answers, and I need to set some boundaries where Lottie is involved. Slow and steady, it's how this needs to go.

> Johanna: How about Tuesday?

> Patrick: Sounds good.

"Daddy, why don't you have a girlfriend?"

I almost choke on the bite of ice cream at Lottie's question. It's harmless, but my child only has one volume setting and we're sitting in the middle of the park.

As I suspected, when I told her we had to take a detour before heading to the park, she laid on the guilt thick. It didn't matter that I told her we would only be twenty minutes, because twenty minutes is a lifetime to her. Her frown turned upside down when I promised her ice cream, though.

I paid Lenny one hundred bucks to hand over the security footage, and I respect that he didn't question why I needed it.

It's a warm day, the sun is shining on us from our spot on the grass, watching the ducks paddle around in the small lake in front of us.

"Why do you ask that?"

"Nora's mommy and daddy don't live together. Her daddy has a girlfriend, and she says it's like having another mommy."

It's a fair observation from her, and something I should have seen coming. I know Carrie has been on a few dates over the years, and introduced one boyfriend to Lottie before they went their separate ways. My last girlfriend was in my freshman year of college and it didn't last long. I've never introduced anyone to Lottie, but it's hard to do that if you don't go on dates.

I attempt to change the topic and point to the lake where some ducks are diving under the water. "Hey, did you see that one?"

She takes a few licks from her chocolate-chip ice cream that's slowly melting down her fingers, but the scrutiny in her eyes makes me nervous. She's obviously been spending too much time with my brothers.

"I'm gonna find you a girlfriend," she declares, tone final.

I lean over and wipe the melted ice cream dripping from her chin. "I don't need a girlfriend, spud. I have everyone I need in my life. You, Grandma, your uncles, and Aunty."

"And Poppa George!" she says excitedly. George has played a huge part in Lottie's life since the moment she was born and loves Lottie like she's his very own grandchild.

"How could I forget Poppa George."

"Is Poppa George a daddy?" she asks and nibbles on the waffle cone.

"He is. He has two little girls, Johanna and Harriet. You know Johanna, or JoJo as you call her."

She gasps, hand dropping to my arm in a sticky grip. "He's Rapunzel's daddy?"

Chuckling at the number of nicknames she has for Jo, I nod. "He is, yeah."

"I like her hair."

She looks thoughtful for a second and then jumps to her

feet. Her mouth gapes open like a goldfish, and I gape right back at her, which makes her giggle. I think she's past trying to play matchmaker, but as always, this child keeps me on my toes.

"JoJo should be your girlfriend," she singsongs, hands me her ice cream cone, skips over to the swings, and calls me over. Leaving no room for debate.

I dump our cones in the trash and walk to where she's bouncing up and down.

"Would you like it if Daddy had a girlfriend?" I ask her. I drop to her level as I grab a wipe from my backpack and clean her sticky fingers and mouth, before helping her in the seat of the swing.

"Uh-huh. I think it would make you happy, and I like it when you is happy."

Well, shit. I can't argue with her on that logic. She has no idea that her innocent proposal was once a dream younger me wished would become my reality. And present me sees it within touching distance.

"Daddy is so happy when he has such a sweet daughter like you."

"I know, but like, extra happy. Like when Uncle Boo makes new friends with the other mommies when he picks me up from school."

Ignoring the fact that Booth has been using her to pick women up, I stand there in the middle of the playground, baffled at how insightful my four-year-old is. That even she can see that something has been missing from my life.

"Daddy?"

"Yes, sweet girl?" I look at her angelic face.

"Can you stop standing around and push me, please?"

twenty-five
JOHANNA

IF SOMEONE HAD SAID TO ME SIX YEARS AGO THAT I'D BE IN Patrick's house playing Barbies with his daughter, I would have laughed in their face. And then probably cried.

Yet here I am, sitting on the plush carpet of his living room and playing with some princess dolls whose names I keep forgetting. Lottie was extremely adamant that I played with the blonde doll with long hair, because we were "twins."

Patrick and I were due to meet up this afternoon to talk. I was just climbing into my car when he called with an emergency, and asked if we could meet at his house instead. Only when I turned up, Lottie was also being dropped off by Graham who was supposed to be watching her after school ended but got called into the office in the city.

Patrick's emergency was a burst pipe in his downstairs bathroom. He's spent the last forty minutes trying to stop the leak before the emergency plumber arrives, and I agreed to help watch Lottie in the meantime.

I don't know many kids, but Lottie is as sweet as pie and pretty fierce for a four-year-old. My heart nearly melted when she gave me my very own nickname, *JoJo*. So like the one her dad gave me when we were around her age.

"Do you have a boyfriend?" she asks from her spot opposite me, not looking up from where she's making her doll do backflips.

I freeze for a second and clear my throat before answering. "No. No boyfriend for me. Don't you think boys are yucky?"

She giggles at the disgusted face I make and then crooks a little finger at me.

I shuffle closer so she can whisper in my ear. "I has one and he's called Malcolm." Her little hand covers her mouth as she breaks into another fit of giggles.

"Ohhh. Does your dad know?"

Her eyes bug out of her head in horror. "No. Don't tell. Daddy says no boys till I'm thirty," she says and holds up seven fingers.

"That's a lot of numbers. Don't worry, your secret is safe with me," I assure her. Though I would love to see the distress on Patrick's face if he found out. He might be the ultimate girl dad who bends over backward for his daughter, although, I think he would draw the line at her having a boyfriend at any age, let alone four.

"You need a boyfriend. You're so pretty like my dolls," she says cheerfully.

"Well thank you, not as pretty as you are though. What's your favorite color? Mine's light blue, like the sky." I try to move our conversation to safer territory.

She thinks for a second, but the next words out of her mouth are not in response to my question. "My daddy needs a girlfriend. He could be your boyfriend. DADDDDDY!" she bellows through the house.

"Oh no, no. That's okay. Let your dad work," I whisper, bringing my finger to my lips.

"What's up, spud?" Patrick shouts from down the hall.

"JoJo needs a boyfriend. Can you do it?" she yells back and is met with silence. She looks at me, gives me a toothy smile, and resumes her playing. I have to pray Patrick didn't hear her, or that something will smite me down where I sit.

"He can do it," Lottie says, her sweet voice oozing with confidence.

Resuming our game, we play gymnastics, the vet's office, supermarket, and school in the space of ten minutes.

"Pink," she randomly declares.

"What's pink?" I ask.

"My favorite color, silly. Pink. My birthday party is princess pink and we're gonna have a tea party. There will be dinosaurs. I'm gonna wear a sparkly crown and so is Daddy and Uncle Boo and Uncle Gray and Uncle Dex." She looks up at me with such excitement and presses the palms of her hands against her cheeks, smushing her lips together. "Can you come? Pleeeeeease."

"You don't want me there," I say, but my heart is already melting into a puddle at how sweet the gesture is.

"You're my friend." Her bottom lip juts out, and *yup*, I'm going to cry.

"That's so sweet. Thank you, Lottie. How about we ask your daddy first?" I can't exactly say no now; I'm not a monster.

"Ask me what?"

Patrick's sudden appearance has us jumping. I didn't even hear him walk in, and when I turn to look at him, he's leaning up against the door frame and wiping his hands on a rag. He's still in the white T-shirt and worn jeans he greeted me in, though they're a little dirty and wet now, making the look even sexier. His T-shirt is almost transparent from how soaked it is, the outline of his abs and nipples visible through the thin material.

It reminds me that although I was practically naked while draped over the pool table the other night, he remained fully clothed. There's something so filthy about that, and it has me desperate to see him stripped bare.

I take him in as he concentrates on wiping his hands and arms. I have no idea how he stays in such amazing shape, however it's clear from the way his clothes hug him that he finds the time.

It's unfair how well he's aged. He said I'd aged like a fine wine the other day. If that's true, then he's aging like a smooth and rich whiskey. One that I would welcome the burn from drinking him down.

I'm so absorbed in watching drops of water run down his arms, that it takes me a second to notice he's looking at me with a smirk on his face. *Busted.* My cheeks heat as I scramble to tidy up the mess of dolls.

Chuckling lightly at my discomfort, he walks over to the sofa and sits behind Lottie and gives one of her braids a light tug. Memories of the night on his bed a few weeks ago flash in my head, when he handled me with such care after my panic attack. My heart warms at the knowledge that he has taught himself to braid hair and doesn't leave the task to Carrie or his mom.

"What did you shout before, Lottie?" he asks.

I'm hoping Lottie sees the silent pleading in my eyes to not repeat herself.

"I said, can you be JoJo's boyfriend?"

Patrick freezes at her words, and now he's the one to blush. He looks at me sheepishly, and I shrug as if to say *Kids, hey,* when really, I'm drowning in mortification.

His lack of reply doesn't faze Lottie, who just moves on to the next question. "Can JoJo come to my party? She said to ask you first."

"Do you think she'd like it? YoYo, do you like tea and dinosaurs?"

"It's *JoJo*, Daddy!" Lottie corrects him with an eye roll.

Patrick's gaze fixes on mine, like he's searching for something, though I'm not sure what. I turn to Lottie, giving her a big smile. "I'd love to come. Which princess should I be?"

I have no idea what coming to his daughter's birthday party means for us, but it feels like a step in a positive direction.

"Rapunzel! And Daddy can save you from the tower and the dragons." She lets out a roar and jumps up to tackle Patrick on the sofa. He catches her with ease and lifts her in the air, peppering her face with kisses until there are tears in her eyes from her laughter. You'd have to be heartless not to get all warm and fuzzy when watching these two. The way Patrick lights up around her is exactly the love a daughter deserves. It's the type of love my dad shows Harriet and me.

Patrick playing plumber is hot. Patrick being a girl dad short-circuits my brain. I'm pretty sure my ovaries are glowing right now. He's an amazing father, so patient, caring, and loving.

A small part of me thinks he might not have this had I stayed. If life is all about silver linings, then this is the glossy strip to our years apart. It will always hurt, but seeing what he gained while I was finding my own way back to myself makes the pain a little more manageable.

I like to think I also gained something. I got to know my mind and body better, to understand my limits, and how to love myself exactly as I am. Had I stayed here, I doubt I would have gotten the help I needed or been truly honest with myself about what was going on, and I'm proud of how far I've come.

From the love pouring out of Patrick, he stayed exactly where he needed to be.

And perhaps this was where we were always supposed to end up.

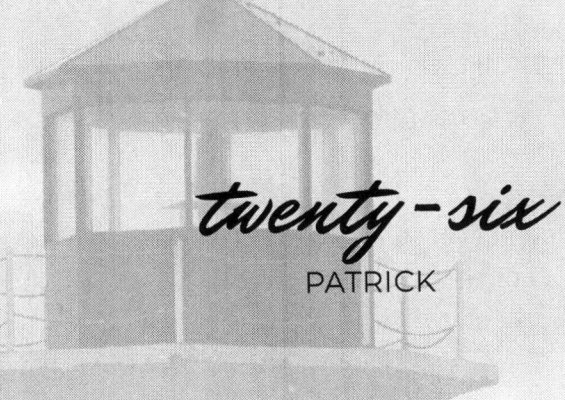

twenty-six
PATRICK

WALKING INTO MY LIVING ROOM AND FINDING JO AND LOTTIE playing together was a sight to behold. Never in all my years since becoming a dad, did I expect to see those two interacting. Hearing Jo speak to Lottie with kindness, showing her patience, and making her laugh, makes me sad that I didn't see it sooner.

I allowed myself to watch them for five minutes, and it pulled at the muscle in my chest, something that's been happening a lot recently. It was only when they started to talk about me that I got curious and made myself known.

Which was fortunate, because it sounded like Lottie was trying to meddle in my love life again.

When I caught Jo looking at me with the same glow in her eyes that I saw at the bar, it lit me up. I could have easily changed into a dry T-shirt, but the appreciative look she gave me let me know I'd made the right call in not changing.

We spent the rest of the afternoon chilling in the living room, until Booth was able to come over and watch Lottie.

Originally, we planned to meet at Dough for pizza, but I made us all a late lunch. Instead, we grabbed coffees from

Quinn and walked down Robin Road to the empty docks, with most boats still out for the afternoon. When we left the house, the sky was a clear blue, and in classic New England fashion, it's now a dull gray. At least spring is in the air.

It's always been Jo's favorite season. Each year she would drag me out to Acadia National Park in the first week of April, the joy on her face was always the same when she took in the wildflowers for the first time each year. She swore she could smell the maple in the air. I smelled it, too, it was just more fun to tell her that I couldn't and watch her get all worked up and sulky.

Aprils haven't been the same since she's been gone.

Though we're not out in the park, she still has a wistful look on her face as she takes in the breathtaking view.

The landscape surrounding us is beautiful, but it holds nothing to Johanna.

It started to drizzle when we got out of her car, and a few strands of hair have escaped her bun and are stuck to her forehead. The misty rain clings to her lashes and fine hairs around her hairline. My attention is drawn to the opening of her coat that reveals her delicate collarbone, decorated with freckles and water droplets. Sparkling constellations across her soft skin.

"Thanks for watching Lottie today, she had a great time."

"She's so great, Patrick. You've got your hands full for sure. You and Carrie should be so proud."

"Thank you. We're pretty fond of her by now. No returns," I joke, and her breathy laugh carries with the wind, mixing with the calls of sea birds circling above. They dip and dive into the water, which encourages me to take the plunge too.

"I know things have been complicated over the last couple of weeks. My life is a bit chaotic, from Lottie to the restaurant and everything that happened with my dad. It just never seemed to stop. Having you here has helped a lot. You've already made so many amazing changes in a short time, things I've struggled to find time for. I want you to know that it's great having you back...in more ways than one. The restaurant is all I have left of my dad, and while you've been gone, it's where I put a lot of my time and energy if I wasn't with Lottie. I didn't mean to suggest that the restaurant is a higher priority than you, I'm sorry for suggesting that, but I can't lose it. I also need to think of Lottie, I don't want to confuse her."

And I can't lose you again. Though I don't say that part out loud.

"This is all pretty new to me. I haven't, umm, dated at all since Lottie was born. I'm not proposing some friends-with-benefits nonsense, Christ knows I'm too old for that, and maybe I'm selfish, but I want to stay in this bubble together for a while longer. Taking the time to find our way and not having our nosy families getting involved. We never got the chance to see where this could go before..."

Finally taking a breath from that word vomit, I study her, looking for a sign I've upset her, or this isn't what she wants. Her face and body language have been indecipherable this entire time. I scratch my jaw, feeling more vulnerable for every second that passes.

When she still hasn't spoken, I accept that Saturday night was about her getting it out of her system. She was the one who suggested it be a one-time thing. Maybe I've massively overstepped, or she's changed her mind.

"I think everything you've said is fair." She interrupts my racing thoughts. "I would never expect you to put me before Lottie. And I agree about the restaurant. We can't let ourselves get distracted from all the hard work we're putting in. Plus, I like the idea of it being between us."

She reaches out, grabs hold of my arm, and we stop walking. The heat of her touch sears through the flannel of my shirt. Her eyes drop, and I know she's about to say something that makes her uncomfortable as her fingers tap against her coffee cup incessantly.

"I owe you answers, Patrick." I go to speak, but she shakes her head and lightly squeezes my arm to stop me. "Don't. I do, and it's not fair for you to pretend I didn't abandon everyone all those years ago." Her voice cracks at her words, and it takes all my restraint not to pull her into me. "I'll explain everything. I want to. Being open and vulnerable about certain things is still difficult for me. It has nothing to do with me not trusting you. I feel safe with you."

"Are you saying 'it's you and not me?'" I joke, but to hear that she feels safe with me is a badge of honor I will wear proudly. "When you're ready, I'll listen." There are so many reasons I want to hear what she has to say, and some of them are selfish. Sure, I was angry once upon a time, however, from the small snippets of details she's told me, it was wrong of me to presume she left this town happily.

I hate that it doesn't put my mind at ease that if I had just been enough for her, she wouldn't have left.

I want to move forward. Together. My heart might want to dive in headfirst, but I have to think about Lottie, and as much as I trust her, I don't want to rush into this.

So for now, we'll take one step at a time.

"Does this make me your dirty little secret?"

"Johanna," I groan, dragging out the last *a* in her name and shaking my head at her in dismay. "Don't start misbehaving now."

"Ohhh da—"

I clamp a hand over her mouth and tug her into me. "Don't you dare drop a *daddy* joke," I growl down her ear.

When I drop my hand, I see her nibbling at the corner of her bottom lip, trying to stifle her laughter. But I love pretty things, and I want to hear it, so I tickle her sides and pull that sweet melody from her, before swallowing it down with a kiss.

THOSE TWO WORDS

It tastes as divine as she feels. With one final brush of our lips, I turn us to face the bay—her back to my chest. I keep her close with my arms wrapped around her shoulders, reveling in how perfectly she fits against me.

"This is happening," I murmur. *It's finally happening*, a quiet voice says in my mind. He sounds a lot like sixteen-year-old me.

"I'm not going anywhere this time, Patrick. I promise you that," she says and places a kiss on the back of my hand.

The certainty in her tone should be enough to erase all the doubts I have. She's proven week after week that she wants to make Sutton Bay her home again, and I want nothing more than to witness that. To be a part of it.

We stare out at the bay, taking in the choppy waves as they crash against the rocks. You can make out Puffin Point Lighthouse on the peninsula north of Sutton Bay, and just through the mist and rain in the distance is the cliffside of Anakiwa Lookout.

"God, I've missed this view. I need to find some time to head up to the lighthouse soon." She rests her head against my shoulder, jasmine and ocean filling my nose.

"We can drive up there one day."

She hums and doesn't say much else as we stand there, content that we're finally making a go of this.

I'd love to know what's going on in that beautiful head of hers, and I know she'll tell me one day, about everything that happened. For now, I soak up this moment, following the slope of her upturned nose, the round apples of her cheeks, her pouty lips, and the pointy angle of her chin. I'm happy to see there are no new freckles to make note of.

Because if everything goes the way I want it to, I'll be here to watch new ones grace her beautiful features.

RONNIE MATHEWS

"She's been lurking on the street for an hour. She's passed by me seven times since I've been out here. I don't know what her deal is, and I swear I saw her snapping some pictures of the restaurant," Dex says with a jerk of his chin across the street.

The moment my eyes lock with Mrs. Stewart's, she turns and hurries away. "No doubt we're doing something wrong. I'm sure I'll hear about it at the next town hall meeting. Just ignore her."

"Are you sure that's the right color?" Jo asks from beside me, both of us shielding our eyes from the early morning sun.

"For the tenth time, Johanna, yes, it's the right color. Midnight navy, the same as the sample you gave me. The same color your dads' picked out twenty-plus years ago," my best friend grumbles with one boot on the bottom rung of the ladder, armed with a paint brush, and a little tired of Jo's backseat management.

She's been the one to take the lead in many of the improvements around here, and I've loved watching her shine. Today she's tasked Dex with giving the front of the restaurant a facelift. He told us he has nothing better to do, and I appreciate his help, even though I know he's lying.

He's probably regretting his helpfulness, especially when Jo stands there *umming* and *ahing* as she compares the paint in the tin to the sample she's holding. She's thorough, I'll give her that, but he does not like to be micromanaged.

"Hey, love, how about we let Dex do his thing?" I attempt to pry the paint tin from her hands, and I see Dex's brows raise in question at the slip of the term of endearment I use for her. He's not exactly going to go around town gossiping about the two of us. It's my own blood I have got to worry about.

Eventually, Jo let's go and begrudgingly hands over the

paint to Dex, who doesn't waste any time in climbing up the ladder and applying a fresh coat of paint to the wooden slats at the front of the restaurant. He spent the morning stripping and prepping, which is when Mrs. Stewart decided to stop by.

"Thanks, man," I call up to Dex, who, for once, is wearing his hearing aid. "Got time for a beer soon?"

"Sure. If you have time for me." He puckers his lips and makes kissing sounds, eyes bouncing between Jo and me. Luckily, she's too busy inspecting the freshly stenciled letters on the restaurant's window to catch on to his jibe.

I flip him the bird before leading Jo inside the restaurant and saving Dex from the list of tasks I know she's desperate to assign him. It's not too busy on the floor right now, that quiet time between the lunch and dinner rush, and from all the out-of-state plates I've seen this week, tourist season is in full swing.

I steer her toward the small coffee machine we have at the end of the bar and start preparing myself a cup.

"Do you want one?" I ask.

"No, I better not. I've had five today already."

My head snaps toward her. "Jesus, Jo. How are you not bouncing off the walls? You have an addiction."

"And I don't want the cure." She's scrolling through the tablet that's linked to the new reservation system, when she suddenly lets out a loud gasp, catching the attention of some of the staff behind the bar and a couple of customers.

"What's wrong?" I ask, abandoning the coffee beans as they fall from the grinder and rush to her side.

Her eyes are wide, but she doesn't look upset or angry. When she finally looks up at me, the biggest grin stretches across her face.

"Patrick. We have a full house tonight," she whispers in shock.

"No way." I sidle up next to her and peer down at the screen she's pointing at excitedly. It takes few seconds for me to take in what I'm looking, and then I see she's right.

"Holy. Fucking. Shit. We haven't had a full house since last summer."

I look up at Jo, who is trying her hardest to contain her excitement. She doesn't want to jinx it, and neither do I, but this feels positive. It feels like we could save the restaurant after all.

And I couldn't have done it without her.

twenty-seven
JOHANNA

"How's your week gone so far?" Amanda asks through the speakers of my laptop. Even though our sessions are now held on video call, they're just as valuable. It took me a while to find the perfect match with a therapist, learning to not settle first time around.

"It's been really good, although a little hectic," I reply. "Tomorrow is the first day of the Easter fair, and it all seems to be going to plan. The busy schedule has helped keep my mind occupied."

"That's great. Don't forget, if it gets too much for you, step away for five minutes."

"I don't know if the familiarity of the crowd is a blessing or a curse yet."

"Who will you be working with at the fair?"

The town has an Easter fair every year, and it's crazy to think this is the first time Our Place will have a table there. We'll be serving a small selection of menu items, with all the ingredients having been sourced right here on the bay or from Hancock County. *"Keeping it local,"* is how I sold it to the town's council members when I put in a last-minute application for a table, who pride themselves on using locally sourced produce and stock.

Everyone was impressed and happy to give us a table, apart from Mrs. Stewart, who was swiftly outvoted. She made sure to warn us of the bullshit penalties we'd receive, should we even dare bring "out-of-county contraband" to the fair.

"I'll be with Booth, our head chef. He'll be cooking, I'll be serving."

"That's Patrick's youngest brother, right?" she asks.

Amanda knows everything about Patrick, and I know I need to tell her about the newest development between us.

"Yeah, that's him." I fiddle with the tassels on the pillow next to me. We only have a few more sessions left together until I start working with my new therapist at the beginning of June. "Speaking of Patrick..."

When I look back at the screen, she's sitting there patiently, waiting for me to finish.

"We've, umm. Well, I guess you could say we picked up where we left off."

"How do you feel about that?"

"Wow, that's the most therapist thing you've ever said." We have a great relationship, never shying away from humor, but she knows just as well as I do that I'm stalling. "I'm scared."

"Talk me through that. What scares you?"

"I'm scared that all his reassurances about being patient with me will wear thin. Or that when he finds out why I left, he'll think it's dumb or a huge overreaction. That I'll cast a shadow over the death of his dad. Scared that if the outcome of the restaurant doesn't turn out how we want it to, will he want me to stick around? He's put so much into that place in the years I've been gone. He wants to try, but what if down the line he realizes I wasn't worth the wait or doesn't understand me on my low days? He has a young daughter he needs to put first, and the last thing I want to do is get in the way of that. She's amazing, such a trip, but I still struggle to accept that we've had these huge life occurrences without each other."

"Those are all valid fears, and I'm sure he has his own. I wish I had the answers or could tell you those outcomes aren't possible. Only you will know if moving forward together as partners is worth the risk. The risk being those fears you have coming true. There's also a risk that everything turns out exactly as you want it. Go at your own pace, and remember, you deserve to be happy, Jo. You've come a long way. Can I ask…Is he worth the risk?"

"He is." There's zero hesitation in my answer.

"Then I think the first step is being honest with him. We're running out of time, but I'd really like us to spend time on our next session helping you prepare for that conversation."

I know I can't avoid it forever, but having her support before I speak to Patrick helps ease my worries.

We chat for another couple of minutes before ending the call. I always feel confident and somewhat validated in my feelings after a session with Amanda, and it puts me in a good mood for the rest of the afternoon. I take an extra-long bath, give myself a pedicure, and finally finish off the puzzle of the Eiffel Tower. I can't wait to rub it in Patrick's face.

It's the perfect Friday, and when I see it's almost time to head to my dad's house for dinner, the drive across town is done with a smile on my face.

My dad has been weird all week. I offered to come over earlier this afternoon before my therapy session to prep dinner, so all he had to do was throw some dishes in the oven and plate it up. He's never one to turn down a cooked meal he doesn't have to prepare, but he shooed the offer away.

When I arrive at my old childhood home, I notice a few

unfamiliar cars on the street. Only they're not unfamiliar the more I study them, because I recognize that light blue Chevy and my stomach drops. Not with the idea of seeing Patrick, but at the idea of him seeing me like this. I'm in ultimate slob-mode right now; with a makeup-free face, hair still damp from my bath, and a zit lurking on my chin. Luckily, my pajamas can easily pass as some knitted loungewear.

I frantically check my appearance in the rearview mirror when movement from the window catches my eye. A small face is pressed up against the living room window and waving frantically.

There's no running away now to change my outfit, and I can't help how my grin grows when I see Lottie fogging up the glass. I can't hear what she's saying, but I do see the look of excitement in her features.

Climbing out of my car, I head up to the house, quickly running my fingers through my hair, trying to flatten it down. Just as I reach the front step, the door flies open. Lottie waves and jumps from where she is standing in the doorway. "Hi, JoJo. Can I hug you? Daddy says I need to ask first."

This kid is so stinking cute. I drop to her level and hold out my arms. "I would love a hug."

She catapults herself into my open arms, and I give her a big squeeze before letting go and straightening.

"Let's get inside before it starts raining," I say, sensing a shift in the air. She takes hold of my hand and pulls me inside. It's only then that I notice Patrick standing in the open doorway, a warm smile on his lips when he sees our joined hands.

"Can JoJo sit by me, Daddy?" Lottie pleads between us.

"You'll have to ask her yourself," he says. When she's not looking, he mouths *You don't have to,* but the thing is, I want to. Lottie is an amazing kid, and being around her is like having a shot of serotonin. The more time I spend with her, the less sad I get about how she came into the world.

THOSE TWO WORDS

"I would *love* to sit next to you, Princess Lottie." I give her a little curtsey that has her squealing in delight.

"You're gonna love your surprise. *Oh.*" Her eyes go wide, and she slaps a hand across her mouth. "Oops, sorry, Daddy," she says before running into the living room.

"What surprise?" I ask suspiciously.

"Nothing special, your dad thought it would be nice to have a Sadler-Thomas family dinner like the old days. You look pretty tonight. Even in pajamas." *Goddamnit.* With a playful wink, he places his hand between my shoulder blades and directs me toward the murmur of voices. I don't think I'll ever tire of the feel of his hands on me, which is why I lean back into the touch.

Before we even take a few steps, a high-pitched shriek comes from the top of the stairs, and someone comes charging toward me.

My little sister.

I have just enough time to prepare myself before she throws herself off the bottom step and plows into me. We cling to each other like it's been years and not months.

"What are you doing here?" I cry happily into her hair, neither of us wanting to let go.

"Oh, you know, I decided I couldn't wait until May to see you, so here I am!"

I look at Patrick over her shoulder, and from the look in his eyes, I know this isn't an impromptu trip. Harriet told me only a few weeks ago that money was tight and she might not be able to afford the trip for a while.

You? I mouth at Patrick.

He just shrugs and walks away. Not realizing how he made an already great day remarkable.

"Look at this one of you and Harriet," Claire coos.

She brought a shoe box full of old photos with her, all of them captured by Ted and his Polaroid camera. We passed them around the table during dinner, and while memories of Mom and Ted still sting, it's nothing like the pain and distraught I would have felt a couple of years ago, or even several weeks ago. The more time I spend in town, surrounded by everyone under this very roof, I can feel my heart healing.

I let out a soft laugh as I look at a photo of Harriet running around in a diaper as I chase her down with a hose in our parents' backyard.

Claire and I are in the kitchen clearing the dishes, but we've been distracted by the black-and-white Polaroids for the past ten minutes. I'm flicking through a small pile when I freeze, and the tears that have been threatening to fall finally spill over.

She catches the change in my body language, and wraps an arm around my shoulder when she peers over at the photo held tightly between my fingers. It's one of my mom standing at the cliff edge at Anakiwa Lookout. "I'm sorry if these pictures upset you tonight, sweetheart. I should have known better."

"No, no," I rush out, hating that she feels she needs to apologize for sharing such happy memories of both our families. "It's always difficult to remember how young she was when we lost her."

"She was," Claire agrees. "I miss her every day, as I'm sure you do. I still remember the joy on her face when she told me she was pregnant with you. We were both so excited to be having babies in the same year. She was glad I was going through it first so I could tell her what to expect." She's laughing, despite the forlorn look in her eyes. My mom and Claire had been best friends since their early twenties, having met when they worked part time at the post office.

THOSE TWO WORDS

"That must have been nice to go through that together," I whisper.

"It was, she was a great best friend. Just remind yourself that even on the bad days, your mom would be so proud of you and the amazing women you and your sister have grown into. Ted would too. I know my boy kept you at arm's length at first, but he means well. He's protective of his heart and the people around him. That includes you."

Patrick has mentioned how he's certain his family knows what went on between us all those years ago. I told him that was ridiculous, however, from the curious look on Claire's face, I owe him an apology.

"I couldn't find the one of you and Patrick from that first New Year's Eve party we hosted. I'm sure it's lying around somewhere. Now—" She shoves the shoe box in my hands and shoos me out of the kitchen. "Get out of here, send your father in, and go hang out with your sister and my boys."

A short while later, we're all cozied up in the living room, passing around the photos.

Harriet and I haven't left each other's side all night, and now we're smushed next to each other on the sofa, laughing uncontrollably at a photo of us as we run away from a swarm of mosquitoes during one of our camping trips. Even though we talk every day, nothing beats catching up with each other like this. I tell her everything that she doesn't already know. Well, not recent progress with Patrick, because I'll never hear the end of it. I also decided not to ask her about the trip he took to visit me all those years ago, knowing she kept it from me for my own good. Looking back, I'm glad I didn't know.

She's here until next week and has plans to see some friends upstate over the weekend. Patrick is still playing coy about how Harriet *suddenly* had the cash. When I cornered him, he simply said, *"Maybe she won the lottery."* The fact he did that for me is one of the reasons I was giving him heart eyes across the dining table all night.

Emotion has been swelling in my chest all evening at how familiar this dinner has been, but not painful emotions.

I wasn't sure what to expect from tonight. Nostalgia was heavy in the air, and it was hard not to notice the absence of two people. Evenings like tonight are what I feared, being reminded of what we've all lost, yet as I look around at the people I grew up with, all I feel is happiness. The love and laughter shared helped remind me how much I loved these nights and how much I've missed them.

Lottie is snoring softly in Graham's lap, having eaten her body weight in Claire's blueberry pie. I was hoping he would have warmed up to me by now, but he's barely spoken a word to me. I try not to take it personally, knowing Graham's always been quiet. Booth was here for a short while, but there was a problem with one of the ovens at the restaurant, and he had to head out early.

"Patrick, how has my big sister been behaving since she's returned?" Harriet asks from her seat next to me.

His glass is halfway to his lips when he freezes at her question, looking around the room like there's another Patrick she's speaking to.

"Oh, umm, yeah, she's been a good girl. I mean, fine! She's fine. No, she's *been* fine." He stands from the sofa and bolts out of the room. No explanation. Harriet and I can't hold back our roar of laughter from where we're curled up under a blanket.

"I'll go check on him," Harriet says and follows Patrick to wherever he's run off to.

An awkwardness settles in the room when it's just Graham and me left. I wish Lottie was awake to fill the silence.

"How's work be—"

"Don't hurt him again," Graham says abruptly, cutting me

off. There's no anger or malice in his tone, and I don't need to question who he's referring to.

"I don't—I never meant to hurt him," I say.

"You might not have intended to, but you did. He won't say it, but he was a mess. Cut up over everything that went on. I don't blame you for it, we were all going through a lot then, and he's not as tough as he makes out. He tries so hard to be the brave one for us all and sometimes forgets to look after himself."

"I'm sorry, Graham." His expression softens just a fraction. "I'm sorry for leaving how I did and at such a difficult time for you all. Leaving this town, my home, wasn't easy. Not a day has gone by where I didn't think about you all. I would never intentionally hurt Patrick. I care for him so much and I want to be the person that he can lean on." I lay my hand across my chest, hoping he hears the sincerity in my voice. "I've missed you all so much, and I understand if it's too late for us to be friends again, but this is my home. And I'm here to stay."

I drop my eyes, waiting for his response. The sound of shuffling from across the room has me looking up to where he is carefully shifting Lottie off his lap. It's difficult not to feel the stabbing of disappointment in my chest when he walks toward the door. I'm about to tell him to stay and that I'll leave, when I'm pulled into a pair of strong arms, my face smushed against the wool of his cardigan.

Graham is hugging me.

He's actually crushing me, and I let out a squeak when the circulation to my lower half starts to cut off. With one final squeeze, he releases me.

He stands up straight and gives me one of those rare smiles. "He's glad you're home. We all are."

As I watch Graham walk out of the room, I sit there speechless. That turned out so much differently than how it played out in my head. I guess we're friends again, or maybe we never stopped.

For years I've held onto the fear that the people who knew me *before*, wouldn't see me the same. Wouldn't be able to forgive me for leaving or understand the reasons behind it.

I should have known that my friends and family, wouldn't do that.

Because these *are* my people.

twenty-eight
PATRICK

I DEBATE FEEDING LOTTIE ANY MORE VEGETABLES WITH THE strength she's pulling me from tent to tent, eager to see all the homemade trinkets and sniffing out anything made of sugar like a bloodhound.

"Lottie, hold your horses," I call out, and she stops in her tracks.

"Where?" she asks, her head whipping left to right.

"Where what?"

"Where are the horses?" she asks, hands thrown up in question.

"Oh, spud, no, sorry. It's a figure of speech. Like when I say, 'Don't let the bedbugs bite,' they're not really there. It's just pretend," I explain, though the wobble in her bottom lip informs me I've said the wrong thing.

"Bedbugs aren't real?" she asks, and I swear tears are pooling in her eyes now.

"I mean, they are—Hey look, Uncle Boo and JoJo are over there. Let's go say hi and tell your uncle his food stinks."

Her head follows to where I'm pointing, and she lets out a cheer before darting over to their table.

Crisis averted.

I make sure to follow the top of her head through the crowd, the purple ribbons in her hair making it easy to spot her. When she reaches Booth, he picks her up and spins her around so many times, she falls on her butt when he puts her down, laughing hysterically from the floor. Jo watches from her spot behind the table, laughing at them as she hands over a lobster roll and a bottle of Moxie to a customer.

From this angle, I see her whole side profile, and I drink up every inch of her from where I'm standing. The black, skintight leggings she's wearing don't leave much to the imagination, and she's wrapped up in a thick, dark green sweater. The shape of her curves is accentuated by the gray apron tied around her waist, tempting me even more.

In the two weeks since our talk on the docks, we've only found the time to steal a few kisses in the breakroom or talk over text. It's not enough, though, and I'm a man starved for Johanna Thomas. She's been working day and night to get the restaurant ready for the fair, and I'm grateful for that, because it's allowed me to concentrate on other things.

There's only so many times I can think about her draped over that pool table with my hand wrapped around my cock, until I go insane. Carrie is picking Lottie up soon, and I know Jo is clocking off shortly, and the moment she does, she's mine.

She thanks the customer and gives them a kind smile as they walk away. I don't make myself known, hiding in the sea of people to watch her. Every day she seems to shine a little brighter, and I could bathe in her light.

She looks up from her spot and glances around the crowd, like she's searching for someone, and when her gaze lands on me, the grin that breaks across her face almost knocks me to my ass. The sun shines on her honey-blonde hair piled on top of her head, a few loose strands framing her face. Her eyes crinkle at the edges as she waves at me over the sea of bodies.

Shit, she's perfect.

Just knowing I'm the reason behind that smile has deep satisfaction thrumming in my chest. Even when we were kids, making Jo smile was one of my favorite things to do.

I make my way over to their table, partially covered by the large marquee behind them. I grab Lottie by the hood of her coat before she dives headfirst into a bag of flour, pulling her gently along as I walk to where Jo is standing.

"Hey," I greet. "This is looking great. How's it been?"

"Crazy. We've hardly stopped since the fair opened," Booth replies from behind us, wiping his station before finely chopping up some cilantro. "YoYo here has been killing it. We're almost out of lobster tails and probably have about eight portions of fried clams left. I think a lot of the customers have been coming over to speak to her," he says, winking at Jo, who rolls her eyes at him.

"What do you mean?" I look between the two of them.

"Just that a few gentlemen callers have been queuing up for some of my famous clams *and* a chance to talk to our lovely server," Booth says, not looking up from his chopping board, but I don't miss the way his shoulders shake. I should know better than to rise to his bait.

I saunter over to Jo while keeping an eye on Lottie, who is twirling in circles in front of the table.

"Hey." She's busy emptying out quarters into the makeshift cash register, and stands a little straighter when I approach her. "Have you been making some new friends?"

"Hey, yourself," she says and ignores my question. "Are you guys having fun?"

Stepping closer, with my hand resting on her hip hidden behind her apron, my voice remains low and face neutral as I whisper down her ear. "I don't share, Johanna."

She bites her lip and slowly shakes her head. "I don't want

you to share me. Can't blame a girl for providing the best customer service there is."

"Be sure that's all it is." I round the table and stand in front of her. "You finishing up soon?"

"In about"—she looks at her watch—"twenty minutes, why?"

"What a coincidence. Carrie is on her way over to pick Lottie up and take her to the fairground. Want to ride the Ferris wheel with me?" My tone is anything but subtle.

She tilts her head to the side and purses her rosy, pink lips. "I don't think you have the best intentions, Patrick Sadler."

"Yeah, I definitely don't. I'm thinking about you in nothing but—"

"Patrick, where's Lottie?" Booth asks, looking around the small space.

"She's here." I turn to point to Lottie behind me but stop short when she isn't spinning around where I last saw her. My head snaps up, and I squint around the crowd looking for her, but there are no purple ribbons in sight.

"Lottie?" I shout, cupping my hands around my mouth as my heart rate increases. She couldn't have gotten far.

Jo and Booth join in the search, looking around the neighboring tables and behind the tent flaps.

"I looked away for a second." My hands run through my hair in panic, and I go to bolt toward the fairground when Booth grabs me by the arm.

"You stay here in case she comes back. She won't be far," he says and squeezes my shoulder before jogging away.

"I'm sorry, Patrick," Jo whispers behind me, but I don't even know what she's apologizing for.

My stomach plummets to the floor, and my chest tightens with worry. In almost five years, I've never lost sight of her, not even for a second.

I continue calling her name, and with each minute that passes, the nausea intensifies.

A tap on my shoulder pulls me from my spiraling thoughts, and I turn to find Carrie standing there.

Oh my god, I have to tell her I've lost Lottie.

"Lost something?" she says with a raised eyebrow and steps to the side to reveal a guilty-looking Lottie, purple ribbons and all.

"Lottie!" I cry out, dropping to my knees and hauling her into me. I crane my neck and peer up at Carrie. "I'm so sorry. I looked away for a second. I don't know what happened."

"I found her a few tables over when I was walking to meet you guys. She feels bad for wandering off, don't you?" She strokes Lottie's hair as she hides her face in my chest and clutches at my T-shirt.

Lottie is safe and Carrie doesn't seem mad, but the last five minutes have aged me by twenty years.

"Pat, don't beat yourself up. I almost picked up the wrong kid from daycare once. She's fine and has learned her lesson. Cut yourself some slack," she says. I shut my eyes and nod, but I still feel like the world's worst dad.

I let out a whoosh of air in relief and I give Lottie one more squeeze, before prying her hands from my front.

"Lottie, you're not in trouble." She sniffles and keeps her head lowered. "I was scared I'd lost you. You have to make sure you have a grown-up who you know with you all the time, remember?"

She nods slowly, twisting her hands in front of her. "I'm sorry. I saw some puzzles over there." She points behind her. "I know you like them."

This is why I can't stay mad at this kid. Her heart is so big.

"That's so kind, my sweet girl."

Carrie pats her head lovingly, and Lottie seems to cheer up

at that. "Hey, why don't we head over there before we go to the fairground? Maybe we can buy your dad one?"

The idea of rides has her perking up even more and she finally releases me.

"That sounds fun." I give one of her pigtails a tug. "Give me a hug goodbye and be good for your mom, okay? I love you so much."

"Love you, too, Daddy." She gives me a hug before taking Carrie's hand and waves goodbye.

Once I'm sure I'm not going to pass out from the panic, I turn back to the table. Booth is now talking to Jules and Simon, who must be here to switch shifts. He jerks his chin at me and mouths *You good?* to me, to which I nod. As I look around the tent, I can't see Jo anywhere.

I make my way over to him and he seems to know what I'm about to ask.

"I told her to hang around. She seemed pretty eager to head out, saying she was tired or something, but she looked upset. You might catch her if you hurry."

I'm already sprinting toward the parking lot before he's finished his sentence. There must be hundreds of cars here and I scan the crowd of people. When I spot a flash of blonde, I race in that direction and call her name. I know she can hear me, but her steps quicken, like she's trying to escape me.

Reaching her, I take hold of her wrist and stop her attempt at fleeing. "Hey, where are you going?"

"Home, I'm exhausted. Raincheck on the Ferris wheel?" I can't see her face, but something about her body language has changed, nothing like the playful Johanna I was talking to earlier.

I know that Jo tends to take herself away when she needs space. I get it, it's just, I want to be that space, and for her to need me in those moments. I want her to lean on me and talk about how she's feeling, or hold her when it becomes too much.

I've begun to pick up on the moments when her anxiety shows, and this isn't one of them, this is something different. I don't want to push her, but I'm also not leaving her right now.

"C'mon." I tug her in the direction of my truck on the other side of the lot.

"Patrick, I'm not in the mood for the fairground." Even with a tired sigh, she follows me.

"That's not where we're headed. I know somewhere that'll be quiet right now. If you need some peace, I can help you find that, just let me be there next to you. We said we'd try right? Well, we need to trust one another, so trust me." I turn to her, and we stop walking. "If you don't want to talk, then we won't. I think you're gonna like where we're going though."

She gives it a few seconds to think it over, then nods her head and walks ahead to climb into my truck.

Once we're out of the parking lot, I drive about ten miles north. The lush canopy traps out the sun, creating a whimsical vibe as we drive down the windy roads curving with the coastline. The tree line ends suddenly, and the road in front of us opens to reveal the endless view of the bay and the vast open ocean. Deep green is replaced with vibrant blue as the water reflects the cloudless sky. We're right on the cusp of Acadia National Park here, and Puffin Point Lighthouse sits on a small, rocky peninsula between the park and Piper Beach.

Jo hasn't said much since we started driving, and I've let her enjoy the silence. Her head rests against the passenger window, watching the landscape pass us by. Once we drive onto the small sliver of land, the waves crashing around us coat the windows in sea spray.

I park the truck in the small lot at the base of the lighthouse and as I suspected, there's no one else in sight. Turning off the engine, I climb out, Jo following silently behind me as we round the whitewash base of the lighthouse. The red rings traveling up the cylinder building need a new coat of paint. It's no longer in use anymore, more of a tourist attraction than anything. I walk a little ahead and stop until I can't walk any farther. The light spray of water hitting my face and the taste of salt on my lips is refreshing.

Jo stops a few feet behind me, the loose strands blowing in all directions. She closes her eyes and takes a deep breath when a strong gust of wind sweeps over us. She looks perfect, standing here with the salty air blowing through her hair and a warm glow painting her cheeks.

"Is Lottie okay?" she asks.

"She's fine. I think I panicked more than her, so it freaked her out."

"I'm so sorry."

Her apology has me jolting in confusion. "What are you sorry for?" I ask. I take a step closer to her and she opens her eyes then, guilt swimming in those deep blues.

"I distracted you when you were meant to be watching her."

"Whoa, whoa." I grab her shoulders before she has the chance to turn away. "I'm pretty sure I was the one who walked up to you and did the distracting."

"That doesn't matter. I never want to be the reason that your priorities shift away from her. I was relieved when Carrie came over with her but then I saw you all together and it looked like..."

"Looked like what?"

"It's stupid of me, never mind."

"No, I want to know." I'm not letting this drop, needing to know what changed from when we were flirting behind the table to now.

"You looked happy, and I was"—she throws her head back and blows out a breath, hands slapping at her sides— "I was jealous, okay?"

THOSE TWO WORDS

I look at this woman. Really look at her.

This beautiful and complex creature who wears her heart on her sleeve yet at the same time bottles so much up, hiding herself from the world. I hate that she feels the need to keep everything locked up, and that she has any reason to be jealous. I thought we were past that.

It's clear she needs reminding that there's no one else who can enrapture me half the way she does.

I do just that as I pull her into my chest, grab hold of her shocked face, and seal my mouth over hers.

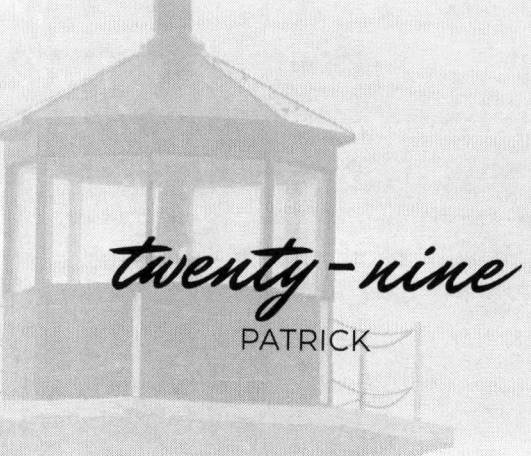

twenty-nine
PATRICK

I SWALLOW DOWN THE SHOCKED GASP FROM HER LIPS AND DRINK up the tiny moan that follows as Jo slowly sinks into the kiss. Her shoulders relax, but I don't dare let go of her, keeping us fitted together.

Despite wanting to lose myself in this kiss, I can't ignore her admission.

"I told you, Carrie and I have never been involved."

She rests her forehead against my chin, mumbling her words into my chest. "I wasn't jealous about that."

"What are you jealous of then?" I ask.

Looking up at sky, she swallows, and twists her well-kissed lips to the side. "I have no right to be. I left. We never even spoke about where we saw our relationship going..."

And it hits me. What she's jealous of. She's not jealous of Carrie and me, but what we have.

Lottie.

A child together.

My heart spasms in pain, but also in hope. When she left, we'd only slept together once, but it was enough to see a future together. Or at least for me it was and it's clear those feelings weren't unrequited like I once thought. I don't have the words to comfort her, because Carrie and I do share a child. I don't need to tell Jo that Lottie wouldn't be here if she hadn't left, that truth is written all over her face. We'll never know what could have happened between us if she'd stayed. But the idea of her carrying my child? Just picturing it sends me wild.

Is that something we could have one day?

Words might be useless right now, so I use my actions instead. I need to show her that she's the only one I want to take each next step with, no matter how slow we take them.

Grabbing her hand, I walk us back toward my truck, pulling Jo behind.

"Patrick, where are we going now?" she asks in confusion.

When I scan the empty parking lot again, I reach for the door handle on the passenger side and fling it open.

"We can't change what happened or our time apart, but I need you to know I'm choosing you now. I never stopped choosing you. There hasn't been a day since you left where I haven't thought about you. If you want to do this, get in the truck, because the last two weeks have been torture. If you're not ready yet, let me know and I will drive you home. We can watch those nineties sitcoms you love so much or do a jigsaw puzzle, I don't care what we do. Tonight you're mine. And I need you to know one thing." I close the short distance between us. "What happened, happened; it's in the past, but this moment right now..." I point to the ground beneath our feet and keep my gaze locked with hers. "It's ours. Let's forget about everyone else and what could have been. I've waited six years, and I don't want to wait another second."

I worry I've stunned her to silence, but when she speaks, her voice strains from all the emotions I see on her face. "Wait another second for what?"

"To be with you again. To feel you around me. *Fuck,* I'm

desperate for you, love. I'll wait, just don't push me away. Let me be the arms you fall into when your days are tough."

Her chest rises and falls rapidly, emotions swirling in her eyes, but I don't see indecision there.

I see want and lust.

When she throws herself at me and our lips collide again, there's not more waiting, and I know there's no looking back.

Turning us so her back is to the open passenger door, I wrap my hands around the backs of her thighs, and she gasps in surprise as I hoist her up onto the bench seat.

Her tits are now at the perfect height, and I waste no time in getting my hands on them, molding my palms to the small handfuls through the soft material of her sweater. My hands trail to the hem of her sweater, and I give her a moment to object before I'm ripping it over her head.

The sight before me is one I would pay an artist to paint, just to hang it up in my bedroom and selfishly hide it away from the world. Baby-blue lace holds up her heaving chest, sheer enough that her rosy-pink nipples poke through, begging for my tongue and hands.

My mouth covers one, sucking it hard through the lace, pulling another sharp gasp from her. I forgot how vocal she is, and I'm desperate to hear all the sounds she's going make as she writhes beneath me, completely at my mercy. Her hand flies to the back of my head while the other stays propped up behind her. I trace her nipple with my tongue and slip it under the delicate material, teasing the soft slope of her breast. One hand remains on Jo's hip while the other pulls down the lace cup, and my lips descend again to suck the hardened peak into my mouth.

"Oh god, that feels amazing." Her legs widen, and I step in closer, grinding myself against the apex of her thighs.

As I continue sucking, biting, and pulling, Jo's hands creep under the hem of my T-shirt. I suck in a sharp breath when her cold fingers sweep across my stomach. She laughs, but it dies on her lips when I close my teeth around her nipple, clamping down, before soothing the sting away with my tongue. Her fingertips trace every dip and curve of my abs, slowly making her way up to my nipples and circling them gently. When she reaches the trail of hair disappearing south, she pauses and hooks a finger into my belt loop and tugs my upper half into the cab of the truck. The teasing touches have my cock growing incredibly uncomfortable in my jeans and my balls feel heavy.

"I want to suck your cock." Her eyes look innocent, but the quirk of her mouth suggests otherwise.

"Jesus, are you trying to kill me?" I laugh between her cleavage while she works on undoing my belt.

When she starts to lower my zipper, I stop her with a hand to her wrists. She pouts as I bring her fingers to my lips, dotting each knuckle with a kiss.

"Why did you stop me?"

"As much as I'd love that, I don't think I'll last long." Reaching out, I trace along her cupid's bow with my finger.

"What are we going to do?" she asks and then nips at the tip of my fingers, before giving me a coy grin.

"I'm going to fuck you in my truck, that's what. I should take my time with you, but it's going to be hard and fast, dirty and rough." I pull at her plump bottom lip until her pink tongue peeks out. "I'll find something to do with this mouth next time."

I lean back and look down the length of her body, trying to work out the logistics of how we're going to do this. My fingers travels over her neck, in between her breasts and taut stomach. Goose bumps follow my path and that blush I love dusts her skin.

When I reach the top of her leggings, I pause. "Can I take these off?"

She nods and chews on her bottom lip, eyes falling to where my index fingers hook into the waistband of her the leggings.

She shuffles backward on the leather seat, shimmies out of her leggings, and kicks off her sneakers. I don't even attempt to hide the appreciative groan that rumbles out of me as I take in the heady view in front of me. Wrapped up in blue lace on the dark leather bench, looking like a fucking vision.

The front of her matching lace panties are darker between her thighs, and because it's my favorite position to be in when around Jo, I drop to my knees on the running board. I don't waste a second before my face falls in between her luscious thighs and I'm inhaling her sweet, musky scent.

My knuckles skate along the damp lace, and when I find her clit through the material, I put pressure on where I know she's aching for my touch. Slow circles have her moaning and writhing, begging for more. Her eyes burn with desire and her mouth is slightly open as she looks down at me with heavy breaths to match my own.

"Is this all for me, love?" My gaze drops to her open thighs. I replace my fingers with my tongue, and even through the fabric covering her, the taste of her drives me wild. Slipping a finger into her panties where they're wedged between her pussy lips, I pull them to the side and groan when I see her glistening in front of me. "Look. At. You. All pink, gorgeous, and wet. This is only ever for me." It's not a question. I'm leaning back in to give her one slow lick with the flat of my tongue, not giving her the chance to say otherwise. "You're all ready for my cock, aren't you, greedy girl?"

Her hips rise off the seat, and a gasp that sounds a lot like *yes* escapes with it. I place a gentle kiss on her clit before rising to my feet. As much as I'd love to feel her come on my tongue again, my aching cock lets me know I'll blow my load in the next few minutes if I'm not inside her soon.

Taking hold of her ankles, she lets out a yelp as I drag her toward me along the bench and secure her legs around my waist. Holding her to my chest, I maneuver us into the truck so

I'm sitting on the passenger seat as she straddles me. The door slams closed, and the moment I seal us inside, our mouths reunite.

I drift my palms up her full hips, follow the dip of her waist, skimming all the way up until my hand frames her face, pulling us apart.

Her eyes are heavy, and as she looks through the fogged-out windows, they widen when she remembers where we are.

"We can do this here, or I'll drive us to my house. You choose."

I'll drive us back if she asks, but she doesn't. She doesn't say anything, just grinds herself against my dick and turns her head until her lips graze my thumb.

When she sucks it into her mouth and hums around it, that's answer enough.

"*Fuck.* You're a filthy girl. Lift up for me," I say and tap her hip lightly. Rising to her knees on either side of my hips, I pick up where she left off with my zipper, and then push my jeans and briefs down. Once my cock springs free between us, Jo sits settles back on to my thighs.

Her eyes heat when they fall to my painfully hard cock. I fist myself and give a few pulls, pre-cum pooling at the tip. Her tongue traces her lips hungrily as she sits there mesmerized by the twist and turn of my fist.

Fuck, would I love to trace and smear myself across those pouty lips.

I bring my index finger to her chin, raising her needy stare to meet my own.

"Johanna, keep staring at my cock like that and I'll be painting those pouty lips with my cum, and this will be over before you know it." Though I doubt I'll last five minutes once I'm inside of her.

"It's a pretty dick," she responds with a shrug. Her words have said *dick* twitching between us. She smirks at the sight and her hands drift to the hem of my T-shirt. I raise my hands in silent offering, and she pulls it off and over my head.

"You know exactly what to say to a man." With a firm grip on her hips, I grind myself up into her, so she knows just how ready I am. "Hard and fast now. Next time I'll spend hours between these thighs and show you exactly what we've been missing out on."

"Next time, huh?" she teases.

"Yes, next time. How about you stop sassing me and sit on my cock? If we're doing this here, I want a perfect view of you bouncing up and down on my lap."

"That mouth," she says and shakes her head in pleasured shock. When she rises to her knees again, I tug her closer until she hovers above me. She might have a sassy mouth, but I don't miss the way she glows whenever I tell her what to do. I wonder what else she would do if I asked.

With a shaky hand, she pulls her panties to the side to reveal her glistening pussy and lowers herself until my tip teases her entrance.

"Oh *fuck*," she mutters as she glides herself across the head of my dick, coating me in her.

Oh fuck, indeed.

I'm not even inside her yet, but her teasing has me feeling tipsy. I grab the base of my cock and rest my other hand on the crease where her thigh and hip meet. Inch by glorious inch, I guide her down my length.

"Christ, you feel amazing." I stare at where I'm disappearing inside her. "So fucking tight. Don't move, fuck, I need a minute."

"Patrick," she whines. My eyes clench closed at the sensation, and I try to find some semblance of control so I'm not rutting into her like my brain is screaming at me to do. She wiggles her hips in a silent plea, and her legs tremble as she hovers above me. "I need all of you. Please don't make me wait any longer."

"Slow, love. Forget what I said about hard and fast, I don't want to rush this with you."

She nods and lowers herself a little more. It really is a tight fit. When she sinks down another couple of inches, her mouth forms into an *o*, but she keeps working her way down my length, and I praise her all the way.

"Look at that." I'm mesmerized at the sight and feeling of her tight heat wrapping around me. "You're taking me so well, love. You're doing so good." The moment her ass meets my thighs, I bottom out, and we groan in unison.

"Oh shit, you're so deep like this."

My jaw cracks as I feel her clench around me. I'm so lost in her that it takes a moment for me to realize *why* it feels so good.

"*Shit.* We didn't use a condom."

Our gazes drop to where I'm fully seated inside of her, and I curse. "I've been tested, I'm good." Swallowing, I bring my hand to the back of her neck, bringing her forehead to mine. "It's been a long time, Jo. A very long time."

Her eyes widen in realization.

"Always you, love. I haven't thought about or wanted anyone else."

"I have an IUD, and it's been a long time for me too. Six years, to be exact...No one else. Not ever."

My eyes shutter closed at her words.

Six years.

I don't know what to say to that. Words have left me. My heart soars and aches knowing she hasn't been with anyone else since our first time. The need for her increases tenfold, desperate to feel what we've only experienced once before.

"Jo," I whisper, my lips trailing across her neck, laying soft kisses across her flushed skin. I pull down the lace cups of her bra to reveal both breasts; the skin so soft and inviting. "Can I move now? I really need to fuck you more than ever."

With a wanton gaze, she nods eagerly.

"Show me what I've been missing and ride me then."

Shock paints her face at first, but then a wicked grin morphs her features, and she raises herself off me. Our moans of pleasure fill the cab when she slams herself backdown. My hands fly to her ass, holding and massaging the soft globes, holding on tightly and hoping I leave marks, as I help her find a rhythm.

Up and down, she moves, over and over.

She lets out the most exquisite moans every time her clit rubs against the base of my dick. I don't know where to look. Everything is intoxicating, from the way her face scrunches in pleasure, to the swaying of her tits each time she meets my thighs, to watching myself glide in and out of her.

It's slow, filthy, and sweaty. Condensation coats the windows, giving us some form of cover, but right now I don't care what's outside of this truck. Only she matters. The only noises that can be heard are our panting breaths, the creaking of leather, and the sounds our bodies make together.

"Look at us, Johanna. Listen to us. Keep riding me like that, baby. What do you need?"

Her mouth falls open as I thrust up inside her, and her brows scrunch as pleasure rolls through her. "My clit, touch my clit," she gasps, as I drop her down roughly on my cock. My balls draw up and I need her to find her release quickly.

With my hand at the back of her neck, I pull her mouth down to mine, demanding entrance with my tongue. The kiss is hurried and messy as she continues to bounce on my lap. I bring my other hand between our sweat-soaked bodies and find her swollen clit. With my thumb, I press down and move it in quick circles, testing the pressure until she clenches harder around me, letting me know I've found the right spot.

"Oh my god, yes, there. Don't stop," she cries against my lips. As I quicken the pace of my upward thrusts, her head falls back. I take advantage and suck, kiss, and bite my way across her neck and chest.

The base of my spine tingles, and I know I'm getting close, but like fuck am I finishing before she comes.

"Eyes here, baby, only on me." I continue stroking her clit, her rhythm becoming sloppy as she edges closer.

"Oh, Patrick. I'm so close. *Fuck.* There. There," she calls out. And when I pull one of her nipples into my mouth, she explodes. The feel of her pussy fluttering around me and the cries that fill my truck have me hurtling toward my own orgasm. I only have a few seconds before I'm following closely behind.

Her hand slaps against the back window, fingers streaking through the foggy glass as she loses herself in her orgasm. Before it ends, I flip us, her back now pressed against the bench. I continue to pump into her as she rides out the last of the waves, back arched, chanting my name like a prayer only I answer to.

The only name she will ever chant again.

That possessive thought and the feel of her still clamped around me is my undoing. My mouth falls to her neck, biting down on the soft skin as I spill inside of her.

I collapse on top of her, both of us breathless and covered in sweat. She rakes her nails over my spine, causing me to shiver as I soften inside of her. I'm light-headed, weak at the sight of her as I raise my head.

I know I'm crushing her, but she doesn't seem to care, and I don't want to move. My face falls to her neck as I breathe her. What have I done in this life to deserve her like this again?

Never has anything felt so fucking perfect.

Being with her again has me feeling whole. Wanted. But I'm also worried. Worried that I'll get addicted to the taste and touch of her, only for it to be snatched away from me again. I don't think she'd leave willingly this time, but the intrusive thought still haunts me.

"I think my legs are broken," she sighs. "Maybe next time we won't be as desperate to fuck."

The way she says *fuck* has my cock hardening again. "I don't know, because that was something else and I'm already thinking about when I can be inside of you again. Also, say *fuck* again?" I beg, with a thrust of my hips.

She slaps my chest with a giggle and pushes me off her. We groan when I slide out of her, but the view in front of me has every carnal urge in me rising to the surface. I watch in apt fascination as my cum drips out of her onto dark brown leather under her ass. Knowing I've had her raw makes me want to push it back inside her where it belongs, needing to mark her as mine in every way possible.

I shake those thoughts away and pull my eyes away from the temptation between her legs.

"You better get changed before I'm inside of you sooner than you think," I warn, but she only finds it funny because she grinds her pussy against the underside of my cock, the feel of the lace rubbing against the sensitive skin has me seeing stars.

"*Johanna,*" I warn.

"Ugh, fine," she says. I rise up on my knees as she sits up. She lets out a satisfied sigh, and much to my disappointment, collects her clothes that have been discarded throughout the truck.

We dress in silence, the only evidence left of what we did is our messy hair and the condensation on the windows. Her satisfaction mirrors my own when we share a look across the bench. The moment we just shared together is something I never imagined I would have with her again and I'm already greedy for more.

It's outrageous that I ever thought I was over Johanna. I'm

the biggest fool to think I could fight this, because I'm falling harder than before. I'm gluttonous for her attention, her touch, her smiles. *Her love.* I look at her, sitting in my truck like it's where she's always belonged, the corners of her lips pulled upward toward her still-hazy eyes.

I've never been more grateful to fall so hard as I have for her.

thirty
JOHANNA

"I know you're my big sister and all, but you totally got railed, didn't you?" Harriet observes casually.

Wine sprays from my mouth and I slap a hand over it to stop it from shooting across the bar. Her unfiltered question wasn't exactly quiet, either, considering we're in a restaurant full of people.

"Actually, don't respond to that." She circles my face with her finger. "Because this says it all. Johanna, you dirty *dawg*."

There's no point in trying to convince Harriet, because she can see right through me.

"I'm *not* talking about it here," I hiss, twirling my finger above my head to remind her where we are—which happens to be Our Place on a Tuesday night, and during the dinner rush no less.

We're perched at the end of the driftwood bar, which gives us the best spot for people-watching, and a great view of Patrick's ass from where he's working behind the bar.

Her head pops into my line of sight, obstructing my view, and she quirks a brow at me. "Look at that blush. I'll have to give Patrick my congratulations on holding off this long before getting his pickle we—"

I slap my hand over her mouth now, checking that Patrick didn't hear her. "Will you behave, you little nuisance? God, you're as bad as Booth."

After our afternoon at the lighthouse, Patrick dropped me off outside my apartment right as the youngest Sadler brother was walking out of Just Brew It. I have a pretty good poker face, but when Booth pointed out that my sweater was inside out and that I had a hickey forming on my neck, I knew we'd been caught. He patted us both on the shoulder and *congratulated* us. But not before telling us public indecency is a crime.

"Please can we change the subject," I beg. "How was your weekend?"

"It was fun, great to see everyone. Now, back to you and Daddy Pat."

"Harry," I groan and bring my head down to rest on the bar. "Listen, no one knows, well, apart from you and Booth, and it's new and we're...We're taking our time, and it feels good. We never got a chance last time, but this feels right. It feels like our time."

"You look good. And I'm not talking about your postcoital glow. I didn't see a lot of this Jo in Tennessee, and I love you in every shape and form, but happiness looks good on you. I've missed this version of you."

She leans into me and hugs me tight.

"I'm really happy here," I say, my voice muffled against her shoulder. "I loved living with you, though I bet you're glad you don't have your big sister invading your space anymore."

She cranes her neck, arm still slung around me. "I miss you like crazy, but this is where you belong. You needed me and it wasn't a question that I was going to help you. You've come so far since that evening in Dad's living room. And I'm so proud of you. For doing what was best for you, finding the help you needed, but most of all, for letting yourself be happy again."

Her words hit me then, because I *am* happy. I'm really happy. And there doesn't seem to be a limit on this happiness, not like when I lived in Tennessee.

"I haven't felt this happy in a long time." I rest my temple against her shoulder.

She stiffens beneath me, mood shifting suddenly as she speaks softly, "We can't lose this place, Jo." I look at her and she has a fond look in her eyes as she stares ahead. I follow her gaze and find the photograph of Mom and Ted where it belongs, in a new, shiny gold frame. Patrick asked me if it was okay that he put it back on the shelf, and let me choose a new frame. "For them. I don't say this to put pressure on you guys, it just feels like we're losing the last pieces of Mom and Ted we have left."

I swallow the lump in my throat. Harriet's worries aren't different from my own, and as I glance at Patrick, he's staring at us with a weak smile on his face, eyes moving between us and the photograph.

The impending news about the restaurant is one of the gray clouds hanging over our heads. The upcoming anniversary of Ted's death is the second.

If I can't save this place for me, I'll do it for him. I've only been in town a short while, but Patrick has been here for every up and down. Putting in his all to keep this place afloat and look after his family. I can survive the loss of the restaurant if I have Patrick, but does he feel the same? And what if once he knows the full story of why I left, he thinks I'm too messy and complicated? All questions I've voiced with Amanda, and as much help as she is, I know I won't know the truth until I rip off that last layer.

Harriet excuses herself to go to the restroom, and I spin on my stool to face the full house of customers we have in again tonight. The light chatter, laughter, and sound of silverware clanking together fill the room, and the mishmash of noises remind me so much of my childhood.

"Patrick, not there. It goes there," I cry as he tries to force another piece into the wrong spot. I jab a finger to the empty one closest to me. "Right here."

"No, that's wrong. It's this one," he argues, and continues to smush it down until the edges bend and it gets stuck. He looks up at me and smiles, but I'm not happy. "Oops."

"I told you!" I turn my head and cross my arms across my chest, not wanting to hear him say sorry for wrecking another puzzle.

"I'm sorry, okay. I can fix it. And my mom bought me a new Sonic the Hedgehog one we can do together at my house next week."

"I don't want to do one of a dumb hedgehog." I can see him making funny faces, twisting his mouth in weird directions, trying to make me smile with no luck. This is the second time I've tried to teach him how to do puzzles, and he sucks at it. Stupid boys.

The scrape of his chair and thud of his sneakers against the floor lets me know he's left the table. Leaving me to sulk.

I look up to see him talking to his dad, who is standing next to mine at the end of the bar. My dad has a big Band-Aid on his hand from when he and George were building the bar. Patrick and I learned a lot of new swear words when they were putting it together, and we made almost one hundred bucks.

Patrick and his dad disappear into the kitchen, right as my mom walks out, carrying a couple of plates. She spots me in the corner, but her smile falls when she sees my face. Dropping the food off with the customers, she comes over and sits across from me.

"Mayflower, what's up? I don't like it when you frown," she says.

I throw my hand out toward the ruined jigsaw puzzle. "Patrick messed this one up too. He's no good at it, Mom. Why do boys suck?"

She laughs and moves the puzzle piece Patrick got stuck. With a few wiggles, she sets it free and hands it over to me. "They can be smelly sometimes. They also make good friends too. He just wants to enjoy something you do, because he knows it makes you smile. Like when you go out and play dirt bikes with him and Dexter."

"I like that."

"I know, but you don't like it when they ride off quicker than you. You'll get the hang of it, just like Pat will get the hang of doing puzzles."

I fiddle with the puzzle piece and look up at my mom. "I think I upset him."

"I think he'll be okay. Don't tell anyone, but I think he's about to get you a surprise." She leans over the table, kisses me on the head, and heads back to where my dad is standing.

I don't know what surprise Patrick is getting me if he's in the kitchen, but I hope it's not bean-hole beans, because they smell like my little sister's diaper. I wait patiently, glancing up anytime one of the servers walks through the swinging doors.

After a couple of minutes, Patrick steps out with his dad, a tray in his hands with something balanced on top.

Please don't be beans. Please don't be beans. Please don't be beans.

"Um, Jo, I got you something," he says, standing in front of me, with the tray wobbling in his hands. "I got Gloria to make you your favorite, plus I swiped us a couple of cookies."

He places the tray next to the puzzle, and my tummy grumbles when I see the gooey grilled cheese on the plate. It looks really yummy, but I need to say sorry first.

"I'm sorry for shouting at you, I just really like playing with you. Do you want half?"

Sitting down in his seat, with half a cookie already in his mouth, he nods his head and swallows. "I'm sorry for breaking your puzzle. I got some money for doing my chores and my dad said he'd take us to the store. I'll get you a new one."

I hand him the puzzle piece my mom freed, and smile at him, laughing when he smiles back with chocolate-coated teeth. "It's fixed. I don't care what game we play. So long as it's with you, I'm happy."

THOSE TWO WORDS

Life was so much easier at that age. When the worst of your worries were broken puzzles, and not hearts.

As I scan the tables of customers, my heart warms when I spy that exact table in the corner of the room. We spent hours in that spot, doing our homework after school or arguing over where the puzzle pieces should go.

My eyes wander around the room some more, but when I spot Mrs. Stewart, the grumbly councilwoman, sitting at table thirteen, my mood sours. She's been very difficult since my return, from putting in an "anonymous" complaint about the makeover we did on the outside of the restaurant and trying to block our application for the fair. Booth assures me this type of behavior is very on trend.

I swivel around at lightning speed, hoping she hasn't spotted me, and find Patrick already watching me. My mind immediately goes to the afternoon in his truck, and suddenly I don't care about the tables of families behind me, or Mrs. Stewart. I care more about dragging him into the stockroom to feel his hands on me again, to hear the dirty things he knows I love, to feel the bite of pain and pleasure as he enters me.

When I sense Harriet return to the bar, I'm about to excuse myself, however, when I turn, I let out a cry at who is actually standing there.

The older woman stares at me without an ounce of emotion on her face. Her face is pinched as usual, inky hair pulled so tight it looks like she's had a botched face-lift. Are her grandchildren as scared of her as I am?

"Oh, Mrs. Stewart, I didn't see you there. Can I help you?"

"No, thank you. I didn't see you at the fair this weekend?"

"Oh, did you come by?" I know she did, because I hid behind the chest freezer when I saw her approaching. "We must have missed each other, what a shame. How's your meal this evening?"

"That's what I came over to tell you."

And here we go.

One of the first things Booth warned me about, was that she comes in twice a week with her husband, and every time, she finds something to complain about. The plate being too hot. The hollandaise being too thick or too thin. The clam chowder being too "clammy."

"My husband had the beef burger; he's never been one for seafood. Honestly, we live in Maine, I'll never know. I had one of the specials. The bean-hole beans. I was shocked to read that it was a *twist* on the classic, something my own grandmother made for me growing up."

Oh fuck. I almost gag at hearing the name of that dish, and also panic, because the bean-hole beans are one of our experimental specials, an ode to Maine traditions. Something we want to put on future menus, if Booth is allowed to make the changes he's been desperate to make. I suggested we test it out with the customers first. I regret that decision now, especially when my ass cheeks start to sweat as I wait for her onslaught of criticism.

Booth is going to blow a gasket when he finds out *who* ordered one.

"Imagine my surprise when it arrives, and I take my first bite..." *Here it comes.* "And it reminds me of my childhood, despite it looking nothing like the original, and the smokiness..." She smacks her lips together, as if trying to relive the flavors. "Peculiar, yet it worked so well. Give my compliments to the chef."

I think I'm drunk or dreaming. Maybe both. There's no way she is saying nice things, and there's no way...she's smiling. I didn't know her face could do that.

"Oh wow, that's so great to hear." I'm surprised I can form sentences. "I'll be sure to let Booth and the team know. Thank you."

"Good. My table is sticky though, please send someone over to clean it." And with that, she walks away.

THOSE TWO WORDS

Well, we can't win them all.

Almost robotically, I stand from my stool, calmly ask one of the bussers to wipe down Mrs. Stewart's table, and push my way through the swinging doors into the kitchen.

I keep my face neutral, despite the excitement bubbling inside. Booth spots me from across the stainless-steel pass and pauses when he sees my face.

"What? What's wrong?" he asks, placing down the sizzling pan in his hand.

"Mrs. Stewart was at table thirteen," I say.

"Oh my god, who sat her at that table? IT'S UNLUCKY!" he cries. "What did she order? Someone get me that check now. I'm going to throw up."

Simon searches through the pile of completed checks and hands him table thirteen's.

"The bean-hole beans?" Booth squeaks out, his voice pitching abnormally high. He paces around the kitchen, and I walk over to him and grab him by the shoulders.

"She..." I don't know why I'm dragging this out, other than it's fun to fuck with him.

"She what, Johanna? Oh god, someone get me a shot of vodka. No, that isn't strong enough. Just sedate me."

Deciding I've tortured him long enough, I look him dead in the eye. "Booth. She loved it. Ate it up and said word for word, 'Give my compliments to the chef.'"

He's actually crying now. His arms shoot up toward the ceiling and he lets out an almighty *whoop*, and then picks me up and spins us around the kitchen.

"Holy shit, we did it! We cracked her." He runs his hands through his hair, his face still glowing with wonderment. "This is all you, Jo. I would have never thought to have trialed it as a special first."

"It was all you. You came up with the dish and your team executed it perfectly."

The creak of hinges diverts our attention to the doorway, where we find a curious looking Patrick peering in.

"What are you two cheering about?" he asks.

"Big bro," Booth says and claps Patrick on the back once he approaches us. "I quit, because my only goal in life was to make that old bird happy."

I laugh at his dramatics, knowing damn well he isn't quitting.

Patrick's eyes meet mine, eyebrow quirked in question. "She liked it?"

With a huge grin on my face, I nod my head, and before I know it, he's wrapping me up in his arms and spinning me around too.

As we celebrate the small success together, I can only hope that whatever the outcome next month, we can get through it together.

Each day that passes, hope returns to Patrick's eyes. Every time a new customer enters the restaurant, or we beat the previous week's revenue, I see the stress stop weighing him down. We're running out of time, and even I'm shocked at how much of an improvement we've made. Will it be enough?

I know losing the restaurant would devastate him. It would gut me, but selfishly I'm more worried about what it would mean for us.

He's been open and honest with me since the moment I returned to town, and as he tucks me under his arm and kisses me on the cheek, I chastise myself for thinking the outcome of the restaurant would change things.

Because it wouldn't, right?

thirty-one
PATRICK

"It looks like a unicorn threw up in here," Graham says to my right. Pink and purple streamers are hanging from his shoulders, complimenting the gold tiara on his head.

"I'm pretty sure that's exactly what Lottie wants." I adjust the crown on my head that my daughter told me to wear; because she said I was a queen.

"Does this tutu make my butt look big?" Booth asks from the other side of the room.

"Yes," Dex says as he slides his own pink tutu up his legs, but halfway past his thighs, it splits in half and falls to the ground. "I'm sorry, I love Lottie, but this isn't going to work. I'm better off being a dinosaur."

The four of us look like some misfit boy band, but we're all too scared of Lottie to not do exactly as she says.

Giving up on the bow I've been trying to tie for the last ten minutes, I let the ribbon hang limply from the chair. I've tried my best to recreate the tea party Lottie described to me. I spent all last night gluing tiny tiaras to plastic dinosaurs, so hopefully the room screams *prehistoric fairy tale*.

Carrie is bringing Lottie over in an hour, then her friends will arrive, and chaos will commence.

I can't believe she will be five. The years have gone by way too quickly, and I wish they would slow down. It feels like yesterday a nurse put this squirming, pink thing in my arms. From the moment I held her, my universe shifted. She doesn't know it, but she came into my life when I needed her the most. I didn't realize how lost and empty I'd been until she opened those big eyes, stopped her crying, and stared up at me. From that one look, I knew I would do everything and anything for that little girl—which includes wearing a crown.

If anything, being a girl dad makes me more masculine.

We finish setting up for the party and share a look of satisfaction as we look around the room. A six-foot inflatable unicorn *and* dinosaur sit at the back of the room, both sporting tiaras. Pink, purple, and white streamers and balloons decorate the ceilings and walls, and a small tea party is set up in the middle of the room. My mom is bringing all the fixings for a classic English afternoon tea, and George is picking up the birthday cake I hired Quinn to make.

Happy that we have some time to spare, we throw ourselves on the sofas before carnage ensues. The moment my butt hits the sofa, however, there's a knock on the door.

"No way is someone here already," I groan, hauling myself to my feet.

"Tell them to scram," Graham says.

"What are you, a 1920s gangster?" I trudge my way over to the front door and swing it open a little too forcefully, prepared to turn away whoever is an hour early.

Only it's not one of Lottie's friends or parents. It's a startled-looking Jo, clad in a purple, floor-length dress.

"Oh! Nice crown." She bites her lips and tugs at one of the layers of her skirt, looking a little shy.

"Sorry, I wasn't expecting anyone yet."

"Is the party not today?"

"No, it is, but not until two."

"Shiiiii—oot. I knew I got the time wrong. I'm trying to practice not swearing around kids and I'm not doing so well. I'll come back when the party *actually* starts. Forget I was here," she says, looking cute and flustered.

Before she can walk away, I hook an arm around her waist and pull her through the open doorway, narrowly avoiding trapping the gift bag she's holding as I kick the door shut behind us.

"No, you don't," I mumble against her shoulder. "Stay, it's fine. I thought you were one of Lottie's friends' parents, and I didn't want to make small talk yet."

She wriggles her way out of my hold, but now I'm able to get a good look at her.

How her hair can look even more golden, I have no clue, but it does as it falls in loose curls down her back. Her long, lean legs might be hidden, but the tight bodice of the dress and the little bow between her cleavage have my mouth watering.

Shit, is this some new kink?

The look is finished off with a pair of Chucks, because of course. How can she look cute and sexy? Suddenly, I'm regretting the horde of children about to take over my home, because all I want to do is drag her up the stairs and peel that dress off her.

"Did you hear what I said?" She laughs, waving a hand in front of my face.

"Nope." My eyes are still glued to her chest, and I'm thinking of all the ways I want to fuck her to Sunday. It's been a week since the afternoon at the lighthouse, and once again, we've done nothing but kiss or grope each other silly in the few moments alone we can find.

Graham walks out of the living room and Jo gives him a warm smile, and for the first time since her return, he returns it.

Okay, it might not be what most people call a smile, but those who know him, know it's genuine, and it's good to see them talking again.

"Hey, Gray," she greets him.

"Jo. Nice dress. I'll take that." He takes the gift bag from her hand and turns to me with a raised brow. "Remember, this is a kids' party, Pat. Stop flirting with Sleeping Beauty and get your *guest* a drink."

"Oh, I'm, umm, Rapunzel, actually," she replies, but I'm already steering her toward the kitchen and away from the three guys currently in my living room who would enjoy nothing more than to wiggle their way into my business right now.

"What do you want?" I ask as I let go of her hand to reach inside one of the cabinets.

"Juice or water is good."

I pull two glasses from the shelf, and watch her from the corner of my eye as she stares out into my yard.

We're not broadcasting what's happening between us, yet from the looks our siblings have been giving us, I suspect they have *some* idea about what's going on.

Okay, they know.

Booth and Harriet wouldn't know the meaning of the world subtle, and when Jo's sister came to the restaurant to say goodbye a couple of days ago, she gave me a wink and whispered, *"Go get 'em, tiger,"* as she hugged me.

Walking over to where Jo is standing in front of the sink, I place our glasses on the counter and loop my arms around her waist, my chin resting on her shoulder. I love that she's always been the perfect height, and I drop my face into the crook of her neck to prove it. She tries to escape my grasp with a squeal as I nip at her skin and breathe her in, scrunching her neck to hide from my attack.

"The decorations look great. Lottie is going to lose her

mind. I can't wait to see her little face," she says, trying to catch her breath from her laughter.

There's something so special about hearing the excitement in Jo's voice when she speaks about my daughter. "She's going to lose her mind when she sees you actually came dressed as a princess."

She cranes her neck and looks up at me with wide eyes. "Please tell me I'm not the only adult dressed up in full princess getup today?"

"Okay, I won't tell you." The grimace on my face must reveal the truth.

"*Nooo*. This is mortifying. She told me at my dad's house all the girls were dressing up."

"All the girls under three feet, yes."

Shaking her head in laughter, she settles against me, and we look out into the yard. I don't have a green thumb, and I don't need to, because my mom comes by every couple of weeks to help keep it maintained. A large spruce sits in the back corner and flower beds line either side of the lawn. Purple, white, yellow, and blue flowers have begun blooming, bringing the space to life.

"I think my mom planted those white ones with your mom in mind." I feel her tense as I point to the small white buds, not quite ready to blossom yet. It's such a fleeting reaction; you'd miss it if you weren't paying attention, but I don't miss a thing when it comes to her.

"Starflower," she whispers. "Or Mayflower, as my mom called it. Her favorite. They don't flower until May."

"Wait, as in your middle name? Johanna *May* Thomas?"

"Yes, you goof," she says, her body shaking against mine. "You're telling me that after knowing me for this long, you didn't know where my middle name came from? My mom literally called me Mayflower."

"Uh, I plead the fifth? I don't know half the names of the plants out there. You'd have to ask my mom."

"Men! You're useless," she gripes and nudges me in the ribs with her elbow.

"Hey now. I taught myself to braid hair, I'm not totally useless," I argue.

"*You* taught yourself?" she asks, gaping up at me.

"Yeah, who else?"

"I don't know, your mom, sister, or Carrie?"

"Nope. All me, baby. Well, and YouTube. It's one of the few times Lottie will sit still for me."

"That's really sweet, Patrick," she says.

I tug her in closer, and from the way she brushes up against me, she can feel how hard I am. Have been since the moment she walked into my house. "I am sweet, aren't I?"

"Mm-hm, so sweet."

I turn her in my arms and push her up against the granite countertop. "Should I show you how sweet?" My lips find hers in a gentle kiss, hands diving into her hair, and running through the soft curls as my tongue runs across her lips. Her nails drag through my hair and across my scalp, sending delicious shivers across my body.

"I love it when your hair is down," I say in between kisses, combing my fingers through her golden locks.

We remain locked in each other's embrace as our mouths slowly explore each other. Her back arches as I push her further into the counter and skim my hands down her body. I gather the many layers of her dress in my hands, until my fingers find her soft, warm skin.

She shakes her head at me, like she knows this is a bad idea, but doesn't stop me as I hitch the material up around her waist. Even through my jeans and her underwear, I can feel the heat from between her thighs as I grind against her.

Gone is my sweetness as I trace along the edge of her

panties, toying back and forth with the lace, so close to where I know she's already soaked for me.

"Can you be quiet, love? We don't want anyone to walk in, do we?" A voice in my head says *yes, we do*. The thrill of someone catching us spurs me on. The tip of my pointer slips under the damp material, and I groan when I find her hot and wet.

"Yes," she rasps out, head falling against the cabinet as my finger circles her entrance.

Before we can go any further, a throat clears behind us, and we freeze.

"Any idea where I can put this cake?"

Noooo. I really wish I didn't know that voice. The idea of being caught now is a terrible, terrible idea.

I might be almost thirty-five years old, but no one wants to be caught in a compromising position with another person at their own kid's birthday party.

Not when that someone is dressed like a Disney Princess.

Especially by that *someone's* father.

thirty-two
JOHANNA

Patrick makes it ten feet across the kitchen in the blink of an eye. His crown sits lopsided on his head, and I'm sure I look like a disheveled version of Rapunzel.

His hands are raised in the air like he's been caught with them in the cookie jar. *Am I the cookie jar?* I could easily brush aside the fact we were found making out in the kitchen, but we were doing so much more than that.

Of all the people, it had to be my dad. I wish the ground would open up and swallow me whole. And from the look on my dad's face as he places the cake on the kitchen island, he's thinking the same thing. Without making eye contact with either of us, he slinks out of the room, like he was never there.

And boy, do I wish he hadn't been.

"He's going to kill me," Patrick whispers, a terrified look on his face. I shouldn't find this funny because he looks genuinely scared for his life, but he knows as well as I do that my dad wouldn't do that.

I think?

"He will not," I say as I straighten out my dress and hair.

"I should go talk to him?"

THOSE TWO WORDS

"I'm sure a conversation with my dad about how he caught you with your hands in my pants will go down well."

"*Jo*," he hisses. "This is serious."

"It really isn't." I'm just as mortified, but Patrick is acting like a scorned teenager. Before he can start to freak out anymore, we're saved by the bell. "Oh look, your guests have arrived."

I usher him to the front door, and with my head held high, go in search of my dad. I'm a grown woman, I can make out with whoever I want. Sure, I didn't plan on him finding out this way, but he was bound to find out eventually.

My dad stands in the middle of the living room with a tiny teacup in his hands. My heart threatens to fall out of my chest when I take in the room. There's no doubt in anyone's mind that Lottie is a very lucky girl, with a dad that loves her unconditionally.

"Hey, staying for a spot of tea?" I ask in a regal accent.

He looks up from the table and smiles stiffly, not the usual reaction my accent gets from him. "You've been doing that accent since you were a kid. Your mom did the exact same."

The mention of Mom has me pausing, but I shake myself out of it. Dad tries his hardest not to talk about her too often, but that's not fair. He loved her and just wants to reminisce about their life together.

"Quite the party, hey?"

He eyes the giant T-rex in the corner of the room wearily. "I'll say."

"Patrick's done an amazing job. Lottie is going to love it."

"He's a great father. A great man," my dad adds, but his tone is off, and I can see he's playing over his next words. "I just want you to be careful, Johanna. You've only been back for a couple of months, and I don't want all the progress you've made over the years to go down the drain because of some old feelings."

"Old feelings?" I ask, arms dropping to my sides from where they were toying with one of the streamers.

"Getting close to Patrick might not be the best thing for you."

"So what, I'm supposed to hide away from the world?" I snap. "You're the one who asked me to come back to town. Your plan to save the restaurant is why we're working together. Now you're worried we're too close?"

"Johanna, please," he pleads and takes a step closer as I take two steps back.

"I trusted you when you said leaving this town was best for me." Hot tears fall down my cheeks, and I swipe at them angrily. "Because you were right. But now that I'm ready to have a life again, the life I put on hold to save myself, you don't think I'm strong enough for that. If he's such a great man, why isn't he good enough for me?"

"That's not what I meant, you know—" His words are cut off with the squealing of children. I use the interruption to flee the room and don't stop until I reach the downstairs bathroom and lock myself in there.

Grabbing hold of the cold porcelain sink, I breathe in through my nose, ignoring the knocks on the other side of the door until I hear my dad walk away. I worry that my purse is in the kitchen where my medication is, but this doesn't feel like panic. There's no tightness in my chest or tingling in my fingers.

Tears still cling to my eyes, but what I'm feeling is anger.

Anger at how anxiety dictated so much of my life for so long, and now that I have a hold of it—learned to live with it—people still think I'm going to shatter with the tiniest amount of pressure. I love my dad, and while leaving Sutton Bay wasn't my idea at first, I know it was the best thing for me. He was the one who saw me at my lowest, day after day, and I know it killed him to see me like that.

So he did the only thing he could do to help. He told me to leave.

It hurts to think that my dad has so little faith in what I can handle. I know it comes from a place of love, but I wish he didn't still see me as that same lost girl from six years ago. I'm the same but not. I'm stronger, more resilient. I know my mind well, can pick up on the signs of a panic attack now, or know when I need to take a step back and listen to what my body is telling me.

I just wish he could see that.

It's not that I want to hide the truth behind my anxieties from Patrick, because he's one of the few people who doesn't look at me like I'm broken and fragile. It's more about finding the right time. We've barely seen each other the last couple of weeks, and we're either in the company of others or end up getting lost in one another.

Patrick makes me feel brave, like there's nothing to be ashamed about. Rationally, I know there isn't, but I've spent years hearing judgmental comments. Questions as to why I don't want to join people for drinks. People whispering behind my back after taking a few days off work following a panic attack or depressive episode.

The things that once had the ability to cripple me, now bring me comfort and joy. Small reminders of my mom. Overhearing people around town talk about Ted. Some are sad and some are happy, but it lets me know that they will always be with me.

Being back in town has also opened my eyes to something else.

My love for Patrick Sadler might have been tested by time and distance, but it never wavered.

The love I have for him has changed over time. From sweet childhood love to something new and scary, to a love I felt he was close to returning. All the different types of love I've had for him have built the foundations for the love I feel today.

A limitless type of love.

It's not some big revelation that I love him, but during our time apart, it was too painful to admit it to myself. A bitter reminder of what could have been. As cliché as it sounds, distance does make the heart grow fonder.

We've said we would give this a go, take our time, but I'm done biding my time. He needs to know I'm all in, and I only hope he feels the same.

Once I'm calmer, the anger having sizzled out, I look up to check my reflection. My hair is mussed from Patrick's hands, but my makeup is still intact, and my eyes aren't as puffy as they feel. I smile at myself in the mirror, despite the whirl of emotions running riot in my mind. After a few more deep breaths, I step out into the hallway.

And run right into Carrie.

"Oh my god, I'm so sorry," she rushes out, catching hold of me to stop me from tumbling backward.

"No, no. I wasn't looking where I was going." We stand there awkwardly, and while I have zero issues with her, we've never really spoken.

"You're all good. I was coming to check on you, actually."

Say what?

"Me?" I ask in surprise.

"Yeah, I was in the dining room when you and your dad were, umm, talking." She must catch the grimace I try to hide, because of all the people to overhear, it had to be her. "I swear I wasn't trying to eavesdrop. I was behind the gift table trying to hide some things, when you came in. I was going to make myself known, but it...I didn't want to interrupt."

"I'm so sorry you had to hear all of that." I sense this is just as embarrassing for her as it is for me. "That was not the sort of thing we should have been discussing at a kid's birthday party."

"Pfft, you should see the arguments my family has at gatherings," she jokes with a flick of her wrist. Her smile softens and she gently pulls me toward the laundry room. "Listen, I have no idea what happened between you and Patrick, and I'm not trying to pry. I suspect he's told you that there has never, and I mean *never* been anything romantic between us. Strictly co-parents and friends. He's a great guy and the best dad for Lottie."

"Oh, that's really not necessary. Me and him, we're not—" Carrie raises her eyebrows at me, the way that moms do, and I stop talking.

"I didn't know him before we got pregnant with Lottie. I know he loves being a dad and managing the restaurant, but from what his friends and family have told me, he's not the same guy he once was. Like I said, I wouldn't know what changed, but I think I do now. It's like someone has flipped a switch and he's finally letting himself be truly happy. I see what was missing now. The Patrick I knew last year, compared to today, is so different, but in the best way. In case I'm not being clear, it's you, Jo. You being in his life again is what changed that."

"I-I literally have no idea what to say." I laugh nervously.

"You don't have to say anything, but I'm glad we had this talk. If you'll excuse me, I need to go and stop a rabble of children from destroying this house." She squeezes my shoulder before heading toward the party but stops and turns when she reaches the end of the hallway.

"I also think you guys are idiots if you let this pass you by," she says with a wink.

Well great. Now I want to be her friend.

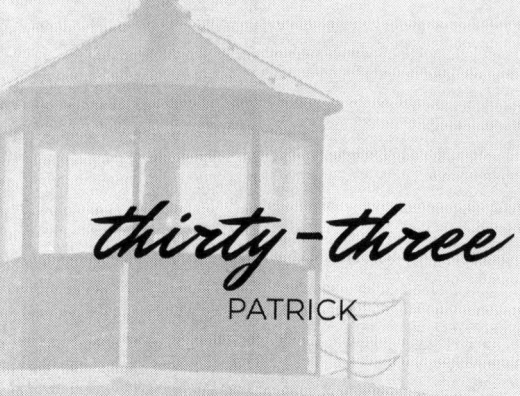

thirty-three
PATRICK

"Happy birthday to you, happy birthday, dear Lottie, happy birthday to you!"

A chorus of people sing to my daughter as she stands in front of a cake bigger than her head. With her hands clasped together under her chin and the widest smile on her face, she looks around the room at all the people here to celebrate her.

And in classic Lottie fashion, she is eating it up.

Carrie and I are on either side of her, and I bend down to whisper in her ear, "Make a wish, Lottie."

She takes a deep breath before blowing out her candles with gusto, triggering a round of cheers around us.

We cut the cake, eat food, and play party games, before people slowly head home. As the last of Lottie's friends waves goodbye, my mom pops up next to me at the front door.

"Hey, Lottie, how about a sleepover at Grandma's tonight?" she asks, looking at Lottie, who is leaning against my leg.

"Ohhhh *yesyesyesyes*. Please, Daddy?" Lottie begs beside me, hands pressed together in prayer. Monday is technically her birthday, so I don't mind her staying out tonight. But I still feel guilty, especially since my mom has helped so much recently. She's usually at Carrie's on Saturdays, but we decided it would be easier for her to sleep here tonight after the party.

"Mom, you had her a couple of weekends ago."

"Exactly. It's been too long since she's stayed with me. Don't keep my grandbaby away from me."

"Only if you're sure. She is high on sugar and life, so good luck to you."

"Yes! Best day ever!" Lottie cheers and darts to the kitchen where my brothers and Jo are tidying up. Not before shouting, "I'm high!" at the top of her lungs. *Yeah,* Carrie is not going to be impressed about that one.

"Thanks, Mom. I love her, but I'm exhausted and my ears are still ringing from all the screaming."

"My pleasure." She starts packing one of Lottie's backpacks with a pair of shoes and a raincoat. "Now that you have a free evening, why don't you ask Jo to stay for a while."

Of course there's an ulterior motive.

"I'm sure she has better things to do tonight." Though I secretly hope she doesn't.

Having her here with me today, among our family and friends, has been amazing, and I know Lottie loved having her here. Her scream echoed through the house when she saw Jo's outfit and dragged her around the party telling all her classmates that her best friend is a real-life princess.

"You won't know unless you ask." She shoves me toward the kitchen with way too much strength for a woman her size. "Go and save her from your brothers."

Squinting my eyes at her suspiciously, I plant my feet firmly on the ground. "What are you up to?"

"Patrick, I have no idea what you're talking about..." *There's always a but.* "But, I think Jo and her dad had a little falling out earlier. She's bound to be a little down now that Harriet has left town too. She could use a friend, don't you think?"

I look at her in question, but she just shrugs, and I take note to ask Jo about this. There was a little tension between them, but I guessed it was embarrassment about her dad walking in on us. I don't bother arguing with my mom, because some time alone, in an actual house, rather than a bar or the bench of my truck, would be nice. I don't mean for sex, either, but spending time together like we used to.

Okay, and potentially some sex.

That afternoon in my truck was like nothing in my life. We were a little tipsy and nervous during our first time together, and even though it was years ago, our bodies remembered each other. I would have waited a lifetime to experience that with her again, but I'm fucking grateful I didn't have to.

My mom snaps me out of my thoughts with a light tap on my cheek.

"Sweetheart, that look you have right now says enough. Go, kick your brothers out, and catch up." She heads upstairs but shouts her next words over her shoulder. "Or whatever it is you kids do these days."

Shaking my head in laughter, I walk into the kitchen, and the sight that greets me has the breath catching in my throat.

The radio is blasting, bubbles float around the room, and Jo is spinning Lottie around in circles.

My heart stalls, and when it restarts, it threatens to burst out of my chest from how much adoration it's brimming with. I rub at the aching spot as I watch Jo beam down at Lottie, who is making up the lyrics to the song with a huge grin on her face.

Graham and Booth have ditched the dishes and are blowing bubbles at the girls as they twirl around the room, still in their princess dresses.

It's chaos, but it's my chaos. And with Jo standing in the middle of it, chaos has never felt so blissful.

"Daddy, look, I'm dancing," Lottie shouts over the music.

"Wow, look at my pretty girls." The words are out before I even understand the meaning behind them. But they don't feel

THOSE TWO WORDS

wrong. They feel so fucking right. These are *my girls* and it's about time Jo knew it.

Jo looks over at me, like she can't believe her ears. She glances over at my brothers, but they don't pay us any mind as I walk over to where they're spinning around in circles.

I don't care what anyone thinks.

She is my girl.

As I approach them, Booth cuts in front of me, bows gallantly at Lottie, and lays a cluster of bubbles on her nose. "Can I have this dance, milady?" Lottie giggles, and before she can reply, Booth is scooping her up and spinning her around the room with a delighted squeal. He sends me a wink over Lottie's head, and I know exactly what he's up to. I've been raised in a family of meddlers. Though, for once, I appreciate the scheming.

"I guess you're stuck with me?" I hold my hand out to Jo.

"You dance?" she asks skeptically, as she takes my hand. I pull her into me, until there's hardly any space between us.

"Nope, so you might need to take the lead." She slides her hands behind my neck and locks her fingers together. I settle mine at the small of her back and we sway with the sound of the music. When the song changes to "Only Love" by Ben Howard, I notice that it's just us left in the kitchen.

I lay a chaste kiss to the crown of her head, before resting my cheek against it. She plays with the hair at my nape as we move with the music. There's no rhythm to our movements, we create our own.

"Stay here tonight," I murmur into her hair.

"What about Lottie?"

"She's sleeping at my mom's. Stay with me."

"M'kay," she says, voice muffled as she nuzzles into my chest.

"Dad—Oh, he is your prince," Lottie abruptly announces.

"Can you stop dancing though, because I found another present," she demands and bounces out of the room.

Cockblocked by my own daughter.

Jo laughs when I steal a quick kiss and pull her behind me. We follow where Lottie has disappeared into the living room and find her grinning up at us like the Cheshire Cat and holding a purple, glittery gift bag.

"Look, another! Can I open it?" she asks.

"Sure. I think that one is from JoJo," I tell her.

She gasps and runs over to Jo, hugging her legs tightly and thanking her repeatedly. Jo smiles at her and laughs, stroking the back of her head.

"You're welcome. But you've got to open it first, silly."

We all sit on the floor as Lottie tears through the tissue paper and gift wrap. A gasp bursts from her lips as she pulls out a rectangular box. "A puzzle!"

I peer over Lottie's shoulder to see a children's fifty-piece puzzle set of the animal kingdom. I look at Jo, who looks just as excited as my daughter. And there comes the ache in my chest again. I've accepted it's a permanent fixture wherever these two are involved.

I think Jo and I were a few years older than Lottie when we did our first puzzle together, and seeing her share something so sentimental with my daughter, leaves me speechless.

An hour later, we're sitting on my sofa together, after everyone has finally left.

Lottie got a bit upset about leaving—I think the sugar high was ending—because she wanted to take all her gifts to my mom's, but I knew they'd get lost or damaged. To keep the peace, I said she could take one and when she picked her new puzzle, I didn't miss the joy on Jo's face. Booth, on the other hand, was devastated she didn't pick the Nerf gun he bought her—the same gun I now have hidden in my room.

It took some effort to kick my brothers out, who took their sweet ass time leaving. Booth said he wanted to help "set the mood," and Graham started talking about safe sex, reminding me it's too soon for oopsie baby number two. They finished tidying up, and then I all but shoved them out of the door.

And now we're alone at last.

Jo's feet are in my lap as we share a bottle of wine and slice of birthday cake. *The Office* is playing in the background, but we haven't been paying much attention to the TV. We're doing something we've never done before—talking about our lives during our time apart. She tells me about the job she had in Tennessee and all the different bars she went to see Harriet perform in. She asks what Lottie was like as a baby and anything she missed about my siblings. The sting I expect to feel hearing about her life without me can't be found, and I don't see the same sadness in her eyes when I talk about Lottie as a baby.

I asked her about her dad, thinking back to my mom's words earlier, but she shrugged it off and changed the subject. I'll let it rest for now, but I hope she'll speak about it later.

She's sprawled out across from me, with a blanket draped over her legs, now in a new dress, thanks to the change of clothes she brought with her. The short dress that's decorated with little white flowers is definitely an improvement, because now her legs are on display. I'm a simple man. Her hair is tied up and the glowing heat from the fire has turned her cheeks a rosy color. It's mostly embers now, but she begged for a cozy night in front of the fire, so that's what she got.

"Thanks for inviting me today," she says, and a small moan escapes her as I press down on the arch of her foot. That little noise does nothing to help the hard-on I've been trying to suppress for the last hour. I'm still in my clothes from the party —sans crown—and I can't wait to get out of this dress shirt. And hopefully get Johanna out of that little dress. I'm grateful she's no longer in the ballgown, because it was getting weird every time one of my brothers caught me checking her out. Even Dex picked up on it, asking me if it was even Lottie's idea to have a princess-themed party.

"I'm glad you came, though it was Lottie who invited you. My mom texted before and said she's already started the puzzle and put up a fight when she had to go to sleep. *Thanks for that.*" Sarcasm laces my tone.

"Oh god, she's going to become obsessed like us." She chuckles.

"Let's hope she's not like you and loses the pieces."

"That puzzle still haunts me to this day. Nine days it took for me to finish that, Patrick. *Nine. Days.* And it came with one piece missing. I was ready to write a strongly worded letter to the manufacturer." She's so cute when she gets angry, her nose crinkles and her arms fly around as she continues to express her outrage over the *mysterious* missing puzzle piece. When she continues to rant, I can't suppress my laughter for much longer.

She tries to pull her feet away, but I tighten my hold.

"It's not funny, and you teased me about it for weeks. You even gave my dad the idea about hanging the dumb thing up in the hallway. It's like you..."

Her eyes widen, and her head turns to look at me like she's got a leading role in *The Exorcist.*

"You," she whispers and raises a pointed finger at me. "And you can't plead the fifth this time."

"I want to speak to my lawyer!" I shout as she throws herself at me. Her hands aim for my throat, murder shining in her eyes.

"I can't believe you! What did you do with it?" she cries. I trap her wrists in one hand to stop her attempt at murdering me, and with one quick buck of my hips, I flip us over until she's lying beneath me. My hand locks her wrists together so they're high above her head.

I didn't think this through, because my cock is now nestled between her thighs and her breasts are pushed upward toward me, giving me the perfect view down her dress.

"I stole it when you weren't looking, and I must have lost it. I'm sorry." I try to keep my face straight, hoping she doesn't see through the lie. "I'm sorry, I couldn't keep it from you any longer. I've been carrying that guilt around for almost two decades."

"I hate you." She pouts.

"Liar." The humor in my tone is gone and my voice comes out all thick now. I trace the bridge of her nose with the tip of mine, leaving kisses in my path. "Do you know how I know?"

She shakes her head.

"Because. If I reached between your legs right now, I'd find your pussy dripping wet." I pepper kisses across her jaw and neck, sucking the pulse point below her ear. My mouth moves lower, and I lick a line across her delicate collarbone, which has her writhing and moaning beneath me.

As much as I want to test my theory, I promised myself when I do this again, it would be somewhere I can worship her body properly.

I let go of her hands and lift myself off her. She looks up at me in a lust-filled daze. Without a word, I stand, turn off the TV, and make sure the fire is completely out.

When I return to where she's still lying on the sofa, chest rising and falling in quick succession, I reach down, take her hand, and pull her up until she's standing.

"C'mon, love. Let me take you to bed."

thirty-four
JOHANNA

We're silent as Patrick leads us up the stairs.

I take in his strong back stretching his dress shirt, the way his hair curls at his nape, and how snug his pants fit over his ass. Patrick in jeans is delicious, but it's a treat to see him in a pair of slacks.

The nervous energy building within me doesn't make sense. It's not like we haven't had sex before, so why does this feel different?

When his eyes meet mine over his shoulder, they're darker, like a forest bathed in starlight. It's not the heat or yearning that has me following him without question. It's the certainty. He looks at me like he's never been so sure of anything in his life.

We enter his bedroom, and I'm glad to be here under different circumstances this time so I can take it in properly. Dark woods mixed with neutral tones; like the rest of his home, it's masculine and intimate. Like the man himself. His dresser is decorated with framed pictures of him and his family over the years, an old watch sits on the side, and a small chair in the corner of the room.

I stand in the middle of the hardwood floor, toying with the hem of my dress as he flicks on a bedside lamp, casting the room in a warm glow. He walks up behind me, wraps his arms around my waist, and pulls me close. "What's wrong? You haven't said a word since we left the sofa."

"Nothing," I reply.

"C'mon Jo, I know you. I can feel something is wrong." He places a gentle kiss at the juncture between my neck and shoulder.

I sigh and try to pull away, but he tightens his hold. "I'm nervous, okay. Don't ask me why, it's my brain being annoying and overthinking everything."

"I like your brain." He lays a kiss on my temple. "I like everything about you. But there's nothing to be nervous about, it's me."

See, that's the problem. It's the fact that it's *him* that I'm feeling all nervous.

"We don't have to do anything, that's not why I asked you to stay." He loosens his hold, but I spin in his arms, stopping him.

"It's not like that. I want to, you know..." I gesture to the bed.

He quirks a brow. "Don't go shy on me now. What is it you want?" His hand creeps down the front of my dress until he reaches the hem but doesn't make another move. "I'd really like to take you to bed. Show you how much I like *everything* about you. But I need to hear you say it."

Something about his tone and the hungry look in his eyes has all my self-doubt vanishing. So without hesitation, I replace his hands with mine, pull my dress over my head, and throw it to the side. "Fuck me, Patrick. I want you to fuck me."

There go my nerves, I guess.

His gaze roams my body, thumb skimming across his bottom lip as he takes in the dark green lingerie set I picked out this morning. The color reminded me of his eyes, and from the heat in them, he knows it.

"I need you to get on the bed right now." The fervor in his

tone sends goose bumps across every inch of my body. I love it when his voice gets gritty like that, not hesitating to tell me what to do. And because I love to please him, I'm already bolting to the bed, his chuckle following behind me.

A scent I only know as Patrick floats toward me as I scramble on top of the comforter. I turn and sit in the middle of the king-size bed, legs stretched out and hands propped up behind me, waiting for his next move. He prowls toward me and the butterflies deep in my belly go berserk. When he crooks a finger, beckoning me closer, they take flight and I feel like I could float away with them, but he keeps me grounded. Moving to my hands and knees, I crawl toward him, not breaking eye contact. My heart beats wildly in my chest when his hungry eyes track me until I'm kneeling in front of him.

He brings his hand down to cup my cheek. "Do you remember what you said in my truck?"

It takes me a second to remember, but when I do, heat rushes over me. "That I want to suck your cock?"

"Mm-hm," he hums as he continues to stroke my cheek tenderly. "You wanted it so badly, didn't you? You were desperate to wrap your lips around me. And I always want to give you what you want."

My eyes drop to the growing bulge in his pants, my mouth watering at the thought of tasting him, pleasuring him that way.

"You're still dressed," I point out.

At my words, he starts unbuttoning his shirt slowly, revealing his hard chest, the *v* of his abs, and that dark smattering of hair on his chest and stomach. Without waiting for his next command, I lower my head, and run my tongue across the grooves between his abs. He allows me a few moments, before he's threading his hands through the bun on my head and pulling me off him.

"Let your hair down and then take my cock out, Johanna."

His irises glow like a wildfire, but other than the steady rise and fall of his chest, he's motionless.

Like clockwork, his hands weave their way into my hair the moment I pull it free from its elastic and it tumbles down my back.

"You have no idea what seeing you like this does to me," he says, eyes following his hands as they glide through the long strands.

I think I do, especially when I take in the view in front of me and reach for his pants.

I try to quell the shaking in my fingers as I slowly flick the button and lower the zip. Any nerves I had have disappeared now. My body only vibrates with desirous anticipation. He watches me acutely as I drag down his pants and black briefs until they're past his ass. It's only when his cock springs free and bounces off his stomach that our gazes break and drop between us. Not wanting to wait, I lean forward and sweep my tongue over the blunt head of him, groaning when the taste of him bursts across my tongue. He hisses as I explore him, the grip he has on my hair tightening with every pass of my tongue.

I look up to find his heavy eyes trained on me.

"I love it when you look at me like that."

"Like what?" I ask, but my attention has drifted back to his length. It curves upward slightly toward his stomach and a vein runs along the underside from base to tip. Lowering his hand, he strokes himself with slow, hard pulls; I'm transfixed with the way the muscles in his forearm ripple with every twist and turn.

"Like your thoughts are just as dirty and desperate as mine."

"They are," I say with a smirk.

"Good. So you know I want you to open that pretty little mouth."

"Jesus, Patrick," I breathe out. My clit throbs at his

commanding words. Even through my panties, I can feel the evidence of my arousal soaking my thighs.

Opening my mouth wide is all the signal he needs. With his hand at the base, he traces and taps my lips with the tip of his cock. A groan vibrates deep in his chest as he slowly pushes past my lips and glides across my tongue.

"I knew this mouth would look perfect wrapped around me," he grits out.

This right here might be the sexiest Patrick has ever looked. Fully in control, eyes heavy with want, and mouth parted in awe. I might be the one on my knees, but the look he gives me makes me feel like I'm the one being worshipped.

Resting his hand on my neck, his thumb strokes the base of my throat encouragingly as he flexes his hips, pumping into me with shallow thrusts.

"Can you take more?"

I hum around him and nod. The muscles of his abdomen flex as he increases his tempo. When he hits the back of my throat, his words of praise feed my enthusiasm. *Fuck, like that. Look at you. You feel so good.* If I wasn't already addicted to him, I would be now. From the taste of him and the sounds of satisfaction I'm drawing from him. All for me. Only for me. My eyes are glued to him, watching to see his reaction as I take him as far as I can.

"You love it when I fuck your mouth, don't you baby?" He enunciates each word, thrusting deeper at the end.

When I gag and he eases back, I shake my head in protest. Grabbing his hips, I pull him back into my mouth and take over. It's as if my one purpose is to bring him pleasure. My palms run up and down his thighs, and I revel in the feel of his strong muscles.

"*Shit,* Jo. You like that, don't you? Choking on my cock like a greedy girl?" The strain and pleasure in his voice spur me on. A salty taste hits my tongue, and I know he's close. But as his thrusts lose their rhythm and his stomach pulls taut with restraint, he doesn't listen to my mewls of protest when he drags me off him again.

He tries to steady his breathing as his hand strokes at my throat. "As much as I want to watch you swallow down my cum, I need to come in that tight, little pussy again. Is that okay?"

This man. How can he be so considerate and assertive in the same breath?

"Yes please."

With a breathy laugh, he jerks his head toward the headboard. "Move up the bed for me and lie back. I think it's time we did this indoors."

"I don't know, I liked it in your truck." I fall on my butt and shuffle backward to settle against the plump pillows, eyeing his every movement as he shucks off his unbuttoned shirt and his pants drop to the floor, revealing him in all his glory. I bask in the knowledge that right now, I have him like this. *He's mine.* And he's stunning. Broad and strong, flexing in all the right places, but it's everything that makes up him—inside and out—that's the real beauty.

He climbs onto the bed and crawls over to me.

"You like the thought of being caught?" he asks, running his hands up my legs.

I bite my lip and think about how to answer that. Do I want someone to find us? The thrill of it excites me, knowing there's a chance someone could catch us at any moment, doing filthy things to one another. *So long as it's not our parents.*

His eyes blaze as I slowly nod at him in response.

"I'm filing that away for another day. For now, I want to show you how you deserve to be treated." Never have I felt so cherished by a man or had someone look at me the way Patrick does, and he's hardly touched me yet.

I prop up on my elbow, and with my other hand, I pull him down until his lips meet mine. The words I want to say are right on the tip of my tongue. My very essence threatens to explode to say those words. Perhaps he can taste them on this kiss. It would be so easy to declare my love for him right here, but we promised we wouldn't rush this, and I know there's more to be spoken before we take that step.

With the gentlest of touches, he kisses me slowly and sensually, rids me of my bra and panties, until we're both completely bare. Every inch of my skin buzzes as he covers my body with his. We explore the planes of each other's bodies lazily. I'm tracing the ripple of muscles along his back but get distracted when he lowers his head and draws my nipple into his mouth. When he traps the sensitive bud between his teeth and bites down, a garbled cry leaves me and I arch off the mattress.

We build ourselves up higher with every stroke of our tongue, scrape of our teeth, and brush of our skin.

He places the softest kisses on my nose, chin, and forehead. Each brush of his lips across my glowing skin is gentler than the last. He isn't just showing me how I deserve to be treated, he's showing me what it would feel like to be loved by him.

Perhaps it is possible.

He pulls back and peers down at me, like he's searching for something. I wonder what he sees when he looks at me. What does he think? What does he want? *Why* does he want me?

Can he see what this moment means to me? How much *he* means to me?

"I have always loved your freckles." He places one final kiss on the bridge of my nose. At his words, I realize he wasn't just kissing my face, he was kissing each freckle. My heart propels in my chest at the sweet gesture, but when he murmurs his next words so softly and with a hint of nervousness I thought only I carried, my heart might need jump-starting.

"Can I make love to you, Johanna?"

This moment *is* different.

THOSE TWO WORDS

We've been waiting for the pendulum to stop swinging so we can finally settle. Settle and bathe in the raw need and desire that grows between us with each day, hour, and minute we're together.

"Please. I've waited so long," I whisper against his lips.

"I know, love. I know." There's a sadness in his words that makes my chest ache.

His lips trail my body, leaving hot kisses as he moves lower. One between my breasts, on my ribs, above my belly button. Lower and lower. He places a tender kiss where I'm wet and aching for him. The teasing, gentle kisses are too much and I'm about to beg him to give me more, but before I can speak, a sharp cry leaves me as his tenderness is replaced with carnal need.

Patrick buries his face into my pussy without warning and I bow off the mattress. My hands fall to the top of his head, pushing and pulling his head, the feeling of his tongue is too much and not enough.

He spreads me wider, alternating between long licks to my lips and flicks of his tongue against my clit. It takes almost no time at all before that telltale sign starts low in my belly. My legs tremble, the need to close them so strong, but the firm grip he has stops them.

"Keep these open, baby, don't hide from me."

"Patrick. Oh, oh, I'm going to come, oh my go—" The words are ripped from my throat when Patrick sucks my clit into his mouth and my orgasm racks my body.

My entire body shakes with the aftermath of what must be the most intoxicating orgasm of my life. But Patrick doesn't give me any time to recover, and when he kisses his way up my body and the head of his cock nudges at my entrance, I'm ready for him.

We lock eyes as he enters me, his movements painstakingly slow. His pupils dilate as he works his way in, gliding easily inside with how wet I am. Despite the fullness and small bite of pain, I don't dare blink, needing to savor all of his reactions, and when he's seated fully, pelvis kissing mine, we relax.

It's utter euphoria, even as we lie there motionless, but I need more. I need him or I'll be convinced this is all a dream.

Gliding my hands up his strong shoulders, muscles quivering at my touch, I dot kisses along the underside of his jaw. "Give me more, Patrick. Give me everything."

"That's all I've ever wanted to give you."

Grabbing the backs of my thighs, he pushes my legs toward my chest.

He pulls himself out of me carefully, but I know the slam home won't be gentle. There's no controlling my loud cry of pleasure as he snaps his hips forward. Not a second later, and he's doing it again. And again. And again. Each thrust more punishing than the last. I cling to his shoulders, nails scraping down his spine as my eyes roll back from how deep he's hitting me. I can hardly catch my breath with how he pistons into me, rotating his hips each time to hit that sweet spot.

Pleasure governs my body. The sounds I make as he takes and takes and takes from my body in the most exquisite way, are like nothing I've ever heard.

Patrick buries his face into my neck, panting with each thrust.

This feels different from our first time together. So different from that afternoon in his truck. Both were amazing, but *this*, this moment is stirring something new between us, something unspoken.

"I've missed this. I've missed you," he confesses into my skin.

"I've missed you too. So much. I'm-I'm..." I don't know what I'm trying to say, but his thrusts become frenzied, and he pulls out almost completely to look down at me, a frantic look in his eyes.

"You're what? Say it, love. Please." His tone is desperate, and I don't know if it's because we're so close, but before I can respond, he's slamming back into me, and just as his pelvis grinds into my swollen clit, already so sensitive from my earlier orgasm, I detonate.

I explode with bliss. Pleasure rolls through me wave after wave. I'm washed with the tide of ecstasy.

All I feel is him.

All I see is him.

All I need is him.

Patrick pistons into me as my orgasm ripples through every cell of my body, like my broken and raspy cries are what drives him wilder. With one last thrust, his body tenses as he groans into my neck. Hot ropes of cum fill me, the feel of it so dirty and erotic.

There's no knowing where I end and he begins as we cling to each other. Hip to hip, chest to chest, heart to heart. The erratic beating of them echoes off one another, like our hearts are speaking their own language.

I know what mine would be saying if it could talk.

Will you keep me and love me?

Patrick lets out a deep breath before he slowly pulls out of me and sits back on his knees, his palms stroking my thighs as he settles my trembling legs onto the comforter. Brushing his lips across my belly, he rises off the bed and walks to the bathroom.

Throwing my arm across my face, I wait to recover from a serious case of jelly legs. Words do no justice to what I just experienced. It was perfect. But I can't shake the feeling that I said or did something wrong when hurt flashed across his features as he begged me to *say it*.

Surely he wasn't begging me to say the words I'm worried are too early to be shared.

My worry disappears when he returns with a washcloth in

hand and wipes between my legs with such tenderheartedness. He helps me from the bed and leads me to the bathroom. I expect his silent care to stop once I'm finished in the bathroom, but that's stupid of me to think. This is Patrick. He sweeps me off my feet and carries me to bed, like I'm suddenly incapable of walking.

"Need you close," he mumbles, answering my unvoiced protests. He keeps me cradled in his arms and settles us back in bed. There's not an inch of skin that isn't touching, and with one firm hand at the base of my spine and the other behind my head, I know he's not going to let me go any time soon.

The feel of his heart slowing in tempo calms my own. I softly run my hands over his chest, tracing odd shapes and patterns across his skin.

When I look up, he's breathing deeply, sleep finding him easily. I kiss the scar on his chin and take in his peaceful expression. I'd give anything to make sure that this beautiful man remains mine, and I send out silent prayers to anyone who's listening, that he does.

I settle my head against his chest and shut my eyes. It's only as my mind starts to drift that I hear a soft whisper. Maybe I'm dreaming, but I swear I hear him utter, "Please be mine."

Sleep pulls me under, but my unconscious mind wants to scream that I am.

That, *I'm yours.*

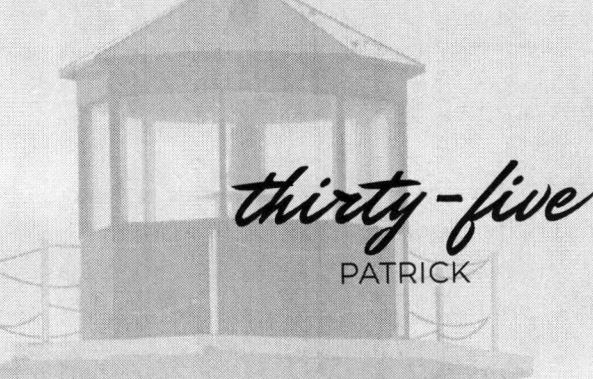

thirty-five
PATRICK

Jo waves at me through the window of her car as she pulls away from my house, the smile that's been on my face all day not faltering. And it stays there well after her headlights disappear into the night.

We've fallen into a routine over the last two weeks, spending time at one another's places and making up for lost time. Last night she came over after her shift and spent the night, though, we didn't do much sleeping.

I'll come to regret that decision later, but right now, I feel on top of the fucking world. Things between us aren't good. They're not great. They're unbelievable.

As much as I love my daughter wholly, I crave the nights I get to be alone with Jo. Finding new ways to bring her pleasure and explore each other's bodies. Cooking her dinner, driving out to the lighthouse to make out like horny teenagers, and lazing around completing puzzles together.

We can't get enough of each other. On the days I don't see her, I call her. If I can't call her, I look at pictures of her that I've snapped on my phone. Anything for a glimpse of her, needing my hit of her even in the tiniest of quantities. That's why we've probably only had two days in total where we haven't seen each other. She seems just as addicted and helpless as I am.

If we're not in the privacy of our own homes, we're working our asses off at the restaurant.

As a last-ditch effort to bring in new customers, we offered a "flatlandah's only" discount. Now that May is here, the discount was a great success, with tourists flocking in from all over the place. Right now, ignorance is bliss, because we haven't really spoken about what happens if the outcome isn't what we want to hear.

I haven't heard her say those two words that I begged her to say after Lottie's birthday party. I was a depraved man, like I would die if I didn't hear her say them.

We also haven't spoken about a date that creeps closer and is a hard day for all of us. Next Wednesday is the six-year anniversary of my dad's passing. A day that comes around too quickly.

It's also a reminder that it's been almost six years since Jo left Sutton Bay.

I won't break my promise to be patient with her, but it's now more than ever that I need to know what happened. Why she left. *Why she left me.*

I want to talk to her about my dad, her mom, to share memories of our childhood together. But I still sense an air of restlessness around her when they're mentioned, so I don't push the topic. And as much as I want to, I don't invite her to family dinner at my mom's, something we've done every year on his anniversary—eating my dad's favorite meals and watching his favorite films.

Shutting the front door, I turn, and silence greets me. My house always feels destitute when Lottie isn't here singing or dancing her way around the place, like the little tornado she is. It feels even more barren when it's void of her and Jo. Even the walls look sadder now, not having Jo's laughter bouncing off them.

Bringing the heels of my hands to my eyes, I rub the building pressure away.

I walk into the kitchen to tidy up the dishes from dinner. Jo calls it dinner, but it was a charcuterie board made up of whatever she could scrounge from my pantry. I reach for the stack of Post-it notes by the fridge to write myself a reminder to always have cheese stocked for her.

When I glance down at the small stack of papers, writing on the top note has my hand freezing where it's reaching for it.

You make me happy.

I read the words over and over. *You make me happy.* Simple words to most, but not to me. *Not to us.* Because those words are the exact four that I left on the pillow after our first night together.

Everything fell apart after that morning, and I convinced myself she never saw it or that I never actually wrote it.

Seeing them written in her neat handwriting, the ink still fresh, tells me she did.

I've always wanted to make her happy. As happy as she's made me most of my life. Jo's happiness is intrinsic to my own, and as I trace the cursive words, I wonder if she even knows how effortlessly she does it.

A buzzing sounds from the other side of the kitchen, my screen lighting up with an incoming call. Walking over to where it's sitting, I see George's name.

"Hey, George," I greet. I balance the phone between my ear and shoulder and continue tidying the kitchen.

"Hey, Pat, how are things?" he asks.

"They're good, busy as always, can't complain though. Everything okay?"

"Yeah, yeah." There's a long pause before he clears his throat and speaks again. "Listen, umm, I've been trying to get a hold of Jo, but she's not answering her phone. Have you spoken to her today?"

Does he know she was here? Jo still hasn't spoken about what went on between her dad and her, but to avoid his calls seems so unlike her.

"Yeah, she was actually here tonight." I'm not about to lie to him about where his daughter is, but also, we're grown adults. "She left about fifteen minutes ago."

"Oh. And she's okay?"

"She's great. Tired like me, but good. Is there something going on, George?"

"I worry about her, is all. Doesn't matter how old your little girl is, you'll always worry."

"I know the feeling." I sit down on one of the chairs at the dining table, abandoning the dishes.

"I've worried about her over the years, more so than I should, but I can't help it. She's...she's been through a lot." I can hear the tiredness in his voice as he sighs through the phone. "I didn't know how to help or if I ever did. Her leaving was hard on us all, for you especially. I always thought it was the best thing for her, but now I worry that I pushed her away when maybe she needed me the most. Needed the people of this town the most."

It takes a second for his words to sink in, and I question what I even heard. "Why would you be the one to push her away?"

The silence that follows feels like it lasts eons, rather than minutes. "I don't—Patrick, Jo never left town willingly. I wish she had, but she fought me on it for weeks. You didn't know that?"

My mouth goes dry. My mind runs through a thousand scenarios as to why she left, none making sense.

THOSE TWO WORDS

It feels like my mouth is stuffed with cotton, but I manage to get my words out. "No. I thought she just...*left*."

"Listen, son. I'm not here to tell Jo's side of the story, that's not my place, only hers. I don't want you jumping to any conclusions about why she left, and I know that's hard, but trust me. Sometimes we reach our limit. She would have stayed here had her sister and I not begged, and I mean *begged* for her to get on that flight. She sees it now, but back then, she was barely keeping her head up. I worry she would have drowned had she stayed.

"I never expected her to stay away for so long, to make a life out there, but it seemed to work for her. When I asked her to come home and work at the restaurant, I prepared myself for her to turn the offer down. Having her here has been amazing, don't get me wrong, but I also worried she wasn't ready to come home yet, that all her hard work would unravel. That the town and its people would remind her of those hard days. That was stupid of me to presume, because if I know anything about Johanna, it's that she doesn't do anything without thinking it through. It took time, but she knew what she was doing out in Tennessee, and she knows what she's doing now."

There's a lot to dissect. The sucker punch to the gut is that she never left willingly. I spent years being angry and bitter about her leaving, right up until a couple of months ago, and it looks like all that was misplaced.

"I don't know what to say, other than, I care for her. So much. Having her back in my life is..."

"I know. And I know you care for her, and I have no doubt she cares for you too. I just worry this is all going to be too much for her to han—"

"With all due respect, George," I cut him off. "Johanna can handle a lot of things. You're right, I don't know the full story, but I'm also not letting that change how I feel about her. She's the strongest person I know."

"She is," he agrees.

"Does she know that?"

There's another long pause. I can picture the discomfort in George's face right now. "I've been so worried about protecting her from the world that I failed to see how resilient she is."

"Maybe that's exactly what she needs to hear."

"I think you're right. It's clear now why she fought me tooth and nail about leaving town. I wish I'd seen it sooner. I still stand by my word that time away was the best thing for her, and I know she carries around a lot of guilt about leaving when she did, but I think she's just been biding her time. Waiting for the right moment to come home. To come home to you."

Hours after George and I hang up, his words still echo in my ears.

To come home to you.

Why would Jo not tell me leaving wasn't initially her idea, even if in the grand scheme of things, she needed it? It's difficult not to type that very question out to her as I open our text thread. Instead, I let her know that I found her note.

> Patrick: You make me happy too.

It's past midnight, so I'm surprised when her reply chimes through.

> Johanna: I wondered how long it would take you to find it.

> Patrick: Not as long as it's taken you to find the puzzle piece.

THOSE TWO WORDS

> Johanna: Goodbye.

Chuckling at her response, I type out another text, hoping it doesn't ruin the moment.

> Patrick: Your dad called me. I think you should speak to him. He's okay, but I think he misses you.

I wait a few minutes for her reply, expecting her to put up an argument.

> Johanna: Okay. I will.

> Johanna: Don't think I won't get payback for that puzzle piece comment.

> Patrick: Oh I count on it. Goodnight, love.

thirty-six
JOHANNA

It's Wednesday.

But not just any Wednesday.

May 17 is a day that will forever be ingrained in my brain. A day that started so perfectly but ended as the catalyst for all future years. It's not to blame for how everything turned out, it's just another devastating day in a timeline of events out of my control.

The evening before is a memory I replay often. It kept me warm when the chill of depression and anxiety tried to suffocate me, reminding me I don't have a bad life.

My journey with anxiety and depression didn't start on this day six years ago, but it took me some time to come to that realization.

I've been on this journey since the summer we lost Mom.

No one is ever prepared to lose a loved one, so when my kind, beautiful mother slipped away in the middle of the night from an undetected brain aneurysm, it was earth-shattering.

What few people know, and something to this day I still struggle to comprehend, is that I was the one to find her.

Dad left for work early, well before any of us had woken up, making the most of lazy Sundays in bed until we had to go back to school. Harriet and I woke up, watched TV, and didn't really question why Mom hadn't come down yet, and presumed she wanted to sleep in.

It's very difficult to describe the emotions of that day and those that followed. Numb and excruciating are probably the most accurate.

Despite my dad pleading with me to see a therapist, I refused. It felt like a way of keeping alive that traumatic memory, being forced to talk about her and that morning with a stranger.

And that's basically how my journey with denial grew, slowly branching off into depression and the root cause for my Generalized Anxiety Disorder.

I experienced bouts of low moods throughout my teens and early twenties, but I brushed it under the rug and hid it well. Being an adult is hard, tiring, and demanding, so nobody questioned if I wanted to stay in bed for days on end or lost interest in things.

Life was busy.

But it was on this day six years ago that everything I'd spent years hiding—the grief, anger, and anxiousness—refused to stay hidden any longer. And like a dormant volcano, it blew up in my face. I was no longer able to put on a mask and show the world I was *okay*.

Because this day six years ago, despite how joyous it started, ended in misery.

Patrick and I had spent our first night together, crossed that line between friends and *more*.

The night before, Patrick and I were closing the restaurant together. It was like any other shift, easy and full of laughter. We worked together like a well-oiled machine, teasing and joking with one another. But in those last few months before I left, the air had been shifting between us. I lived with my dad at the time and Patrick had a small apartment a few blocks away from the restaurant. After we closed, we weren't ready for the night to end. I think we were full of energy from a busy shift and sleep wasn't going to find us anytime soon.

We headed to Patrick's for a nightcap, which turned into half a bottle of whiskey—which led to more, so much more. The *more* I had wanted for so long. That night confirmed that we'd held the same quiet longing for one another for years, both too afraid to make a move.

It felt like we went from zero to sixty in the blink of an eye. Like the moment his lips touched mine, a switch was flipped. I'd been looking at him with tinted glasses all my life and when we finally stopped fighting it, I saw him in a kaleidoscope of colors.

It wasn't love at first sight, because I had loved him my whole life. It just shifted to something I hadn't realized was possible.

We made plans to go on our first date later that week, though when I look back, it's funny to think what difference a date would have been compared to all the other outings we had been on together.

We never did get to go on that first date.

The restaurant was closed the following day for some scheduled maintenance. Patrick left me in his bed to head over there and meet his dad. I showered and locked up with the spare key I had to his apartment, but the moment I turned the key in the door, my phone rang. And I just knew. I knew something was wrong. I can't explain it, but I did.

I'll always remember that phone call. The sheer panic and distress I heard over the line. How he couldn't get his words out to tell me what was going on. My heart broke at the sound of tears in his voice, begging me to come to the restaurant.

It's bad, Jo. It's so bad.

Ted's death, much like my mom's, was without warning and

cruel. He was refitting some light fixtures and on top of a ten-foot ladder when he fell.

He never felt a thing, and we had to take comfort in that knowledge.

Only I couldn't. Because another person I loved had been torn from my life.

When I reached the restaurant, medics and police were already there. It wasn't chaos like I expected. It was eerily calm. The air was heavy with misery and grief. When I saw Patrick sitting on the curb, eyes bloodshot, skin blotchy, and pale, I threw myself into his arms. The devastated look on his face was one I knew all too well. I held him as he sobbed and sobbed in my arms, clutching my T-shirt like he was petrified I would slip away too.

He was living my worst nightmare, while I relived it.

I didn't cry. Not until I got home that evening. At first, I thought I was desensitized to it all, but the second I shut my bedroom door behind me, the blocker my mind put up fell away. Crumbling and bringing me down with it.

I crashed. Flashbacks of my mom's death hit me with the force of a freight train.

And I had my first panic attack in four years.

My brain switched off after that, giving me just enough energy to carry out basic tasks, like eating and sleeping. We kept the restaurant closed while we all mourned. I went to see Patrick a couple of times, going with my dad to be there for the Sadler family, helping them grieve.

I was there, but I wasn't present.

It was after my eleventh panic attack in eight days that my dad met the end of the line, the one I'd been dangerously tightrope walking across for so long.

"Do I need to call an ambulance?" Dad says from beside me on the sofa, his hand rubbing in wide circles across my back.

"It's over. I'm fine," I rasp out.

But I know I'm not. *I just want this to stop. The constant panic. Feeling like an alien in my own skin. Every day clouded by crippling fear, with no forecast for hope.*

I'm reminded constantly that every day is numbered with the people I love and there isn't anything I can do about it.

Today's funeral confirmed that desolate fact.

Harriet passes me a glass of water, her face etched with worry, and when I turn to my dad, his worry mirrors hers.

The black dress that's been choking me all day is now covered in sweat.

"I-I'm fine, Dad," I say, but my voice shakes so badly, the words barely make it past my lips.

"Johanna, I'm worried about you. Have you spoken to a doctor?"

"I don't need a doctor. It's just grief."

"I don't think this is grief. You haven't had panic attacks like this in years, not since your mo—"

"No, Dad, please. I can't think about Mom now." I'm shouting now, fresh tears cling to my lashes as the tremors start in my hands again. "Everywhere I look, there they are. Mom. And now Ted. They're here, but they're not."

Harriet takes my clammy hands in hers, the cool feel of her skin pulling me from the after-fog that usually hangs around after I hyperventilate. "Dad's right, Jo. I think you need to speak to someone. You're trying to do too much. No one would judge you if you took the next couple weeks off work."

Next week the restaurant reopens for the first time since Ted's death.

"I need to be there for Patrick...h-he needs me. I can't leave him right now." As the words leave my mouth, my voice cracks and I break down into a fit of sobs.

"Patrick will understand, Jo." My dad tries to soothe me.

"I have to be there for him," I whisper. Someone helps me lie down on the sofa and places a pillow under my head. "Like he was there for m-me."

THOSE TWO WORDS

"I can't watch you fall apart like this, Jo. You're losing weight, barely sleeping, I...I don't recognize you. We all grieve differently, but I'm worried something more is going on here. Something I can't stop or help with. Go with Harriet tonight, take some time away from town, from work. It will be here when you get back."

"Y-you want me to leave?" I whisper.

"I want you to put yourself first."

From the torn and distressed look on my dad's face, I know I'm fighting a losing battle, and it's time to hang up my cracked armor. This is like after Mom, only worse.

I'm losing myself in this town, the memories of people I love suffocating me.

So I stop fighting and leave with Harriet that evening.

Only when I get to Tennessee, somehow things escalate. Weeks turn into months. I ignore Patrick's calls and texts, so ashamed with how I abandoned him, but also, not wanting to give him an excuse to see me this way. Every day is a struggle. I beg my sister and dad not to tell anyone what's going on, just that I'm safe and need some space.

I wanted to stay but needed to leave.

And I'm not sure he will ever forgive me.

The rest is history.

Only we got our timelines and stories a little wrong. Patrick didn't stop waiting for me, he came to find me. I didn't leave him behind to start a new life, I was trying to find myself. We've been through so much, together and apart, and we're stronger for it.

What I accepted as the end of our story, now feels like the end of part one.

Yesterday, I spent my second-to-last session with Amanda preparing myself for what I knew I had to do. I know he's looking for answers, and something deep within me feels like today, of all days, is when he needs them the most.

I don't fear the loss of my loved ones like I once did.

I fear the loss of never feeling love.

I came back to Sutton Bay worried there wasn't much left for me here, but deep down, something other than my dad and the restaurant lead me home.

Patrick Sadler was that beacon guiding me home. My lighthouse in a stormy bay.

On a day I usually hide away from the world, I seek out the person I know needs comfort. A person who always puts others' needs above his own.

And hopefully this is where part two begins.

thirty-seven
PATRICK

Am I a good father? Do my employees respect me? Do I spend enough time with my siblings? Why wasn't I enough for Jo?

Those are some of the questions that float around my head regularly.

Today, there's only one.

Would my dad be proud of me?

I'd like to think he was when he was alive, but would he be proud of the man I am today?

My dad was always a straight talker to all four of his kids, never making us feel like we'd disappointed him. He'd listen carefully as we talked through our feelings before offering up his guidance.

One piece of advice that's always stuck with me was from when I was eight years old.

I was crying in the mud with grazed knees and hands, probably more embarrassed than anything. Jo and all our friends watched me eat dirt after I tried to show off on my new bike along the trail behind my house. My front wheel didn't even make it off the ground before I was thrown over the handlebars.

Dad calmly walked over, sat in the mud with me, and cleaned my cuts. He picked up my bike and said, *"Tomorrow is a new day, Patrick. Make it count. Let the failures of today build the foundations of tomorrow."*

At eight years old, those words didn't make much sense, but he repeated that phrase over the years. The older I got, the more I understood the meaning.

I've lived my life by those words. We all make mistakes—I still make them—I just try not to dwell on them. I'm only human, and perhaps that's naïve of me, but life's too short.

Losing my dad proved that.

Not telling Jo how I felt all those years ago was a mistake. Holding her at arm's length when she first returned was another.

But she doesn't speak about her years in Tennessee as a mistake. And having Lottie was most definitely not a mistake.

I'd assumed Jo had given up on us, and the pieces of herself she'd given me were all I was ever going to get. I suppose that's why I always keep a piece of her with me at all times.

I'm not ashamed of crying; I want to show Lottie it's healthy for men to be open with their emotions. But when she asked me if I thought Grandpa Teddy would have liked her, I excused myself from the table, kissed Lottie on the head, and walked out of the family dinner being hosted at my mom's tonight.

Mom gave me a look of understanding, not questioning or asking me to stay. Giving me space she knew I needed.

Lottie's innocent question gutted me. I should have stayed and told her that of course her grandpa would have liked her. He would have loved her and spoiled her rotten. Knowing he never got the chance to meet his first grandchild is one of the most painful realizations about my dad's passing.

I stare out across the horizon. The dark storm clouds reflect exactly how I'm feeling. The sounds of the crashing waves and birds usually calm me, but today they're drowned out by a torrent of emotions. I stand there for what feels like hours, trying not to think about anything at all.

It's not the squeaking of footsteps on the sand that lets me know she's here. It's the presence I felt moments before. The tips of my fingers are going numb from the biting wind, but having her close by warms me.

Jo loops her arms through mine and rests her head against my shoulder. We look out at the bay together, the whirls of dark grays and purples painting the sky. The storm hasn't reached us yet, but it will soon.

"They loved this view," she murmurs softly. I turn my head to look at her as she continues to stare out at the choppy waters, looking peaceful as she takes in the moody horizon. "Do you remember that barbeque we had on the beach one year? I think it was before Harriet and Florence were born. Your dad convinced us there was treasure buried in the sand. We spent hours digging holes; there were so many of them along the beach, I'm surprised we weren't charged with ecocide. After every hole he would act confused and say he forgot what the treasure map said. Right as the sun was about to set, he suddenly remembered."

I nod, a weak smile pulling at my lips as I recall that memory.

"I don't know how your dad did it, but I remember the excitement of digging that final hole and finding one hundred gold chocolate coins. We didn't even wipe the sand off them before we started devouring them. I was so sick that night. I'm pretty sure Graham and Booth ate them with the foil still on." She laughs and nuzzles closer to me. Dropping her hand from my elbow, she intertwines our fingers, her warm ones a reminder of how long I've been out here.

"That's how I always like to remember Ted. Making memories for us at every opportunity, a smile on his face as long as the people he loved were happy." Her smiling doesn't stop as tears fall freely down her cheeks. She strokes her fingers against my knuckles, soothing the pain away in so many ways.

Her words. Her touch. Her presence.

It settles me.

My tears join hers as she shares more stories about my dad, ones about him dressing up as Santa Claus every year at the restaurant, or how he asked George for advice when he had a daughter after three unruly sons. She doesn't tense up or falter like she has on other occasions when talking about my dad but laughs and smiles through the tears. It's such a welcome sight and sound.

"You remind me of him, you know." Her hand remains in mine as she turns to face me, and brings our woven hands up to her chest, the other coming to rest on my cheek. Leaning into her touch, I shut my eyes, feeling relaxed for the first time all day.

"Every day I see pieces of him in you. He'd be so proud of you, Patrick. I'm so sorry I wasn't here for you after you lost him. I'm sorry for a lot of things, and I need you to understand that leaving wasn't easy for me, but I'm here now, and I don't ever plan on leaving unless you're with me.

"When my mom passed, I buried away a lot of feelings and trauma from her death. And even years later, I never really addressed them. I thought it was best to hide it, especially from Dad, who was dealing with his own grief after losing his wife and adjusting to being a single parent. I slapped a label on it and called it grief, and most people accepted that. It took a long time for me to be honest with myself. Grief was present, but what I was trying to keep hidden was severe anxiety and depression.

"Before I even knew what Generalized Anxiety Disorder was, I suspected my moods and emotions weren't what most people experienced. I found my own ways to cope with them and, worked for a while, but it wasn't healthy. Pretending I was okay when I wasn't was probably the worst thing I could have done. On the day your dad..." She takes a deep breath, and I squeeze her hand, letting her know I understand what she's trying to say.

"Everything I'd been hiding or was too ashamed to talk about refused to be kept in the dark any longer. Those last few days in town were some of the most difficult in my life. I was holding on by a tether." She looks off into the distance, and I want to pull her into my arms and kiss away her tears, but I know she needs to finish.

"My anxiety disorder and depression come hand in hand. After a lot of therapy, I began to understand the reasons behind my disorder. An intense fear that everyone I care for will be taken away from me, and everywhere I looked, I was reminded of it. Loss of loved ones. I know it sounds ridiculous, but—"

"It's not," I say hoarsely, her eyes darting to mine. It's the first I've spoken since she arrived, content in listening to her stories, but I won't stay silent when she says things like that. "Nothing about how you feel is ridiculous."

"Sometimes I need to remind myself of that." She runs her thumb along the scar on my chin, like that small contact keeps her going. "The day of the funeral was too much for me to take. Putting on a brave face for everyone was too much. My dad was worried sick about me. When I saw how ignoring my feelings was impacting my family, I knew it was best for me to get out of town for a little while. I left, thinking I'd be back soon, a couple of months tops. But it got a lot worse before it got better. The panic attacks were less frequent but more intense. I ended up in hospital on two occasions.

"It was never you, Patrick," she says, and the sobs she's been holding break free. The moment fresh tears fall, I pull her into my chest. "I can't stand the thought that you'd think I would leave because of you. I never moved on; I never forgot you. Whatever you saw the day you came to visit me wasn't how it looked. The guy, Davis, he's a therapist. He's a friend of Harriet's, and she put me in touch with him...who then put me in touch with Amanda. My therapist."

I understand now why she might have felt apprehensive about sharing all of this with me, like it would make me see her differently. But I only see her as this incredibly brave, selfless, resilient woman.

"That day was the first time I left the apartment in a while, and I went to go and thank him for connecting me with Amanda. It took a while to find the right fit, and I was so grateful for his help."

"That's good. That you didn't settle for just anyone, right?"

"Yeah, it is." Bending her neck, she places a kiss on the tops of my hands, which are wedged between us. "I never wanted to leave, and as much as it pained me, I don't think I would be the person I am today if I didn't. It was only meant to be short term, that's the truth and I don't tell you this to hurt you, but when I found out about you and Carrie...I was already in a really bad place. Eventually, the idea of coming back to town felt so overwhelming; too many reminders of what I'd lost. I went from trying to confront my fears face-on, to running from them entirely. I think leaving when I did was the best thing I could have done for myself."

I know she's not being spiteful in sharing how the news of me and Carrie landed with her, but I hate to think I played any part in hindering her recovery.

She brings her hand to my jaw and runs it over my skin lovingly, catching across the stubble I didn't have the energy to shave this morning. "I'm so happy you found joy when you had just lost so much. Sometimes it takes hitting rock bottom to find the way out. That's how I see my time away from Sutton Bay. But you were always with me."

Pulling away from me, or as far as I'll let her, she reaches into her pocket and pulls out a little slip of paper.

"On my hardest days, this note reminded me why I could get through it. It reminded me that not all days are bad, and though it didn't feel like it then, I would be happy again. Even before our first night together, you made me so fucking happy, Patrick." She unfolds the paper and holds up a Post-it note. It's been folded a lot of times, wearing thin at the edges, but I can still make out my messy handwriting.

You make me happy.

I take hold of her face, staring deeply into those stunning blues, so warm and welcoming. "I'm so proud of you, Johanna. Proud of what you've overcome," I whisper and lay a soft kiss to her forehead. "I don't want you to ever feel shame for having a bad day or if your anxiety gets too much. I'm so happy you came back to me, love. I can't begin to put into words how much I've missed you, and I'm sorry for not chasing after you, for not trying harder to reach you." I kiss her nose and cheeks. Those freckles I love so much. I bend at the knees so our mouths are level, barely touching. "But you're here now, and I've got you."

"Being here, with you right now, this is why I had to come home. I had to come back to you."

We waste no time in letting our mouths meet. The kiss feels like our first. Not the one on my sofa, but the one I stole on New Year's Eve as kids. Because that was the moment I knew Johanna Thomas would be in my life forever.

I feel weightless as we deepen the kiss. Pride and relief flood my veins.

When the first raindrops splat across my cheek, we pull away from each other and look up at the sky as the heavens open. The rain washes away the tears, but our smiles remain.

"You were always going to find your way back to me. This is your home, Johanna, and you're mine." I watch water droplets glide down her face and coat her skin.

She watches me attentively, recognition shining in her eyes. She was so close to whispering those words that evening after Lottie's birthday. I need them. I need those two words like my next breath.

"I'm yours."

And there they are.

I'm yours.

I bring my mouth to hers with fierceness. As much as I love seeing her smile, it feels and tastes even more incredible. I taste it as our tongues entangle, and sense it in my soul. I feel *her* in my soul. Because she's mine and I'm hers.

As I hold her in my arms, I know what I want.

This.

A hundred more moments like this. The sad, happy, and angry ones. For every sad day, I'll give her one hundred happy ones. On the days we find ourselves angry at each other, I know the making up will be incredible. I'll take on anything, so long as she is by my side.

Since I was seven years old, I knew one thing for sure.

I love her.

I love her so deeply I think it's one of my life's purposes.

As the rains falls on us, I know this moment is one I'll carry with me for the rest of my life.

On a day that's filled with such sadness, she brought me joy. She showed me love.

thirty-eight
JOHANNA

Patrick and I spent the rest of the evening sitting in his truck and sharing more memories about his dad and my mom.

It's not just the elation on his face as he listens, but the comforting presence it brings from talking about my mom with someone so openly that has us talking well after the sun sets.

We didn't care about our wet clothes as we cried and laughed together. But as we peeled them off each other back at my apartment, I was happy to be rid of them. I knew we didn't have long, so when he joined me in the shower, claiming it was better for the environment, I didn't argue. I most certainly didn't care when he fucked me hard and fast, with my face pressed against the shower tiles, our moans being lost under the spray of water.

He stands by my front door now, hair wet and curly from the shower and a cocky smile on his face.

"If I didn't have Lottie tonight, we wouldn't be sleeping in separate beds, know that," he says, before giving me another kiss. The last five have all been followed by "Just one more."

"It feels a little anticlimactic, doesn't it?" I laugh as he zips up his jacket.

"Johanna. When we're alone together next, it will be anything but anticlimactic," he retorts, his voice gravelly and deep.

Now I really don't want him to leave, but I know if he doesn't, I'll climb him like a tree.

"I don't think we're on shift together until Friday. And then it's Monday..."

We share a worried look.

"God, Monday," he groans, and I want to echo his discomfort.

The past few months have flown by so quickly, and I can't believe we'll know the outcome of the restaurant next week. It feels like yesterday I stumbled into the restaurant and his life. I know whatever we're told, we've tried our hardest, and if anything, I'm grateful for how it's brought us back together.

I can deal with that potential failure, but I still worry about how Patrick will handle it.

I shake the pessimistic thoughts away. "It'll be fine; you've worked so hard."

"*We've* worked so hard," he corrects. "I've been doing what I've been doing for the last six years, you're the one that came in and made all these amazing changes. That's all on you."

"Yes, yes." I start to push him toward the door. "Get out of here, or you'll never leave. And I need to sleep."

I rise up on my tiptoes, plant one last kiss against his lips, and pull away when his arms start to slink around me, trying to pull me closer.

"Ah-ah," I chide, taking a step backward and pointing an authoritative finger at him.

"You're so *cunnin'* when you're angry."

"Oh god, you sound like Lenny. You've spent way too long in this town, Patrick Sadler."

He throws me a wink and walks out the front door. When I hear the door at the bottom of the stairs shut, I run to the window and watch as he climbs into his truck. He looks up to where I'm standing, kisses his hand, and lays it over his chest.

Be still my beating heart.

As my finger hovers over the doorbell, I let out a little laugh at how ridiculous I'm being. This is my childhood home; I have a key. I doubt it's even locked.

I've avoided my dad since Lottie's birthday party, and I hate that we've hardly spoken in the last couple of weeks, only talking business when he's been at the restaurant. I called yesterday to check on him, but it was a short conversation as he was on his way out to see some friends.

I try the handle and when I find it unlocked as suspected, I push my way in and shut it behind me.

"Dad?" I call through the house.

When I'm met with silence, I can only guess he's in the basement listening to old records. Kicking off my sneakers, I walk toward the basement stairs, when a familiar gold frame catches my eye.

The jigsaw puzzle that was and still is the bane of my existence stares at me. When I was twenty-three, I came home drunk and attempted to pry the damn thing off the wall. My dad caught me, and the next day, he reinforced the frame to the wall, arguing that it's his favorite piece of "art" in the house.

It wasn't a complicated puzzle by any means, just the sun setting over a mountain range somewhere in the world. I've stared at the scenery so many times, I could probably draw the missing piece by memory. Blue, purple, and pink hues for the sky and a tiny speck of white for the tip of the snowy mountain.

Now, whenever I look at it, I'm reminded of Patrick's betrayal.

I can't believe he was the one to take it all along, and then lost it! I run my finger along the glass where that piece should sit and shake my head, a small laugh breaking free. I suppose in a lot of ways, it was always him.

The raw sounds of a saxophone greet me as I enter the basement, and I find my dad sorting through my mom's old records that line the back wall.

"Hey, Dad," I shout above the music.

He looks up and smiles when he sees me. "Hey, kiddo, what are you doing here?"

"I wanted to pop by and see you." I settle in the recliner in the corner of the room.

"I'm a lucky guy. Do you want to stay for dinner?" He's texted me a few times asking me to come for dinner, but I'd say I was too tired or had already eaten. I'm not proud of it, but I was feeling bitter after our conversation at the party.

I know my dad didn't mean to upset me; all he's ever done is care and support Harriet and me, but it hurt to think he doesn't trust my own strength.

"I'd love that. What are we having?"

"Pizza?"

"I'll make us something. You eat way too many frozen pizzas, it's gonna catch up with you one day. What are you doing?"

Patting his stomach, he purses his lips and shakes his head. "Oh, just sorting through your mom's records. She had so many, I bet she didn't even listen to them all."

"You bought them for her."

"Oh yeah, so I did." He winks, before sitting in the recliner opposite me. "It's good to see you. How are things?"

"They're good..." I tap my fingers against my thigh but stop myself, because there's no need to feel anxious about this conversation. "I'm sorry I haven't been over, or that I didn't come to see you yesterday."

I called my dad yesterday afternoon, before I found Patrick at the beach. Ted was his best friend, and yesterday would have been hard for him. He went around to see Claire in the morning and took her out for lunch, something I know they do every year. When we spoke on the phone, he was halfway out the door, off to Shirley's to meet some of his and Ted's old school friends for a drink.

I feel bad for not seeing him, but Patrick needed me more.

"You're fine, kiddo, I kept myself busy. Did you see Pat?"

"Yeah, I saw him." I let out a sigh. "I told him everything."

My dad's brow raises at that, but not so much in surprise. He slowly nods, eyes crinkling when he smiles softly. "I'm glad. I know it can be hard for you to share that, but I'm proud of you."

"I'm sorry, Dad," I mutter as my chin drops to my chest.

"What on god's earth are you sorry for?"

"For everything." I try blinking away the tears, but my vision starts to blur. "But especially for putting you in a position like that after Ted's funeral. For fighting you, when really I knew I needed to find help. You'd just lost your best friend; you shouldn't have been dealing with my mess."

"Johanna," he says and places his hand on top of mine. "I'm going to stop you right there. Never, and I mean *never*, should you have to apologize for what happened. And if anyone ever makes you feel that you should, well, then send them my way and I'll give them a talking to. What you've been through isn't a *mess*, it's a small blip, one that you have overcome with grace and strength. You deserve to find someone who stands beside you during your bad days, but also someone who makes your good ones even better. I'm guessing you've found that person, huh?"

I nod my head immediately, no question about it.

"And that's all a father can ask for his little girl. I never doubted your strength, but I'll always worry about you, Johanna. Protecting you is like second nature, so I can't promise I won't be overly dad-ish from time to time, no matter how old you are." His eyes sheen with love, and I'm reminded how lucky I am to have a parent who cares so deeply for me the way he does. He tilts his head with a knowing smile. "I'm guessing Patrick's that person?"

"He's *my* person," I confirm. My cheeks ache from how wide I'm grinning, and from the satisfied look on my dad's face, it's all the answer he needs.

"Can't say I didn't see that coming. I know he'll treat you right." He rises and pulls me to stand with him. "Now, go cook dinner for your old man, I'm starving."

As I laugh my way up the stairs, my dad's own laughter following behind me, I think how different this day was six years ago. Barely staying afloat. I'd still be treading water like my life depended on it, if I didn't have the amazing support network around me.

And though it was hard, I found my way home, and that's all that matters.

"Booth. I swear if you don't stop fidgeting, I'm going to punch you in the dick," Patrick snaps beside me.

We're all antsy, but Booth hasn't stopped pacing the office since we got here, slowly wearing a hole in the floorboards.

"Honestly, it might help me stop feeling so sick. Where are they?" Booth whines and continues his persistent pacing until Patrick tugs him to sit next to him. I'm surprised the worn leather sofa we're sitting on doesn't cave with the weight of our combined nerves.

Booth continues to annoy us as his knee bobs up and down, foot tapping against the floor.

"Booth, if you don't quit it, *I'll* punch you in the dick," I say, peering around Patrick with a warning glare.

"Pat, please get a hold of your woman," Booth says, suddenly calm as he leans against the sofa with his hands behind his head. Patrick and I stare at him. "Oh, don't look at me like that, you idiots. I saw that hickey on Jo's neck outside the bakery weeks ago. You guys are shit at hiding things. About time you quit dancing around each other, it was getting old."

I gape at Booth, but Patrick only chuckles softly next to me. My warning glare is aimed at him now, but Patrick shrugs off his little brother's comment and takes hold of my hand like it's the most natural thing to do in the world.

Today is the day.

It came around too quickly *and* slowly at the same time. But the wait is over when Dad and Claire finally walk in. Even with our parents present, he doesn't pull his hand away and satisfaction blooms in my stomach that we've come to some unspoken agreement and our relationship is no longer hush-hush.

Claire takes a seat in the chair behind the desk while my dad sits in a wooden one beside her. It almost feels like an episode of *The Apprentice* with how we're all sitting.

"Thanks for coming in today," my dad starts. "I don't want to drag this out, and I know you're all eager to know what the plan is, but before we get to that, I just want to say that the last few months have been some of the best performing months the restaurant has seen in a long time."

Does he sound nervous?

The tension melts from Patrick's fingers, but something in my dad's tone only has me tensing more. Patrick must notice, because he turns and gives me a reassuring smile, like he knows it's all going to be okay. I just wish I shared his confidence.

"We can't thank you enough for all the hard work and extra hours you've put in. I know the news in February came as a shock to you all, and it wasn't a decision we took lightly. You kids went above and beyond to put this place back on the map. Even Mrs. Stewart left us a positive review online."

We all chuckle at that, though the humor is shrouded with foreboding.

"Booth, the food was perfect as always, and we loved what you did with the specials. The taste of Maine with a twist. Good job, son." Booth puffs his chest out, and I know the praise from my dad means a lot to him. My dad looks at Patrick and me next. "You two have really outdone yourselves. I know it was a rocky start, but the way you've worked together has been nothing but tremendous. It reminded me of the days when you were youngsters, fighting over who would bus the tables on a Friday night. I'm glad it all worked out." There's more behind his words than just working together at the restaurant. His lips turn up at the corners when he sees our fingers laced together.

He's glad *we* worked out.

"I wouldn't want to be anywhere else than right here. I couldn't have done it without Johanna and Booth by my side," Patrick says, eyes flitting between his brother and me.

"G-man, I'm sorry, but please put us out of our misery," Booth pleads, scrubbing his hands down his face and voicing what we're all thinking.

My dad lets out a big exhale and turns to Claire, both sharing an indiscernible look. When he faces forward again, my stomach drops, because his expression is riddled with regret. Despite the warmth of Patrick's hand, I feel cold and hollow before my dad's next words even leave his mouth.

"It wasn't enough, guys, I'm so sorry." The disappointment in my dad's tone is palpable.

Patrick's hand slackens in mine, and I tighten my grip, not wanting to lose the contact, but it slips away. A fissure opens between us at the loss of his touch, and all I can do is stare at my empty hand.

"Do we have more time? Surely there's more we can do. The summer is almost here, tourists are coming back." Patrick is trying his best to sound calm and collected, but the pitch in his tone betrays him.

"We simply don't have the time or money," Claire says. "We've put this off long enough. We've been funneling in our own savings to keep this place afloat and ensure everyone gets paid. The revenue's been slowly increasing, but it isn't enough for restaurant to be viable in the long run."

"So that's it?" Patrick bites out. The hurt in his voice twists at my heart, but I don't know what to say. He runs his hands through his hair in frustration and lets out a sigh of disbelief. I debate reaching out to comfort him but think better of it, having already been rejected.

He's just hurting, I try to assure myself.

"We don't want you to think we haven't seen how hard you've worked, and how much this place means to you all," my dad says. "But we must be realistic here. If we don't do something soon, I worry it'll be too late. I don't want to let people go before they have time to find another job. At least now we can—"

"I'm sorry, I can't listen to this," Patrick says, and he stands abruptly from the sofa. Booth—who, like me, has remained silent since the news broke out—shares a concerned look with me. I reach toward Patrick, no longer able to sit back and watch his struggle, but retreat when I see the tremble in my hand. I squeeze my palms together, hoping to hold off the incessant need to tap my fingers against my thigh.

"It's as if no one cares about this place. How are you all so calm?" He looks at us, though I'm not sure he's even taking us in from the look of betrayal on his face. "How do you know that whoever you sell this place to won't rip it apart and destroy everything you've built? Everything my dad built."

Claire gets up and walks to where Patrick stands, arms raised at his sides in question.

She takes a breath before she speaks. "We're hoping to avoid that, Patrick. The potential buyer we've—"

"*Wait*. There's already a buyer? Since when?" His hands are shaking now, but not from anger. Pain radiates off him in waves, and in this small office, there's nowhere for it to escape. From the uneasy feeling snaking its way through me, it's as if I'm acting as a conduit for all his emotions.

"We were approached by an anonymous buyer a few weeks ago; we didn't openly seek them out," Claire says, her voice firm. "It's not common knowledge, let alone listed anywhere, so we don't know how they knew to reach out."

"So why not tell us then? Why make us waste our time and force us to work with each other? What was the point in the last few weeks if you already knew?"

I glance down to check my heart hasn't fallen out of my chest. When I see I'm still intact, the gravity of what he's saying settles. *Waste of our time. Force us to work. What was the point?*

He doesn't know the impact of his words. I remind myself of that, but they cut me deeply anyway. There's no way he thinks the last few weeks are a waste, right? Because outside of the restaurant, we've seen each other almost every day. And those days don't feel wasted.

The tingling in my fingers works its way up my arms, and a familiar tightness pulls at my chest. I straighten my spine, hoping it eases the discomfort, but it draws four sets of eyes in my direction instead.

It's Patrick's gaze that rocks me the most. His eyes widen as he takes in my shaking hands and quick breaths. All the fight leaves him as his shoulders sag, realization dawning on him.

He moves toward me, apology written all over his face, but

my skin feels too tight. I don't know if it's the news about the restaurant or seeing how torn up Patrick is, but the bubbling panic propels me from the sofa.

It's nothing too severe, but I know I need my medication.

Which is in my car.

Internally cursing at almost making the same mistake twice, I scurry toward the door. "I'm sorry, I really am, but I need a moment," I mutter, not daring to look at anyone. Not even Patrick.

Inches from the door, a gentle touch on my hip halts my movements. I almost don't make out his murmured words they're so quiet. "Love. Don't run, not now. I'm sorry, I wasn't thinking."

"I'm not running, Patrick. I really do need a minute. I promise, I'll be back."

Without a backward glance, too scared to see the hurt on his face, I leave.

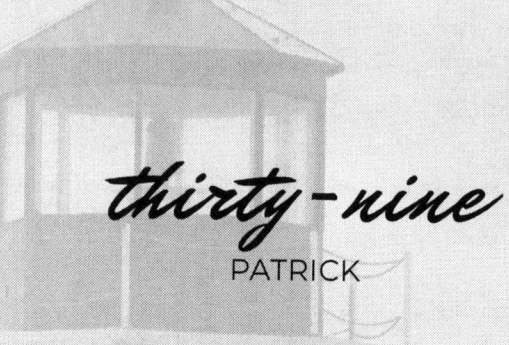

thirty-nine
PATRICK

The open doorway Jo just disappeared through feels more like a blackhole, sucking up any energy I have left.

I'm frozen in place. Torn between running after her or giving her the space she pleaded for.

The moment I saw the tearful and desolate look on her face, I knew I fucked up.

I was so blinded by my failure and denial that I let my emotions feed my words, not thinking how they would sound to her. And they couldn't be further from the truth.

"Should we go after her?" Booth says from where he's perched on the sofa.

"She needs a moment, she'll be okay," George says, but it makes me think about the words he said to me all those years ago when I found out Jo had left Sutton Bay.

She's fine, she just needs some time.

No.

This isn't the same thing and I trust her when she says she's not running. I know she's putting herself first, and I'm proud of her for doing what she knows is best for her. I just wish I wasn't what drove her away.

THOSE TWO WORDS

My mom takes hold of my hand. "Sit, sweetheart. I'll go check on her. She'll be okay, she's a strong one."

"I know." My agreement echoes down the hallway behind her.

Despite my desperation to go and find her, I take my seat again. I'm embarrassed at how I reacted, pacing around like a toddler having a tantrum, but arguing and trying to negotiate seems pointless now. Not when Jo isn't beside me.

George gives me a pitiful look and picks up where he left off. "We kept the buyer at bay until this morning. There's no denying our cash intake has gone up, but the forecasts don't look good. We might last another six months, but I don't want to take that risk."

The disappointment from earlier feels different now. The news about the restaurant is meager in comparison to the anguish I'm feeling over my behavior and thoughtless words. I allowed my own insecurities to take the driver's seat and in return, I hurt Jo. I could see it in her pained expression, and it made me sick to my stomach, because I put that there.

The indent in the leather sofa taunts me as George continues. "Nothing's final and we have another meeting lined up in a few weeks to discuss it further. We've been clear that we will only sell to them if it's written into the contract agreement that they don't change the name of the restaurant and keep on all the staff currently working here."

My head snaps up. "You can do that?"

"Of course we can. That's what we were trying to explain to you earlier," George says pointedly, and I cringe at his subtle scolding.

"For now, we have enough money to keep us going until fall, but we need to come to an agreement with them soon, or we risk losing the offer they've put on the table altogether. I'm not sure we'll get another opportunity like this. We don't know who the buyer is, because we were contacted by a third party, but they've explained the buyer isn't interested in the operations side of things. They prefer to take a backseat approach with their investments. We didn't argue with that, it's all kosher, and we couldn't ask for a better proposal."

George is talking to me like it's a sales pitch, as if I need more persuasion. But I don't really care what happens to this place if it means Jo won't be by my side when it happens. I'm not sure we would have lasted this long had she not come back and accepted the job.

She's the reason we've made it this far and she's the reason I need to go. *Now.*

"Do it. Do whatever you need to do, but I have to go. I'm sorry for how I reacted, I trust you guys," I rush out. "I fucked up, and I love this place, but…"

He seems to know what I'm trying to say.

I love her more.

I love her more than this place, because it's not *Our Place* without her. It hasn't been for a long time.

"Go," Booth urges. "You've waited long enough, dickhead."

With my middle finger raised at my brother, I run out of the office and into the restaurant. I look around the room but don't see them anywhere.

One of the servers walks by and I stop them. "Sorry, have you seen my mom or Jo?"

"Oh, they left about five minutes ago. Your mom told me to tell you they've gone for a coffee at the bakery."

"Thanks," I call over my shoulder, my feet already carrying me out the front door.

Dodging people as I race down the street, I head in the direction of Just Brew It. When I stop outside the window of the bakery, I don't waste time trying to catch my breath.

Gasps and stunned faces greet me as I barge through the door, and I know I look deranged on my hunt for Jo right now, but I don't really care. Scanning the tables, I don't see a head of golden hair, but suddenly something is sniffing at my shoe. Looking down, I see Curly, Graham's dog, and follow the lead up to where my brother is standing.

"Hey, have you seen Jo?" I rush out, still winded from my run here.

My mom appears over his shoulder, a wary look on her face.

I do not like that look.

"You don't—yeah, she was with Mom before she went to the back to find Quinn. She seemed pretty upset." Graham's a direct person, so when I catch the edge to his tone, worry churns in my stomach.

I slide past him and my mom and walk over to the counter. Quinn looks up from her spot behind the glass cabinet, and I don't like the look she greets me with either.

"Hey, Quinn, is Jo here?" I ask, pointing to the small kitchen behind her. I don't wait for a response, though, and maneuver my way past the cakes and breads. Her arm shoots out and grabs me by the bicep.

"She just left," she says and drops her arm.

"Left to go where?"

"I don't know, umm, but she said..."

"What did she say?" I ask, with a little too much bite.

"Watch it," Graham says in warning from behind me. I turn to look at him and raise my hands in apology before turning back to Quinn. She doesn't seem fazed by my outburst, but a subtle blush colors her cheeks.

"I'm sorry, Quinn. I just—I just need to find her. Do you know where she went?" I ask, more calmly this time.

"I do, but she said that if anyone came looking for her to not tell them. I don't want to break her trust, but I promise she's safe."

"*Fuck.*" I don't let the dread trying to bully its way out of me take root. She's probably in her apartment, upstairs. I respect Quinn's loyalty, but it won't stop me from searching for Jo.

Only when I knock on her apartment door until my knuckles start to swell do I resort to calling Martin Willis and somehow convince him to let me into her apartment. But she's not there.

She doesn't answer her phone. Every call rings out until it goes to voicemail.

Graham and my mom assure me that she wouldn't have gone far, presuming I'm thinking the worst and that she's left town. But that's not what I'm concerned about; that worry is a thing of the past.

It's that I have no idea where she is, how she's feeling, or what she needs.

And she doesn't know I love her.

I'VE BEEN STARING AT THE CHIP IN THE COUNTERTOP FOR WAY TOO long, I'm beginning to go cross-eyed.

My chin rests on my folded arms, as Lottie sits across from me, doodling away and humming a song. Her tuneless serenade helps distract me, but only a little, which confirms how deep in my head I am.

Jo must have turned off her phone, or the battery died, because it goes straight to voicemail now. That doesn't deter me from leaving her a message each time I call. I think we're up to twenty-five now.

Graham and I drove around town for an hour looking for her. Shirley's, Dough, her dad's, Piper Beach, Puffin Point Lighthouse; we looked everywhere and no Jo.

I would have driven around town all day, but duty called,

and I knew seeing Lottie would ease some of the regret I'm stewing in after today's meeting. My mom and Quinn assured me that she was relaxed when they saw her. I just need to see her. I need to apologize and explain my words were a knee-jerk reaction, and nothing to do with us.

I need to hold her, kiss her, love her.

Instead, I'm sitting in my mom's kitchen, agonizing over my words.

Tracing the granite countertop with my finger, I think of all the ways I'll apologize to her. Iced coffees. Grilled cheese. A new puzzle every week. I'll even let her win at a game of pool.

I need her here.

"Daddy, why do you look sad?" Lottie asks, with a tilt to her head.

"I'm not sad, spud."

"Are you mad?"

"No, not mad."

"Then why is your face doing this?" she asks and scrunches her eyebrows together and pouts her lips. Even on her cute little face, it's not a good look.

"I'm just disappointed in myself."

"What's *spis-a-pointed* mean?"

"*Dis-ap-point-ed* means I'm not happy with something I've said or done," I explain.

"Are you spisappointed in me?"

Jesus, will I ever say the right thing to women today?

I stand and round the counter, bending at the knees until we're eye level.

"Not you, sweet girl. Never you. Not when you draw such pretty pictures like this," I say, pointing to the big blob of pink and yellow.

"It's me and JoJo," she announces proudly and shoves it in my face. She peeks around the edge of the paper, her bottom lip curling. "I miss her. Can I play Barbies with her again? That was fun."

"We'll see her soon." Standing up, I stretch my arms above my head and decide I need to distract myself until Jo is ready to talk. I ruffle Lottie's hair, when a thought pops into my mind. "Hey. Why don't we make a fort, snuggle up underneath it, and watch *Tangled*?"

She gasps and drops her pencils on the table, before scrambling down from her stool in a frenzy. She runs out of the kitchen, shouting for my mom, and I take that as a yes.

"Let me grab the sheets," I call and make my way upstairs.

Walking into my mom's room, I search the closet for some spare sheets and pillows. When I don't find any, I try the one in the guest room across the hall and nearly get flattened by all the crap piled high and leaning precariously on the shelves.

Board Games. Cassette tapes. Old baby booties. Fishing poles. You name it, it's in here.

I'm about to give up the hunt, when I spot a pile of white sheets hidden behind an old boom box and...*no way*. The sight of my dad's old Polaroid camera pulls at my heartstrings, and I wonder when my mom last cleared out this space.

Carefully, I pull the sheets down and try not to bring the contents of the closet crashing to the floor. Just as the sheets are freed from the carnage, my elbow knocks a stack of shoe boxes, and they tumble to the ground. A flurry of photos and pieces of paper float down to my feet.

"Shit," I curse and bend to tidy up the mess.

When I have most of the contents stacked in neat piles, I shuffle them back into their worn, cardboard homes, but pause when I see four envelopes, one with my name on it and the rest with each of my siblings' names on them. I pick up the one addressed to me and turn it over, inspecting it to work out what it is and who it's from. My name is written out in big, block letters, so it's hard to decipher whose handwriting it is.

THOSE TWO WORDS

The longer I look at it, the more my curiosity gets the better of me. It has my name on it, so it's clearly meant for me. I tear the seal of the white envelope and pull out a folded piece of paper, but before I finish unfolding it, something flutters to the floor.

A Polaroid photo.

It's lying face down, but when I turn it over, a hearty laugh mixed with astonishment breaks loose. Looking up at me from the monochrome film is a photo of a young boy and girl. They look the same age, and the boy is leaning in and planting a kiss awkwardly on the girl's cheek. A look of shock and disgust on her face. Even in black and white you can make out the flush of her cheeks.

I don't blame Johanna; I was a gross kid.

I've never seen this picture before, and even though it was taken almost thirty years ago, I remember the night clear as day. I trace my finger across the black-and-white image, amazed that my dad managed to capture this moment.

Our first kiss.

But not our last.

I admire the photograph for a few moments, when I remember the piece of paper in my hand.

Once it's unfolded, I recognize the handwriting immediately. Probably because it's the same handwriting that taught me my ABCs.

When I start reading, I don't stop, despite how my heart tumbles with every word.

To the boy who made me a father,
I have no idea why I'm writing this letter. I'm sitting in my office as you finish up your first shift as bar manager and I thought I would share some sage

words of wisdom. We know I'm good at that.

But first I'd like to tell you a story, so bear with me.

I once met a woman who I instantly fell in love with, but I was too chicken shit to talk to her. When I finally found the courage, I didn't ask her out on a date like I had planned, no that would come later, but we did become good friends. I cherished those years of friendship, but I knew deep in my bones this wasn't what fate had planned for us. When I finally asked her out, she rolled her eyes and responded with, "Well, what took you so long?"

That woman soon became my wife, made me a father, and is the love of my life.

But you call her Mom.

Your mom was my best friend before anything else, and I can't believe I almost let a future with her pass me by.

I suppose my advice is to not make the same mistake I almost did. It can be scary to ask for what we want, but isn't that what life's about? Facing our fears and not living with regrets.

Get your head out of your ass, son, and go after what you want.

I'm so proud of the man that you are.

Tomorrow is a new day, Patrick. Make it count. Let the failures of today build the foundations of tomorrow.

All my love, Dad

A whoosh of air leaves me and I realize it's the first breath I've taken since I read the first word. A broken sob follows closely behind as I read my dad's words over and over, until I can no longer make out the letters through my blurred vision.

I can't begin to understand what would make him write a letter like this, and over a decade ago no less. Was he ever planning on giving it to me?

It doesn't take a genius to know what my dad is referring to in the letter. Clearly my efforts at hiding my feelings for Jo really were useless.

I've always trusted my dad's advice, and that doesn't stop today, even if he's no longer here to see his words come to fruition.

If I only knew where she was.

Folding the letter up, I tuck it back in the envelope. From where I'm still kneeling on the floor, I pull out my ratty old wallet, knowing exactly where the Polaroid picture is going.

Jo told me the Post-it note I left her kept her going through the hardest of days, and as I slide the multicolored piece of cardboard out of its home, I stare at the one thing that helped me through mine. As I look down at paint strokes of blue, white, pinks, and purples, I'm reminded that Jo has always been close by.

Who knows why I never reunited it with the 999 other pieces, but when Jo left, I was grateful to have a small piece of her to carry with me wherever I went.

Despite its missing piece, the puzzle created a beautiful picture of a mountain range, with the sun setting behind it. The painting of the sky always reminded me of the sunset you could see from Anakiwa Lookout.

And it hits me.

I know where Jo is.

I'm still following my dad's advice, because Johanna is my tomorrow, and every day that follows. But I'm not waiting until then to find her. I'm going after what I want *today*.

Ten minutes later, after rushing out of the house and trying to answer the slew of questions my mom was firing at me, I'm about to turn the key in the ignition of my old Chevy truck, when I stop to take a breath.

I bring my hand to the dashboard and tap it three times.

"Thanks, Dad. Love you."

Then I start the engine and drive off to find the owner of the missing puzzle piece and my heart.

forty
JOHANNA

It's taken me longer than usual to get to the lookout point.

I've spent my time on the hike up taking in the view and collecting my thoughts. The effects of my anxiety had disappeared by the time I snuck out of the back of Just Brew It, swearing Quinn to secrecy about where I was going. I wasn't stupid enough to not tell anyone I was headed to the park, not wanting to risk spraining my ankle and no one knowing where to find me.

About halfway up, I notice a manmade path branching off the main trail. My watch tells me I have half an hour until the sun sets, so I go to investigate. Rays of sunshine stream through the thick canopy of pine trees, and like little spotlights, they light up a small clearing of wildflowers. Bluets, Marigolds, and Wild Strawberry. Picking a few of the larger stems, I make up a small bouquet before finding my way back to the trail and continuing my trek.

Once I reach that familiar ridge on the horizon, I'm met with the most stunning sky. The once-white clouds are now backlit with all different shades of pinks, purples, and oranges, each melting into the other. The horizon glows brightly, shifting ever so slightly as the sun begins its descent. The smaller islands and pine trees sitting out on the bay are black silhouettes, with the sky stealing the show behind them.

I feel at peace up here, like the calm waters in front of me. There's no breeze in the air as I tip my head back and bask in the sun's last few moments.

With the small bouquet of flowers, I slowly walk up to the strikingly large and thick pine tree, a few feet from the cliff edge. It must be at least two hundred feet tall now, overshadowing all the other pines, spruce, and oak surrounding it. I run my fingers over the rough bark before placing the flowers at its base.

I've only been out here once since I've returned—when I took Quinn hiking—but I didn't want an audience for what I'm about to do. Craning my neck to stare up the length of the tree, I find my voice.

"Hi, Mom," I whisper, voice cracking. "I'm sorry we haven't spoken in a while."

I've never put much thought into what happens once we die, but I do like to think we leave a presence behind. Something that allows our memories to live on. This spot is exactly where I always feel closest to my mom. It's my favorite place on the bay, because it was hers, and it was where we came to scatter her ashes before the first snowfall that year.

"I've missed you. But I know you're watching over us all. I hope Ted is with you too. We all miss you both so much, but I'm glad you have each other. I know Dad misses you too. He says he comes up here a lot to see you." I crouch down and run my fingertips across the soft petals of the flowers, ignoring the tears that splash on the dirt beneath my feet. "I hope you haven't been too disappointed or worried about me. I had—I had a tough few years, but I'm okay now. I'm more than okay.

"I finally came home and I'm so glad I did. I miss Harriet,

but I missed Dad too. I missed the memories we made here together as a family. I missed seeing reminders of you in the restaurant, at the beach, and in the flowers that bloom every spring. I didn't want to miss you more than I had to. The memories of you weren't what kept me away, I realize that now. And although it hurts, I've learned to treasure all the time we had together.

"I met someone. Well, you know who Patrick is." I chuckle, just as a light breeze cuts through the trees. "I have never been so sure of something in my life, but I had to make sure my heart and mind were ready to give him the love he deserved. You always told me that to love, we had to love ourselves first. I hope you're glad we found our way back to each other. Patrick makes me feel complete, treasured, and so happy. Some days are hard, but I'm loved by so many people, and I still feel your love."

I wipe at my cheeks with the sleeves of my sweater. Kissing the tips of my fingers and pressing them into the wood, I slowly stand. "Thank you for creating so many memories for us, Mom. I promise I'll visit again soon. I love you."

Peace washes over me.

I needed to do this before heading back into town and finding Patrick. I turned my cell off after his first few calls, but not because I'm avoiding him; I just know I would have begged him to come up here with me. This is something I had to do alone. With one final look at the sunset, I turn to make my way down the trail.

Only my feet stop working when my eyes meet another pair so green, they rival the trees surrounding us.

Patrick.

His are bright with tears, and I have no idea how long he's been standing there.

But he's here.

One of his hands is tucked into the front pocket of his jeans, while the other is behind his back. The sunset paints him in orange, making him look ethereal, as if he fell from the sky itself. So many emotions are etched into his handsome face, but relief and tenderness shine the brightest.

"Are you following me?" I ask. Despite the humor in my voice, tears collect in the corners of my eyes.

"I think I've been following you my entire life, why stop now?" A gentle smile pulls at the corners of his mouth as he takes a few steps toward me. "Do you mind?" He nods toward the large pine tree. Before I can ask him what he's doing, he's leaning forward, placing a kiss at the corner of my mouth, and walking toward the tree. It's only then I see what's behind his back.

As Patrick crouches down in the same spot I was at moments before, he gently rearranges the small bouquet I collected as he adds delicate, star-shaped flowers.

Mayflower.

My heart flutters, and I suspect it's going to be doing that a lot now.

"My mom's—"

"Favorite flower, I know. *And* your namesake," he adds.

"Are you going to finish all of my sentences for me?"

"If you let me do it for the rest of our lives, then yes, I am." His smile grows wider, but I'm in too much shock to respond. He turns toward the tree and like me, he places a kiss in the palm of his hand and lays it against the bark but doesn't remove his hand when he speaks.

"Hey, Valerie. I hope you remember me." *There goes my heart again.* "This will be short, because there's something important I need to tell your daughter. But I just wanted to stop by and thank you for bringing Johanna into my life, and for being the best friend my parents could have asked for. I suspect you know this already, but Johanna is one of the strongest people I know. You and George should be so proud of the woman she's grown into." His voice drops a level; I almost don't make out his words, but when I do, there's no controlling the flow of tears. "If you see my dad, thank him for me and tell him this. I'm finally chasing after what I want, and I won't waste a second of it once I have it."

He slowly stands and walks back to where I'm standing stock-still. An air of calmness radiates off him, so different from the man I saw earlier today. My chest aches and vibrates with every step he takes.

"I know you wanted your space," he says, standing in front of me now. "And I promise I'll always give that to you, but I needed to say two things. First, I'm sorry for how I reacted at the restaurant. I didn't mean a word of what I said and I'm an idiot."

"I didn't need space from you, Patrick. I just needed space in general. I had to take my meds, and then the idea of coming out here suddenly felt like the right thing to do. Like the final step in my journey to coming home. It's always been so special to me, and I'm sorry if I had you worrying or thinking I'd left you again."

"I didn't think you'd left. And even if you did, I would have followed you and waited until you were ready. You're worth the wait. I know what this place means to you, I'll bring you here whenever you want."

He holds out his hand to me and I look at it in confusion. "Friends?" he asks and nudges his outstretched hand, palm facing down, against my arm. "I promise I won't spit in it this time."

Laughing, I decide to go along with it. My head is spinning too much to try to make sense of it.

I reach out and slip my hand under his, when something hard digs into my palm. My head tilts in question, and when I see what he's handed me, something between a gasp, cry, and laugh echoes around us.

The colors of the sky. The white tip of the mountain. Even

down to the curvature of the edges, is exactly how I imagined it would look.

"The missing piece," I whisper. "How did I not know you had it this whole time?"

I look up at him and expect to see his face lit with a smug smile, but he stares at the puzzle piece with such fondness.

"I'm not even sorry for taking it. It's a good thing I did, too, because it told me where I could find you." He points out at the bay and to the sunset behind us, the sun minutes from sinking behind the horizon.

"You found me."

"I found you."

"What was the second thing you wanted to say?" He closes the distance between us and cups the side of my face with his hand, the other looping around my back and pulling me close until there isn't a sliver of space between us. It's amazing how his touch stokes a fire within me and keeps me steady simultaneously.

"I thought it would be obvious by now." He shakes his head, and his smile grows even bigger as he looks at me. "I love you."

And off my heart goes, taking flight in my chest with such a force, I might float up into the orange-tinted clouds if he didn't have such a tight grip on me.

He doesn't give me a chance to respond, because he lowers his head and brushes his lips teasingly, not quite a kiss, against mine.

"When I felt lost or sad, that missing piece kept me grounded. It reminded me of all the amazing times we had together, and I suppose of all the times I spent too scared or nervous to chase after you. I never stopped loving you, not when you left, not ever. You make me so happy, love. The type of happiness I can't put into words. The kind that hurts when I think about it too much, but it's a good type of hurt. I won't regret our time apart, not if it brought us to this very moment.

You have and will always be the holder of all my joy and my heart.

"I want to spend the rest of my life making you happy. To see that beautiful smile on your face every day when I wake up, and every night when I go to sleep." He cradles my face in both hands and whispers his next words against my lips, exhaling the love he has for me deep into my bones. "Can we spend the rest of our lives making each other happy?"

Does he not know he's been doing that my entire life?

On my darkest of days, Patrick was there. In my memories, in the note I kept, and in my heart. Even when I thought our time together was short lived, knowing we shared years of memories together was such a comfort.

"I love you. I have loved you for as long as I can remember. That love is what led me home. *You* led me home. Loving you was never a question. I had to love myself first. I'm sorry it took me so long, but my heart is yours, if you'll give me yours in return?"

He slowly shakes his head, the green of his eyes glowing brighter from the burning sky.

"Johanna, my love. You can't have my heart, because you already own it. I don't want it back, but please don't make me watch you walk away with it again." His fingers caress the back of my head as his thumbs wipe away my tears.

I bring my hand up to his chest and place it over his heart, the beat of it matching the tempo of my own. "Never, Patrick. Never again."

We decide we've done enough talking, as we close that small distance between our lips, allowing ourselves to become even more consumed with the other. If that's even possible. And with this kiss, and our words, everything clicks into place.

Like the last piece of a puzzle.

He tugs me closer and lets me know how much he loves me

with this kiss. It's slow and sweet, needy and desperate. Our lips glide over each other before we're nipping and sucking.

There are only two words left to say.

"I'm yours," I say between kisses.

"And I'm yours. Forever," he declares.

We lose ourselves in the kiss but never loosen our hold. Only when the sun is about to wink out of the sky do we stop, not wanting to miss the sunset. Patrick wraps me in his arms, and I lean into his strong chest, as we watch the fiery watercolors disappear behind the ocean.

By the time we get back to town, twilight has faded, and the stars twinkle and flicker high in the sky.

We tumble into my apartment, half of our clothes already gone from our journey up the stairs. We come together in a frenzy of limbs right there on my living room floor.

Hours later, Patrick wakes me up in the middle of the night and makes love to me slowly. With his body curled against mine, he whispers sweet promises of our future together, the children we're going to have, and how he wants to watch me walk down the aisle with a bouquet of wildflowers.

I whisper my promises to care for him until the end of my days, how I'll love Lottie like she is my own, and how I hope to make him even half as happy as he makes me.

I fall back to sleep in his arms.

Feeling so happy. So loved. And finally his.

For all the unspoken words, it took only two to put us back together.

forty-one
PATRICK

ONE MONTH LATER

I LEAN MY HEAD BACK AS THE SUN BEAMS DOWN ON ME, THE GRASS tickling my wrists, and sweet laughter ringing in my ears.

It's not just any laughter, though. It's the laughter from two very important ladies.

With one eye open, I squint over at them from across the picnic blanket. Lottie and Johanna are whispering and giggling to each other. My daughter is attempting to braid Jo's long hair, the blonde locks shining the brightest I've ever seen them as the sun kisses the tops of their heads.

My girls.

I'd find the interaction sweet, if I wasn't suspicious of them secretly plotting something against me.

"What are you two up to?" I ask, both eyes open now.

"Daddy, don't sneeze-drop, it's rude," Lottie scolds.

"It's *eaves-drop*, spud. And it can't be eavesdropping if you are sitting right next to me and cackling away like a pack of hyenas."

"It's a need to know, sorry. And you need to be a girl to

know," Jo says. She's lying on her front, head turned toward me as Lottie plays with her hair. She doesn't seem to mind the knotted mess Lottie is causing at the back of her head and lies there looking serene and radiant.

Things have moved quickly since that initial meeting at the restaurant, and although it didn't end conventionally, we all met up a week later to discuss the prospective buyer's proposal. It didn't feel right not to include all our siblings, so Graham came along to the meeting, and we dialed Florence and Harriet in. It was a unanimous decision, and a no-brainer. I still have my apprehensions, but for now no changes are being made and we take each day at time.

My mom and George are waiting for the final purchase agreements to be written up, and once signed, the restaurant will officially have a new owner. They've remained anonymous, and I don't know if that's a good or bad sign, but no one dares question it.

Graham has decided to take a step away from some of his bigger clients, handing them over to other accountants at his firm, claiming he wants to spend more time around the restaurant. He's not the only one to be suspicious of our prospective new owner, but he's been hanging around Robin Road an awful lot lately.

As for Jo and me, there was no big announcement about our relationship. There didn't need to be, either, because it seems everyone knew what was going on before we did. We just took some catching up. And now that we're all caught up, we aren't wasting a second.

We're not sad about the years we spent apart, because it only made us stronger. Time allowed us to grow and heal into the people we are today. That doesn't mean I'm not making up for every missed smile, kiss, and night we could have spent together.

I show her exactly how much she means to me every

moment I can. I'll never stop showing her, and soon, I'll show her by asking her to be my wife. By growing our family.

I won't stop, even after my last breath.

I no longer have to guess where one of her new freckles is from, or what made her smile that day. Because I'll be by her side the second a new one appears, and I'll be the one putting that stunning smile on her face.

I'll be the one making her happy.

Jo's not a new person in Lottie's life, but I still want to speak to her about Jo being around more often. I can't imagine she will complain, because Jo has quickly become one of my daughter's favorite people.

Once we finish our picnic, and Lottie has had the chance to burn some energy off in the park, we settle on the blanket and share a bowl of blueberries as we look out at the lake.

"Hey, Lottie, can I talk to you about something?" I ask.

She looks at me with purple-stained lips and fingers and nods her head.

"You know that Jo is one of my best friends?"

"Uh-huh," she says and grabs another handful of berries, before shoveling them into her mouth.

"Well, I'd really like it if she would be more than that. Sometimes she might stay for dinner or be over for breakfast. Would that be okay?"

"Like a best-best friend?" she asks.

"A bit more special than that."

She gasps and bounces on her knees. I'm grateful she caught on so quickly, because it was making me uncomfortable having to explain my relationship to a five-year-old, no matter how persistent she was about setting us up a few months ago.

"Like a big sister?" she whispers excitedly.

Nope.

I look toward Jo in panic, hoping she will help me out, but she's too busy trying to control the violent shaking of her shoulders before a gut-busting laugh breaks free. I can see it in her eyes. I won't hesitate to leave her here if she makes a single *daddy* joke.

"Johanna, please help me here," I plead, feeling a headache coming on.

"Lottie," Jo says, catching her attention. "You remember when you asked me if I had a boyfriend?"

"Yes." Lottie shoots me a side glance and leans in toward Jo. I know she thinks she's whispering, but I hear every word. "Like my boyfriend, Malcolm?"

"Malcolm who?!" I all but shout, sitting up straighter. Jo glares at me over Lottie's head, and I bring it down a notch. "Umm, yeah, like that." I try to act cool, and pretend I'm not going to find out where this Malcolm punk lives and ask what his intentions are.

"Well, you said your daddy needs a girlfriend, and I don't have a boyfriend, so we thought we'd help each other out. I'd be your dad's girlfriend, and he'd be my boyfriend. Whaddya think?"

Lottie looks between Jo and me. Her expression gives nothing away as she continues to gobble down berries. She swallows her last mouthful, and with a shrug, she stands up and reaches for her bubbles. "That's cool. I'm going to blow some bubbles." And then walks off.

I stare after my daughter as she skips away and spins around in a cloud of bubbles.

"That was a bit underwhelming. How did you make that so painless?"

"By not talking in code, just get to the point. It's a good thing you have me," she says and army crawls toward me. "Although, I would have loved to call you *daddy*."

"That's it!" I shout and dive for her. I grab hold of her wrists in one hand and start poking her in the sides. She squeals at

THOSE TWO WORDS

me to stop, laughing so hard, until tears are streaming down her face. The moment she surrenders, I steal a kiss.

"I love you."

"I love you too," she breathes out, gifting me with a smile.

The afternoon sun begins to cool as we walk to my truck, Jo's hand securely in mine as Lottie snores softly against my chest.

I settle behind the wheel of my truck, with Johanna tucked into my side and my daughter dreaming behind us. I'm reminded that this town has always been home. But with Johanna in my life again, my home feels whole again.

And that makes me so happy.

She makes me happy.

JOHANNA

EIGHT MONTHS LATER

"Did you want another glass of wine?" Patrick asks as I pop a grape into my mouth.

"Mm, maybe later. I think I've eaten too much cheese." I'm leaning up against the small sofa as Patrick lies sprawled out in front of me on the brown, fluffy rug. His back is to the wood stove, its bright orange flames the only light source in the small, log cabin.

When Dex mentioned one of his cabins had a last-minute cancellation, we snapped it up and headed north the next day. A weekend getaway is exactly what we need after the last couple of months, and this is the perfect location to hide away in the woods, not another soul to be found for miles.

"That's impossible." He laughs and picks up a puzzle piece from the few remaining in the pile between us. We've been dipping in and out of completing the puzzle but keep getting distracted by one another. Only Patrick Sadler would have the ability to make jigsaw puzzles sexy. It wasn't even an hour ago

EPILOGUE

that he stripped me bare and fucked me on all fours in front of the fire. Now we're acting like a civilized couple, sipping on expensive wine and grazing on a cheese board.

Life is great.

I've lived with Patrick for almost six months now. He asked me to move in with him when he found out my rental agreement was renewing each month, but I argued it was too soon. He argued we'd already spent enough time apart.

Touché.

After two months of standing my ground, I finally relented. Lottie took to our relationship and my moving in with ease. Poor Patrick, on the other hand, is officially outnumbered, and I think he's started sprouting gray hairs since Lottie and I have teamed up.

I stretch my legs out in front of me and wiggle my toes in my fuzzy socks.

"You're getting bad at this with your old age, these ones are easy." I point toward the errant pieces waiting to find their homes, and wave in the general direction they need to go, too cozy and relaxed to move from my spot.

"You finish it, then," he says. I sigh and lean toward the puzzle, easily slotting in two pieces. He distracts me for a second when he stretches his arms above his head, revealing that line of dark hair that runs low on his taut belly. He really does get better at everything with age.

That need for one another hasn't lessened; if anything, it grows stronger with each day. Now and again, we will climb into his truck, park it off the beaten track, and steam up the windows some more.

"Where's the fun in that?" I ask. Excitement hits me when I see we only have two pieces left to place. I slot the first one in easily, but when I look at the final piece, something doesn't look right. I pick it up and turn it in my fingers. "I think this is from a different box. All the colors are wrong."

EPILOGUE

Patrick peers over at my hand and rolls his eyes before letting out a *tsk*. "This one is brand new. I'll have to take it back to the store."

"Oh my god, it's happening again. I'm cursed when it comes to jigsaws." I groan and throw my hands over my face.

He chuckles softly as I hear him searching around for the missing piece, but I'm still too busy being dramatic to help him look.

"What about this one?" he asks, his voice closer now.

"No, I give up, you put it in. I'm officially done with jigsaws."

"Love, I don't think this piece is for me," he says softly.

Opening my eyes, I look up, and as my vision refocuses, I find him kneeling in front of me. His eyes shine bright and warm like the fire glowing behind him, but it's the love firing off him that sets me alight.

It's only then I notice he's down on *one* knee.

My eyes dart from his face to his posture, before widening. That's when I spot his outstretched hand between us. Between his fingers is *my* puzzle piece. And taped haphazardly to that piece, is a sparkling rose gold ring, with a large solitaire diamond sitting in its center.

I stare at it, then at Patrick, and then at the ring again. I'm dizzy from the speed my eyes move from him to his hand, but when I settle back on the man in front of me, I get light-headed for a whole other reason.

"Wha-what's that?" I ask, pointing a shaky hand at the ring.

"It's for your hand, silly," he says as he reaches out and takes the hand I'm pointing at him with—that just so happens to be my left. "I thought I could place it here." He taps my ring finger, before placing a kiss on the same spot. "And then I can continue to make you happy for the rest of your life, only this time you'll be my wife."

I think I'm crying; I don't actually know. *No, I am.*

EPILOGUE

"Will you marry me, Johanna?" Patrick says, his fingers stroking along my wrist. He brings his other hand up to cup my cheek and leans his forehead against mine. "C'mon, love. What'll it be?"

My head bobs up and down, heart soaring, and I'm too awestruck to formulate words. As he slides the ring onto my finger, I hold my breath until it passes my knuckle. Through the tears and smiles, I manage to whisper one word.

"Yes."

When he finally settles the ring at the base of my finger, he dots kisses across my hand before pressing his lips to the top of the diamond. "Perfect fit," he says, and when he looks up at me again, his eyes shine with unshed tears and love.

So much love.

Laughter peels out of us as I throw myself at him and he tumbles backward with me in his arms. I rain kisses on his face and say *yes* over and over again. He takes hold of my face and kisses me with so much love and adoration, I know I made the right decision in giving this man my heart.

Because he will fill it with love and happiness for the rest of our lives, and I'll do the same to his.

Right here is my happy, and it was absolutely worth the wait.

***

Thank you so much for visiting Sutton Bay! I hope you enjoyed Johanna and Patrick's story.

Want more from them? Read their bonus chapter on my website. www.ronniemathews.com

***

EPILOGUE

Just One Moment is #2 in the series. Quinn and Graham's fake dating story between a shy MMC and sunshine FMC is available to read now.

acknowledgements

It won't come as a surprise for a lot of you that I'm crying while writing this. There are so many people that I am so grateful for in helping me finish this story and helping me find the courage to complete this first step in this new journey. There is one person who, while they posed some challenges and would tell me I couldn't do this, or I didn't belong in this space, I couldn't have done it without them.

That person is me.

If there is anything I want readers to take away from this story, it's that you need to love yourself, listen to your mind and body, and don't be afraid to take a step back from your busy lives to look after yourself. Jo's journey with her mental health is very similar to my own. We both ignored, denied, and felt ashamed when we first felt things weren't "right," and thought it was best to turn a blind eye. It took a lot of bravery and hard work until we felt comfortable being vulnerable and honest with ourselves and the people we love. But it was the best thing I ever did, and as you can see from Jo's happy ending, putting herself first helped her find her way back to the love of her life and find her happiness.

To my husband, best friend, and biggest cheerleader. Thank you for never letting me talk myself out of this. Thank you for listening to me vent, cry, and get angry during each step of writing this book. The love and support you show me every day means the world. When you have no idea what I'm talking about, you listen and make me feel validated, even when I'm being a hot-headed mess. You are the calm to my storm, and I am very lucky to have you. Don't worry, there is a main character inspired by you coming soon. Love you to the moon and back.

To my friends and family. If you decide to read this, just remember, you don't know me. Unless you're my mum, who is a lover of smutty books. Without your constant support, I couldn't and wouldn't have done this. You all showed me such kindness and love during my hardest times, and I love you all so much. You are my people.

Isla, I am convinced I wouldn't have written this book, had you not convinced me to start a Bookstagram page almost two years ago. You've been a constant presence and supporter of mine, and I am forever grateful for our friendship.

Katie. My critique queen, fellow Type 4, sharer of unhinged texts and voice notes, and friend. Your friendship and support have meant so much to me, and you are one of the authors who inspired me to take the plunge and publish my own book. I can't wait for us to become even more unhinged as we navigate this crazy life together. When I say I couldn't have done this without you, I truly mean that. Thanks for putting up with my crying voice notes. I don't really hate you.

Hannah. Who would have thought that you DMing me about your debut and me asking, "Is it spicy?" would lead to such an amazing friendship? Thank you for loving baby Guinness and being no nonsense, because we know I'm full of it. Thank you for giving me my first review on Goodreads and for being one of the best beta readers. Jo and Patrick wouldn't be near the quality they are now without you.

To my early readers, Kerry, Courtney, and Tabitha, who read Jo and Patrick's story in its rawest form. Thank you for being gentle with me, for loving TTW in its infancy, and hyping me up every step of the way. You helped a very scared and anxious girlie, and I couldn't have done this without you. I hope you're ready for tentacles.

To my other betas, Jules, Lauren, Albany, Kristen, and Karla. I couldn't have picked a better group of ladies to call me out on all my British-isms, gently guide the story in the direction it needed to go, and make me believe I could actually do this. I will forever be grateful for each one of you. And for those begging for Booth's book, it's coming, I swear.

The moment I saw the cover from Mel, I knew this was all real. Thank you so much for bringing this story to life with your beautiful talent. I am so excited to work with you on the rest of the Sutton Bay series, and extra thanks for being my go-to for all things Maine.

Paisley, you really helped this over thinker not overthink, especially during one of the most vulnerable stages in my author career. Thank you for taking care of my babies and helping to polish them up. Don't worry, I've saved your man for last...sorry, not sorry.

Caroline, thank you for being one of the last set of eyes to read Johanna and Patrick's story, and for helping it be the final story it is now.

To the bookish community. Wow. If someone had told me two years ago that making a Bookstagram account would have led to me publishing a book, I would have snorted in their face. But here we are. To all my fellow readers, authors, and anyone who has supported or hyped me up since I joined the community, thank you so much. It truly is one of the most welcoming places on the internet.

To my Street Team, thank you for all the hype you continue to give *Those Two Words*, even though I was a baby author with no way to prove her worth. You are all amazing, and I'm so glad to have you spreading the word about single dads who can braid hair.

And to the readers, thank you for taking a chance on me. I

hope you loved Johanna and Patrick's story and will stick around to see what's next in the Sutton Bay series.

about the author

Ronnie Mathews writes small town, swoon-worthy stories with lots of feels and delicious spice. If she isn't writing or reading, you'll find her in the kitchen or out with friends and family trying to balance being an ambivert. She lives in the North West of England with her husband and black Labrador, Jake.

Made in the USA
Middletown, DE
29 September 2025